Praise for *A Nov...*

"A romance lovers dream of a book. V...........,, ... packed with charm, Ashley Poston is the queen of high concept love stories."
—Sophie Cousens, *New York Times* bestselling author of *The Good Part*

"Ashley Poston has done it again. I fell into these pages just as effortlessly as Eileen tumbles into Eloraton. Whimsical, emotional, and tender. . . . Another enchanting romance from Poston."
—B.K. Borison, author of *In the Weeds*

Praise for the novels of Ashley Poston

"Consider me Ashley Poston's greatest admirer!"
—Carley Fortune, #1 *New York Times* bestselling author of *This Summer Will Be Different*

"This is a book to make you laugh during the funeral scene and cry when the dance party begins."
—*The New York Times*, on *The Dead Romantics*

"Funny, breathtaking, hopeful, and dreamy."
—Ali Hazelwood, #1 *New York Times* bestselling author of *Love, Theoretically*, on *The Dead Romantics*

"Warm, funny, and heartbreakingly hopeful, *The Seven Year Slip* is a magical love story."
—Sangu Mandanna, bestselling author of *The Very Secret Society of Irregular Witches*

"Off-kilter, romantic, and irresistible."
—Emma Straub, *New York Times* bestselling author of *This Time Tomorrow*, on *The Seven Year Slip*

A Novel Love Story

ASHLEY POSTON

Berkley Romance

New York

BERKLEY ROMANCE
Published by Berkley
An imprint of Penguin Random House LLC
penguinrandomhouse.com

Library of Congress Cataloging-in-Publication Data

Names: Poston, Ashley, author.
Title: A novel love story / Ashley Poston.
Description: First edition. | New York : Berkley Romance, 2024.
Identifiers: LCCN 2023053552 (print) | LCCN 2023053553 (ebook) |
ISBN 9780593640975 (trade paperback) | ISBN 9780593640982 (ebook)
Subjects: LCSH: Literature teachers—Fiction. | Bookstore owners—Fiction. |
LCGFT: Romance fiction. | Novels.
Classification: LCC PS3616.O8388 N68 2024 (print) |
LCC PS3616.O8388 (ebook) | DDC 813/.6—dc23/eng/20231117
LC record available at https://lccn.loc.gov/2023053552
LC ebook record available at https://lccn.loc.gov/2023053553

First Edition: June 2024

Printed in the United States of America
1st Printing

Book design by Daniel Brount

To the author of my favorite book,
I wish I could've met you,
but I hope my books find your books on the shelves,
and I hope they're friends

Also by Rachel Flowers . . .

Daffodil Daydreams

Unrequited Love Song

Honey and the Heartbreak

Return to Sender

[Unfinished Book 5]

An Ending

THERE ONCE WAS A TOWN.

It was a quaint little town, in a quiet valley, where life moved at the pace of snails and the only road in was the only way out, too. There was a candy store that sold the sweetest honey taffy you ever tasted, and a garden store that grew exotic, beautiful blooms year-round. The local café was named after a possum that tormented its owner for years, and the chef there made the best honey French toast in the Northeast. There was a bar where the bartender always knew your name, and always served your burgers slightly burnt, though the local hot sauce always disguised the taste. If you wanted to stay the weekend, you could check-in at the new bed-and-breakfast in town—just as soon as its renovations were finished, and just a pleasant hike up Honeybee Trail was a waterfall where, rumor had it, if you made a wish underneath it, the wish would come true. There was a drugstore, a grocer, a jewelry store that was open only when Mercury was in of retrograde—

And, oh, there was a bookstore.

It was tucked into an unassuming corner of an old brick building fitted with a labyrinthine maze of shelves stocked with hundreds of books. In the back corner was a reading space with a fireplace, and chairs so cozy you could sink into them for hours while you read. The rafters were filled with glass chimes that, when the sunlight came in through the top windows, would send dapples of colors flooding across the stacks of books, painting them in rainbows. A family of starlings roosted in the eaves, and sang different songs every morning, in time with the tolls of the clock tower.

The town was quiet in that cozy, sleepy way that if you closed your eyes, you could almost hear the valley breathe as wind crept through it, between the buildings, and was sighed out again.

There once was a town, and I was so certain that it would feel like home if I ever made it there.

There once was a town, and it didn't exist.

1

Country Roads

I WAS LOST.

Not metaphorically—at least, I didn't think so—but physically lost, hundreds of miles from home, in the middle of nowhere.

No cell service. An outdated map. A gas tank running on empty.

Oh, and I was alone.

When I started this road trip yesterday, before eight hours on the interstate and a pit stop at a dinosaur-themed hotel, and eight more hours today, I didn't think I'd lose my way on the last leg of the journey. I was so close—the cabin where I'd be staying for the next week was within reach—but Google Maps kept glitching as I drove my way through Rip Van Winkle country, until my phone screen was nothing more than beige land and my little blue dot roamed, without a road, in the middle of nowhere.

I'd taken the same road trip with my best friend for the last two years to the same cabin in Rhinebeck, New York, to meet the same people in our Super Smutty Book Club. I *shouldn't* have gotten lost.

But this was a year of firsts.

Overhead, angry-looking clouds rumbled with thunder, dark purple with the coming night and heavy with rain. I hoped the weather held up until I found the cabin, unearthed a bottle of wine from my back seat, and settled down in one of the rocking chairs on the front porch with a romance book in my hands.

The promise of a week of wine and happily ever afters had kept me sane all year, through boring English 101 classes with half-asleep students and AI-generated papers on Chaucer and colleagues who swore that *War and Peace* was a riveting read. The English department was rife with people who would love to talk to you for hours about *Beowulf* or modern literary theory or the intersectionality of postmodern texts. But for one week out of the year, I looked forward to shucking off my professorial robes and disappearing into the twisting roads that hugged the soft hills of the Catskills, and reading about impossible meet-cutes and grand romantic gestures, and no one would judge me for it.

And when everyone else pulled out because life got in the way, it was just going to be my best friend, Pru, and me—and that was perfect, too. I *needed* this. Pru didn't understand how much. No one did. So when she told me last week that she couldn't go, either, it surprised me. No, that was the wrong word—it *disappointed* me—but I didn't want it to show. I sat on the couch opposite her, *The Great British Baking Show* in the background, digging my fingers into the comforter I'd pulled over my legs because she always kept her and Jasper's apartment freezing.

"I'm sorry," she'd said, twisting the rings on her fingers nervously. Her dirty blond hair was done up in a sloppy ponytail, and she was already in her pajamas and fuzzy slippers. She was petite and perpetually sunburnt in the summers, with wide brown eyes and a scar on her chin where my teeth went into her face when we were twelve and trying to do backflips on a trampoline. Through the crack in her open bedroom door, I could see her suitcase half-packed already with warm sweaters and cute knit hats. Definitely not summer apparel. "Jasper surprised me with a trip to Iceland, and this is the only time we can go because of, you know, his job," she gushed quickly, like saying it faster would make it hurt less—ripping a proverbial Band-Aid off a very hairy leg. "I know it's not ideal but he *just* told me. We *just* found out. And . . . we can all go to the cabin again next year?" The question dipped up, hopeful.

No, I wanted to tell her, but I couldn't quite muster up the word. *No, we can't. I needed this. I* still *need this.*

But if I said that, then what would happen? Nothing good. She would still go off to Iceland, and I'd be stuck exactly where I was. Besides, we both knew what Iceland meant: a proposal. *Finally.*

It was something she'd been waiting for for years.

So, what did it matter if she couldn't come to the cabin this year? It was nothing, really, in the face of what she had to look forward to. So I put on a smile and said, "Obviously. Next year we'll be back to normal."

"Absolutely," she promised, and she didn't suspect a thing. "Oh, and maybe this year we can all get on a video call together instead?"

"C'mon, Pru. You know if Jasper's taking you to Iceland, you won't have time to video call with anyone." Then I held up my hand and wiggled my bare wedding ring finger. "You know what he's gonna do."

My best friend squirmed anxiously. "He might not, and I know how much this trip means to you . . ."

"*Go,* have fun, don't think twice about it," I urged, draining my glass of wine as I stood to leave, because I didn't want her to see how upset I really was. Jasper was a pretty low-level attorney at his law firm, so he only had certain days off once in a blue moon, and this was a last-minute trip that he'd managed to snatch up for them. I would be a monster to be mad at that.

Prudence might've been able to sacrifice this trip, but I certainly couldn't. I was desperate for it—I needed to get drunk on cheap wine and cry over happily ever afters, even if I'd be the only one in the cabin this year.

So, in the summer of my thirty-second year, with no money and no prospects and one too many AI-generated papers waiting for me to grade for my college English 101 class, I set off on a sixteen-hour road trip alone.

I *needed* to get lost in a book.

More than I needed anything else.

Besides, it was the ten-year anniversary of the publication of *Daffodil Daydreams* by Rachel Flowers, and that was something that I wanted to celebrate. The author had passed away a few years ago, and her books had brought the book club together.

And, I think, deep down I just wanted to get away—no matter what.

On the sixteen-hour drive, I listened to *Daffodil Daydreams*. The audiobook narrator was in the middle of my favorite scene. I fished out a stale fry from the fast-food bag in the seat beside me and turned up the volume.

"Junie crossed the rickety bridge to the waterfall, searching the plush greenery for any sign of Will, but she felt her heart beginning to break a little with each beat. He wasn't here."

"Just wait," I told her. "Love is neither late nor early, you know." Then I frowned at my half-eaten fry, and dropped it back in the bag. I was so sick of fast food and gas station bathrooms. Almost twenty-four hours of it could do that to a person.

My puke-green hatchback, lovingly nicknamed Sweetpea, had started making this sort of high-pitched whining noise somewhere back in DC, but I'd elected to ignore it. After all, Sweetpea *was* a 1979 Ford Pinto, the kind that had a penchant for exploding gas tanks. So I was just betting that it'd want to go out in style rather than by a faulty gasket or an oil leak.

I probably should have turned around, because I couldn't imagine anything worse than being stranded in a no-name town, but I was a part-time English professor who filed her own taxes and knew how to change her own tires, goddamn it.

Nothing would stop me. Well. *Almost* nothing.

A fat rain droplet splatted on my windshield. Then another as, in the audiobook, Junie worked up the courage to leave the waterfall, succumbing to the awful nightmare she'd been afraid of all along—that Will didn't love her. Not in the way she did him.

I knew these words like Holy Scriptures. I could recite them, I'd read them so many times.

In just a few paragraphs, Will would come running up the trail to the waterfall, out of breath and exhausted. He'd pull her into his arms and propose that they fix up the Daffodil Inn together— make it their home. Their happy ending.

I knew what she'd say, but my heart fluttered anxiously anyway.

I knew her voice would be soft, and it would be sure as she took him by the hands, and squeezed them tightly, under the glittering spray of the waterfall. And there would be magic there, in that moment. The heart-squeezing, tongue-tying, breathless, edge-of-your-seat magic of Quixotic Falls. Of true love.

What did it feel like to love someone so much you ached?

I thought I'd known once.

If life were like a storybook, I would be a premier scholar on the material. Most of the year, I taught English classes at my local university. I waxed poetic about history's greatest romantics. I taught at length about Mary Shelley's devotion to her husband, and Lord Byron's . . . promiscuity. I handed out the letters Keats wrote, and challenged students to see the world through rose-tinted glasses.

I graded papers on *The Vampyre* and Lord Byron, and I taught that Mary Shelley kept Percy's calcified heart in her desk drawer because that was the closest thing to romance as real life could get.

I didn't *need* love. I didn't need to fall into it. I didn't need to find it at all. Not again. Never again.

Because love stories were enough. They were safe. They would never fail me.

The rain came down harder, and my hands grew clammy with nerves. I hated driving in the rain. Pru always drove whenever we went anywhere. I rubbed my hands on my jean shorts, muttering to myself that I should've planned out another day and booked a hotel for the night. Maybe I still could, because I didn't know where the hell I was.

Shit.

I gave up on trying to fix Google Maps and returned my eyes to the road.

Somehow, the rainstorm seemed to get *comically* worse, until I found myself driving through a complete washout. I think I passed a town sign, but I couldn't make out what it read. The rain on the roof of my car was so loud, I couldn't hear the audiobook anymore.

"Will pressed . . . kiss . . . whispered . . . 'It sounds . . . lo . . . dream . . . forever?'"

"Damn, that's my favorite part," I muttered, turning up the volume, but it was already as loud as it could go.

Then—the road seemed to veer off ahead. Thank god, maybe I could find some civilization and wait out the storm.

Putting my blinker on, I turned off onto the exit. There was an old barnlike covered bridge ahead, crossing a small river that overflowed and frothed with white water. I slowed down to putter over it. I was sure in the sunlight this drive was gorgeous, but right now I felt like I could go hydroplaning off into the wilderness at any moment and never return. The road beyond the bridge turned around a steep embankment of pines and wound down between more tall firs, plush and verdant with summer. I thought I'd made a mistake, because the road didn't seem to end, until through the haze of gray rain a tall clock tower appeared, and with it came the soft lines of buildings and light posts and cars—a small town.

Night was coming fast. I tapped my phone one last time to see if I could refresh the map—there *had* to be cell service in the town, right?—but I must've tapped it too hard, because my phone came dislodged from its magnet holder and fell down onto the floorboards, ripping out the cassette converter with it.

Almost immediately, Junie's quiet musings about walled gardens and true love turned into a blaring pop song, so loud it startled me straight in my seat.

"*Come on, Eileen,*" the eighties song sang.

A blur of something caught in the headlights. I saw it out of the corner of my eye a moment before I looked up to the road again—

A man. There was a man standing in the—

"*Shit!*" I cut the steering wheel to the left. Sweetpea's tires squealed. My car swerved into a parking spot, tires slamming against the curb. My car gave a *clunk* (a disastrous *clunk*, actually), and came to an abrupt and final stop. The pop song died with it.

2

Meet-Cute

MY HEART HAMMERED IN my chest. Oh my god—oh my god, did I hit him? Did I kill him? Oh god, I still had student loans to pay off. I couldn't go to jail *yet*.

Clawing my seat belt off, I gulped in a breath and took in my surroundings. There wasn't blood on the windshield, so I hadn't hit him, right? Where was he? I'd come to a stop in front of a bar. The red lights on the sign flickered as the rain came down harder.

I shoved open my door and forced myself to my feet. "Hello?" I called, whirling back toward the road, the rain drenching me almost instantly. I pulled my fingers through my matted copper hair. *"Hello?"*

The man was sitting on the ground, his oval glasses lopsided and foggy. He slowly turned to face me, dazed.

Oh no.

Oh no no no n—

"Oh, sir—sir, are you okay?" I asked, hurrying over to help him to his feet.

He was tall and wiry, soaked to the bone, his white button-down clinging to his muscular torso, looking like the brooding, blond-haired pale ghost of Darcy, his angles all sharp and solid. An electrified zing tingled down my spine. In the pinkish-gray light of evening rain, he was very handsome . . . and very much glowering at me like I'd just tried to murder him.

Which, to be fair, I *hadn't*. On purpose.

"Are you okay? How many fingers do you see?" I held up four fingers, but really three because I angled down my fourth one—

He grabbed my hand and lowered it. "Three, trick question—you almost ran me over," he accused, his words clipped. The warm streetlights made his eyes glitter like peridots.

I yanked my hand away. "Well, why were you in the middle of the road?"

His mouth twisted into a scowl. "I was crossing it."

"No, you were just standing there."

"You almost *hit* me."

"You were standing in the middle of the road!"

He bent down to grab his keys from the asphalt. "Not anymore." Then he turned and stalked across the street.

I watched him go, dumbfounded. "What the hell?" I muttered, pushing my wet bangs out of my face, and looking around.

Now *I* was the one standing in the middle of the road.

At least I'd parked in front of a bar. Most of the neon letters were out, save for two Os in the middle that, every time it thundered, flickered so it looked like they were screaming OOOOOOOOOOO in angry red lights. Not ominous at all. If nothing else, I could get dinner there and directions to the nearest hotel. My heart was hammering too fast to drive, anyway. So I dug my wallet and cell phone out of my car and gave the steering wheel one last loving pat before I left for the bar.

I sent a text to the book club—MADE IT TO A TOWN.

Who knew *which* town. Then, for good measure, I put a smiley face at the end, which was far more optimistic than I was feeling. A moment later, my phone pinged with a notification—the text had failed to send.

Perfect.

"Well," I said to myself, "this is certainly how all horror movies start."

Alone. In a rainstorm. In a no-name town in the middle of the woods. Without cell phone reception. If Freddy Krueger or the *Saw* guy came out from behind a building, I'd pull Sweetpea back onto the road and drive until I hit Nova Scotia.

This was going to be worth it—I kept telling myself that. The alternative was . . . that this was all for nothing, and I'd wasted gas, sanity, and my time on this ill-begotten adventure. Like Bilbo Baggins as he left the Shire, I was beginning to wonder if I'd made a *horrific* mistake.

A bolt of lightning crossed the sky, quickly followed by a clap of thunder, and I was running for the bar.

The door closed behind me with a slam, and all seven patrons at the bar turned to look at me. I dripped rainwater onto the scuffed hardwood floors. Well, this was certainly awkward. I quietly took a seat on the barstool closest to the door, and as I did the patrons went back to their drinks.

This night *really* couldn't get any worse.

At least I wasn't in the rain anymore.

"What can I get for you?" the bartender asked, sliding over a dry towel. I took it gratefully, and began to squeeze out the droplets in my hair. The bartender was an older woman with dark brown skin, gray-streaked short hair, and bright orange nails, wearing frayed jeans and a T-shirt with a flaming rooster logo. She had a kind of openness about her that told me she often played therapist to most of her patrons. It was a good thing I was just passing through, I doubt she had time for all my baggage. "Beer? Wine? A fruity little drink with an umbrella? We just got pink ones with flowers on them."

"Um—whatever your house red is, is fine, and do you have a food menu?" I asked hopefully, and she produced a beat-up menu. The plastic was peeling at the corners, and there was a strange stain near the wine section.

"Sure thing. Take a look at the menu, and I'll go fetch your drink," she replied, taking a glass from the rack, and left.

The barstool was leather, and my wet thighs stuck to it as I tried to get comfortable. The bar was chilly, and I shivered as I checked out the menu. Or *tried* to. The words were blurry, so I rubbed my eyes, but it didn't seem to fix them at all. The place probably had the normal bar food, anyway. I'd eaten at enough of them in my lifetime to know that there was at *least* a burger on the menu, some cheesy fries, and a chicken tender option.

I was still so riled up from my run-in with that strange man that I wasn't hungry at all, but I could hear my mom's voice chide and tell me that if I didn't eat now, I'd just be crabby later with a migraine. She wasn't wrong, but it was annoying. Even a thousand miles away, off on her *Eat, Pray, Love* adventure, she was pestering me without even knowing it.

The bar was small, lit with neon signs promising PARADISE BY THE DASH(BUD) LITE, and SMOOTH RUMMING. The smell of cigarettes was unmistakable, despite the large NO SMOKING sign behind the counter. The smoke had permeated the worn leather barstools years ago, and no amount of deep cleaning could scrub that odor out now. I didn't mind, though. It smelled a lot like those dives Pru had dragged me to in college. She'd always find a Beatles cover band and shout at them to play "Dear Prudence" just to hear a stranger sing her name.

When you were named after a song, you had to make the best of it somehow.

There weren't many people in the bar, just a few locals at the high tops in the back, watching some sports game on the flat-screen. Soccer, I think.

When the bartender came back with my wine, I ordered a burger and gave the menu back. She jotted it down on her pad, nodding. "Good choice, good choice. It'll be up in a jiff. You need anything else, I'll be over on the other side watching the rest of the match," she said, pointing to the TVs in the back. Then she leaned in close, and whispered—as if in a secret, "I've got fifty on Wimbledon."

"I wish I knew what that was," I replied.

She gave a shrug. "Beats me, but I can't pass up a bet. Ooh—I think someone scored!" she added, and fled to the other side of the bar.

The house red wasn't half-bad—a fruity, sweet blackberry merlot. The burger came out a few minutes later, with a side of soggy fries. By then, my hair wasn't dripping anymore, so I pulled it up into a bun and tried a bite. I almost immediately regretted not getting the chicken fingers. The patty was closer to charcoal than beef, and hard as a rock. I debated sending the burger back, but the bartender was deep into the match, and I didn't want to distract her from fifty bucks.

It's fine, I told myself, taking a bottle of ketchup from the condiments rack. The label had been peeled off, probably to disguise the brand. People were weird about ketchup. It was waterier than most ketchups, but as long as it disguised the taste, I didn't care.

And when I took another bite, I learned it wasn't ketchup at all. It was hot sauce.

It was hot sauce so hot that after just one bite, I could no longer feel my face.

"Everything good over here?" asked the bartender, returning as if she could sense my distress.

I swallowed my pain. "Yeah, I'm fine," I gasped, and then downed most of my wine. Somehow, it made the burning *worse*. Whatever was in that bottle of Satan's revenge had turned my lips to jelly.

"The hot sauce got you," she inferred, and dug something out of the refrigerator below the bar. A small carton of milk—probably used for late-night coffees. She poured me a glass and I gratefully drank it. "It'll calm down in a second. The heat's always at the front, but after, it leaves you with a nice, sweet aftertaste. It's quite good, considering," she said as I finished the glass of milk. "Gail, by the way."

"Eileen," I said, grabbing a napkin and mopping my nose with it. "And I'm sorry, I didn't realize I'd be this leaky. What's *in* that hot sauce?"

"It's a secret, Frank says. But you get the sweet now, right?" she added, grinning.

I did, actually. "It almost . . . tastes like honey?"

"Don't tell Frank you said that," she warned.

"Noted."

I didn't know who this Frank guy was, but he was suddenly my sworn enemy. In the back of my head, I could hear Pru laughing at my luck. She'd say that I must've picked up a penny on tails or crossed a black cat; I better throw salt over my shoulder and spin counterclockwise three times. She never looked like a fool anywhere she went—she knew what to order at bars, and she could pick out the best appetizer on any menu. She was the kind of person who the world just unfolded for, and I missed her glow.

I hoped she was enjoying her flight to Iceland. I hoped she got seated next to a crying baby. I hoped she got to see lots of boring glaciers and ate a lot of tender reindeer and . . . and had a good time.

I was really bad at staying mad. And I *was* still mad.

The group of townsfolk in the back of the bar cheered as their soccer team scored a goal, and clapped each other on the shoulders. Someone had just won some money—and maybe ended a friendship.

"Damn, there goes my fifty," Gail muttered, shaking her head.

I took another sip of my wine. One bite from the burger was enough for me, so I started picking at the fries. There had to be *one* that wasn't soggy . . .

Gail turned back to me and asked, "So, did the rain bring you in?"

"Yeah, I got caught in it, so I decided to pull off and wait it out." *Oh, and I almost killed a guy.*

"You'll probably be waiting until morning, then," she replied, taking up a few glasses from the sink, and putting them on the drying rack.

I almost choked on a soggy fry. *"Morning?"*

She gave a shrug. "It is what it is."

Easy for *her* to say. I had a cabin to get to and a vacation to start. Alone. It wasn't like anyone was expecting me this year. "Is there a hotel you recommend?"

"There *was*," she replied, "but it's under renovation. Bad luck you came tonight."

That seemed like the theme of this trip so far, and it didn't look to be turning around anytime soon. Hotel Car it was. I'd slept in worse places. Mainly, the floor under my desk in the cramped windowless room the university called an *office*. Also, allegedly I'd slept on a park bench in the middle of the college green my junior year of undergrad, but I didn't remember that even though Pru *swore* she spent all night looking for me.

The front door opened, and a blast of loud rain and wind swept through the bar. Gail flicked her eyes to the newcomer, and her concern turned into a revelation. "You know," she added, scheming, "hang on real tight, I think I might have an idea."

"Oh, you don't have to—"

"Gimme a sec," she said, holding up a finger as someone crossed behind me and sat down three barstools away. He shrugged out of his sage-colored raincoat, tall and angular, like a chiseled statue come to life. He was her plan?

I glanced over at him—and my hope dropped like a stone into my gut.

Oh *no*, not *him*.

"Anderson, honey," Gail greeted, producing a glass and pouring him a water. "You're just the person we need."

The man I had almost run over shifted his gaze from Gail to me, and then back to Gail again. His hair was still damp honey turning white-blond, and he'd changed into a dry T-shirt and jeans. He folded his raincoat in half and placed it neatly on the stool beside him, cautious, like he was a rabbit caught in the crosshairs of a rifle. "I . . . am?"

Gail put on a smile. "You certainly are. You've still got that loft of yours, don't you?"

He hesitated. "Yes?"

"And it's vacant, right?"

"At the moment." Though he sounded like he didn't want to admit it.

"Excellent! This young lady here needs a room for the night"— she motioned with her thumb at me—"and I was just thinking about you. She's new in town. Just swept in with the rain."

He finally slid his gaze to me. In the light of the bar, his eyes turned out to be a lovely bright green—almost minty. I felt that shiver again—starting in my scalp and going all the way to my toes. There was fresh stubble across his cheeks, and as he pursed his lips, it made the scar that cut down the left side of them turn into a thin white thread. "Did she now," he said wryly, giving me a long look. He narrowed his eyes. "How fortunate."

Embarrassment flooded my cheeks. *You were the one standing in the middle of the road*, I wanted to point out. *It wasn't* totally *my fault.*

Just mostly. Probably.

I think I would rather eat my own shoe than take his hospitality. "I'll be fine, really," I said to Gail.

"Nonsense! Where will you sleep otherwise?"

"My car—"

"You will *not* sleep in your car!" she said, positively scandalized by the thought. "Bears can open car doors."

"I'll lock them." Though, to be honest, it didn't fill me with excitement imagining waking up beside Smokey Bear. *Only you can prevent forest fires, nom-nom.* I'm sure it was someone's fantasy, but not mine. "Or something."

"Anders, tell her she can sleep in your loft," Gail went on, not taking no for an answer as she brought him a plate of food that had been sitting on the pass-through window since I'd gotten there. I guess he came to the bar often for dinner. "Andie?"

He popped an onion ring into his mouth. "I mean, if she'd rather take a chance in her car with a bear, who am I to intervene?"

"Anderson!" Gail threw her bar rag at him.

He caught it, cracking a grin for the first time. So he *wasn't* just a good-looking, moody lump. Who knew. "I'm joking! I'm joking," he said, and then angled his head toward me. "Unless you would *rather* take a chance with the bears?"

Tricky, tricky, I thought, as he tossed the ball into my court. I obviously didn't *want* to sleep in my car, but staying in the loft of someone I'd almost run over . . .

I hated him, I realized. Not vehemently, but just a light hate. A casual dusting of hate. Enough hate that, if he were standing at the edge of a cliff, I'd seriously debate pushing him over. I *wouldn't*, but the temptation would be there.

I crossed my arms over my chest. "I'll take the loft. Thank you," I said forcefully.

The edges of his lips twitched—just slightly—as if he were fighting a smirk. "Then you're welcome to it for the night, as long as you don't mind the starlings in the eaves."

Starlings. Like the tattoo tucked behind Prudence's and my left ears. *To remind us that like a starling's song, all stories are different*, Pru had said as she held my hand, the tattoo feeling like an ice pick going straight through my skull. *Also, they're cute as shit, yeah?*

Absently, I rubbed at the tattoo. It was faded now, always covered by my mess of copper hair.

I studied him.

He looked to be about my age—early thirties—though no wedding ring on his finger. His white-blond hair curled gently around his ears, giving him a boyish charm under all the Darcian bravado he exuded. His nose was slightly crooked, and his cheekbones were high, his lips full, eyelashes long and fair.

He definitely wasn't my type, but I couldn't take my eyes off him, either, like my brain was trying to place him. Did he look familiar? Had I met him before? No, that was impossible. I was just tired, starved of any sort of human interaction in the last twenty-four hours, and suddenly more aware than ever that my Fleetwood Mac T-shirt was too threadbare, and my pink sports bra was too bright, and my tennis shoes were too wet, and—I'm sure my face still looked flushed and melty from the hot sauce, my hair a damp and tangled rat's nest that I hadn't washed in . . . three days? Was it three? Or four? I wished I knew as I tugged on the end of my ponytail, trying not to sink underneath the counter and disappear forever.

"I don't mind starlings," I said finally.

"Excellent!" Gail crowed. "It's settled."

He turned back to her and said, "How could I say no to you, Gail? I'd starve without you and your brother." He waved at the cook through the small window into the kitchen, and the chef back there—a bigger guy with dark brown skin, bushy gray eyebrows, and an even more impressive mustache—silently waved back.

Gail patted the top of Anders's hand like a doting grandmother. "Oh, trust me on this, you two will get along like peas and carrots, I can tell."

Yeah, well, I wasn't sure how long it took peas to look carrots in the eyes, but I certainly was avoiding it like it was an Olympic sport and I was gunning for gold.

Gail, proud of herself, left to close out the soccer fans at the end of the bar.

I drained my glass of wine, my lips still numb from the hot sauce, and wondered if maybe Smokey Bear would've been the better option after all.

3

Signatures

ANDERS HELD THE DOOR open for me as we left the bar and hovered beneath the awning. The rain hadn't let up any, and however dry I'd gotten inside, I was immediately very much damp again the second I left. The night was so humid, the air itself felt like I was swimming in it. He pulled up the hood of his raincoat, and I kicked myself for not having an umbrella—until he pulled one out of his pocket and popped it open.

"I assume you have an overnight bag?" he asked, and motioned to my car.

"Yeah, it's in the trunk."

He held the umbrella over me as I went around and opened the hatchback. When I'd parked the car, most everything had slid up toward the back seat, so I had to climb in to drag my duffel bag back out. As I did, he looked into a cardboard box wedged between my spare tire and a jumper kit, and inspected one of the books. The second Quixotic Falls novel. It was tattered, the cover bent and waterlogged, the pages crumpled, spine broken.

All of the books were signed by Rachel Flowers, personalized in elegant, loopy handwriting—

To Elsy

I'd met her once—Rachel Flowers—a year before she died. She'd been my age. It was a tragic accident, the news outlets had said, but I barely remembered the year at all. I didn't *want* to remember most of it, actually.

"Short for Eleanor?" he asked, guessing the name. "Elvira?"

"Do I look like an Elvira?"

He replied, "I'll know in the daylight."

I snorted. He was a little funny, I had to admit, in an awkward way. This man was made with tweed and argyle, and sewn together with an Oxford comma. I debated whether to lie and say the book was a friend's—he didn't seem like the type to appreciate the finer qualities of romance—but ended up simply telling the truth. I wasn't very good at lying, anyway. "Eileen."

He returned the book to where he'd found it in the box. "You have the entire series."

"I like to read." I pulled my duffel bag over my shoulder. "Okay, let's go. How far's this loft of yours?"

"Right across the street," he replied, nudging his head in the direction he had stalked off to after I'd almost pancaked him with my car. We waded across the street in the inches of rain to a charming old brick building. The windows were all fogged up from the humidity, the front door a dumpy grayish color in the dark.

He unlocked it and pushed it open.

A bell chimed above our heads.

"This way," he said, and headed down the aisle on the far left. I stood in the doorway for a moment, inspecting the rows and rows of shelves—no, bookcases.

It was a *bookstore*.

Somewhere between the stacks, I heard him clear his throat impatiently, and I pulled my duffel up higher over my shoulder and followed after him. Tall, shadowy bookcases loomed overhead as he led me through them, like a guide through a minotaur's maze. The store wasn't big, but it was intricate and tightly packed. He had to angle himself sideways a little bit so his shoulders didn't brush the spines of the books on the shelves. It should've felt suffocating and small, but the store just felt cozy—like being trapped under a warm blanket.

In the back left corner of the store, beside a cozy reading area with a stone hearth and a weathered fainting couch, there was a spiral staircase to the second floor. I followed him up, and the loft was off to the left of the cookbooks, behind a narrow blue door. He took his keys out of his pocket and unlocked it.

"It may smell a bit musty," he began, opening the door for me, "but it's secluded, and you have your own bathroom and shower. The sheets are fresh, too."

I stepped into the room. It was surprisingly quaint, with a double bed on a brass bed frame, a dresser, and a window seat that looked out toward the street. On the far side of the room was a doorway that led to a bathroom with a claw-footed tub and a toilet.

"Oh, wow," I murmured, because I'd expected a cot squeezed into the corner of a dusty old attic. He went over to open a window and air out the room. "It's perfect. How much do I owe you?"

His eyebrows jerked up a fraction as he glanced over his shoulder to me. "Nothing."

"No way, there *has* to be a catch."

"No catch—*shit*." He gave the window another yank, to no avail. I came over to help him, grabbing the bottom lip of the window, and with another pull, we finally managed to push it up. The hush of rain swept in, along with the smell of wet grass and clean sky. He rubbed his hands on his trousers, shaking his head. "Peas don't pay carrots, don't worry about it."

"Why am I the pea?"

"Because I hate peas."

"Oh. Well then." I rolled my eyes and turned to sit on the window seat. He was close enough that I caught a note of his cologne— cedar and black tea and, faintly, the subtle scent of a well-loved paperback. Familiar and yearning. It was mystifying. "Good thing I hate carrots—sorry," I added as my shoulder accidentally brushed his.

He didn't seem to notice at all as he looked up into the eaves. "Carrots are delicious."

I scrunched my nose. "They're gross."

"So are peas."

"Well, at least one of us has taste," I quipped, "and—"

"It's certainly not you," he interrupted before I could say the same. I gave a squawk of indignation, and for the first time his stoic expression twitched a little into what *might* have been a smile. If he hadn't fought it off. Pity. I think he might've had a nice smile. His laugh was probably good, too. Deep and throaty, coming right from the center of his belly. He pushed away from the window. "Though what should I expect from the woman who almost ran me over?"

"You shouldn't have been standing in the middle of the road," I pointed out. "In the rain."

"Have you ever done it?"

"Killed someone? No. But I've thought about it," I said, and— were we getting closer?

He subtly shook his head, his mouth twitching at the edges again, fighting some kind of semblance of a smile. He was like a cat batting around a ball of yarn, and I was just knocking it back to him. "I mean get caught in the rain."

"Not if I can help it." My voice had gotten quiet, almost too quiet to hear above the downpour outside. There was something magnetic that made me look at him, and I couldn't figure out why. I'd met plenty of handsome men before, whose eyelashes were just as long, and who wore scars like pickup lines. But the scar on Anders's lip was so infuriatingly apparent, I couldn't stop looking at it. Not because it was on his mouth, surely not. Not because I was a lightweight when it came to drinking. Not because of the house wine. "I don't really like the rain."

He sucked in a breath through his teeth. "What a pity, then."

If this was a romance novel, we'd kiss. That's what always happens—the gumptious heroine meets her match in the first chapter. A meet-cute. Something memorable. Remarkable. In old Harlequins, we'd be intimate by page one hundred, and a part of me intimately wanted to know what it felt like to unbutton this stranger's shirt. To let go of this plot and just fall headfirst into someone else's.

My story wasn't that interesting, anyway. A three-star read at best. I could imagine the trade reviews—*Though she tackles the mundanity of her life with aplomb, nothing happens to Eileen Merriweather. Angst-ridden backstory told in deeply regrettable prose. An utterly skippable read.*

I sat back on the window seat, sobering at the thought. Prudence would've taken him by the face, she would've crushed her mouth against his, making him fall in love with peas, anyway. But I wasn't Prudence, which was why I was here. Alone. In a no-name town.

But I wasn't Prudence, and I didn't need to fall in love.

He leaned back, a frown tugging at his delicate mouth, as if he was puzzled about why it hadn't happened. Or maybe why he'd toyed with the idea in the first place. But then he shook off the thought, and pushed himself to his feet. "I best take my leave. Should you need anything, I live in the house behind the store. If the starlings wake you up in the morning, I warned you."

He retreated to the door, his long fingers curling around the brass doorknob. My heart was hammering, quick like a rabbit, and I hoped he didn't notice. That he attributed my blush to the wine.

The question slipped out of my mouth before I could stop it: "Why?"

He gave me a curious look. "Why what?"

"Why *were* you standing out in the rain?"

He tilted his head in thought. "Why did you take the road here?"

"You can't answer the question with another question, that's not fair!" I replied, frustrated. I threw up my hands. "Because it was raining! And I was lost."

"Then it was raining," he echoed, "and I was lost. Good night, Elsy," he said, his voice a low rumble, and closed the door behind him.

That *still* wasn't an answer.

Downstairs, a door near the back of the bookstore opened, and closed again, and I was left alone in the quiet. The rain drummed against the window in the bedroom like tiny fingers. I sat down on the edge of the bed and closed my eyes, listening to the way the water trickled down the sill.

When Pru and I were in school, we'd plan our reading days based on the weather. She'd circle the spring rains on her calendar, mark off the weeks when hurricanes came through in the fall, and then when the storms hit, we'd have at least a dozen books ready—library reads and wilted paperbacks from the secondhand shop.

We'd curl up on the couch for hours on end, playing hooky from school.

Then in college, we built sheet forts like we were twelve again, and had weekend escapes into quaint rose-tinted towns.

In the rain, I could hear the flick of a page as we imagined moments and scenes and lives never lived, falling in love with the heroines of happily ever afters.

And we swore that when it was our turn to chase our happy endings, we'd do it together. But that was before all the heartbreak, all the broken promises, because life never panned out like a romance novel, no matter how well plotted and meticulously planned.

As I turned off the lights in the loft and listened to the tiny taps of fingers on the windows, I wondered if there was a way back to before, when happily ever afters felt real.

4

Star(t)ling Realization

MORNING LIGHT POURED INTO the loft from the skylight. And there was a sound. A voice? Yes. Maybe.

And it was *humming*.

I blinked slowly in a puddle of sunlight, forgetting for a moment where I was because the mattress was comfortable and the pillow smelled like fresh laundry. I couldn't remember when I'd gone to sleep, though it was sometime after the rain had let up. That's right—the *rain*. With a start, I remembered: the storm, the bar, the grump, the loft above the bookstore.

I quickly sat up in bed, rubbing the sleep from my eyes. The loft looked different in the daylight. The cushions against the window seat were a bright mango, the hand-embroidered pillows stitched with the same color in blossoming wildflowers. The artisan had painted floral designs on the dresser, on the wardrobe, and around the floor-length mirror. Outside, the rain had given way to verdant foliage and strong redbrick buildings, interspersed with colorful colonial row houses and Victorian homes.

Faintly, I heard someone downstairs in the main area of the bookshop.

Anders? I checked the time on my phone, stifling a yawn—

Shit.

It was almost eleven! How had I slept for almost *ten straight hours*? I had a cabin to get to and a vacation to start. Even if there was no one there to welcome me this year, pour me wine, sit with me in front of the stone hearth, and ask if I'd read this month's club pick, I needed to *get* there.

My phone still had zero bars. No Google Maps, no satellite, I was cursed to roam forever. Maybe there was Wi-Fi downstairs. I'd ask, and then once I left this no-name town and hopped back on the road, I'd figure out where I was.

Probably.

There—the humming again. So it wasn't Anders.

A soft, warm breeze rustled the sheer white curtains hanging in front of the open window, a nest of starlings sang up a storm in the eaves above. I sat on the window bench for a moment, listening to them, watching them fly off and turn back again. The sound came from the birds. They could imitate anything. Pru was obsessed with that fact in the Quixotic Falls series.

"Of all the birds—she chose *starlings*," Pru had said. "It's going to be important. I just *know* it."

To which I'd replied, "Just because fanfic ran with it doesn't mean anything."

"I can't wait for you to be wrong," she said, and picked a sweater out of a rack. We were shopping at her favorite secondhand store, trying to find vintage pieces for something. I no longer remembered what. "Rachel Flowers never puts in details for no reason. I'm telling you, it's going to be important at the end."

I had rolled my eyes and let Pru have her theories. I had my own, after all. There were a few plot threads that hadn't been tied up in the fourth book, and rumors were the fifth one would be the last in the series. We were still waiting to see whether Junie and Will would open their inn, or if the grumpy possum would finally return to the café, if Maya Shah's wish would come true, or if the magic of Quixotic Falls had finally run its course, with no more magic left to give.

It was all coming to a head like all good romantic epics did. I couldn't wait to find out how everything tied up in a neat bow. It felt impossible. A magic trick for a magical series. I never would find out how Quixotic Falls ended, sadly.

A few months later, Rachel Flowers died. She was thirty-two. My age now.

After her death, it came out that she hadn't planned the ending at all, and she'd told no one her ideas. Everyone was bereft. Not only for her, but for a happily ever after that would never come. A series, half a decade in the making, left without a proper ending. A story just stopped. No THE END. No epilogue to assure you that everything would be okay.

Nothing.

It was a year I'd rather not remember. Mom said that everyone had them, when your entire world is upended and you can't seem to get your footing again. Except, I never found my footing again, and I'd been stumbling ever since.

I took a quick shower, which was a pity because the claw-footed bathtub was *gorgeous*, and it would've been the loveliest bath, and pulled out my last pair of clean shorts and an old Stone Cold Steve Austin T-shirt that had somehow survived in my closet since the late nineties. I tucked it into my high-waisted shorts, slipped into my still-damp tennis shoes, and made sure that I'd packed everything into my duffel before I left the loft.

Anders was talking to someone at the front of the store as I came out of the loft. I paused at the top of the spiral staircase, and soaked in the view.

In the daylight, the bookstore took on a new life.

Motes of dust danced in the sunlight that streamed through the windows. It looked a lot cozier, as the colored glass window ornaments threw rainbows across the bookshelves and pirouetted across the hardwood floors like flecks of dappled sunlight on sand.

Bookcases, filled to the brim, reached up to the ceiling, cluttered with so many colors and kinds of books, short and fat, long and wide, that it almost felt like an assault on the senses. The center of the bookstore was open to the second floor, where tall bookshelves towered so high you had to reach them with ladders. Heavy oak beams supported the roof. Planetariums and glass chimes and other ornaments hung from the rafters, catching the morning's golden light and throwing it across the store. The shelves were made from the same deep oak as the ceiling beams and the banisters on the second floor, signs hanging from the eye-level shelves detailing the different sections of the store: MEMOIR, FANTASY, SCI-FI, ROMANCE, SELF-HELP, NATURE, HOW-TO . . .

This place was *beautiful*.

I wondered, briefly, what it would be like to own a place like this. It was magical. A shop that sold the impossible inked onto soft white paper.

"You can try this instead?" Anders was saying in a voice I hadn't heard him use before. It was tender, a bit sweet.

When I descended the stairs to see whom he was talking to, I could guess why.

A young girl—maybe eight, with warm brown skin and thick dark hair pulled up into a ponytail with a yellow ribbon—stood by the counter, a tattered book in her arms. The cover was missing, and the pages were bent and crinkly with water damage. The girl scrunched her nose at the book in question and then held out hers. "Can't you just order another one, Uncle Andie?"

Anders pushed his glasses up the bridge of his nose. "I am not a wizard, sadly."

"But . . ."

"I'm sure I have some duct tape . . ."

She gasped in alarm and quickly returned her damaged book to her tote. "Never mind! I'll deal with it. I'll just read it . . . gently."

"Or," he ventured, "you could try a new book?"

She rolled her eyes. "Yeah, *okay*. Sure."

"Hey, your favorite book could be one you haven't read yet."

"Or it could be the one *you* want to duct-tape. I'll take my chances elsewhere, with someone more *tactful*," she quipped, and moved over to the corner of the counter, where a blond-and-orange cat snoozed on a well-loved cat bed, and scrubbed it behind the ears. "See you around, Mr. Butterscotch."

"No goodbye for me?" Anders asked.

"You don't deserve it," she replied severely, turned on her heel, and marched out of the bookstore without another word. The bell above the door jingled as she left.

I bit the inside of my cheek to keep myself from laughing. Whatever ill will I had toward Anders from yesterday went out the door with that little girl. I hadn't seen someone so thoroughly annihilated by a child since I made the mistake of subbing for a middle school art class before I realized I was better off teaching college.

Anders sighed, having not yet noticed me, and studied the cat in the pool of sunlight. The cat returned his bored look and yawned. He muttered something to it, and poked it in the side. The cat turned over and showed his belly, and went back to sleep.

"You couldn't just order her another one from Amazon or something?" I asked, stepping up to the register.

He jumped, startled, and then turned a glare at me. The sunlight lit his minty eyes, making them almost glow. "Really, you suggest *that* in a bookstore?"

"Two-day shipping," I replied with a shrug, trying to ignore the weird twist in my stomach. Not butterflies, surely. I barely knew this man. "You can't beat it."

"I hope all your bacon burns," he muttered. "Who hurt you?"

"How much time do you have?"

He gave me a lingering look. "Not enough to ask. Did you sleep well?"

"Like the dead. Well, with the exception of the starlings."

"I warned you."

"I thought they'd tweet. Not . . ."

"Sound like chain saws?"

I scoffed. "That'd be *better*. They sang this creepy song. Have you heard it?" I hummed a few bars.

"Can't say I have," he replied, and glanced over at the orange cat. "Butterscotch is very bad at catching birds. At catching anything besides sleep, actually."

"Oh, I think Mr. Butterscotch is doing a great job," I said, and went over to pet the cat.

Anders gave a start. "Wait, he doesn't like—"

Too late. I rubbed Butterscotch behind the ears, and he started to purr. "Oh, who's a good kitty? You're a good kitty. What doesn't he like?" I added as the cat tilted his head up so I could scratch under his chin.

Anders looked like he'd just been betrayed. If I knew him better, I'd have said he almost *pouted*. "People, usually."

"Ah, see, there's the difference. I'm not people. I'm Elsy," I pointed out.

"Indeed," he replied, clearly not impressed.

I motioned after the girl. "So, what happened to her book?"

"Read it so much it fell apart," he said, giving one last look of betrayal to his cat, before he went over to the old Compaq to wake it up. The computer hummed to life like an ancient being crawling out of its crypt a century too soon. "I knew it would, eventually."

"That's heartbreaking. I remember when my favorite book fell apart."

"And what did you do?"

I'd run into the kitchen where my mom was making chili, sobbing, the cover of *Inkheart* in one hand, the pages in the other, like I'd just killed my favorite pet by playing with it too hard. My mom tried to console me, but I was absolutely beside myself, and we really didn't have the money for a new book back then. She was good at looking on the bright side of everything—sunshine and rainbows even when you were in the seat of a volcano and it was filling with molten lava. She sat me up on the counter, and told me that we could fix it instead. She was a librarian, after all, so even the most mangled picture book she could cut, glue, and sew back together. Maybe it wouldn't look *new*, but well loved, and those always looked better, anyway.

I found myself grinning at the memory. "Well, we actually *did* use a little duct tape—no, wait, packing tape."

"And it looked . . . ?"

"Perfect," I replied. "I mean, not really, but I could still use it. A book doesn't have to be pretty for you to read it."

"I have seen some god-awful covers in my time," he agreed. "Well, Lily won't go for packing tape, either. I'll have to think of something else for her." He chewed on the inside of his cheek, and wrote a note down on the far side of the cash register, on a yellowed notepad that already had a list going for the day. He scrolled through some accounts on the computer—a library of titles, it seemed. "Maybe I can find something here. Something close enough."

"Would you settle for anything less than your favorite book?" I shook my head. "It's not the same."

"Hmm," he muttered, and I had the feeling that was as close to an agreement as I'd get.

He and the bookshop were more similar the longer I looked at them. They were both tidy in that cluttered way—you weren't sure where to look, but everywhere you did, you found something surprising. There wasn't a book out of place, and there wasn't a hair out of place. His shirt was wrinkle-free, his trousers knife-pleated. The smattering of freckles on his cheeks carried across the rest of his skin, too, including the back of his neck, hidden just beneath his orderly collar. "Is there something you need?"

I leaned over the counter to look at his screen. "You wouldn't happen to have internet, would you?"

He looked at me over his oval-shaped glasses. I'd never seen eyes that green or bright before. This close, I could tell that the green was mixed with a light gray, making the strange minty color. They were very pretty.

I caught myself before I stared too long.

I dug my phone out of my back pocket. "Because I don't have cell service here. Do you have Wi-Fi? I need to figure out how to get out of here."

"The storm knocked out the internet last night," he said, brushing off a speck of invisible dirt from the counter, not meeting my gaze.

I wilted. "Oh . . ."

I must've looked quite forlorn, because he sighed and plucked a map from a kiosk beside the register. "Here. This should help. Obviously you'll want to head out the way you came, across Charm Bridge—"

"'There was only one road in, and one road out of Eloraton, New York, and most people never took it,'" I quoted, taking the map, and unfolded it on the counter.

His eyes widened. "Excuse me?"

"It's the first line in a book, *Daffodil Daydreams*—"

"You memorized the first line?"

I hesitated. "I mean, you're a book person, too. Don't you memorize your favorite lines?"

He started to reply, and then frowned, stumped by my question. "No. I can't say I do. But I'm sure I'll remember our little meeting for years to come. Safe travels, Eileen. It was . . . an experience to meet you."

"You too, Anderson," I replied with a fake smile, resisting the urge to roll my eyes with every fiber of my being. I gave the cat lounging in the window a final scratch on the head, and left the bookstore behind me.

The late morning sun was so bright, I shielded my eyes and realized—with a wince—that I'd forgotten the map on the counter. And I certainly wasn't going back for it. It couldn't be that hard to find the main highway again and just . . . retrace my steps until I found something familiar. Or ran into Poughkeepsie.

Preferably not Poughkeepsie.

I slung my duffel bag into the passenger seat, dug my key out of my pocket, jammed it into the ignition, and cranked it up.

The car gave a sputter, yowling like a dying animal.

I tried again.

And again.

"Not now, not now," I prayed. "*Please* not now. Let me get to the cabin first. Let me get lost in a book."

But my car betrayed me, and the engine refused to turn over.

It wouldn't even *try*. I guessed the noise it had started making back in DC was bad, after all. Everything was falling apart—*everything*. Maybe I shouldn't have gone on this trip. I shouldn't have come *alone*. This was a mistake.

"Stop it," I told myself. "Everything's fine, you're fine. You can fix this."

Then I unbuckled myself from my seat, and rounded to the front of the car, where I unlatched the hood to look underneath.

I . . . didn't even know what I was looking at.

The Pinto sat there like an aged, decrepit dinosaur, leaking oil like that was its last mission on Earth, and I knew about as much about car mechanics as I did brain surgery. So it looked like an engine, and it wasn't like one of my Barbie cars from my childhood, where I could just switch the batteries and give it a few more hours of life.

I pressed my forehead against my forearm as I held the hood up.

"Okay, maybe you *can't* fix this, but you're in a cute town! Someone's gotta know something about cars," I said, turning around to survey the town. "Or have a number for AAA."

There were two old men walking their schnauzer. I waved to them, but they turned down the next street too quickly to notice me. The bar was closed, but the garden shop beside it had just flipped its sign over.

Perfect.

Hopefully, the owner would be a *little* more friendly than Anders.

I closed the hood and hurried down the sidewalk to the garden store.

The smell of wildflowers and freshly cut stems filled my nose as I stepped inside. Enormous pots of ivy hung from the ceiling, and fresh-cut flowers stuffed into tin vases hung across the walls in various colors: black-eyed Susans and roses and bright lavenders and soft asters, cornflowers and daisies and forget-me-nots. A woman was at the counter in the back, humming along to an old radio perched atop a shelf behind her. She looked about my age, with long copper-red hair braided into a fishtail down her back, dressed in a crop-top T-shirt and jeans that were already dirty at the knees. She wore a worn-looking apron in a cactus print, her fingers wrapped with multiple Band-Aids, as if she pricked her fingers often. She glanced up at me and smiled; there was a gap between her front teeth.

I felt a sudden rush of déjà vu—I'd seen her before.

But I couldn't place where.

"Good morning," she greeted happily. "You must be the one who stayed in Anders's old loft last night!"

"I guess word gets around," I said.

"It's a small town," she replied with a laugh, and then leaned forward a little to add conspiratorially, "You'd be surprised how quick news spreads. I'm Lyssa." She extended her Band-Aid-wrapped hand.

"Eileen," I replied, accepting it—and then frowned. "Lyssa with a *y*?"

She brightened. "Yes! How did you know?" She glanced down at her cactus-print apron. "I didn't even put my name tag on yet! Has Gail been gossiping about me? Ruby? Oh, it was probably Ruby. Whatever you heard, it is definitely not in any way *true*."

I hadn't heard anything at all, but I knew everything was true. Because I realized where I'd seen her before—well, *seen* wasn't exactly the right word for it. My mouth opened and closed like a goldfish gasping for water. Because surely it was a coincidence. *Surely* it was. A ginger-haired woman named Lyssa with a *y*, tending to a garden shop in a small town. Surely she hadn't threatened to bury a man when she'd caught him cheating on her sister. Surely it was a fluke.

The song on the radio ended, and the DJ came on with—

"*Buzz buzz*, Eloraton! Hope you're kicking serious beehive butt on this glorious Saturday morning. That was the hit single from Dexys Midnight Runners, 'Come On Eileen' . . ."

I stared up at the radio. Beside it were certificates of BEST IN SHOW and TOP BLOOM from the state fair and local garden shows.

But that didn't—

That didn't make *sense*.

"Eloraton? Like the book series?" I added, because she looked confused. "You know, the Quixotic Falls series by Rachel Flowers? *Daffodil Daydreams? Honey and the Heartbreak? Unrequited Love Song?*" She stared at me, nothing ringing a bell. "*Return to Sender?* Small town in the Hudson Valley, with a magical waterfall?"

"Well, I don't know if the waterfall is *magic*," she replied, "but we are a small town in the Hudson Valley, true."

This was a really elaborate joke, right?

It had to be.

Eloraton was a fictional town like Virgin River or Stars Hollow or the countless other made-up places manifested through someone's imagination.

I must have paled a shade, because Lyssa asked, "Are you all right there, friend?"

"This isn't funny," I said, shaking my head. She even looked like I imagined. Freckles dotted across her cheeks, a heart-shaped face, a gap-toothed smile.

"I'm not sure what's the joke?"

"This is a theme park, then? A—a roadside attraction?"

Her smile faltered. "I . . . don't follow."

If this wasn't a joke, then she was Lyssa Greene, the botanist who opened a flower shop instead of joining the family business, who grew the most dazzling blooms with the greenest thumb in the state, whose laugh sounded like wind chimes, who'd kissed Maya Shah under the waterfall—

That Lyssa Greene.

And if this was Lyssa, then . . .

She tilted her head. "Are you sure you're all right? Can I get you some water?"

"No, yes, I'm sure I'm fine—I'm sorry." I retreated out of the garden shop, almost knocking over a vase full of wildflowers. "Bye!"

She picked up her hand to wave, but I was already gone. I stumbled into the middle of the road, where people began to stare, but I wasn't paying any attention to them. Not at first.

Because the first thing I noticed was the sign above the bar, which read THE ROOST. Last night all I'd been able to see was the *OO*. The mural on the side was painted by Junie Bray herself, of a town overflowing with flowers and bees, the banner strung from one side of the painting to the other—WELCOME TO ELORATON! HOME OF THE FIGHTING BEES. Then in smaller letters: THREE-TIME SPELLING BEE CHAMPIONS. I spun around.

In the bright midday sun, I could see everything.

The one road in curved down from the hills, through the trees, and fed through the main thoroughfare of Eloraton, straight toward the town square, where a tall clock tower stood over the rest of the buildings like a sentry, its face grinning under mustached hands of time. I'd seen many idyllic towns on my road trips up here, old Main Streets and quaint villages nestled in the woods, but this place was different. In the storm, I hadn't been able to tell, but contrasted against the blue sky and deep green woods—it was hard to miss. This town looked like every good part of every lovely town I'd ever seen, all jigsawed into one. Main Street burgeoned with life, buildings housing SWEETIES (advertising honey in the window), and DRUGS (just Drugs), and the corner grocer, and all the little eclectic shops that sold paper crafts and hardware and pet clothes and bath soaps. The streetlights were covered in crawling ivy, the brick faces of buildings cracked in that old yet well-loved way buildings got. Cars parked diagonally outside of various businesses, but most of them were in front of the Grumpy Possum Café.

And when I looked back at the bookstore, I noticed the name on the display window, too.

INEFFABLE BOOKS

If this *was* a joke, it was very elaborate, down to the people actually looking like the people I'd read about dozens upon dozens of times, until the spines cracked. I kept trying to see the flaws here, the man behind the emerald curtain, but all I saw were pages—pages and pages—of words and scenes and moments that Pru and I giggled over. The kiss in the rain at the corner of Bluebell and Main, the confession in the garden of the bed-and-breakfast, the breakup at the Grumpy Possum Café . . . it was all here.

Impossibly.

I was . . .

This was . . .

My heart knew the word long before my brain did. My heart said it with every beat as I walked down the only road in and out of this fictional town, passing business after business, person after person. It was all here—

Even the Daffodil Inn, standing quiet and vacant in the corner of the square.

I kept walking until I found the courtyard beneath the clock tower, and there I sank down on the bench donated by one Frank Greene of Frank's Hotties, the premier hot sauce of Eloraton. The hot sauce without a label last night—Gail had said it was local. It was Frank's. A soft breeze rustled the trees, and the smell of wild-flowers and pine curled through the air.

It wasn't a dream.

Or if it was, I was dead on the side of the road somewhere and this was heaven.

A droplet of rain splatted on my nose. Then another on the sidewalk in front of me.

Rain? But it had been clear just a moment ago. I held out my hand, and another raindrop landed in my palm.

There was a *pop*, and I glanced up just as the bookstore owner navigated a large umbrella over my head. Rain drummed on the open fabric, loud and hard. There were questions—so many questions—right on the tip of my tongue.

And he already knew all of them.

"Every day is about the same here," Anders said after a moment. "A storm blows in around noon, and then another in the early evening. The inn is always under renovation, the burgers at Gail's bar are always slightly burnt, the honey taffy is always sweet, and the starlings always make their nests in the eaves."

I stared at him, unsure of what he was getting at.

"The clock tower is always three minutes behind," he went on, "and Lily's book is always losing its pages, and Lyssa always pines over Maya when she passes the flower shop. Nothing ever changes. Nothing ever will."

The rain had begun to let up a little already. Bits of sunlight broke through the clouds.

"If I ask you a question," I said, scooting to the edge of the bench to look up at him, into those bright mint-colored eyes, "will you promise to tell me the truth? The actual truth?"

His hard expression softened a little. I tried to place him—somewhere in all the pages Pru and I read. White-blond hair and green eyes, a strong jaw and a nose that looked like it'd been broken at least once, but I couldn't for the life of me remember. The last I recalled, the bookstore had been for sale. In want of a new owner.

"I promise to tell you the truth." He surprised me, because he sounded as sincere as he had with the girl—Lily. Who was she to him? A niece? A cousin? She called him uncle, but I didn't remember Lily Shah having an uncle.

Anders, Andie, *Anderson*—I didn't remember the name in any of the books.

He was the only part of this town, this story, that wasn't familiar. Maybe he had been hidden somewhere in the pages, some strong-jawed man sipping tea at the Grumpy Possum Café, and I'd just skimmed over him in search of the happily ever after.

"Is this really . . ." I hesitated, because it couldn't be, it *couldn't* be—

The clock tower behind me began to chime noon in that bright, distinct song that hummed across the buildings, so loud I vibrated with it. I closed my eyes. Let the hum pass over me, through me, around me, until it faded into the sounds of the town again: birdsong and bug noises and the distinct chatter of life.

He inclined his head and tilted the umbrella back. The rain had stopped, and the way the afternoon sunlight danced across the town reminded me of light at the bottom of a fish tank. Down the street, shop owners propped open their doors and set out their chalkboards again, waving to each other in that small-town way, as if they were perfectly happy with every day being the exact same, one hour bleeding into the next, into days and weeks and months, where nothing ever changed, ever transformed, until the turn of the page.

"Welcome," he said, closing his umbrella, "to Eloraton."

5

Beginnings of a Book Club

S OMETIMES, A BOOK CAN change your life.

It's hard to explain that to someone who doesn't read, or who has never felt their heart bend so strongly toward a story that it might just snap in two. Some books are a comfort, some a reprieve, others a vacation, a lesson, a heartbreak. I'd met countless stories by the time I read a book that changed my life.

At first it didn't really *feel* like anything special. It was a romance, one I'd picked up at my local independent bookstore because it had a fun cover, and I liked small-town stories, and I'd been in my hardest year of undergrad. The world felt gray, and just the sight of a book made my stomach turn from all the anxiety of late-night essays and GPAs and scholarship funding. And the book was just sitting there. It was the copy on the shelf, wedged between Brontë and Gabaldon, on a single bookcase set aside for romances.

The book had just come out, but it was already 50 percent off, and I figured with the change I could get a cup of coffee across the street at Starbucks, too.

The moment was so unassuming, so *normal*.

Sometimes, that's how it happens. Sometimes your favorite book just hits you out of the blue like a bolt of lightning.

Daffodil Daydreams was a paperback original. First in a series of five called the Quixotic Falls Quintet. It was written by a woman not much older than me. I imagined we could've been friends in high school, maybe classmates in college. I'd sidle up beside her and casually tell her that she wrote a novel that changed my life.

She made me remember why I loved to read.

I'd heard of books doing that, but I always figured it was metaphorical, a nice sentiment.

I never thought it actually happened.

And because of it, I went on to grad school to study library and information science, and I took an adjunct job at my alma mater, and that was how I wound up as an English professor, where more than a few of my mutuals questioned my taste. Then again, they always lied when they said their favorite book was *Lolita* or *Fight Club*. (There was one guy who said his favorite was *The Hobbit*, and I believed him, at least.)

So when Pru came to my windowless office one autumn day four years after I first read *Daffodil Daydreams*, bringing with her a pumpkin spice latte and a warm cookie she'd freshly baked at home, and told me about a romance book club, I was intrigued.

"And how did you find these people?" I asked, taking a bite of the snickerdoodle. Pru always made the best cookies. Warm and gooey, melt in your mouth. If I didn't break out every time I ate sugar, I'd have a mouthful of cavities because of her.

She sat down in the threadbare chair on the other side of my paper-filled desk. "The internet."

"Absolutely not," I said instantly.

Pru leaned forward. "C'mon, Elsy, just hear me out for a second? I did bring you coffee," she added, and I took another sip of my latte. I guessed I owed her a listen, even if the answer was going to be an emphatic *no* either way.

I sighed. "Fine. So you met them on the internet, but how do you *know* these people?"

She tried to hide a grin, thinking that maybe she was going to win me over after all. "I started chatting with JakesNob42 about the publisher pushing *Return to Sender* back a few weeks, and we just started . . . talking. About a book club. They know a few people. I know you . . ."

"So you planned an online book club with someone who willfully chose their username as JakesNob42 . . ."

"Oh my god." She rolled her eyes. "You were just complaining the other day about not being able to talk to anyone about the books you read, and now I come to you with a great idea and you can't get over a username. Which, I might add"—she held up a finger—"is a bit ironic, if I recall your username from high school."

I sipped my latte loudly. "I don't know what you mean. Sparkle-LlamaCullen was a great username."

"It was—what do the youths say? Cringe?"

"Youths don't say 'cringe' anymore," I replied.

I sighed dramatically, and shook my head. "Bless their little hearts . . ."

She resisted the urge to roll her eyes again, and took out her phone. "I'm just saying, I'm joining this super-smutty book club, and you should, too."

"Is it *really* going to be super smutty?"

To which she replied, "We're starting with Rachel Flowers. So

Emily Henry–level canoodling, but I think we're going to transition nicely into omegaverse and sex spores."

I opened my mouth. Closed it again. Gave it a long, and very, very deep thought. It *would* be nice to sit down and talk about novels with people who liked browsing the romance section of bookstores. Or, at least, it'd be more entertaining than chatting with Elmer Williams, for the third time, about the newest translation of *Beowulf.* Not that there was anything *wrong* with academic discussions—I was an English professor; I loved waxing poetic about the nuances of Apollo and Dionysus's relationship in Ovid's *Metamorphoses*, or the Byronification of *The Vampyre.* But to sit down with mostly strangers and just talk about a lovely little meet-cute? A grand romantic gesture?

Oh, be still, my beating, bloody heart.

"I do like Rachel Flowers," I finally admitted, and Pru wiggled her eyebrows. Because she had me. She *knew* she had me.

"No, you *love* Rachel Flowers. And as luck would have it, so does everyone else in the book club. It's how I found them. We're starting with the first book, and reading the next two over October and November, so when the fourth book comes out in February . . ."

"We'll be ready," I finished.

"*We?*"

I took another sip of my latte. "All right. You've caught me."

She winked. "Hook, line, and sinker. I knew you'd come around." Then she stood, and stole a peppermint out of the bowl on my desk, reserved exclusively for the college freshman boys who, somehow, didn't understand that hygiene meant brushing your teeth before your 8:00 a.m. class. "We're meeting over video call on Thursday. Right after your English 101 class. Come over and we can hop on the call together?"

"Fine, fine." I checked my watch. It was almost time for

Shakespeare's Comedies, a class I didn't teach, but the professor had taken a leave of absence after contracting mono (along with, mysteriously, another professor in the nursing school), so it fell to me to teach about taming shrews. "I hope it's not going to be too weird."

"Nonsense. We're *way* past the point of weird." Then she popped the peppermint into her mouth and took her leave just as swiftly as she'd come.

PRUDENCE NEVER DID ANYTHING IN HALVES, WHILE I DID WELL if I remembered to bring *myself* to things, which is exactly what happened that Thursday of the inaugural meeting of the Super Smutty Book Club. She'd gone all out, with a cheese plate and veggie tray meant for at least ten people, and our favorite bottle of Riesling.

"About *time* you got here," she said as I slipped in through the front door to her apartment. She wore her I GOT WET IN QUIXOTIC FALLS T-shirt, and I took mine out of my satchel and quickly changed in the hall bathroom. "We're just about to start!"

"Sorry, sorry," I called, pulling off my Caesar salad–stained top and tugging on my T-shirt. "I had a rather heated discussion with one of the students about *Romeo and Juliet*."

I heard Pru pause on the other side of the door. "I thought you were filling in for Shakespeare's Comedies?"

"Oh, I am. The student argued that *Romeo and Juliet* is satire, like most of Willy Shake's comedies." I pulled my hair into a ponytail, checked my eyeliner, and opened the door to find her waiting outside. "So I should be teaching it with the comedies."

"But the two kids die," Prudence replied matter-of-factly.

"Yes, *but*—and this is the really interesting part—the student posed that because Rosaline denied Romeo's advances at the beginning—which is what any normal girl would do, right?—the story is actually a satire about the very real problem in the sixteenth century of marrying girls much too young. Juliet *is* thirteen in the play, after all. Romeo's sixteen. And, to back up the student's claim, they pointed out that the Montagues and Capulets originated in *The Divine Comedy* by—"

"Dante, is it?"

"Exactly. It was really, really fascinating."

Prudence shook her head. "Nerd," she said lovingly.

I smiled at her. "Takes one to know one. So, where are we meeting these strangers who will find out our deepest and darkest secrets?"

She laughed. "C'mon, it's not *that* bad. It's not like we're giving them our fanfic usernames."

In the living room, she already had her laptop set up on the coffee table, with the aforementioned cheese board and veggie tray. We sat down, and waited for someone named Janelle (aka Jakes-Nob42), to email us the link to the video call. It came three minutes late, and when we were finally let into the room, I knew we had found our people. There were five others on the call. The youngest—Aditi, wearing a beanie reading SPACE QUEEN pulled far over their dark hair—was videoing in from their dorm room under the covers, while Janelle, a slender woman in her thirties, sipped something from a Twihard mug, already in her pajamas with a wrap over her box braids. There was Matt, a larger middle-aged white man with scruffy blond hair and black-framed glasses, and Olivia, who looked about my and Pru's age, with pink-dyed hair and a white cat pawing at her keyboard. Then there was one of the most handsome men I'd ever seen. Dark hair, long pale face with a regal nose, where thin glasses sat on the edge, moles dotting his face like a constellation. He was reading something off-screen until we came on, and then quickly exited out of it. This was Benji.

Pru waved at everyone with an "Evening, everyone! I'm Pru, and this is Elsy."

I gave a brief wave. "Hello."

The woman with pink hair tossed her cat off her keyboard for a third time. "*Finally!* Pru's told us a lot about you!"

I gave my best friend a cautious look. "She has?"

"Nothing bad!" Pru quickly added. "I promise."

"But you *do* have to answer a question," said Matt. "To settle an argument we're having."

Aditi rolled their eyes under the covers. "It's not an argument. There's a *clear* answer."

I nodded. *Okay.*

Janelle ate a fuego Taaki chip and asked, "Favorite love interest in Quixotic Falls, go. Team Will or Team Jake?"

Benji muttered, having gone back to reading something just off-screen, "No love for Thomas, I see."

"Or Maya!" Olivia added.

To which Benji replied, "Maya isn't a love interest."

"*Yet,*" Olivia corrected. "I can dream. Oh, or *Ruby.*" She gave a pleasant sigh. "She has such bi wife energy."

And was one of the best characters, in my opinion. The books were sectioned off into couples, and they were all companions of one another. The first was Junie and Will, the second Ruby and Jake, the third Gemma and Thomas. The fourth was Bea, but her love interest was a mystery. The book wouldn't come out for a few months, after all.

I gave a laugh. I guess I should've been nervous, but there really wasn't a wrong answer. There were just fun answers. "Will, *obviously.*"

Pru gave a gasp. "Seriously, not Jake?"

Olivia sighed. "And still, no love for Maya . . ."

Matt said, "What about Frank? He was the real MVP of the third book . . ."

Two hours later, after we'd all said goodbye, my cheeks hurt from smiling so much. We didn't talk at *all* about the first book, because we'd read them already, and the conversations filled my heart so full, I thought I just might burst.

Pru ate the last piece of cheddar from the cheese board and asked, "So? What do you think?"

I tried to stop smiling, but I couldn't. For a very long time, it'd just been Pru and me, talking about books we read together, so I didn't think how different it'd feel to be a part of a group that was just as unapologetically enthusiastic. I didn't know it then, but it would sate a part of my soul that had been thirsty for connection— for community—for so long, I'd forgotten to water it. I'd forgotten that in it, joy could bloom.

"I think," I said, feeling like I was still in a dream, "I'm in love."

~

THE SUPER SMUTTY BOOK CLUB DIDN'T MEET IN PERSON UNTIL two years later, during the Year I Wanted to Forget. Pru had to drag me out of my apartment to go because I hadn't wanted to—I would just ruin the mood. I was still picking up the pieces of my broken heart. I wasn't in a state to be a person. But she dragged me along anyway. The book club picked a cabin in the middle of Dutchess County, New York, a nice breezy jaunt from Rhinebeck and the seat of the Hudson Valley, and we all met there. Aditi came from some remote part of Canada, and Olivia came from Seattle. Matt flew in from Texas, and Janelle came down from Maine. Benji had the shortest trip, since he lived in New York City, so he was in charge of all the big foodstuffs. Pru decided to make a road trip out of it, packed our bags and two cases of wine into my Pinto, and we drove up.

I squirmed in the driver's seat as Google Maps inched us closer and closer to our destination. What was thirty minutes turned into fifteen, and Olivia was blowing up our phones asking about our ETA. Google Maps led us up one of the winding hills of the Catskills to a small, secluded cabin. There were a few other cars parked in the dirt lot out front, and I pulled in beside them and turned off the engine.

We were the last ones at the house. It was a secluded A-frame cabin with six beds and two pullout couches, a Jacuzzi that Benji later ended up passing out in after one too many glasses of Riesling, and rocking chairs on the back porch, where Janelle took a cat nap every afternoon. We decided to all read a series together while we stayed in the house for a week, nothing but paperback romances and box wine and good conversations.

Or at least, that's what I had hoped would happen.

"What if things go wrong?" I asked, looking out the windshield at the A-frame cabin. "We'll be trapped here for a week with them. What if they get tired of me, and what if I burst into tears, and what if—"

Pru grabbed my hand and squeezed it tightly. "Hey, hey, look at me."

I did.

"These are our friends. They aren't Liam. Okay?"

Liam. It was the first time we'd said his name aloud in . . . *months.* The name made my stomach twist, but I squeezed her hand back and gathered up my courage. This wasn't like me. I had to get over this. "Okay," I said.

Pru said, "Repeat after me: we're going to have a great time."

"But—"

"Repeat it," she said.

I swallowed the stone in my throat. "Great time. We're going to have a fucking great time."

Pru smiled. "There's a glimmer of the Elsy I know. Now come on!" She dropped my hand, and shoved herself out of the passenger side. I took a deep breath, unbuckled my seat belt, and followed.

The woods were quiet, the sound of birds bright and twittery in the summer afternoon.

Breathe, I told myself. *It'll be okay—*

The front door burst open, and a bear of a man walked out. Blond hair, black-framed glasses. It took a moment to recognize him, because he looked so much smaller on video. Matt grinned and threw his arms wide.

"Let the debauchery begin!" he boomed.

My stomach dropped. Oh, no. This was going to be horrible. This was going to be bad. This was going to be—

"And by 'debauchery,'" added Olivia, who had dyed her hair teal to match the cover of the newest Quixotic Falls novel, "we mean put on your bunny slippers and bring in that wine, because if the cops don't find us in a week half-dead under a mountain of Romancelandia, then we did it wrong."

Amazing. This was going to be amazing.

I couldn't unload Sweetpea fast enough. As Pru and I hauled our things from the hatchback, she winked at me as if to say, *See? Trust me.*

Because for Prudence, things always worked out. She was the main character, and I was happy just being along for the ride. It was safe that way. Easy. Her heart never led her wrong—not once.

I wished I could say the same about my own.

6

Honey, Honey

ARE YOU HUNGRY?" ANDERS asked, shaking out the rain from his umbrella. Sunlight streaked through the clouds, and slowly ambled in golden splotches across the town.

I glanced up at him, squinting. He was right in the sun, so I couldn't read his expression. "Am I dead?"

He snorted. "No. You're not."

"Oh," I said, looking down Main Street again, "then I'm running out of ideas for how this is real. Because it's not—I know it's not."

"No, it's not."

"Then I'm dead."

"No," he repeated. "You're here."

"In a town that doesn't exist," I replied.

He twirled his umbrella around his hand. "Stranger things have happened, Elsy. Now come on," he said, outstretching his hand to help me up off the bench.

I took it without really thinking. His grip was strong, his fingers soft and gentle, as he pulled me to my feet. If I was dead or dreaming, he certainly felt real. His skin was warm, and he was solid, and I clung to his presence like an anchor. Pru would judge him for his too-short trousers, the way the hem barely reached his ankles, and she'd ruffle his perfect hair and ask him if he was trying to be a romance hero with that cut. It looked just curly enough that my fingers would snag if I raked them through it—and that thought in and of itself startled me out of my head.

What was I even thinking? I didn't know this guy. He was a character in a book series. He wasn't *real*.

"The café starts serving lunch at noon," he went on, checking his watch, "and look at that, it's quarter past."

"By café, do you mean . . ."

"The only one in town," he confirmed and I followed him down the street, back toward the main thoroughfare.

It was half-past by the time we reached the café. On the walk, I caught glimpses of people I felt like I'd met once in a dream. It was the strangest sort of déjà vu, and each time it happened, it sent a stronger shiver up my spine.

He reached for the door handle, and then paused and turned back to me. "Don't act weird. Pretend you're a stranger. You don't know anything. You don't know anyone."

I squinted. "Who are you?"

He rolled his eyes in exhaustion, and opened the door. The café was charming, just like I'd imagined, the booths a worn black vinyl, the tiles checkered. The logo of the restaurant, Grumpy Possum Café, was on the window, a cartoon possum holding both a pancake and a waffle, looking ready to bite the head off a person. I scooted into one of the booths, and he took the other side and handed me a menu. I blinked, thinking my eyes were playing tricks on me, and then I squinted a little more. Most of the menu was normal, but there were a few items that were just . . . half-printed. I rubbed my eyes and looked again. The words didn't change.

"They weren't imagined," he said simply, flipping over the menu and skimming the back. "The pancakes are good. So are the waffles. And the club sandwich."

I barely paid attention to him as I glanced around at the other people in the café, wondering if I remembered them from the books as well. Pru would—she *certainly* could—name them all. My brain was finally beginning to shake off the shock. Curiosity, giddy and insatiable, swelled in me, growing larger and larger like a snowball rolling down a hill.

Eloraton.

This was *Eloraton*.

I set down my menu, leaned over the table toward Anders, and whispered, "How is any of this possible? The town? The people? Did Rachel Flowers base everything on a real town? No, that can't be right. Even on Google, the town doesn't show up, and there's a plaque on the side of the road—"

"She based Eloraton on all the romance novels she fell in love with as a teenager," he said, setting down the menu. "I can't answer how this is real, or how you found it—but you did. And didn't I tell you not to act weird?"

I gave a start. "How else do you expect me to act?"

"Normal."

"I am being very normal, thank you—oh my god, I can get the Honey Surprise," I said excitedly. "The special. I can get the special!"

He sighed, and it sounded like his soul had left his body. "Yes. You can. Then you'll get back in your car, and you'll leave."

Oh, I realized. *He doesn't know my car's dead.*

I thought about correcting him, but that might upend this

lovely lunch, and I really wanted that Honey Surprise. "Yeah, of course," I said lightly, inspecting the menu, hoping he didn't sense my lie. "I will . . . *eventually*."

He narrowed his eyes further. "Don't you have people who are going to start missing you soon?"

"I mean, not *immediately*—" I began to reason as a peppy waitress hurried over to us, a notepad and pen in hand. Anders already knew what he wanted: plain black tea.

"You're so boring, Andie," she sighed.

"I like it how I like it," he replied simply.

"And that's why we love you. And coming in with a *girl*?" she added, pressing a hand over her heart with a mock gasp. "Andie with a friend, I never thought I'd see the day! What's your name, friend? Got an eye for what you'd like?"

They both looked expectantly at me. I was still staring at the waitress, my mouth agape.

Anders cleared his throat.

That was—the waitress was—

Anders pressed the heel of his shoe over my toe, and I yelped. "Ow! Oh, I mean—uh—" I snapped my attention back to the menu. "Um . . ."

My mind had gone completely blank. What had I wanted?

"This is Elsy," Anders introduced. "She stayed in the loft last night. She got a little lost in the rain."

The waitress snapped her fingers. "Oh! Gail said something about that this morning. Well, welcome to our little town. It isn't much, but it's home." She had a thick Tennessean drawl, just as I imagined it. Her hair was long and glossy and blond, her eyes brown, her white skin tinged with a bright summer sunburn. She had a kind heart-shaped face and a tattoo on her wrist in the shape of a compass, to remind her that she was the captain of her own life, and to navigate it well. The name tag on her apron read BECKA, but her name was—

"Ruby!" someone called from the back. Frantic. Followed by a lot of little somethings falling to the floor. "The ice maker!"

Ruby, to match her bright red lipstick.

"Oh shit," she cursed, taking my drink order before shoving her pad and pen into her apron. She said apologetically, "I'll be right back!"

Then she was gone, and suddenly I was back in my last semester of grad school, stress-eating my way through the spring, while Pru lay on the floor and read *Unrequited Love Song*. She had decided to skip the whole grad school thing and go to work at her parents' printshop, so she usually came over to my study sessions for moral support. Rain drummed against the window, and it beckoned both of us onto a cozy couch to finish the book—but *some* of us had critical theory to pass.

"Oh my god, I love her already," Pru kept saying, flipping the pages as fast as she could read.

I glared at her from the shitty kitchen table in our shitty apartment. It was only a few blocks from the campus, so it made walking to class easy, but the toilet ran most nights, and Pru could swear there was something living in the walls. "Can you stop torturing me with that book?"

"You're the one who's studying when it's *raining*," she replied, then licked her fingers, and turned the page. "You know the rules."

"I'm going to fail this class," I muttered, flipping back into my notes. "When the hell did we talk about *Heart of Darkness*?"

"Come join meeee," she pleaded, patting the carpet beside her. "Eileeeeeen."

I studiously ignored her. "Roland Barthes . . . 'Death of the Author.' Maybe my death, too."

"Pity," Pru said, "I'm reading about a great little death right here."

"You're the worst."

"You love me."

I highlighted a passage in my notes about genre theory.

And from the floor, she began to hum the one song that I hated more than I hated anything else in life—and that included my visceral hatred for the rubber smell that comes with Halloween, and men who crop dust on dates.

She started to hum "Come On Eileen" and shimmied her shoulders. The more I resisted, the louder she got until she was singing the words at the top of her lungs, and mimicking a rope to lasso me over to her, and what else could I do but melt out of my chair and join her on the floor, and read about Ruby Rivers and her second-chance love songs?

I passed the exam, but mostly I just remembered the feeling at the end of Ruby's book, when she traded her dream of spotlights and glitter and world music tours for a small café in the middle of nowhere, and I hated that she had to choose.

7

Like a River Runs

RUBY RIVERS CAME BACK a few minutes later.

"Figured out what you'd like yet, friend?" Ruby asked, delivering our drinks, and pulling out her scratch pad.

I knew how to talk—really, I did—but the only thing that came out of my mouth was . . . nothing. My mind was blank. This was Ruby—*the* Ruby. The woman who punched her ex-boyfriend in the face, who made out with Jake in the rain, who sang soft lullabies to the café's possum when it was her turn to close for the night. I knew her. I knew her so intimately, it was like we'd been friends for years.

Anders cleared his throat. "She'd like the club s—"

I pulled myself together. "The Honey Surprise."

"Great choice," Ruby replied with a wink. My heart felt like it could explode. "Bacon on the side? Grits?"

"No thanks, just Grumpy," I said, thankful that my mouth seemed to be working again. Grumpy was the code word for a sprinkling of a special blend of powdered sugar and cinnamon—I couldn't *not* order it grumpy.

Ruby's face brightened. "*Someone* came prepared! Did Anders tell you about us?"

"I've just read about this place a thousand times."

"In the local *Buzz*," Anders quickly added, giving me a warning look.

"That's fantastic," she said, scribbling down my order. "I'll have to tell Jake we've got a fan."

"The *biggest*. Do you sell T-shirts? With the logo? Or, um, hats, or, ooh! An apron?" I went on, because now that my mouth worked, it couldn't stop. "Christmas ornaments? Specialty pens?"

If looks could kill, Anders would have murdered me ten times over by now.

Ruby laughed, and stuck her pencil into her ponytail. "You know what, we *should*, but we don't, sadly. I'll tell you what . . ." And she unpinned the name tag from the apron, rubbed off the name BECKA, and handed it to me. It had the name and logo at the top. "There you go. A souvenir."

"You're too nice," Anders deadpanned as I excitedly pinned it onto my shirt.

"Better than boring," Ruby shot back.

He handed her our menus. "I prefer routine."

"So a club sandwich, hold the greens?" she guessed.

"As always."

She rolled her eyes, jotting down his order, as someone else called her away. She seemed stretched in four different directions at once. A customer wanting her in one place, another one wanting her at the counter, her cook wanting her at the window—it looked a little overwhelming.

When she was gone, Anders hissed. "I said act normal."

I scoffed. "I'm not quoting from the books yet, am I? This is normal." But I couldn't hide my excitement, looking down at the name tag. My insides felt like squirming, giddy worms. Ruby gave me her name tag. She actually gave me her name tag! "Totally, totally normal— Is it crooked?"

He glowered.

I tilted the name tag to the left. "There, good enough."

He sipped his black tea. How boring.

When I was satisfied with the tag, I realized that I hadn't stopped smiling. "I can't believe that was *Ruby*! Is Jake here, too?" I glanced around for the café owner, but the only people working were Ruby, and the cook and dishwasher in the back.

Anders said, "Jake's probably still asleep. Or doing the accounts in the back. He takes the evening shifts."

"And she has the morning?"

He nodded. "Every day."

My excitement dulled a little. "It must be hard for them to see each other."

He gave a one-shouldered shrug. "I don't ask."

"She seems overworked, and he probably is, too," I went on, remembering the end of her book. *Unrequited Love Song* was divisive among readers. Some said it was a happy-for-now, like Bea's story in the fourth book, but others said that Ruby found her happy ending. That *this*—the strong coffee, the all-day breakfasts, the checkered-tile floors—was her happiness. I didn't believe that for a second, but I also didn't think this was her happy-for-now, either. "I wonder if Rachel meant it this way. I wonder if Ruby's happy."

If he heard me, he decided not to respond. At least, not at first. Not until he said quietly, "The worst thing that can happen here is a burnt hamburger and a rainy afternoon. How can she not be?"

True. Some people would call this place perfect, even.

I was just overthinking things. Trying to find some flaw in this wonderland—and I needed to stop. Enjoy myself. *Relax*.

My attention wandered out the window, to all the people and the shops. Down the street, I thought I saw the flash of pink hair and my heart leapt into my throat. There was only one person with pink hair in Eloraton. I scooted closer to the window to see. As I did, my watch caught on the handle of the syrup pot, and I dumped it into my lap. "Shit," I cursed, quickly righting the syrup, and grabbed a handful of napkins. It was a good thing the syrup was slow, because it only got me a little bit. I scooted out of the booth, muttering about going to clean myself up in the restroom. Anders pointed in the right direction, but I was already on my way.

The restroom was on the far side of the café. The door was squeaky, and the only functional stall didn't have a very good lock on it. On the back of the door, there were names etched into it, secret messages and smiley faces and signatures, all real, indented under my fingers.

The soap smelled like lemons, and the water from the sink was cool, and I couldn't shake the feeling that Ruby was very good at faking a smile. Because I was, too.

I still remembered lying on the living room floor, the carpet scratchy and the bookcases impossibly tall, after finishing Ruby's story. We stared at the speckled ceiling for a long while, listening to the toddler in the apartment above run back and forth, sounding like a miniature elephant.

"Well," I had said, after a while, as Pru got up to make us some tea in the kitchen. "I guess that was a happy ending."

"Of course it was," Pru replied, coming back into the living room with two cups of chai, and she offered me one as I sat up. "Ruby got her guy. And that kiss in the rain? Delicious. God, I thought she'd strip him down in the waterfall scene and do him there."

I wrinkled my nose. "Under the waterfall? That can't be comfortable."

"Live a little, Elsy," she chided, curling up on the couch. "What didn't you like about it?"

I sipped on my chai. The honey had a lavender taste to it. "What about her own dreams?"

"She found new ones. I mean, it's not really *realistic* to go off and become a pop star."

"That's what bothers me, I think," I replied, as I joined her on the couch. "Because a romance isn't supposed to be realistic. If it was, every story would end with everyone dying alone in an old folks' home."

"Wow, Elsy. Tell me how you *really* feel."

I gave a frustrated sigh. "All I'm saying is why couldn't she have both? Her dreams *and* Jake?"

Pru tilted her head in thought. "And Jake's dreams?"

"Exactly, why couldn't he settle instead?"

She rolled her eyes. "Elsy, I love you, but I think you think too much about all this. It was a fun romp! They get to stay in Eloraton with their friends and have fun! It's not that deep."

Maybe not, but I was sure that if I was ever presented with that sort of choice—between my career and true love, I knew what I'd choose.

So did Pru.

And we were on opposite sides.

So I pushed my feelings down and said, "You're right. I mean, that kiss in the rain? To *die* for."

"Right?" Pru sighed. "I want to be kissed in the rain."

I leaned closer to her and wiggled my eyebrows. "By Jasper?"

She seemed scandalized by the thought. *"Eileen!"*

I feigned innocence. "What? I thought he was hot . . ."

"He is but he's—he's our *neighbor*."

"A tale as old as time," I pointed out, and she went pink around the ears.

"You're the worst."

"Thank you." I bumped my shoulder against hers. She ended up dating Jasper. They fell in love. And now they were adventuring around Iceland and I was . . . here. We grew up on the same romances, we read the same stories, so how after all of that did she get it right, and I got it all so very, very wrong?

In the bathroom, I splashed myself with cold water and dried my face. *Stop it*, I thought. Tossing the paper towel into the trash can, I swung open the bathroom door to return to the table.

". . . Sugar, I can't cover your shift tonight," I heard Ruby say. She was leaning against the end of the counter, on a red landline phone, twirling the cord around her finger. "I can't—I promised Junie I'd help her with wallpaper." Then a pause, a frustrated sigh. I eased myself back into the bathroom, pretending that I wasn't eavesdropping at all. The rest of her words were mumbled, and then—"Yeah. All right, I'll talk to her. Love you too, bye."

She must've been talking to Jake. Everything was okay, right? The worst that could happen here was a burnt hamburger and a rainy afternoon—that's what Anders said.

I was reading too much into it.

I counted to three, and left the bathroom.

Ruby was standing at the other side of the counter, directing the poor dishwasher to sweep up the ice from the ice maker. Then she noticed me and smiled. "Oh, Andie's friend! How're you liking the town?"

"It's . . . very quixotic," I said, a little tongue in cheek.

"It's definitely quiet. Nothing ever happens here. It's slow as fuck," she added with a forced laugh.

"Do you think you'll ever leave?"

Ruby shrugged. "I used to, but if I did I wouldn't meet all of Andie's fun friends, now would I? You're the first, but I'm sure he has more."

"Oh, no, I'm not—"

The cook in the kitchen called her name and shoved three plates through the window. "Order up, Rubes!"

"Oh, sorry, excuse me." Then, with an apologetic smile, she took the plates and turned toward the other side of the café. "It was nice to meet you!"

"You, too," I replied, and as she left, I fought to keep my mouth closed. I thought back on my conversation with Pru, about Ruby settling instead of Jake, and I knew she thought she was in the right. She had a loving boyfriend, after all, a perfect relationship, and probably what was about to be a fantastic proposal, and I just wanted—I wanted to be right about one thing. That maybe Pru was wrong. So I said, "Ruby—you can go after your dreams, you know."

She tossed a curious look over her shoulder. "What?"

"This can't be what you want, is it?"

She turned back to me, and the eggs on the tray sloshed with the movement. "I'm sorry?"

I nervously glanced across the café. Anders was sipping on his tea, and gazing out the window with a distant sort of look. Like he was a hundred miles away. It emboldened me to press on. "You just—you don't have to settle."

The woman blinked. She wasn't quite sure what to say, and I hoped I hadn't overstepped my bounds, but she needed to know. She just needed a little push, a little shove. That's all it ever took, right? She was a fictional character. How hard could it be? I think I got through to her, because her breath hitched. Her eyes widened.

And then, to my utter dismay, things went south.

Very, very quickly.

"You don't know me," she said, her words so sharp they made me wince. "And even if you did? *Fuck you.*"

Then she left for the table destined for the discombobulated eggs and pancakes, and I felt a blush creep up my neck as the scraggly dishwasher glared at me.

I retreated back to Anders and slid nervously into my seat, glancing back at Ruby. Anders, for his part, didn't even acknowledge me at first, still staring out the window. I followed his gaze to Gail, the bartender, walking beside a tall and burly man I could only imagine was Frank from Frank's Auto Shop (and the owner of Frank's Hotties), though I couldn't see his face. Gail was laughing at something he'd said, and then they turned down the street and were gone.

I asked, "Penny for your thoughts?"

His minty eyes focused, returning, and he pushed his glasses up the bridge of his nose reflexively. "Oh, no. My thoughts are a little more expensive than that."

"Ah, had to adjust for inflation?"

"The ever-depressing climb of late-stage capitalism." He shifted in his seat, and finally pulled himself all the way out of his thoughts. He asked me coyly, "Besides, a penny? What can you buy with a penny these days?"

"I *thought* I could buy your thoughts, but seems I was mistaken. I should up my prices, too, I guess." I glanced nervously again toward the kitchen.

He caught on this time. "Is everything all right?"

"What? Oh, yeah, everything's fine. Peachy keen."

He pursed his lips. "Right." Because now, of course, he was

suspicious, and the guilt of *not* telling him tugged at my conscience, so I took a gulp of soda and was starting to tell him—really, I was—when Ruby came back with our orders.

She slammed food down in front of us. My Honey Surprise leaked across the table, sticky and golden. She asked Anders, "Hot sauce?"

"No, I'm g—"

"Because here at the Grumpy Possum Café, we don't just sell Gemma's Honey-Honey honey, but give equal attention to our town's other infamous product—Frank's Hotties," she went on in a voice that had done this spiel too many times, and pulled a small bottle of hot sauce from the pocket of her apron. I recognized the shape of the bottle from last night, though at least this one still had the label. "Frank's Hotties is locally sourced and—"

Anders held up a hand. "I promise I'm g—"

"—grown right here in the great town of Eloraton, New York. When you think of hot sauce, think of Frank." She took the hot sauce bottle and squeezed it with a vengeance atop his club sandwich, pinning me with a glare as she did. Anders watched as the mountain of liquid fire drowned his club before he, too, turned a pointed glare at me. When the bottle was empty, Ruby slammed the bill onto the table, and stalked away without another word.

When she was gone, Anders gave me a tired look.

I tried to feign innocence, unfolding my napkin. There was a spot of hot sauce on his shirt. "It's so *weird* that she did that."

"What did you say to her?"

I reached over and dabbed the hot sauce off his shirt, but all it managed to do was smudge the stain. "I didn't—"

He let out a breath that sounded a little like a growl.

I snapped my mouth closed. Honestly, if he hadn't been looking at me like he wanted to punt me off Charm Bridge, the sound would've been a bit sexy. As it stood, I'd just ruined one of his shirts and probably his eating experience at this café for the fore-seeable future.

Retracting myself into my side of the booth, I gave a one-shouldered shrug. "I just . . ."

"Go on."

I finally admitted, "I overheard her and Jake talking, so I gave her some advice, all right? I mean, you know her story, too! She didn't want *this*—to work herself to the bone—and neither did Jake."

He sat back in the booth and massaged the bridge of his nose tiredly. "Look," he sighed, taking a napkin to wipe as much hot sauce off his sandwich as he could, "no one here knows they're in a book."

"No one?"

"No."

"Save for you?"

"I'm an exception," he replied, and I wondered what kind of character he was to be an exception. The narrator, perhaps? No, his personality was too dry for that. He didn't explain it, either. "How would *you* feel if some annoyingly peppy stranger—"

"I'm not annoying."

He went on, unfazed, "—came up to you and told you that you weren't living your happily ever after right. How would that feel?"

I frowned. "A . . . little angry."

"Exactly." Then he ate a fry, and another. "At least she didn't get the hot sauce on everything."

The pancakes and French toast were topped with locally sourced Honey-Honey honey, made grumpy to order with powdered sugar and cinnamon, with a perfectly star-cut strawberry on top. I took out my phone to take a photo of it, when he cleared his throat and I wilted.

"One photo?"

"It won't show up."

"Seriously?"

"Try it and see."

So I did. The camera app immediately quit. I tried again. Same thing. "Huh. And I guess your Wi-Fi is perpetually out? And there's never any cell service?"

"Oh no, everyone has cell service here, and the Wi-Fi is perfectly fine. For everyone except you, I suspect, since you don't belong here."

"So you lied to me."

He shrugged. "Would you have believed me otherwise?"

"No," I admitted, and unrolled my utensils from my napkin, and looked down at my breakfast for lunch. Pru and I had tried to make the Honey Surprise a hundred times at home, until we'd perfected the art of French toast and the perfect golden-crisp pancake, but nothing prepared me for the fluffiness, the buttery sweetness, the crispy crunch of my first bite.

It was so good, I moaned.

Anders choked on a fry, and chased it with the rest of his tea. By the wrinkle of disgust on his face, the combination tasted terrible. "Can you *not*?" he whispered to me, coughing.

"Have you *tasted* this? It's delicious. You should have what I'm having."

"I don't eat sweet things."

"You're missing out. What do they put in this stuff? It's *so* good."

"Butter, flour, and love, or so the sign says," he replied, motioning to the slogan painted on the back wall of the restaurant.

I rolled my eyes. "Thank you."

"You're welcome. And after we finish, I'll escort you to your car, and you'll be on your way. You *will* be on your way."

"Oh," I said distractedly, shoving another bite of honey-covered pancake into my mouth, "most definitely."

8

Sweet as Whole

TO BE ABSOLUTELY FAIR, I *was* planning on telling him about my car after lunch. Probably. But then we passed Sweeties and I couldn't *not* stop in and buy a bag of honey taffy. Locally sourced from Gemma Shah's honeybees. I thought I'd see Gemma at the counter, but she must've been out to lunch. Maya Shah, her younger sister, was there instead. Sleek dark bob, tongue stud, black-painted nails to match her eyeshadow, striking against her warm brown skin. Olivia's favorite character and crush-haver of Lyssa Greene. She could shoot a fly out of a tree with a compound bow from fifty feet away.

"Andie!" Maya greeted, throwing up her hands. "Well, isn't this a surprise. I thought you were allergic to me, you never stop by."

"I don't like sweets," he replied tiredly, as if he'd had to repeat that fact a thousand times already.

"Well, we all have our flaws," Maya said, and turned to me. "I hope you have better taste?"

"Much better," I agreed, and sampled every single bit of candy in the place. Anders brooded over the lollipops, looking more and more like he was planning on tying me up and carrying me over to my car, as I chatted with Maya about flavors and bees. She was bubbly and sharp, like a bubble gum with razor blades inside.

"Ready to go?" Anders asked as I said goodbye to Maya.

"Oh, come *on*, Anders," I said, and opened the bag of taffy I'd purchased. "Everything is here. Everything! I can't *not* see it."

In reply, he sighed.

"Fine. You can leave, you know, if I'm boring you."

"I wouldn't say boring. See you, Maya," he added and held the door open for me. I rolled my eyes as I stepped into the sunshine, and he followed.

I unwrapped a taffy and popped it into my mouth. The sweetness about knocked me to my knees. "Oh my *god*," I said as I tried to chew the honey-flavored candy, "it's actually sticking to my teeth! Like in the books! I can't believe it!" A laugh bubbled up from somewhere so deep in me, I didn't think I could sound that bright.

My chest was filled with a fuzzy Pop Rocks feeling. I hadn't felt it in so long, I'd forgotten what it felt like.

The realization hit me like a train.

I was *happy*.

Everything—everything was real. Sweeties, the Roost, the Grumpy Possum Café, the Daffodil Inn, the *bookstore*. No wonder I slept so well last night. Because even though I hadn't known where I was, my body knew.

I felt like I was home.

My face hurt from smiling so widely, but I couldn't help myself. The taffy was sweet, and the afternoon was warm and clouds were beginning to roll in from a distance, thunder rumbling between the trees. An afternoon shower, like yesterday.

Anders studied me after we passed the art gallery. "You're like a kid in a candy store."

"We *did* just come from a candy store," I pointed out, and offered him a taffy.

He shook his head.

"Oh, right, you don't like sweets."

I unwrapped another one, and this piece was just as sweet and sticky as the first one. "Okay, so, I have a question for you."

"Different than the hundreds of questions you already asked?"

"Smart-ass," I muttered.

I stepped in front of him, bringing him to a sudden stop. "Who are you?"

"A small-town bookstore owner who desperately wants to get you on your way."

"Yeah, I know, but I don't remember you—and I remember everything from these books."

"Ah"—and he put his hands into his neat knife-pleated trouser pockets—"everything?"

I frowned, studying him.

Ever since I was little, I was excellent at remembering what I read. I could pick up a book from ten years ago and recite the plot, almost chapter by chapter, though that might've been because I was a slow reader, and as a slow reader I just absorbed useless knowledge like a sponge. But in all the Quixotic Falls novels, I didn't remember this man. The last I'd read, the owner of Ineffable Books had sold it, but to whom the author never said, and then that brought up more questions—where in the story were we? What book? It was after the fourth one, because all of the couples were together and neither Beatrice Everly or Garnet Rivers were anywhere to be found. So, Eloraton was drifting, unmoored, in the possibilities that Rachel Flowers left when she passed.

"Well," I finally admitted, "I thought I knew the series. Clearly, I don't, since I don't remember you. And why *do* you know you're in a book series but everyone else doesn't. Are you related to Lily? Thomas's brother? Maybe a cousin of Frank's . . . ?"

He inclined his chin. "I'll let you keep guessing."

"Will you tell me if I get it right?"

"Yes," he replied.

I wasn't sure if I believed him, as I folded my taffy plastic into a neat square, and put it in my back pocket. I took a deep breath, closing my eyes. "I can't believe that I'm *here*. The taffy, the café, the inn, the bookstore . . ."

It was all here. Everything that I loved.

"I have to see the rest," I decided. "The inn, the clock tower, that little jewelry store that's only open when Mercury's in retrograde, and—" My breath hitched as I realized. The most important part of the town. The place where everything started, where everything ends. I spun to him. "The waterfall! I have to go see the—"

"No," he said decisively.

"Why?"

"It's not magical, it's the middle of the day, it's hot, there's a storm coming in, and you need to leave," he said, picking at his fingernails, as if it was matter-of-fact.

"How do you *know* it's not magical?" I challenged.

He slid his gaze to me. It was sharp. Testy. "How do you know it is?"

"I don't! Which is why I want to go."

"To see if the magic's real."

"Maybe I just want to see it."

He scoffed. "I doubt it. Besides, what good would the magic do you?" he asked. "Even if it is real, it won't work outside of Eloraton.

It'd be wasted on you. Besides, and you've got no one to stand under it with, anyway."

Suddenly, the taffy didn't taste all that sweet anymore. "You don't know that."

He looked me over, his minty eyes bright in the sunlight. They looked like drops of melted Mentos, and there was a guardedness behind them, and—pity? "It's not going to give you what you want, Elsy."

I felt my entire body stiffen, like a cat spooked. "I don't *want* anything—"

"You're obsessed with a fictional book series. You're alone and you don't want to leave," he said, bending close to me. "You're desperate, sweetheart."

An ember of anger lit in my stomach. "I'm not desperate," I snapped. "And you're mean."

"I'm sure someone broke your heart, left your texts on read, whatever, and trust me when I say a waterfall won't make them come back—"

I'd never slapped anyone in my life, and my hand stung by the time I realized what I'd done. A red mark bloomed on his cheek. I was mortified that I'd slapped him—and mortified that I'd let him get to me. I quickly reeled away, blinking back the tears that came to my eyes.

"Sorry." My voice trembled. I wasn't sure if it was in rage or apology. "I'm sorry."

Then I spun on my heel and fled toward my useless car, pushing back tears, but they just kept coming, and I couldn't stop them. Because, even though he was awful to me, Anders was right. I was alone, and nothing—nothing at all—could make Liam come back to me.

9

Good Enough

I WAS TWENTY-SIX WHEN I fell in love—really fell in love—for the first time.

When the night started, I didn't think I would end up kissing a stranger at midnight. I'd spent the last two New Year's Eves with boyfriends who ended up finding the loves of their lives while dating me, so spending another one with a man who'd fall for the person behind him in line for coffee was something I didn't want to go through again.

I'd read enough stories where a heroine gets dragged to a New Year's Eve party, only to fall for the most unattainable man of the evening, but I always figured those kinds of moments were saved for Prudence.

After all, she bumped into Jasper—our neighbor—at the grocery store three weeks after we read *Unrequited Love Song*. In the soup aisle. Both reaching for the last can of chicken noodle.

What's a better meet-cute?

So when Prudence begged me to come to Jasper's law firm's

New Year's party, because she was nervous to go alone, I couldn't say no, even though I had plans to sit at home and watch *When Harry Met Sally* and drown myself in chocolates. So I put on a sparkly silver dress that still fit from undergrad and that made me look like a walking disco ball, and followed Prudence into battle.

To the surprise of no one, I ended up in the corner of the room for most of the night, while she and Jasper danced under the twinkle lights and kissed in vacant hallways. It turned out I wasn't needed at all, forgotten in a large wingback chair beside the open bar, and I was perfectly content with just people watching. Making up stories of all the meet-cutes, the soft hand touches, the way people bent together, whispering and giggling. I wondered if there was a series of romances set at a law firm, two competing lawyers vying for the same partnership. I made a note in my phone to look that up when I finally got home. *If* I got home. By the looks of it, I might have to call an Uber.

By eleven thirty, I decided that maybe Uber was my best bet, and if I left then I could make it home before the rush after midnight. I found Pru in the entryway to the historical house the law firm had rented for the evening, and told her my plan. She was aghast.

"Oh, come on," she said, her cheeks rosy from the champagne, "at least stay for the ball drop!"

"I'm tired," I replied, and besides, I didn't have anyone to kiss, and the closer it crept to midnight, the more apparent that felt.

"You got up at noon! You *can't* be tired. Is it the hors—horse—whores . . ." She frowned, her eyebrows furrowing, and said instead, "The finger foods? Are your shoes too tight? Is it the music? Did they play—" And she looked around conspiratorially before whispering, *"The bad song?"*

Oh, my sweet, lovely Prudence. I hugged her. "I'll be fine."

"You sure?"

"Absolutely, now go have fun with Jasper," I said, because he was being a gentleman and hanging out a few feet away, trying not to eavesdrop. "Speaking of music, I think your favorite song is playing."

Prudence perked at the music. "Oh, I'm named after this song! Jasper, Jasper, this is the song!" she cried, spinning around and taking him by the arm. "Dance with me?"

He glanced back at me, to make sure I was okay. I mouthed, "Happy New Year," to him, and waited until they'd gone back into the party before I left out the front door and sat down on the steps to wait for my Uber. The night was chilly, and I hadn't thought to bring a coat, so I shivered in my disco ball dress—until someone dropped their jacket onto my shoulders.

"Not enjoying the party?" asked a soft voice.

I glanced up, and there was the bartender I'd sat beside all night, watching him dole out drinks and charm pretty girls. He had a rugged look about him, his brown hair cut short and his blue eyes sharp, his tan finally fading from a long summer in the sun. He sat down beside me, taking a long drag from a vape pen. It smelled like strawberries, mixed with the lingering sharp scent of vodka on his fingers. He looked disarmingly debonair in a white shirt and charcoal vest to match his trousers, and shined loafers.

"It's a lovely party," I replied. "I just . . ."

"It's the kiss, isn't it?" he guessed.

My mouth dropped open. *"What?"*

He took another hit off his vape pen, and blew it out. "You know, the cliché?"

I glanced down at my app. Why was my Uber driver still sitting exactly where he'd been five minutes ago? "And what if it is?"

"I'd say it's a pity, then."

"That I'm leaving?"

He leaned closer. "That you've got no one to kiss." His gaze flickered down to my mouth.

My heart started to race. Was he—*flirting*? I swallowed the knot rising in my throat. "Do you?"

A smile curled across his mouth. "Sure, if she'd like."

Then one of his coworkers called him back in from his smoke break, and I handed him back his jacket. He seemed surprised that I did, but I wasn't accustomed to keeping what I wanted. He pulled his jacket back on as he climbed the steps to the building, and left me alone to wait for my Uber, which *still* hadn't moved.

I shivered again. And the time climbed and climbed toward midnight.

And then—

Cheers.

Calls of "Happy New Year!"

"Auld Lang Syne" played from the speakers inside, accompanied by a drunken sing-along by half the firm.

In *Daffodil Daydreams*, Junie kissed Will for the first time on New Year's, on the rooftop of the Roost, under a meteor shower. There wasn't a meteor shower tonight. And there wasn't snow. And I had no one to kiss but—

I shoved myself to my feet. Climbed the steps into the house. The large clock in the main room chimed *three, four, five*—

The room was full of people kissing, and laughing, sharing each other's space and time, and I wanted that. I wanted that so badly that my body was moving before my brain caught up with me.

It was like that moment in a love song, when the bridge changes key. He glanced up from a mixed drink, and locked eyes with me, and the crowd parted as I crossed the room.

The clock chimed *eight, nine, ten*—

I took his face in my hands, and pulled him down toward me.

Eleven, twelve—

I crushed my lips against his. He wasn't even surprised, as he wrapped his arms around my waist and pulled me closer. He kissed like he talked—sharp and bold, with the slightest aftertaste of strawberry nicotine. "Auld Lang Syne" sang loud in our ears, about old acquaintances being forgotten, though I'd never forget the way he looked at me as we finally broke apart, like he wanted to devour me—body and soul.

"I'm Liam, by the way," he said, breathless, tracing my lips with his thumb.

"Eileen," I replied, and I fell.

One kiss turned into two, turned into a night together, and then brunch, and then he was taking me home and asking me what my dinner plans were—and that was it. I didn't think I'd look into his eyes and fall so hard and so suddenly that when I woke up four years later, it would all feel like a dream.

But I did.

Liam Henry Black became my entire life, like how a bold wallpaper overtakes a room and all you want to do is find pieces to complement it. As it turned out, he was an architect between jobs, which was why he'd taken the gig at the New Year's party. His father owned a firm on the other side of town, but he wanted to make his own way, and the second he set those disarmingly beautiful blue eyes on me, he made me feel like I was that cool, go-getter girl who'd kissed him on New Year's.

In all the books I'd read, in all the romances I'd devoured, from Jane Austen to Nora Roberts, from fairy tales to dark erotica, not a single one of them prepared me for how hard I fell.

There were some love stories that seemed perfect.

This was mine, I thought.

After the first week, Prudence caught on that I'd fallen head over heels. She found me that Friday evening, coming in from dinner with Liam. We were supposed to have a girls' night, and I'd forgotten, but she wasn't angry at all as she dragged me to the couch, and demanded the story.

"Is that the guy from the party?" she asked, her eyes glittering.

I chewed on my bottom lip. "Yeah . . ."

"And was this a first date or . . . ?"

"Fourth," I replied, and she squealed.

"Oh my god! Oh my god, it's happening. It's *happening*. I *knew* you would find someone at that party! Honestly, I thought it'd be one of Jasper's coworkers, but the bartender's good, too."

I laughed, and told her that he was an architect between jobs, and that I liked him. "Like, *really* like him," I added, quieter, like it was a secret. Maybe it was, and I was afraid that if I told the universe that I was falling for a guy so far out of my league, it would course correct, and Liam would realize that he could do better.

She scooted a little closer. "Tell me *everything*."

Everything—like how I loved the way he gushed about the climbs he'd taken, and the ones he wanted to take. Half Dome in California. Devil's Tower in Wyoming. A dozen others. Or how he put his wallet into his back left pocket, or how his brown hair lay so perfectly over his ears, or how he kissed me like I was meant to be savored, or how he was just the right height for me to lean my head against his shoulder in a movie theater.

It would've taken all night to tell her everything.

So I just told her the easy things—how we loved some of the same nineties movies (*Tremors* and *Twister*), and how he took his burgers (so rare they bled), and how he'd been raised by his uncle in Montana, until he decided to come down to Georgia for college. I told her about the year he volunteered for AmeriCorps, building houses, and how he'd skydived over thirty times, and wanted nothing more than to climb Everest and Kilimanjaro and Fuji, and every impossible rock face from here to California.

He was so different from me. He rarely read, but he listened to me recount every book with patience, and our music collections would've waged war against each other—but none of that mattered.

"He makes me feel like I'm not Elsy Merriweather. He makes me feel like I can be someone new—*should* be someone new. I want him," I told her. "I want him so badly."

She hummed, closing her eyes, and wiggled her fingers in front of my face. "Then you'll have him."

And I wanted to believe her.

"Just . . . don't lose yourself to it all, okay?" she added, a little quieter. "I like you the way you are."

"Of course I won't," I replied, and if this had been a romance, it would have been foreshadowing.

For years, as we went on double dates with Jasper and Pru, and vacations, and bowling nights, and hikes along the Appalachian Trail, and indie rock concerts, I was so blissfully happy with Liam, I could explode. I drowned in whatever he loved, I soaked in the rays of his joy, and I followed him. We shared plates, and shared memories, and shared beds. We shared a life that was comfortable, and good, and I was someone he loved.

And when he proposed to me at the top of a rather difficult hike, about half a mile from a waterfall I'd wanted to see, I hadn't paused to consider the question. It was known. Of *course* I would say yes. I knew this was my forever—as corny as that sounded. When I closed my eyes at night, I could still see him on his knees at the peak of the trail, the sign to Looking Glass Falls behind him

on that brisk autumn day, his dark hair short and his eyes matching
the color of the sky. Everything was orange and red through
rose-tinted glasses.

There was no doubt in my mind that I loved him, so of course I
said yes.

He swept me up, and we kissed, and everyone loved the photos
Pru took when she posted them to Facebook.

I thought it was the beginning of the best year of my life. It was
supposed to be. He'd proposed, and we began to plan our wedding.
It was going to be a small affair—his idea—just our closest friends
and family. I didn't really care about weddings at all; I would've
been happy with a courthouse sort of deal. Maybe it was because
my mom's wedding was big and boisterous, and it ended in a di-
vorce when I was four. My dad had found a new family, and left my
mom and me to pick up the pieces of the life he wrecked.

But Liam asked, so I did what would make him happy (because
wasn't that love?), and I had to admit that I was looking forward to
it—at least a *little* bit.

The venue would be a converted barn, with twinkle lights in the
rafters and an antler chandelier, and we'd eat a three-tiered red
velvet cake and toast with flutes of bubbly prosecco and dance to
"Modern Love" by David Bowie. A week before the wedding, we
visited the venue to make sure everything was in order. The wedding planner stepped out to take a phone call—or at least I thought,
maybe Liam had told her to go—and we were alone in the red
barn. I felt on pins and needles. My entire body felt electrified, because in a week I'd marry the one person I loved more than anyone
else.

"Eileen," Liam had said, coming up beside me. He was gorgeous in the way that outdoorsy men were, his skin tanned and his

brown hair streaked with blond from the sun, and I felt so, so lucky to be with him.

"Liam," I replied in the same stoic voice, because I thought it was funny, and moved over to him, planting a kiss on his strong jaw. "You were right."

He hesitated, threading his fingers through mine. "About?"

"A wedding. This wedding." I squeezed his hand. "You've got good taste. I was skeptical of the barn at first but . . ." And I grinned at him. "I guess the rustic charm is growing on me, and the antlers."

"Yeah," he said absently, glancing up at the chandelier. He took his hand out of mine, and rubbed it on his jeans as if it was clammy. "I've something to ask you," he said, and his voice was soft and tender. My heart skipped a beat—

I didn't know why. He already proposed. We were getting married. Whatever he was going to ask, I'd say yes. (Within reason. And experimentation.)

Then he said, "Do you really want to do this?"

I laughed. "The antler chandelier *is* a bit much."

He glanced at me, and his eyebrows furrowed, and he looked away again. "No, I mean—you know what I mean."

I stared at him. Why did he look nervous? "The venue? I thought you liked the rustic look—"

"Why do you always *do* this?" he muttered.

I didn't understand. "I . . . what am I doing?"

He started to reply, and then closed his mouth and frowned. After a moment, he said, "I don't think I want to do this."

Oh, I thought, my eyes widening.

"I'm not ready," he went on, shooting me a pleading look. "I thought I was but—I'm not. I don't think we should."

"I don't think I follow," I said, feigning naivete, because he couldn't possibly be telling me what he was. I was misunderstanding. I had to be. "Is it the venue? I can ask about a different one?"

"You didn't want a wedding," he interrupted.

"I wanted what you wanted."

"And you hate this barn."

"I don't *hate* it," I murmured.

He turned to me, grabbing my hands tightly. "Elle," he said, and he was the only person who ever called me Elle. "Where are you in this wedding? I keep looking around and I don't see you at all. What are you looking forward to here?"

My eyebrows furrowed. "Being with you."

His lips pursed into a thin line. And—to my utter horror—he let go of my hands. "There has to be more to it. Think, is there anything?"

"I . . ." I looked around. "I mean, I . . . like my dress? And—and the red velvet cake is going to be great. And—why are you asking me all this? What's gotten into you?" My heart was in my throat. I felt like I wanted to vomit. "Is it something I did? Something I said?"

"No," he quickly replied, shaking his head. "No, I just . . ." He pulled his hands through his thick, dark hair. "I think I want a break."

I stood, numb, in that rustic barn under the antler chandelier as it loomed over us like some sort of witness. "A—a what?"

"I think we should see other people," he clarified.

"We're getting married," I said, and my voice sounded a hundred miles away. "In a week, we'll be married." Then my brain began to work overtime. It began to tally up all the different facets of this wedding that he wanted but didn't *actually* want to be in charge of. "We've already paid for this venue. We have family coming from across the country—they probably can't get their flights refunded! What do I tell them? What do I tell the caterers? The DJ? What do we do with the little gift baskets we got for everyone?" Then, looking him in the eyes, I asked, "What about me?"

He ran his hands through his hair again. "I don't know, Eileen. I don't *know*. I just—I can't do this. I just—I realized . . ." He turned his piercing blue gaze to me. "That I don't really know you."

That sounded silly. "Of *course* you do. We've been together for—for what, four years?"

"Yes! Four whole years, and I just know you when you're with me."

"Because I'm *with* you," I tried to argue, but he turned and started to pace away from me. "You know my favorite color! My birthday! You know everything—"

"I don't know what you *want*, Eileen!" He turned on his heel back to me, and reined in his voice. "I don't know what you want."

I stared at him, mouth agape. "I . . . I want . . ."

Whenever I thought back on that conversation, there were a hundred things I could've told him. I wanted a courthouse wedding. I wanted that red velvet cake. I wanted to dance with him to our favorite song, and I wanted to forget it all and squeeze into a taxi with him, bound for some far-distant beach to elope, because more than anything else I just wanted *him*.

So, that's what I said.

"I want you to be happy."

And in a perfect story, that would be enough.

But the words made him shrink away. Shake his head. "I met someone else," he said, unable to meet my gaze.

Oh.

Oh.

"But . . . what about the wedding? The people coming? The . . . the . . ." I felt like a broken record. "The *everything*?"

His voice cracked as he said, "You'll figure it out."

You'll figure it out. Not *we*. No *us*.

There would never be an us again.

"Alone?" I asked.

He gave a nervous laugh. "I mean, what can *I* do?"

Because I'd done everything, anyway. I'd planned the wedding, I'd invited the guests, I'd picked out the cake and the music and the—

The everything.

I didn't remember a lot of the rest of that afternoon after he drove back to our apartment—the last time it would ever truly be ours—and he made good on his word. He was done. Moved out that night. I had to call everyone. I had to cancel the wedding. I had to get as much money back from vendors and catering as I could.

He went on a hiking trip up the Appalachian Trail with a work friend to clear his head, and that was the last time I heard from him.

Six months later, he was engaged to the "work friend" he took on the trail. A person he'd met while we were still dating. A person he'd flirted with, charmed, courted, all the while engaged to *me*. Pru had threatened to castrate him, to drag her keys down his pretty Tesla, to "Goodbye Earl" him somewhere in a remote area of North Georgia, but I didn't have the energy to be angry.

Apparently, he had wanted to get married. He just hadn't wanted to marry *me*.

I felt like a fool. Even as I read back through our text messages, listened to the voicemails he left, trying to find any crack in our relationship, any signs that I had missed. Sure, we didn't take each other to the airport anymore when we had to travel for work or kiss each other goodbye every morning, but we'd been good. We had a routine, and we had a lovely story—a perfect kiss on New Year's. The rest of it should've been perfect, too.

So who could blame me for sinking into books, where I knew the people weren't real, but they also never disappointed me? I knew everything would work out in the end. I knew happy endings were destined, ever afters fated, and no matter what trials and tribulations and, well, surprise fuckups happened, things would end up okay.

I just needed a story—or maybe a few hundred stories of happily ever after—to escape mine.

Then Rachel Flowers died later that year, and the happy ending I was looking forward to fell through my fingers like sand.

What started as the best year of my life became the worst. The only bright spot was the book club, when we finally met in person, and I got to cry my heart out while sharing a box of Riesling with five of my closest friends, and it healed me a little.

For two whole years, it was bliss.

Then, this year, life got in the way.

First, Janelle couldn't come because there was no one to cover her shifts at the hospital. Then Aditi failed an undergrad math course and had to retake it over the summer. Olivia broke her foot. Matt had to go to Wisconsin to take care of his mom. Benji pulled out of the retreat this year to plan his own wedding.

Then Prudence.

I had half a mind to not go, to make up some life excuse, but then while I was looking through Airbnbs I couldn't afford in places I didn't have the money to fly to, I checked social media, and I saw the photos.

The ones of Liam's wedding.

He wore the same tux that I'd picked out with him three years ago, though the pocket square now matched the new bride's bridesmaids—a lovely lavender. The wedding was in an old red barn in the middle of a farm, hay bales stacked to the ceiling. There wasn't an antler chandelier, but there was a DJ, and there was dancing, and the cake was red velvet, and Liam looked at his now wife like he used to look at me and—

I just didn't want to be here anymore. I wanted to get lost. I wanted to burrow myself somewhere out in the woods with my favorite books and a bottle of wine, and never see anyone ever again. Never have the opportunity to meet someone new. Never give my heart the chance to fall again.

Because if it hurt this much to let go?

I never wanted to fall in love again.

I didn't tell Pru about the wedding photos. She was on cloud nine, and I didn't need to mess that up with my terrible life choices, so I made the decision to pack up Sweetpea and road-trip to the cabin alone, because I couldn't stay in my tiny apartment, surrounded by books and work and everything that told me that I'd put my life on pause because it felt better than risking heartbreak again.

I couldn't do it again.

In my head, I'd be in a different story, sharing shitty wine and good books, lighting vigil candles and singing *Fleetwood Mac* at the full moon in Rachel Flowers's honor with my best friends.

It was a good dream.

Too bad Pru caught me the day I'd packed up Sweetpea to leave. She saw the duffel bag and box of wine in the hatchback, shook her head, and said, "You aren't seriously thinking about going alone, are you?"

"Sure, why not? It'll be fun," I replied, pulling on a smile that I hoped didn't look too fake. I was already dreading the sixteen-hour drive up the Northeast alone. "Your flight's tomorrow, right? Remember to take Dramamine before—"

"Stop deflecting," she interrupted, and curled her hands into fists. "You're seriously going alone? No one's going to be there, Elsy."

"I'll be there." I carried my box of books and set them in the trunk, probably with more force than necessary. "Besides, I'd rather be *there* than here."

The realization dawned. "This is because of that asshole's wedding, isn't it? You're just running away."

I winced. So she *had* seen the photos. "I'm taking my vacation."

She rolled her eyes. "Sure you are, Elsy."

"Really! It's not because . . ." Because they had the wedding I would've had. Because they looked so happy. I curled my hands into fists. "It's not."

But Prudence could see right through me. "You haven't dated since he left you—three *years* ago! It's like you just put yourself on ice and you don't even want to *try* anymore."

I turned back to her. "This isn't about cabin week anymore, is it?"

"No! It's not! It's about everything! You think I can't tell when my best friend is hurting? I've been waiting for you to—I don't know—just confide in me! Ever since Liam left! I just thought you needed time. But instead you just . . . stopped. And I've missed my best friend."

I threw up my hands. "What do you want me to say, Pru?"

"Just tell people what you *want*!"

It didn't matter what I wanted, anyway, so I just marched to the driver's seat and cranked up my antique Pinto, and left.

What I *wanted* was for us to do these things together. All the things. Engagements. Weddings. Kids—well, maybe not kids.

I wanted us to grow together.

And now I was too scared to try.

But I couldn't say that, because that would be admitting that maybe a little part of me *was* still hung up over Liam, who clearly no longer even thought about me. Maybe I did still creep on his and his new wife's Facebook sometimes, wondering why it couldn't be me, but those secrets were between me and my internet history.

Pru just didn't understand.

I *knew* what I wanted. I knew what I didn't.

I knew I never wanted to feel like I had the day I found out Liam was engaged not even a year after we'd split. I still had my wedding dress in my closet. The guest list was still saved on my phone. I never wanted to fall asleep crying on my couch, wondering why he didn't want that life with *me*. What was so wrong with *me*?

I knew I never wanted to feel so foolish, so—so *embarrassed*—ever again.

So I was out of my neighborhood before those angry tears could crawl out of my eyes and stream down my face, and I only stopped crying as I got out of Atlanta traffic, on my way up north, determined to spend a week in a world where there were only ever happy endings.

Where no one was ever alone.

So who could blame me for wanting to stay in Eloraton a little longer? I wanted to soak in the afternoon sun, and I wanted to fill my lungs with summer breeze.

I wanted to get lost—and stay there.

10

Plot Twist

S O THERE I WAS, back at my car that wouldn't start, wondering what to do. I drummed my fingers on the hood. It was propped open, and I was trying to see if I could guess which big metal bit was the *engine*. I wiggled one of the hoses, kicked the fender, and returned to the driver's seat to try the engine again.

Sweetpea sputtered.

I rested my forehead against the steering wheel.

So what if I *did* want to go up to the waterfall and kiss some stranger underneath it?

You don't realize how much of life is built for relationships until, newly single, you find yourself with a broken ankle, cooped up on the couch in your one-bedroom apartment, and you need to go to the restroom. The problem is, you've knocked your crutches over and the pain prevents you from moving too much at all. You go through the Rolodex in your head of whom you can call, and every one of them has someone more important than you in their lives to take care of. You have to weigh how much of a bother you're going to be, and how much you can rely on them. (Obviously you can rely on your friends. Obviously I'm not saying you can't, but there is always a limit of *how much* before you're a burden.)

And in the end you just . . . sit on the couch, and cry.

At least, alone, no one is there to watch.

So what if a secret, soft part of me hoped that a magical waterfall could cure me of that sort of loneliness?

I got out of the car again and dropped the hood closed. Pretending I knew how to fix my car clearly wasn't working, and I wasn't sure what else to do. Anders had disappeared after I'd slapped him, probably returning to his bookstore across the street. I felt mortified remembering the slap—I didn't know what came over me—and I doubted going over and apologizing would win me any favors.

Think, Elsy. I put my hands on my hips, looking up at the blue sky speckled with clouds. There had to be someone in one of the books that—

I stood up straight. The idea hit me like lightning.

Frank.

I checked my watch. In the books, he closed up his auto shop around four on Saturdays. It was ten till, so maybe I could still catch him. Grabbing my cross-body purse, I slung it over my head as I took off at a very speedy walk toward the center of town, and then at Mulberry I took a left, and there it was. Just like I had imagined.

Frank's Auto Shop was housed in a large brick building that, at one point, probably had been some sort of factory. Painted murals of the waterfall and the surrounding woods decorated the brick walls, interspersed with glowing fireflies and buzzing June bugs, which bled right into a large ad that read FRANK'S HOTTIES SOLD HERE! And, underneath it, the flame-throwing raccoon that served as its logo said in a speech bubble, THE BETTER CONDIMENT IN ELORATON!

Which was shade thrown at Honey-Honey.

The mural was Junie's work. The dig definitely Frank's.

The lights in the auto shop were off, and there was a sign on the window that read GONE FISHIN'. Shit.

"No no no no, *please*," I muttered, hurrying up to the rusted blue door. I knocked and waited. When no one answered. I knocked again. "Hello? Mr. Frank?"

If he was gone already, he wouldn't be back until Monday. I didn't care if I was breaking every rule Anders had laid out for me. I couldn't be *stuck* here all weekend.

But why not? a small voice asked, toying with the idea like a cat with a ball of yarn.

Because.

Because . . .

I pounded on the door harder. "Mr. Frank? Hello?"

Still, nothing.

I sat down hard on the curb. No cell service, no car, nowhere to stay, and the sun felt like it had a personal vendetta against me. I pushed my sweaty bangs out of my face. Okay, think.

Think.

I squeezed my eyes tightly closed. If I was dead, and this was some delusion of my dying brain, I didn't want to imagine what state my body might be in, if they ever found me. A morbid thought, but honestly the most *realistic* out of the two options.

A) I had hydroplaned off the road and was currently dying in some ditch in nowhere New York.

Or . . .

B) I was in the imaginary town of my favorite romance series.

And if this was real, and I was stuck here . . .

As I tried not to panic, a timid voice dragged me out of my thoughts.

"Lyssa?" the voice asked.

I cracked open an eye.

On the sidewalk, a freckled young woman stood, holding on to the thin strap of her purse tightly, in a paint-splattered T-shirt and baggy jean shorts. Her pastel pink hair was pulled back into a messy bun, her hazel eyes more blue than green today, her lips pink with gloss. Her thick, expressive eyebrows furrowed when she realized I wasn't Lyssa.

Junie Bray.

The Junie Bray.

Main character of *Daffodil Daydreams*. Fell off a horse at six and cut her brow open, leaving a scar. Knit when she was anxious. Baked the absolute *best* brownies. Smelled like vanilla and acrylic paints. Had worn the same pair of pink Converses since senior year of college. She was brilliant, and brave, and everything that I wished I could be but never amounted to, beautiful and wild like a Monet painting come to life.

And she had saved me. More than once. When I was at my lowest she had been there to reach her hand down and pull me out of that horrible pit—

Her eyes widened. "Oh—oh shit, I'm sorry, I thought you were . . . sorry. Wow, that's embarrassing."

I swallowed the knot in my throat. Tried to be cool. "It's the hair, right?"

She scrunched her nose, and it wrinkled the skin between her eyebrows. "From a distance, and there aren't many redheads around."

"Well, I'm all natural. Mostly. If you don't count the color over the gray hairs," I added, and she laughed.

"Why do you think I dye mine pink? I'd be all white with the way this year has been going," she said. "I'm guessing you're the newbie who slapped the hell out of Anders?"

My eyes widened. "Oh, fuck. People saw that?"

"Only, like, three people," she replied, and just as I was about to sigh in relief, she added, "and that means soon the entire town'll know."

I buried my face in my hands. "Of course."

"For the record, *I* didn't see it, but Maya sure as hell did," she said, motioning back toward the sweets shop. "She said she's never seen Andie piss someone off so thoroughly before. I mean, he snipes at Will often but, *wow*, he really said something to you." She stepped off the curb, closer. "Are you okay?"

"I—" My voice caught in my throat. I closed my mouth. Frowned. That was the last question I expected anyone to ask. "Yeah," I said, though I didn't sound convincing. I cleared my throat and tried again, because whatever was going on in my head was my business. I didn't need to drag anyone else into my solo pity party. "Better than my car, at least."

She glanced back at the auto shop, putting two and two together. "Ooh. The green thing in front of Gail's is yours?"

"Heeey, that green thing is Sweetpea, and she's never let me down before."

"Hella bad timing." She checked her watch, and shook her head. "He probably just left."

"Of course I just missed him."

Junie winced. "Yeah . . ."

"And there's no chance of him coming in tomorrow?"

"On a Sunday? Sure, when hell freezes over."

It was worth a shot. I pulled my hair over my shoulder, and gave it a tug, racking my brain for anyone else who could fix my car. "Is there another mechanic in town?"

"Garnet left with Bea, and Lyssa doesn't really know much about cars so . . ." Junie frowned, and sat down on the curb beside me. "Not really. Did I mention—I'm Junie, by the way."

"Elsy," I replied, and took a deep breath. Okay, so Frank was out of the question—at least until Monday. "I guess it could be worse."

"Right," Junie agreed. "You could be stuck in Poughkeepsie." And she shivered dramatically.

I snorted a laugh. It was one of the running jokes in Quixotic Falls—everyone hated Poughkeepsie. All the Bad Boyfriends came from there.

For a moment, I mulled over the thought of staying until Monday. I could try to walk out of Eloraton, up the road and across Charm Bridge, but would I make it before the rainstorm came again? Probably not today. And even if I got to the main road, who knew how far it was until another town? "I guess staying until Monday won't be so bad. Though, do you have any suggestions on places to stay? I sort of slapped my only option."

She grinned, bright and excited, and it made her hazel eyes glitter. "Well, you've met the right person, then. You're looking at the co-owner of the only bed-and-breakfast in town."

I was confused. "I thought it wasn't done with renovations yet?"

"I mean, it's *mostly* done," she pointed out. "*Mostly* done is only *slightly* not done."

"Ah . . ."

She waved off my confusion. "Don't think too hard on it. C'mon," she added, getting to her feet, and outstretched a hand to help me up.

Sunlight glinted off the half dozen rings on her fingers, and shimmered against her silver and gold bracelets. I looked at her outstretched hand, and then up at a woman I had read about countless times—I'd highlighted passages about the way her heart beat brighter whenever Will Carmichael walked into the room—while trying to find those feelings in real life. Her outstretched hand wasn't a trap, but it felt like one, regardless.

If I accepted it, then I was going to stay here until Monday.

What was the worst that could happen?

So I took her hand, and she pulled me to my feet.

11

Monsoon Season

JUNIE CHATTED ABOUT THE local drama as we walked back toward my car. Most of the things I already knew from the novels—like how Gemma and Frank were currently fighting over who would have *the* condiment in Eloraton, and how the Grumpy Possum Café was named for the possum that lived in the ceiling that kept evading them every time the owners tried to capture him.

"Though the possum hasn't been seen in ages. We're all hoping he just went off to make babies or something," Junie said. "I feel like he's just lurking somewhere, waiting to be found. Don't tell anyone, but Jake is *bereft* over it."

The Grumpy Possum Café without the possum? I'm sure he was just hiding.

There was a small grocery store, and the pharmacy beside it had a real and working soda counter. There were little boutique shops and a general store and clothing stores selling fashion that had been in, well, *fashion* probably half a decade ago, and most of the shops that weren't important to the books were forgettable in the way that the menu had been unfinished in the café—half-thought-out and blurry.

We retrieved my duffel bag from my car, and I eyed the box of books in the back. Should I take them with me, too? No, they should be fine where they were. After all, who was going to steal a bunch of paperbacks? I closed the hatchback.

A heavy raindrop landed on my nose. Then another on my forehead. I glanced up—and the sky was dark. The clouds had turned in a matter of minutes.

Junie held out her hand, and watched a few raindrops pool in her palm. "Again with the rain," she muttered. The clouds looked about ready to give. The storm looked angrier than the one earlier, like the one from last night. "I don't think we're gonna beat the rain. Wanna go to Gail's for an early dinner?"

"Sounds like a plan. Ah! It's starting!"

We ran for the Roost, but by the time we slipped into the cool bar, we were both halfway to soaked. Gail brought us over towels as we took seats near the middle of the bar. We dried off as we ordered house wine and burnt burgers.

"You really need to stop getting caught in the rain, darling," Gail said to me, and I ducked my head in embarrassment.

"I don't know, Gail, getting caught in the rain is *so* romantic. Just ask Ruby," Junie said.

"It wasn't," I quickly assured, because I'd almost killed a man and I really did not want to think about Anders at all right now. When Gail left to go put in our food order to the cook leaning against the kitchen window, Junie turned and asked me, "Okay, so, I've got to ask—what brought you this way in the first place? Not to be creepy, but I noticed your license plate is from Georgia. What brings you all the way up here?"

"A book club, actually. A romance book club."

"Oooh." She wiggled her eyebrow. "The spicy kind?"

"Do I look like someone who reads anything else?"

She grinned. "I'd hope not." Gail brought over our wines and a basket of roasted peanuts. Junie took a timid sip, thought for a moment, and then decided that she liked it. "Okay, so, you came up here for the book club?"

I nodded, cracking a peanut shell between my fingers. "We started meeting at this cabin in the Hudson Valley the year Rachel— a few years ago," I corrected. Meeting the book club had been the only bright spot during the worst year of my life. "So we decided to keep going every year after that."

She gave a start. "Oh, shit, so people are waiting for you?"

I winced. "Well . . . no. No one could make it this year."

"Except for you," she inferred.

"I know it's silly . . ."

She shook her head. "I think it's brave. I mean, staying in a cabin alone for a week sounds terrifying."

I barked a laugh.

"Why the Hudson Valley?"

"Our favorite book series is set here," I replied, hoping she didn't ask anything else, "and it's pretty easy for most everyone to get to. It's weird, I didn't think some of my best friends would be strangers on the internet, but here we are. My mom doesn't *quite* get it, but she understands enough. She said that once you find the good ones, you keep them around no matter what." I frowned, thinking about Liam, whom I did try to keep around no matter what, and he'd just left me anyway. "Though, they don't always stay."

"Then they weren't the good ones," Junie replied matter-of-factly.

"My mom would say the same," I said, eating a peanut. "She's on a Nile River cruise right now. My folks divorced when I was, like, four, and she never looked back. She met a woman a few years ago who had a passport filled with stamps from all around the world. Mom realized, while talking to her, that she'd spent so much time *reading* about far-off places, she finally wanted to see them for herself. She figured if that woman could travel the world alone, why couldn't she? So, off she went."

"I couldn't imagine. That must be so scary," Junie said, propping her head up on her hand. "Traveling alone."

"She'd agree with you, but she does it anyway. You do the things you're most afraid of."

"Is that why you came up here alone?"

I thought about back home, about the Facebook post detailing Liam and his fiancée's wedding, the pictures of the venue and the ring and the flower arrangements and how unbearable it all felt. "Yeah," I lied.

Gail came back with our burgers and fries, and leaned over the counter conspiratorially. "I got a question to ask you."

"No hot sauce this time," I said.

She pulled a ketchup bottle from behind the counter. "No, no, that's not it. Is it true?"

I blinked, confused, as I took the condiment. "Uh . . . is what true?"

Gail scoffed that I'd even ask. "That you and Anders had a *fistfight*!"

"A fist— Oh no. No no no, we didn't," I quickly replied. Junie snickered. I slapped him once and now it was a fistfight? I wanted to crawl under a rock and die. "I didn't even mean to hit him!"

Junie added, "But if she *had*, she'd win."

"You think so?" I asked, and then thought about it. "He might be scrappier than he looks—"

"Oh, *sweet*!" A man with dusty hair, sunburnt skin, and a lopsided grin slid up to the bar beside Junie and leaned against it. His white T-shirt was paint stained, as were his fingers. If I didn't know better, I'd think he was a painter or some sort of construction worker. But no: he was worse. My heart did a flip when I recognized his face. Broken nose, scar on his upper lip, dreamy sky-blue eyes, just like in the books. "You're the chick who stabbed Andie in the thigh, right?"

I denied it, flustered. "I—I did *not*—"

"Does she *look* like she stabs people in the thigh?" Junie asked, rolling her eyes. "Honestly, babe."

The man replied, leaning in behind her, putting his chin on her shoulder, "But, Junebug, I try not to put people in boxes."

My mouth was dry. It was him—it really was him. It was—

Junie kissed him briefly on the lips. "Elsy, meet Will."

I know.

I tried not to stare, but it was hard. Like seeing Aragorn step out of the pages, or finding out you're seated beside sparkly-skin-of-a-killer Edward Cullen himself.

"Is it true you tried to take out his eyeballs?" Will asked, and Junie punched him in the arm.

"*Seriously*, Will?"

"Ow! What? I heard she had!"

She rolled her eyes. "Please ignore him. He's huffed too much paint today. We're finishing up the kitchen in the inn. Babe, she'll be staying there tonight, is that all right?"

He gave a gasp. "What, we get *roomies*? Amazing. It'll be a pleasure to have you."

"I'm just happy I don't have to sleep in my car," I said.

"We'd never let you do that," he replied, and slid onto the bar-stool beside Junie and stole a French fry from her plate. "Heart of my heart, love of my life, daffodil of my eye, how was your day?"

"Lovely. Yours?"

"Still looking for a new plumber."

At that, Gail came over with a beer for Will. "New plumber? What happened to the one you had?"

"Fell," June replied. "He's been down on his back for six weeks now and we don't know when he'll be up to working again, so I think we need to just find a new one." She sighed wistfully. "He was *so* close, too. All we had left was the haunted toilet. It works sometimes, and then sometimes it just . . . floods for no reason, and water ends up everywhere."

Will stole another fry, until Junie slapped away his hand with a glare. "We aren't sure if it's actually haunted or if it's just the leaky pipes."

"Shush, we can market it if it's haunted—it *might* be haunted." She added toward me, "You'll be far away from it, I promise."

"Junebug, who would come to a town of two hundred people *just* to see a haunted toilet?" Will asked, not unkindly. There was adoration in her nickname, in every syllable. I wondered what it was like to have someone call you by a name like that.

Junie inclined her head and replied, quite certainly, "You'd be surprised, William."

And I raised my hand to prove her point.

A *ghost story* in the middle of Quixotic Falls? I felt like this was a story written *just* for me. There was no part of this that I wasn't about to thoroughly enjoy.

After Gail took Will's order so he'd stop absconding with his fiancée's fries, I asked Junie, "If it's just that little thing . . . can't you open up without it?"

"Sadly, no. It's the *origin* of all our . . . waste issues . . . to begin with," Junie admitted. "It's the biggest fix, and there isn't another plumber in town so . . ."

"It's a waiting game," Will finished for her.

She agreed. "A long one."

Will wiggled his eyebrows. "That's what she said."

Junie gave a sigh so tired, it sounded like her soul was leaving her body. She planted a hand on his cheek and said, in all serious-ness, "You're awful. I love you."

"I know," he replied.

As they bantered, a familiar figure sat down at the corner of the bar, the exact same seat he'd haunted the night before—and before that, and before that, and before that, I was sure—and Gail brought over his dinner without so much as a glance. Like clock-work. He must come here every night and order the same thing. He cracked open a book, dog-eared like the heathen he was, and munched on an onion ring as he read, having not spared anyone else in the bar a single glance.

I picked at my cuticles, wondering how to approach him to tell him that I was sorry. I *was* sorry, wasn't I? Either way, I needed to be an adult about this.

Pushing myself off the barstool, I excused myself from Will and Junie's conversation about inn renovations, and went up to him.

He didn't even look up from his book as he turned the page and said, "Gail told me that your car broke down?"

My shoulders squared. Already I knew this was a bad idea. "It must've broken when I dodged you in the rain."

"Oh, believe me," he said. "I'm regretting standing out in the rain as much as you probably regret missing me."

"Nonsense, I didn't want to dent my car."

He snorted.

I winced. How come every interaction with him felt like I was trading barbs? Just being near him made my body feel like it'd been jolted with electricity, and I wished I could say it wasn't addicting. I hated that if he wasn't always so moody, he could've been hand-some. Well, I guess he *was* handsome, regardless, but unattainable, like an ice block in the freezer you could never thaw. And I hated that it kind of made me want to get to know him more. Like a puzzle I couldn't quite solve, but I was stubborn. His white-blond hair had gently curled in the evening's humidity, his minty eyes sharp and bright, as he finally flicked them to my face, and studied it.

"Are you here to stab me in the thigh?" he asked snidely. "Go for the throat? Carve my heart out with a dull spoon? Finish the job?"

"We both know that you don't have a heart." I tsked.

His eyebrows jerked up, but he didn't argue. His gaze drifted behind me to Junie and Will. "Remember that you're gone Monday," he said, returning to his book. "Whatever waves you make, you aren't sticking around to see what they wash away. So don't ruin their lives."

"Like you think I've ruined mine?"

"I didn't say that."

My fingers curled into fists. "You're awful."

"Yes, I am." Then he licked his thumb and turned the page, effectively dismissing me.

The red mark was still on his cheek, and a bead of shame bloomed in my chest. How could I hate someone so thoroughly and still want to apologize for being awful? I swallowed that feeling, though, because he didn't deserve my apology tonight. He was wrong—about me, about what I wanted from the waterfall, about my *life*.

I returned to my seat, and neither Junie nor Will questioned my interaction. They probably realized it wasn't a good one, so I ate my burnt hamburger and listened to Junie and Will talk about remodeling the inn, and tried to forget about the fight earlier, or why his words still stung.

You're alone.

I wasn't, but he certainly was.

12

Haunted

WILL FINISHED HIS BURGER, and ducked out of the bar to go back to the inn early. He wanted to take a shower, and clean up his mess before I arrived. I assured him that I wouldn't care if there *was* mess—they were giving me a place to stay, and that was more than enough—but he wouldn't hear a word of it. So that left Junie and me to finish our burgers, and take the slow walk back to the Daffodil Inn. As we strolled, crammed under the small umbrella that Gail lent us, Junie and I talked like we'd known each other for decades. It felt like meeting a part of my heart that had broken off years ago, and remembering exactly how it beat.

Often, during lunch breaks at the college where I taught, I'd get into postmodern and critical theory with some of the other professors, and we'd talk about readers' parasocial relationships with authors, and fanfiction, and ownership. There were always varying opinions—some professors believed that the story belonged to the author, and we were merely peeking through a window. Other professors thought that all stories should be part of the global collective, free to use and transform however we liked.

I argued, often, that once a book was done, once it was written and published and sent out into the world, it was no longer *yours*. It turned into *ours*—together. You, telling the story, and us, interpreting it.

So, I knew that this Junie wasn't *my* Junie—not the one I had imagined in my head. There were bits of her that were unfamiliar. The birthmark on her neck didn't look exactly as I imagined, and she walked with her shoulders hunched forward a little, like she was always charging ahead. I was relieved, honestly, because if she hadn't sprung from my imagination, then I probably wasn't dying on the side of the road somewhere.

Then again, it meant that either she was part of someone else's imagination, or she was real. That *this* was real.

Which was also very hard to wrap my brain around.

As we came to the town square, I was telling her about the time Prudence and I took a pottery course in college, and ended up making phallic-shaped vases. The teacher had not been amused. "But they worked great as bongs," I added, and Junie howled with laughter.

"Oh my god, I *love* this Pru girl. Where's she now?" she asked, wiping a tear from her eye.

I hesitated. Above us, the clock struck seven. The bells chimed loud and bright, the reverberating buzz ricocheting along the buildings like a hum.

Junie could sense she'd said something that upset me. "Fuck, I'm sorry, that was rude. You don't have to tell me."

"It's okay." I gave a one-shouldered shrug. We stopped at the corner of the street. Across the way, sidewalk gave way to a green park at the base of the clock tower, and a family running around, chasing after a small corgi named Augustus. It wasn't that I didn't want to tell Junie, but I was afraid that it would sound silly. That *I* would sound silly. "She's in Iceland with her boyfriend. I think he's going to propose."

"Ooh, that's so fancy."

I agreed. "He's been wanting to do this for *ages*. I'm happy for them. Genuinely."

Under the light thrum of the rain, she studied my face. "But . . ."

"Is it that obvious?"

"No, but I would feel a little disappointed, if I were in your shoes."

"It isn't really about the cabin week. I mean, it *is*, but it isn't. We . . . were supposed to do everything together," I said finally, and it felt like I'd finally moved a heavy weight off my chest. I could breathe. "We *did* do everything together, actually. We got our ears pierced together when we were twelve, and we flew on a plane for the first time when we were sixteen, and we both had our first kiss at prom—hell, our *periods* started within a week of each other. We went to college together, and we graduated together, and we fell in love together and went on vacations and celebrated milestones and . . . and . . . I can't shake myself out of this—this place I've fallen into. She's going to get married and have kids and I'm just . . . standing still." I squeezed my eyes shut. "And I'm afraid."

She stopped and took my hand in her free one. The rain dripped off the edges of the umbrella, a curtain around us. "Hey, it's okay."

But it wasn't.

I should've seen the signs, but for years I was just . . . contented . . . following Liam down hiking trails, and curling my fingers around the back of his shirt like a child as we swam through concerts, and letting him lead us wherever he wanted to go. I should've realized that he never looked back to see if I was still there. His gaze was always trained ahead, and that's what I'd loved about him, but in the end it turned out that I simply wasn't important enough for him to look back at.

Not even once.

Junie squeezed my hand again. "It's okay to be afraid. Some things are hard, and sometimes you can't go it alone. Have you spoken with Pru about any of these feelings?"

I let out a bark of a laugh. "And say what? That I'm afraid she'll leave me behind? That I'll be alone? That I'm sorry I'm broken and she's—"

"You're not broken."

"I am, Junie. I really am." I pulled my hands out of hers, and wiped the edges of my eyes, glad that I hadn't started crying. I was never going to cry over Liam again—I'd promised myself that years ago, and I was going to stick to it. "And anyway, that's what the vase-shaped bong is for."

She rolled her eyes. "You and Ruby have the exact same humor."

"Is that a compliment?"

"No," she replied, and I gasped, pressing my hand over my heart. "I'm telling her that the next time I see her!"

"You better not!" She shoved me in the shoulder, and I smiled, stumbling away from her on the sidewalk. When I came back to her side, she put her head on my shoulder. "It's weird, but I just met you and I feel like we've been friends for years."

"Yeah," I agreed, remembering when I'd curl up on the couch, flipping to a dog-eared page, like the heathen I was, and reading my favorite parts, and how they ferried me through so many sleepless nights. If only she knew. "Me, too."

And then we came to a stop in front of a large yellow Victorian house that sat, so stately, between two brick buildings, like a misplaced Lego piece, overgrown with ivy and bluebells and honeysuckle vines.

The Daffodil Inn looked exactly how I'd imagined.

The bed-and-breakfast was fresh and bright, the dentils all painted across the edging on the roof, the corbels replaced, the sawn spandrils and turned spandrils all given proper attention. The bay window was set with a stained-glass daffodil, the same one that encrusted the window in the front door. Around the inn, encasing it like a lovely cage, was a wrought-iron fence overgrown with ivy and honeysuckle that bled into the rose garden that surrounded the house.

A small wooden plaque hung on the front of the gate, reading 102 MERRY LANE.

It looked just like the description from the first book, when Junie stumbled into town, and asked for a room from the bored-looking young man at the counter, who later turned out to be Will. They'd met there, their first kiss was out back near the water fountain with a statue of two mermaids intertwined, he *proposed* to her right in the foyer—

And all of it, so sweetly, felt like home.

Junie opened the gate of the white picket fence, and I followed her up the delicate stone walkway to the front porch.

"Welcome home," she said, opening the door, and my heart skipped in my chest as I stepped into the foyer and took a slow turn. It felt a little like coming to a place I'd been a hundred times before. The air was thick with memories. The house had belonged to a couple who'd moved here to escape the city. They threw lavish parties and filled the pool in the back with champagne, and celebrated New Year's for two weeks straight. Then the husband had a heart attack and the woman died of a broken heart—or that's how the story went.

Then Junie had stumbled into town, and she'd fallen in love with the wooden design of a daffodil in the foyer floor, and the glass mosaic windows that threw colors across the hardwood floors, and the delicate molding along the walls. And, most importantly, she'd fallen in love with the man at the front desk, the grandson of the woman who'd died of a broken heart.

I took a slow and deliberate pivot. "Wow," I whispered.

I wished the book club could see this. I wished Pru was here.

God, they'd have a field day.

"Sorry the inn's a bit of a mess. We're still trying to finish up," she said, waving her hand flippantly toward the basement door, and the haunted toilet in question.

"It's beautiful, though. The daffodil motifs. The bright colors . . . it feels warm. Homey."

Her expression softened, and she patted the railing knob at the bottom of the stairs. "She's a good old girl. You should see the wallpaper in the third guest room upstairs. Want a tour?" she added, her eyes glittering.

How could I say no?

She took me through the parlors and the kitchen, and I marveled at the beautiful ceiling molding, the wooden banisters up to the second floor, the crystalline chandelier in the dining room. The furniture was tasteful and sparse, plastic over the fainting couches and coffee tables and wingback chairs, so that as they stood in stasis they wouldn't collect dust.

The second floor was just as gorgeous, the rooms all themed in different flowers. The yellow daffodil room was my favorite. The wall with the headboard had an entire mural of huge daffodils blooming across it. Junie's handiwork, I was sure. Just like the mural on the side of Frank's Auto Shop, and the logo for the Grumpy Possum, and even Gail's bar scene. She showed me all the different rooms, each with a different flower theme and a different focal color—lavender and coral and sage. They even *smelled* like the colors of the rooms. The pink one—roses—matched Junie's pastel hair. After she showed me the last room—sunflowers—she said to me, "And that's it. That's the Daffodil. You know, even with all the hang-ups we've come across, what with the roach infestation, the leaky floorboards, the dry-rotted eaves, the century-old love letters hidden in the attic, I still love this place."

The love letters were part of the fourth book's plot, where Beatrice went on a road trip with the recipient's grandson (a man she allegedly hated who was, as it turned out, Ruby's little brother) to return the letters to his grandfather's lost love from forty years ago. It was Rachel's saddest book by far, sadder still with the tragedy of the author's passing herself, because at the end Beatrice left Eloraton. Bea was the only one of the heroines who ever did. So many heroines had come to find a home in Eloraton instead. Junie wandered in looking for a safe haven. Ruby found shelter in Jake. Gemma found acceptance in a small honey shop owned by the town's eccentric self-proclaimed witch. But Beatrice? It was the wild blue yonder that filled her with wonder.

Junie ran her fingers along the banister on the second floor— looking so lovestruck with the life she'd found.

And a feeling so visceral struck me then and there—I *wanted* that.

I wanted to *find* that.

The feeling was so strange, and so heavy, it felt like a fishhook tethered to my toes, pulling upward. It was a yearning so deep, it went all the way into the parts of me I hadn't even discovered yet. I felt it as Junie dragged me into the kitchen to make brownies, because the wine had given her a sweet tooth and Will loved her brownies even when she burnt them, and I felt it as we drank lemonade on the front porch and rocked in the rocking chairs, and she told me about things I already knew—about how she and Will met, and her life before Eloraton, feeling unmoored from her job and her passions. She talked about it all with the sort of distance of someone who had figured out where to drop anchor, and build a life. And too soon, it was midnight and she was showing me how to unlatch the windows in my room, and where the spare blankets were if I got cold in the middle of June, but my mind was five hundred miles away, thinking about my lonely apartment and my cluttered office in the English department and the syllabi I still needed to submit for next semester, and the sinking feeling in my gut.

"Elsy?" she asked, and I realized that she'd been talking to me.

I pushed the feeling away. "I'm sorry, what?"

"I asked if you needed anything. Will and I are in the main bedroom downstairs—closer to the haunted toilet, don't worry. The toilet down across from the main hall is the only one working right now . . . you know, the plumbing issue. So we all share that one. And if you want a shower in the morning, you can take one in the main bedroom, if that's all right? And I think that's it?"

"This is perfect," I replied, dumping my duffel bag on the foot of the bed.

"Even with the awkward plumbing?"

"It's better than sleeping with bears."

Her eyebrows scrunched together. "I . . . would hope so?"

"Thank you, really. If there's anything I can do to repay you—"

She waved her hand. "Please, don't mention it." Then she grabbed the doorknob and paused just before she shut it, a thought occurring to her. "Also . . . if you hear something in the middle of the night, don't mention that, either."

I schooled my face to keep myself from looking too sly. At least, unlike Ruby and Jake, Junie and Will seemed to be getting on—and getting *it* on—perfectly well. "Mention what?"

"Exactly! Well then—good night. Oh, we usually get up around eight, but feel free to stay in bed as long as you want," she added, and with one last awkward wave, she closed the door behind her. The floorboards creaked as she retreated to the stairs, and then down to the first floor. I waited until I heard the door close in the main bedroom, and then I fell onto the creaky bed in the yellow daffodil room, and smiled to myself.

This was so much better than any stuffy old loft.

I CHANGED INTO MY PAJAMAS AND SHUT OFF THE LIGHTS, JUST about to push up the windows and crawl into bed—there wasn't any central AC in most older New York houses—when movement in the garden behind the Daffodil Inn caught my eye. At first I thought it was a trick of the rain, but then the streetlight caught on the spoke of an umbrella. There was someone letting themselves in through the gate, and heading toward the pergola in the back of the garden. I couldn't see a face, but his knife-pleated trousers and spit-shined shoes gave him away.

Anders.

What was he doing sneaking around?

He hadn't noticed me up in the window as he dipped beneath the pergola, and disappeared through the narrow vine-covered alleyway beyond. Where was he going? I tried to think whether there was anywhere connected to the Daffodil Inn's garden, but nothing came to mind.

Curious.

If I had time tomorrow, I'd see what was so important that he'd go visit it in the rain. Then again, I'd almost hit him standing out in that same rain, so maybe wandering around in storms wasn't such an odd thing for him.

I retreated to bed. The mattress was comfy, if a little old, and the linens smelled like fresh laundry and lemons. The sound of the rain whispered in between the gauzy sunlight-colored curtains, and I sighed back into the feather pillows. This was it. Heaven. I didn't understand what was holding Junie and Will back from opening the inn—everything seemed perfectly copacetic. Surely the plumbing couldn't be that—

Then I heard it.

At first, I thought it was just a noise of the house settling. So I rolled over in bed, and admitted to myself that I might actually *miss* the starlings in the eaves . . .

But then I heard it again.

I sat up.

Was that . . . no. It couldn't be.

Rachel Flowers wouldn't write a *ghost story* into her books. It must have been Junie or Will getting up to go rustle around the kitchen.

The sound didn't . . . *seem* like rustling, though.

Slipping on my still-damp sneakers, I grabbed my phone and turned on the flashlight, and crept out of the room and down the stairs. I wasn't very sneaky, as it turned out. If my shoes weren't squeaking, then the floorboards were.

But the sound persisted as I reached the bottom of the stairs and turned my light down the hallway.

The ungodly demonic gurgle was coming from the door beneath the stairs. The door to the basement.

The haunted toilet.

To my utter dismay, the door to the basement was unlocked, so of course down I went into the bowels of the Daffodil. I ran my hand along the side of the wall until I found the light switch at the bottom of the stairs. If it was a ghost, who would it be? Would Rachel Flowers bring back a character she killed off? No, the only people she killed were the ones no one *wanted* back. Gemma's ex and Bea's stepmother, and a host of unnamed parents because Rachel Flowers was nothing if not a sucker for the orphan trope.

Another low, awful gurgle rumbled. It really wasn't a terrible basement, all things considered. If the toilet wasn't *haunted*, I think Junie and Will would've turned it into a recreation room. There were a pool table, extra couches covered in plastic, and a door at the back that led out to the private garden with the mermaid fountain.

If this—this *ghost*—was the reason Junie and Will didn't have their happily ever after yet, then maybe I'd just . . . give it a small talk.

I followed the sound to the perpetrator in the far corner, and opened the door. The toilet in question looked like any other basement toilet, though it did have a worrisome ring of rust around the base that looked, a bit too cryptically, like blood. I tried to flush the toilet, and but it just bubbled and burped—like there was something clogging it.

Huh.

I tried it again—but nothing this time.

Then, even worse, there was another strange noise—like a high-pitched screech in the walls, and I jumped back out of the bathroom and swung the door closed.

Okay . . . maybe it wasn't going to be so easy. I knew enough about toilets to unclog them, but this? This was above my pay grade.

The pipes above me gave a tremble, and whatever ghost Rachel Flowers had written into this story could stay dead.

I was up and out of the basement by the time the rattling stopped, taking the stairs up to the second floor two at a time. I'd barely gotten my tennis shoes off before I dove into bed again, and pulled the covers high.

Junie was wrong. I was not brave at all.

13

All By My Shelf

JUNIE WASN'T SURPRISED TO find me up and dressed the next morning when she came into the kitchen. In fact, she looked a bit sheepish. Because she knew what I had endured last night. Oh, she definitely knew. I couldn't remember the last time I'd been awake on a Sunday before noon. Nursing my coffee, I watched her sleepily shuffle over to the coffeepot and pour herself a cup, before joining me at the table. I set down my cup, and looked her in the eyes.

"When you said 'noise' last night, you didn't mean . . ." And I made a motion with my two hands.

She dipped her head down, embarrassed, and her tangled mop of pink hair fell into her face like a curtain. "Oh, so you heard it."

"I'm not an expert, but I am going to say this with all the love in my heart: don't find a plumber." I leaned against the table, closer to her. "Find an exorcist."

"I'm so sorry. It was worse last night than most—did you get any sleep?"

I waved her off. "Sleep is for the weak. And lucky. What I want to ask is how do you and Will sleep with that? Isn't your bedroom, like, right over the basement?"

"Earplugs," she replied simply, and then took a sip of coffee. "Ooh, this is so good. Is this *our* shitty coffee?"

"You learn how to make good coffee when you live on it for your entire grad program." I leaned back in my chair again, and cast a suspicious look at the basement door. "Honestly, it sounds like something's alive in your pipes."

"Right? I don't know what it could be. We've tried everything, and if you go look now, I can bet you there's water all over the floor."

"A ghost who likes to get a little wet, who knew?"

She almost spewed her coffee. "Elsy!"

I giggled. "Couldn't help it."

"Couldn't help what?" Will asked, coming into the kitchen with a stretch, his rumpled shirt lifting to show his tanned midriff. He yawned, and sniffed the air. "Is that coffee?"

"Elsy made it," Junie said, and he quickly grabbed a cup and joined us at the table.

He hummed as he took a sip. "Junebug, get her recipe."

"My dude, it's just coffee. There is no recipe," she replied, looking offended, "and my coffee is *great*."

I bit the inside of my cheek, because I wasn't about to point out that she, also, had just complimented me on the taste. There really wasn't anything to it—I just made it so strong you could stand a spoon up in it, and hoped you had a taste for molasses.

"Your coffee *is* great," he agreed, nodding, "but Elsy's is better."

She narrowed her eyes at him. "You're sleeping in the basement tonight."

He blanched. "Babe!"

"Don't you *babe* me, it's too early. Oh, by the way, give her an extra pair of your earplugs tonight."

He took another sip and eyed me. "So, you heard it, too? The bane of our existence?"

I hesitated, looking between the two of them. "It wasn't *that* bad," I finally amended. Besides, I didn't want them to feel like their hospitality had somehow turned out worse than sleeping in my car, ready for a visit from Smokey Bear. I'd gotten to sleep in *the* Daffodil Inn, and no matter what, no haunted toilet had mucked that up. It was still memorable. Just maybe not in the way I'd imagined. "It was fine, really. And I *did* get to sleep." Finally. At four in the morning. For thirty minutes. "So I'm good."

Junie didn't seem all that convinced, but Will was. "Man, you gotta tell me your secret, then, because I can sometimes hear that sucker *in my sleep*."

I shrugged nonchalantly. "I guess I'm just a heavy sleeper."

Which was a lie. I was just good at pretending to be awake for all those 8:00 a.m. classes that my dean somehow *always* scheduled me for. I was convinced that she had it out for me ever since I told her that Nora Roberts had as big an impact—if not bigger—on the modern publishing landscape as literary giants like Franzen or Tartt. She'd been scheduling me for the ass-crack-of-dawn classes ever since.

I took another long sip of coffee. Will didn't have to know that. Neither did Junie.

I'd deal with the haunted toilet for the next few nights—after all, this was a place to sleep and they were already so gracious. I wasn't about to complain any more than I already had.

"What do y'all have on the docket today?" I asked, steering the conversation elsewhere, and they told me about the molding they had still to paint, and some aesthetic work on the wraparound porch, but otherwise it was simply a waiting game until they could find a different plumber.

Or an exorcist.

Neither of which Rachel Flowers wrote in abundance. Too bad she hadn't written a hot priest romance. That could've really come in handy here. No, instead she wrote a grumpy, handsome man in a bookstore. What an abysmal waste.

Will made breakfast, and afterward I decided to get out of their hair for a while and go explore Eloraton. Do all the big stops—the clock tower, the jewelry store that was only open when Mercury was in retrograde, Sweeties (again), the art gallery, the old movie theater, the waterfall . . .

Anders's sharp gaze flashed in my mind, and the sound of the slap, and I winced.

Or maybe *not* the waterfall . . .

It was so frustrating—why would he care if I went there or not? Or was his character flaw the curmudgeon who didn't believe in true love? The worst that could happen, if I went, was . . . what? I'd get wet? I'd stand under the waterfall alone and wish I had someone to kiss, just to see if the magic worked on people outside of fiction?

But even if it did, I had no one to kiss.

The magic would be wasted on me.

Speaking of Anders, what had he been doing, sneaking around in the rain? I descended the steps out back into the garden, taking a to-go cup of coffee with me. Junie and Will had gone to get dressed, and get started on painting for the day, so I was sure I wouldn't be followed.

The pergola sat unassuming at the back of the property, almost hidden between the overgrown rosebushes.

I had begun to pick my way through the garden, when something caught the corner of my eye. Across the street, in front of the butcher shop, Lily stooped to pick up the pages of her book again. A few of them had fluttered out into the middle of the road. I glanced back to the pergola. It could wait, I figured, and I hopped the side fence in the garden and crossed the road to her. I picked up the pages in the street. They were hazy, the illustration blurred, like the menu at the café. Another thing half-imagined.

I handed them to her.

Lily thanked me, and shoved them back into their proper place. "I keep losing them," she said with a frustrated huff, and then squinted at me. "You're Uncle Andie's friend, aren't you? The weird girl who almost ran him over?"

"I guess I am," I replied dryly, not surprised at *all* that Anders had slandered my name even to an eight-year-old. "That book looks really well loved."

"I guess you could say that."

"What are you doing out here?"

She shrugged. "Mom had to go tend to the bees again, so I had to go get Maya to open the shop. Apparently, the bees want to murder the queen."

"I'm sure your mom will stop them."

"Or the bees will raise a new queen in secret, and when she's old enough, the hive will rise up and kill the old queen." She gave it a thought. "I feel bad for the new queen. Well, the old one, too, but especially the new one. What if the new one also does bad? Then the hive'll raise *another* one and then the new queen'll be killed by the same bees that raised her. They're ruthless."

"When you put it like that . . ." I muttered, thinking that maybe this kid needed to read about unicorns and princesses a little more. Or maybe tardigrades.

"Bees can form a hive in three months, and start making honey in forty-five days," she went on matter-of-factly, and looked down at her book, keeping it so tightly closed her fingers were turning pale. "And I can't even fix my book."

"To be fair, books are hard to fix."

Lily frowned, squinting up at me in the morning sun. "How do you know?"

"Because I've done it."

"You have?" She sounded skeptical.

I couldn't blame her.

"Sure." I shrugged. "I've done it plenty of times."

Lily eyed me suspiciously. "If Uncle Andie couldn't do it, how can you?"

"Because I might just be better than Anders." I tried not to sound *too* smug.

She narrowed her eyes. This kid really was a tough sell.

I held out my hand. "Here, can I see it?"

She handed over the book. I took it gingerly and turned it over in my hands. It really was in terrible shape. The cover was missing, as was the title page, and the spine was broken, so at least half of the glued-in pages were already in the middle of falling out, or had already done so. Since the book was perfect-bound and not coptic stitched, it was both an easier *and* a harder fix. The cover itself was toast—it'd need a new one. But overall . . . I'd done worse to my own books, and Mom had fixed those.

Lily waited impatiently. "Well?"

"Yes, I think I can do it. I don't have my tools from home, so it might be a bit hard . . ."

"The bookstore has a craft section," she pointed out, biting on her dark hair nervously. "Maybe you can find some stuff there?"

The bookstore was the last place I really wanted to go, but it sounded silly to tell her that I wouldn't just because I wanted to avoid Anders at all costs. And here I thought I could spend a day without seeing his face. Well, I could still try.

"Okay," I caved, "but we'll have to be a little sneaky. Anders . . .
doesn't really like me right now."

She nodded knowingly. "Because you assaulted him?"

I winced. "It's . . . more complicated than that."

She rolled her eyes. "Grown-ups are weird."

"You're not wrong," I admitted. "So . . . to the bookstore?"

"The bookstore," Lily said, and left down the street toward Ineffable Books. I hurried after her, the broken book in tow.

14

Spine(less)

ANDERS, BLESSEDLY, WAS NOWHERE to be found. Neither was his cat, Butterscotch.

I set the book down on the front counter. The longer I could sneak around the grumpy bookstore owner, the better. Apologizing was the adult thing to do, but I didn't know exactly what to say yet, or how to say it. *I'm sorry I slapped you, but you were an asshole?* That seemed contrary. No, best to avoid him for as long as possible.

I whispered to Lily, counting on my fingers, "Okay, I'll need some Elmer's glue, some tape, a cardboard box, scissors, and a ruler—oh, and a ribbon, too, if you've got it—"

"*What* are you two doing?" came the cold, articulate voice of Anders.

I spun around with a gasp. "Ah! You're here."

Anders stood, quite unamused, between Nonfiction and Memoirs, and took a bite of his bagel with—what smelled like onion-and-chive schmear. "And, regrettably, so are you."

Today, he wore a loose heather-gray T-shirt and dark blue jeans that he most definitely looked horrible in. He didn't have an ass for jeans, I told myself, and I didn't take note of the way he fit in them. Not at all.

I narrowed my eyes. He returned the glower. "You don't have to sneak up on people," I said.

"It's fun." He shifted his gaze between me and Lily, and then back to me. "Let me ask again: What are you two doing? Nothing good, with you two together."

Lily held up her book. "She's going to fix it for me! Oops," she added as a handful of pages fell out and fluttered to the floor.

Anders shoved the rest of his bagel in his mouth, dusted his fingers off on his jeans, and stooped to help her pick them up. When he'd swept them together, he handed the pages to her, squatting down so he had to look up at her. "Is she now?" Again, another one of those piercing looks at me. I winced, wanting to melt into the floor, and diverted my gaze to my shoes. "And she knows how to fix it?"

"I do," I interjected, and Lily nodded excitedly.

He didn't say anything for a long moment as he studied me, pushing himself back to his feet. The way he held himself, cold and composed, made him seem like a giant. It made me stand straighter, too, so I didn't have to look all the way up his nose. Then his attention returned to Lily, and he said to her, his shoulders melting a little into a friendlier stance, "Well, aren't we in for a treat, then? What can I help with?"

I began to say, "Oh, you don't need—"

But Lily held up her hands and counted on her fingers, "Glue, tape, cardboard box, scissors, ruler and—um—what was the last thing?" she asked me.

"A ribbon."

"Right, that. You got it, right?"

Lily and I both looked at Anders expectantly, and he gave a one-shouldered shrug. "I think we've got most of that in the back." He went to go get the supplies. "Not the ribbon, though. Butterscotch has made it his life's mission to shred them all. You'll have to find that elsewhere."

Lily looked around. "Where *is* your cat?"

"Probably hiding somewhere," he replied, though there was a note of uncertainty in his voice as he looked around the bookstore. "Probably crawled into an alcove and fell asleep. He'll come out eventually. *You* need to go find a ribbon."

"Hmm." Lily gave it a thought before an idea dawned on her. "Ooh, I know where some ribbon is! I'll be right back," she added, and before I could ask her where she was going, she fled out the front door and down the sidewalk.

I could feel Anders's judgmental gaze on me.

"I know what I'm doing," I said, answering his unspoken question. Then I said, "Truce? For Lily?"

He rolled the thought around. "Depends."

I didn't want him to hate me. I didn't want anyone to, really. It was a flaw of mine. I took a deep breath. Now or never, I guessed. "Look, about yesterday—"

"I've got some boxes in the back," he interrupted, and left.

I snapped my mouth closed. Oh, dear. He must *really* hate me.

A few moments later, he came back with a cardboard box, a box cutter, and a few other supplies that Lily had listed off.

I riffled through them. "This should work, thanks. I mean, I wish I had *my* supplies: a bone folder, PVA glue, my stitching needle, but this'll do in a pinch. What?" I asked, when I found him staring.

He snapped out of whatever thoughts he had in his head, and

quickly retreated toward the children's section, muttering something about finding his damn cat.

"Weird," I muttered, and got to work.

First things first: I had to tear off the remaining cover and reinforce the spine, which I did with Elmer's glue. By the time I was done, Lily had come back with a pretty ribbon that—clearly—she used in her hair.

"Will this work?" she asked, breathless.

I took it, and ran the inch-thick ribbon between my fingers, measuring it against the book. It was the color of milk and honey. "It's gorgeous. Are you sure you aren't going to miss it?"

"Nah. I don't like ribbons in my hair anymore."

"Then I'd love to use it."

She pulled up a stool and sat on the other side of the counter as she watched me work, swinging her feet back and forth underneath her chair. I glued her ribbon to the cardboard spine at the top, giving her a built-in bookmark. Lily watched, amazed.

"So how did you learn all this?" she asked as I measured her book and then set the glued pages to dry under five heavy tomes I pulled from the closest shelf (History). The weight of the books would compress the pages so they would end up gluing tight together. From the measurements, I drew boxes on the cardboard. "A special school?"

"No. My mom was a librarian, so I learned from her," I replied, double-checking the measurements, and then started to cut with the box cutter. "We didn't have a lot when I was your age, and I read *so much* that my books would also start falling apart. She was used to bandaging up books for the library she worked at—our district didn't have great funding—so she taught me how to fix them. Bind the spines. Glue the pages. Tape the covers. She knows how to fix it all."

"Are *you* a librarian, too?" Lily asked.

"No. I teach English at the local college."

"That sounds boring."

I laughed, finishing cutting out the cardboard that would become the cover. "It is, sometimes, but I get to talk about my favorite stories. So it makes it worth it."

She watched as I took a piece of card stock and laid it flat under the cardboard spine, and glued the two covers to either side. "What's your favorite?" Then she scrunched her nose. "Are they kissing books, like the ones Uncle Andie likes?"

Startled, I asked, "What?"

"You know, *romances*."

"I mean . . . I . . . yeah. I like them a lot."

She nodded sagely. "You should talk to Uncle Andie, then. He's not married, but he almost was. I think that's why he likes to read them."

That surprised me. Anders once had a fiancée? "I wonder what happened," I muttered.

Lily shrugged. "Guess it wasn't MTB."

"MTB?"

"Meant to be."

Years ago, when I first met Liam, I believed in things like that, too. Stars crossing, and fated mates, and couples who were meant to be. Stories better suited for books, where the plots were predictable and the endings were always happy.

I tried to imagine Anders engaged, how he proposed, what the ring looked like. Who was his ex-fiancée? How did they break up? He wasn't very forthcoming with any sort of information, so I doubted I could outright ask him. I thought of everything that I'd already gleaned—he was still single *and* he didn't have any prospects, he walled off his emotions, he owned a cat, he came to town and took up the bookstore . . . but everything else was a blur. Fill in the blank. He was a blond-haired Darcy looking for his Elizabeth.

That at least made him sound interesting. Gross.

I picked at the drying glue on my fingers. *An ex-fiancée, huh?* In the back of the bookstore, I heard him clicking his tongue, pushing books aside, looking for his cat.

It must have been awful, however they ended the engagement.

Anders and I were more alike than I thought.

"Wanna help me with this next part?" I asked Lily to distract myself from *that* idea. "Let's pick out some endpapers. There's an art to it." I handed her the book of card stock, and we finished putting together the casing.

I told Anders I would pay for the supplies I used when I saw him peeking out around the Romance section, but he just waved it off with a tinge of embarrassment on his cheeks, and disappeared again, saying he thought he heard a meow.

Lily picked out her favorite colors of the card stock—pink and yellow—so we wrapped the cardboard in them (she said they made her feel like she was in her happy place), and then chose a glittery purple for the endpapers, and set to gluing it all together. It wasn't my best work, but the afternoon with Lily was nice. Peaceful, even. It reminded me of all the times Mom and I had fixed up tattered library books in her office.

I'd been happy then. Really, *really* happy.

Not that I wasn't happy now, teaching college-level English courses. I was. Keats and Byron and Shelley. It was a dream to be able to read as much as I wanted, and discuss the bard's greatest turns of phrase with fresh eyes. But there was also something . . . a little divorced from those conversations, too. Something missing.

"There," I said, gingerly opening the book and then closing it.

The pages crackled a little, still delicate from the glue. "It's not the best, but . . ."

She gasped and took it and held it out in front of her, the ribbon she picked out the perfect size to fit between the pages. "I *love* it!"

"You sure?"

"Yes, and now I don't have to pester Uncle Andie anymore!"

I barked a laugh, and then gave a start when Anders materialized from the innards of the bookstore, his hands in his pockets. Still without his cat. He said, "You could never pester me."

Lily made a face. "You're a bad liar."

"I'm not *that* bad," he muttered. Lily showed him the book, and surprise flickered across his face. "Oh, that is very . . . bright."

"I love it! I love it!"

He caved almost instantly, and agreed. "It looks charming, Lily. Did you thank her?"

Lily spun back around to me and then dove into my stomach for a hug. She buried her face in my torso and squeezed me tightly. "Thank you! Thank you, thank you, thank you!" she said, and then let me go. "I used to want to be a marine biologist, but now I want to be something else."

Anders put a hand atop of her head. "And what's that, Lils?"

She pushed his hand off. "A book fixer who *also* saves the whales, duh."

"Ah." And he rolled his eyes in that endearing way that adults could only do to kids who *knew* they were right and so no one could tell them differently. "Silly me for asking."

She stuck out her tongue, and he stuck out his in retaliation. "I'm going to go show Mom at the honey hives!" she announced, and said thank you to me one more time before she scrambled out of the bookstore in a whirlwind of pigtails.

I watched her go, unable to keep myself from grinning. What

a sweet kid. I wondered if, when Pru and Jasper had children, I'd make a good eccentric aunt. The weird one who came over on weekends and brought with her even weirder gifts, and knew how to mend books and wore different-colored socks and had a story for every occasion. I never imagined myself with kids. It never felt like *me*.

But this? I could do something like this.

Then, of course, Anders had to ruin it.

"I see you're making friends," he remarked dryly, putting his hands in his jean pockets, and inclining an eyebrow. He looked so cool, so composed, so *good-looking*, it was infuriating.

I took my cross-body purse from the counter, and slung it over my shoulder. "Yes, well, I prefer to hang around people who like me."

"I didn't say I hated you."

No, but he didn't *like* me, either. I still needed to apologize to him, but would he just interrupt like last time, not wanting to hear it? "You've got a great romance selection," I said instead, motioning to the shelf of paperbacks.

And then I left.

15

The Cemetery of Deleted Things

I GOT A LATE LUNCH at the café. Jake had just showed up, breezing in like he'd rolled out of bed two seconds ago, five-o'clock shadow and scruffy dark hair. He high-fived the teen behind the cash register, as if to tag him out, and slid over the counter to stand behind the bar. He put on his name tag, tied his apron around his waist, and got to work. I assumed that Ruby had already left, but I wanted to try to apologize for—well—telling her that she'd settled, because Jake really was doing his best, and he never really got enough time on the page doing *this* work—the work Ruby had settled with. And to be honest, he was great at it. He schmoozed up customers like he'd been doing it since he was born. He knew their orders, he knew their names, he knew how to smile and when to laugh, and he was very good at getting people to buy a little more than they originally came in for. Oh, just a coffee? Are you sure you can't make room for a cheese Danish? They're fresh and better than Starbucks could ever be.

It was truly a sight to behold.

As I finished the rest of my soda, Ruby tore out of the back office like a storm. She pecked a kiss on Jake's cheek, and said hello to the customer he was attending, and quickly made her way for the door. Her shift must've been up.

"Ruby," I called, putting down a ten for my lunch and scooting out of the booth. I probably could've just let her go, but I didn't want her to think I was—well, I didn't want Ruby Rivers to hate me because I'd been thoughtless.

She paused at her name, looking around for the source, but when her gaze settled on me, she frowned. "Oh, Anders's friend."

"Not quite friend," I replied with a wince.

"Right, right, you slapped the shit of him. Poor guy," she added, putting a hand on her hip. "What do you want?"

Blunt and to the point. I couldn't blame her. "Can we talk?" I asked, twisting my fingers together. I glanced back at Jake, who was leaning against the counter, chatting with a customer. "Please?"

There was a defiant purse to her lips, but then she sighed and motioned out the door. "Can we walk, too? I just really wanna go home and crash for a bit."

Relief swelled in my chest. "Sure."

So I put a ten down on the table for my food and followed her out of the Grumpy Possum and down the sidewalk toward the center of town. Ruby and Jake shared an apartment above the old movie theater—the place had been vacant for years, until she and Jake decided to fix it up and move in together. The theater—THE GRAND, as the light-up sign said—was across the square from the inn, so old that it still had a marquee out front, and big bulb lights that needed constant replacements.

The early afternoon was hot, and rain clouds had already retreated to the edges of the valley, leaving behind puddles against the curbs of the streets, and muggy windows.

"So," Ruby asked, digging into her purse for a mint, and offering one to me, but I declined. "What do you want?"

"I want to apologize," I replied, "for saying those things to you. I was out of line and I barely know you, so . . . I'm sorry. Anders just told me about how you and Jake met and—I guess—I just . . . I'd seen it before. But I know my experiences aren't yours and I was wrong. I'm sorry," I repeated, and if I could say it a thousand more times, I would.

"You're right," she replied, rolling the mint around on her tongue, "my experiences are different, and I'm not you, and it was more than a bit uncalled-for."

"Yeah . . ."

We walked together for a moment in silence. Was that it? Should I leave now or—

She sighed. "But you remind me of another do-gooder."

"Oh?"

"Junie. You're staying with her. Two in the same town is one thing, but in the same house?" She shivered. "It's probably all sparkly rainbows and butterflies."

I laughed self-consciously. "I think I'm too selfish. Like, I just wanted you to hear what I thought, never mind whether or not you wanted to hear it. Which, in hindsight, of course you didn't."

"No," she agreed, and tilted her head, "*but* . . . it did get me thinking. When was the last time we had a day to be with each other? Am I there for me or for him?"

"When you're in love," I said, remembering all the years with Liam, "the lines sort of blur."

We stopped at the corner, in front of us the square and the clock tower that reached high into the sky, and the minute hand snapped to the twelve.

The bell at the top gave a groan as it tipped to the side and rang. The sound reverberated through the town once, then twice, dissipating in the buzz of a thousand bees.

Ruby turned to me and said, "You're forgiven. This *once*. But only because you seem pretty interesting, and I like shiny things. See you around, Elsy."

Then she broke off from the corner of the sidewalk, crossed the street, and made her way toward the movie theater. I watched her go for a moment, my heart swelling because she remembered my name.

She remembered it! I'd only told it to her once, and she still knew it.

I was grinning to myself before I realized it, and turned on my heel—

And ran right smack into Maya Shah.

"Sorry, sorry," she said, stumbling out of my way, pulling her headphones down around her neck. A dark heavy metal murmured from the earphones. She gave a start as she recognized me. "Oh, you're the new girl! With the broken car!"

"Eileen, but everyone's called me Elsy since before I can remember," I introduced, my brain still buzzing from my chat with Ruby, and she jutted out her hand.

"Maya, and everyone just calls me Maya," she added, tongue in cheek. She motioned down the street. "You came in to Sweeties yesterday, right? Got a whole half pound of that honey taffy."

I laughed self-consciously. "I did. I haven't regretted it yet."

"Eh, it'll take at least two pounds to rot your teeth," she said jokingly, and glanced behind me. "Were you and Ruby just chatting? That's frightening. Usually when she hears her brother's coming back into town, she gets in a *mood*. Doesn't want to talk to anyone. Garnet does that to people. But you're still standing," she added, inspecting me up and down, "so miracles *can* happen."

"Only in Quixotic Falls," I replied. "Isn't the rumor the town is magic?"

"Only the falls, and only if you believe that sort of thing," she added with a roll of her eyes. "If you see Garnet Rivers, don't let him trick you into going to the falls. It's always his M.O., and I doubt his Great American Road trip changed him that much," she added, a bit sour. In the last book, Garnet had left Eloraton with Beatrice Everly. Was he coming back without her? I wanted to ask, but Maya said, "Though, it doesn't seem like you have a problem with difficult men. You just slap the shit out of them."

I gave a sigh. "Does everyone in town know?"

"Well, Gail saw it, and if Gail saw it then . . . yeah," she confirmed. "Probably everyone."

"Great."

"It could be worse."

I sighed. "Right. I could be stranded here without a car. Oh, wait."

"I can't think of a worse fate."

"Really?" I asked. "Eloraton can't be that bad." And I never knew Maya to hate the town, either.

"Well, no, it's not bad, it's just . . ." She took out her phone, and finally paused her music.

"Just what?" I prodded, and she chewed on her bottom lip, debating.

The Maya in the books wouldn't have hesitated a moment to speak her mind. The Maya who could shoot an apple out of a tree at fifty paces, and painted her nails to match the equinox in the summers, and adored the first day of spring and the river that ran through Charm Woods, and every day she got to see Lyssa Greene.

She would've shouted about her life, her lovely life, from the rooftops, but this Maya felt different from the one I'd gotten to know in the series.

Something had happened to her.

At the end of book four, Lyssa and Maya were left sharing secret glances at each other, and going off and sitting in the projection booth of the old movie theater, eating popcorn and watching terrible nineties monster movies.

This woman wasn't her.

"It's just," Maya finally caved, "sometimes when I think about it too hard, it feels like I'm just . . . sort of this sidenote in my own life, you know? Like I don't have one of my own here in Eloraton."

"Like . . ." I hesitated. "A secondary character?"

"*Yes!*" she crowed. "I just feel like I'm stuck. And the only person who understood was— Oh." She froze, staring at the woman on the sidewalk. "Lyssa," she said, her voice barely above a whisper.

The redhead stood in front of us, about ten feet away, carrying two paper bags full of groceries, her wide-brim hat shadowing her face. At the sound of her name, she pulled herself to her full height, shoulders square. "Maya," she replied.

I could see how, yesterday, Junie confused us. We both had long reddish-copper hair and a heart-shaped face, but that's where our similarities ended. She wore hers in pigtail braids, and dressed in green rompers, and had a sleeve of flower tattoos that she kept adding to, even though it was already stuffed full.

I expected Maya and Lyssa to blush at each other, to make flirty small talk, like they had in *Honey and the Heartbreak*, but there were no teasing smiles, no moony eyes. There was a wall, and jagged spikes, and man-eating plants between them.

She simply gave a polite hello, and recognized me. "You're Anders's friend from yesterday!"

"Not quite friends," I clarified.

"Oh . . ." She shifted awkwardly, and then asked Maya, "How's your family?"

"Good," Maya replied woodenly. "Except for the mutiny of bees."

Lyssa nodded. "That reminds me, I'm going to go help Gemma figure out a solution. I'll . . . see you around?"

"Yeah," she replied, her hands curled into fists, and she didn't move again until Lyssa had passed us on the street and migrated across the road toward Sweeties.

Beside me, Maya held her wrist with her grandfather's fixed watch, and gave a long sigh. "Look at me, babbling. It was nice chatting with you," she added, and pulled her headphones back over her ears.

I watched her go, and when she turned down the next street, I began to wonder if *all* of the characters were stuck like that— somewhere after the happily ever after of book four. In that span, Anders appeared, Maya and Lyssa split, the bees started a mutiny and . . . what else had changed?

That's when I remembered.

"Wait," I said quickly, and she glanced over her shoulder, taking off an earphone.

"Sorry, yeah?"

"Do you know what's behind the inn at the Daffodil? You know, there's a pergola and there's an alleyway, but . . ."

She gave me a strange look. "Yeah, it's abandoned. There's nothing back there." Then she left down the street toward home, and I decided where I wanted to go next.

~

THE PERGOLA STOOD AT THE EDGE OF THE DAFFODIL INN'S
garden, so that's where I went. The path beyond it squeezed between two old buildings crawling with ivy. Clover and weeds grew
from the cracks in the pavement and in the edges of the building.
At the end of the alleyway was an iron gate, though it didn't look
locked.

I stopped under the pergola, looking down the narrow way. All
day, I'd been racking my brain about this space, this nook behind
the inn, but I didn't remember it at all. This had not been in the
books.

This . . . this was something *new*.

I stepped through the pergola into the alley, the temperature
between sunlight and shadow making my skin prickle with gooseflesh. The air felt like it was filled with electricity. I followed the
alleyway down to the wrought-iron gate, and pushed it open.

The gate led to a courtyard, boxed in on all sides by buildings,
so there was only one way in and one way out. There was an overgrown fountain in the middle that somehow still worked, marked
with algae and moss as the water poured from the maiden at the
top. Honeysuckles and wildflowers crawled across the carpet of
grass and broken stone pathways, and oak trees grew, their branches
swaying in the breeze, sending ripples of sunlight down through
the leaves like the bottom of the ocean.

This place felt . . . *impossible*. Like there was something new
lurking just under the clovers. It was right in the center of town,
but how come it'd never been brought up before? Was it in the
town maps in the front of the books?

At first glance, it looked like just a forgotten courtyard.

But then the shadows shifted, the trees blew the other way, and through the weeds there were glimpses of . . . stranger things. Statues, mostly. Old and forgotten, all broken and lying in different states of disrepair as nature slowly reclaimed them. There were mannequins huddled together in an embrace that reminded me of the couple found in Pompeii, and there were cat statues missing teeth, and birds missing wings. There were half-written epitaphs on tombstones jammed into the overgrown ivy, but none of them had names.

No, they said things like:

DRAFT4_TOEDITOR_3.docx.

RTS_FINAL_COPYEDITS.docx.

When I brushed off the ivy from another one a few feet away, it read **IDEAS FOR #5.docx.** Another one read **MAYA romance .docx. GARNETCOMPANIONv8.docx. JUNIEHEA_other.docx.**

GarbagePickings.docx.

On and on.

What *was* this place?

I moved across the carpet of clovers under my feet, to the shade of an oak with quite a few statues beneath it. The ivy wasn't as overgrown over here, so I picked the closest statue and tore the vines off the face—

I gave a start.

The impossibly cold stare of Anders looked back. Or, at first glance it *looked* like Anders, but the nose was wrong, and there wasn't a scar on his lip. The hair was too messy, and the eyes weren't quite right. It was like looking at a fun-house mirror that was so subtle, you didn't notice the change at first.

Did *Anders* make all of these? I pulled the ivy off another one. The ears were too big, the scowl too ugly. No, he couldn't have made these. They looked old. Worn from all the weather and rain.

This couldn't be the kind of place I was thinking of—that was impossible, wasn't it? A graveyard of deleted scenes?

And if Anders knew about it, and he knew this place was a story, then who *was* he? I still couldn't place him, no matter how much I tried.

He was annoyingly attractive, grumpy as hell, had a developed backstory, an appealing profession . . .

Wait—fuck.

What if *he* was supposed to be the main character in Rachel's last book, but his story had never truly gotten started? Left in some limbo, somewhere in the dark night of the soul?

I began to pace across the courtyard, my mind whirling.

It made sense, in a weird way. He *looked* like the kind of hero that Rachel Flowers would write. Gangly limbs, bright eyes, handsome face picked out easily from the crowd. Her heroes always had charming qualities, even if they were a bit of a wreck at the beginning of the books, with a sad or mysterious backstory. Maybe she just went a little . . . *harder* . . . on the unlikable qualities this time around. Overkill. Something her editor would have highlighted and asked her to tone down.

Maybe this was why I felt that zing of tension every time I saw him, why I stared at his lips. It wasn't me. He was a would-be hero walking around exuding bookish sexiness with no heroine to use it on . . .

Ohhh. Is that why he's so protective of this town? Because it's his story? I thought.

It had to be.

Because *I* definitely wasn't interested in him. He wasn't *interesting*. Not in that way, not to me. I didn't want to have a crush. I didn't need one.

No, he was the hero of the fifth book. His allure was simply baked into the plot—whatever this plot was. It wasn't me or my faulty heart at all. Tall, wiry, broad shoulders, and a penchant for glowering. Mint eyes and blond hair and a scar on his lip from a childhood accident. He was probably an orphan—most of Rachel Flowers's main characters were—and his long fingers had probably been dreamed up just for gratuitous descriptions about the way he licked his thumb and turned the page in the book he was reading. Oh yes, I could see it now. I didn't know how I'd missed it before.

But then why didn't he want anything to change, to *move?* Surely he wanted to find his heroine and his happily ever after, right?

I closed the gate behind me as I hurried out of the courtyard, and through the garden of the Daffodil Inn. The sky looked like it was going to rain soon, so I picked up my pace, determined not to get caught in it again, as I headed back to the bookstore to prove myself right.

16

Heroic

THE BELL ABOVE THE door jingled as I let myself into the bookstore. "Anders?" I called, and stepped inside. "Hello?"

He wasn't at his usual haunt behind the counter. I searched the first floor of the shop. In the office, in the rare editions alcove, in the reading nook with the fireplace, but he was nowhere to be found. Neither was Butterscotch.

"Anders?" I called again. "Butters? Here kitty, kitty." I clicked my tongue to the roof of my mouth, but there wasn't even a peep. Just the bookstore, creaking in the evening heat. A rumble of thunder shook the rafters, distant, but getting closer. I frowned. Where the hell could they be? If Anders was out, then wouldn't he have flipped the business sign to CLOSED?

I pursed my lips, frustrated. I'd be gone from Eloraton tomorrow morning, once Frank fixed my car, so this was really the last chance I'd have to ask him.

I turned the sign over for him, about to leave the bookstore, when I heard a *thump*.

Coming from . . . above me?

Then again, two more.

Well, that was odd. I'd had enough of weird sounds thanks to last night, but something told me to climb the spiral staircase, so I did, and followed the knocking. There was a line of windows on the right side of the bookstore that looked out to a small rooftop ledge. I hadn't really explored this area of the store yet, mostly because it was cookbooks and poetry, and there were also some window seats lined with lush velvet cushions. The windows all had latches on them, so on nice days you could open them from the inside and let the breeze in. And framed in the third window was none other than Anders, his back pressed against the glass, sitting as far up on the sill as he could.

On the *outside*.

"Anders?"

On hearing his name, he gave a start and glanced over his shoulder and through the window. Butterscotch was tight in his arms. Upon seeing me, the hope in his eyes flickered out. "Oh *god,*" he replied dreadfully, "did it have to be you?"

I took in his predicament, kneeling up on the bench inside the window. "What are you doing on the *roof*?"

"Admiring the view," he replied sarcastically, throwing his free hand out toward the view of . . . trees. Lots and lots of trees. In his other arm, he clung tightly to a fat orange-and-white cat who looked more terrified of the rain than of anything else. "I'm *trapped*, that's what. Butterscotch snuck out here and he wouldn't come in so . . . I crawled out." He glanced at the edge of the rooftop, and then back at me. "And now I'm stuck. The window is jammed."

I inspected the lock. It was stuck fast. "Can't you just slide off the roof?"

He gave me a pained look. He motioned to the cat. "It'd be a bit hard."

"Ah." I nodded. "You couldn't just draw him in with treats or whatever?"

"I tried, but he was after the starlings."

"So now you're stuck," I echoed his earlier sentiment. "And I'm standing by the only window that will let you in." His mouth twisted, thinking that I was taunting him. I shoved off from the window. "Hold on, I think I saw a screwdriver down under the counter. I'll be right back."

He shouted something after me, but I couldn't understand it through the window as I hurried down the spiral stairs again, and searched for the screwdriver under the counter. I found it, beside a tape dispenser, and quickly returned to the window. The sky outside was looking darker and darker by the moment. A few errant raindrops splattered against the roof.

"What did you say?" I asked as I returned, kneeling up on the window seat, and beginning to jimmy the clasp free.

He hesitated, watching me. "I . . . didn't say anything," he decided, and slumped back against the window. Butterscotch looked quite fretful in his arms, his eyes wide as another roll of thunder carried itself across the valley. He muttered to his cat, "Learned your lesson? Is *this* really worth a damn bird?"

"Meow," the cat replied, which sounded a lot like a resounding no.

The clasp to the window was rusted, and held fast as I tried to pry it loose. "Damn," I muttered, and tried from a different angle.

"I'm sorry," he mumbled, so quiet I didn't think I'd heard him correctly.

"You're what?" I pried the screwdriver out of the clasp, and decided I'd just pull the entire sucker off.

"Sorry," he repeated, turning his head to the side so I could read his lips. "I'm sorry for being so rotten to you."

I froze, letting the words sink in. He was apologizing? *Now?* "Ah," I replied levelly, trying to get purchase on the screws in the hardware, but most of them had been stripped years ago. So, plan B it was. "So you're sorry now that I'm useful to you?"

"What? No," he quickly replied. Another roll of thunder quaked through the air, and Butterscotch's ears went back in fright. "Ow ow, stop, Butters," he muttered, and then told me, "I meant to tell you earlier, but you said I hated you."

"You don't *like* me."

"I don't hate you," he said, and he sounded earnest. "I was—I am . . . sorry. I'm sorry."

Honestly, I was very close to believing him. Hell, I'd had bad days before, and I had a bad day yesterday, too, when I slapped him. He just said the exact wrong thing at exactly the right time. It wasn't just him who needed to apologize, I realized.

But I wasn't about to let him get off easy on it.

"Could you say it again?" I asked, changing the screwdriver to a flathead, and jabbing it between the wood of the window and the clasp. "The apology? I didn't hear it the first time. A little slower, maybe. Let me relish it."

"You heard it the first time."

"I did," I admitted, and began to twist the screwdriver, "but I'd like to hear it again."

He breathed in deeply. Then he looked at me with those mint-colored eyes, and I felt my entire body tingle. He was so close to the window that his breath, when he spoke, fogged up the glass. "I'm sorry, Eileen."

The smallest shiver crawled up my spine.

Eileen. It wasn't the first time he'd said my name out loud, but it was the first time I noticed him saying it like a song, instead of a curse. *Eye-lean*, sharp at the front, soft at the end. Maybe that was his character quirk—that he could make any name sound wanted.

"For?"

"Being a bit too harsh."

"And?"

"Saying those terrible things to you."

"And?"

He hesitated, thinking. "For . . . implying Lily's book was ugly?"

I reeled. "You thought it was *ugly*?"

"I . . . feel like I am in a trap," he observed. "For what it's worth, I am sorry."

"Thank you. And I'm sorry, too. For destroying your window."

"My wh—"

With one final push with the tool, the clasp popped free, and because Anders had been leaning on the window, it swung inward. He toppled through it, onto me, and we hit the ground hard.

Butterscotch squirmed out of his arms, fur standing on end, and went scurrying for the opposite corner of the bookstore with a yowl.

Through the window, the rain began to come down harder.

We lay there for a moment.

Then he said, "Thank you."

I looked over at him on the floor beside me. I held up my hand, pinkie out. "Truce?" I asked.

He eyed my hand. "I'm not giving you my pinkie."

"*Truce?*"

He begrudgingly hooked his finger through mine. "Truce," he mumbled. "For now."

I rolled my eyes. "You're such a pessimist."

"Realist," he corrected.

"A glass-half-empty sort of guy."

"No, I'm a the-liquid-could-be-poisoned sort of guy."

That made me laugh, and if I didn't know better, I would've thought he actually cracked a smile, too, but I must have been seeing things. He finally returned my gaze, and held it. A knot lodged in my throat, because he was closer than I expected, and his eyelashes were darker than I expected, and long, and there was a gray rim around the inside of his irises that looked like crowns of storm clouds surrounding a peridot. His gaze made the butterflies in my stomach shake off their hibernation and want to remember how to flutter again.

Oh yes, he had to be the main character.

Book boyfriend material, once someone fixed him up.

But then: Where was his heroine?

I tore my gaze away from his, and pushed myself to sit up. "It's getting late. I should get going to Junie's—"

"You can stay in the loft again, if you'd like," he said.

I paused. Waited for him to go on.

"I mean, I . . ." He pushed himself to sit up, too, and rubbed the back of his neck nervously. "I doubt you got much sleep last night, and the inn isn't *finished*. Is the plumbing even working?"

"One bathroom is. Shared among the three of us," I replied.

"You'd have your own bathroom here. And it wouldn't be haunted."

"According to Junie, the haunted bathroom might just be a plus."

"You and I both know Junie is just saying that because she's your kind of optimist."

I inclined my head. "Is that a compliment?"

To which he replied carefully, "Is the sky blue?"

"Technically? No. Blue light just travels in shorter, smaller waves so we can see it."

And he bit the inside of his cheek, as if resisting the urge to smile. "Ah, so it does."

I inclined my head, studying him. When I first found the courtyard, I'd thought I would come here and ask him point-blank about it, but I'd just gotten on even footing with him, and I was leaving tomorrow anyway. What did it really matter? I thought about what he'd said earlier, about making waves, and telling him that I'd found that strange courtyard might just inadvertently make more. Not right now, not when he almost *smiled* at me.

"Okay," I agreed. "I will."

The rafters rattled again with another rumble of thunder, and the wind began to blow raindrops inside, so he stood and closed the window.

"Well," he said, "when the rain stops, you should go and get your things—" He turned back from the window, and almost ran into me when he realized I hadn't yet moved. His eyebrows furrowed, and he tilted his head. I stared down at his polished loafers. They were a soft, warm brown, polished to a shine.

Why was it easy to stare at his shoes and muster up the courage to say—

"I'm sorry. For slapping you. It was uncalled-for and awful, and I should have restrained myself. I'm sorry," I repeated, and to my surprise his hand came up and gently caught my chin, and raised my gaze to meet his. His eyes were soft, and there was an amused curve to his lips.

"Could you say that again?" he purred, and the rumble in his voice made my toes curl.

"I'm sorry."

"Hmm." He studied me, our faces so close I could count his individual eyelashes, see the specks of gray and gold in his eyes. Then he dropped his hand from my chin, and stepped away, and as he did the space around me suddenly filled with cold, cold air. "Apology denied. I still deserved it."

"Fine." I said, hoping he didn't see the blush rushing to my cheeks. "So now we're *actually* even. Good, great. Happy to help. So, I'm going—um—to go get my stuff. From the inn. And tell Junie and . . ." I pointed across the bookstore, about to retreat, when he asked—

"Do you have dinner plans?"

"Dinner?" I asked, and the word sounded strangled. With *him*?

He said, "Yes, dinner. You know, that meal where people eat in the evening time?"

"I know what *dinner* is," I said. "I just . . . I . . . with you?" Because I needed to know for sure, and I was at a loss for words. Dinner—with *Anders*?

He nodded. "Me. Unless you already have plans . . . ?"

I could lie and say that I did. That would have been the smarter thing to do, and then cover my ass by inviting Junie to dinner. But . . .

"I'll have to check my dance card," I replied. "Though, I'm getting very sick of burgers."

He tilted his head to the side, deciding. "How do you feel about spaghetti?"

It sounded better than burgers, I had to admit, but I kept waiting for the little voice in the back of my head to tell me this was a terrible idea. The voice never spoke up. So maybe it wasn't that terrible an idea? And maybe I could find out more about his back-story, and piece together what Rachel Flowers had planned.

Maybe I'd find an ending to Quixotic Falls, after all.

The idea was electrifying.

I rolled the thought around in my head for a moment, and then realized—"Wait. Are . . . you asking to make me Sorry Pasta?" I asked. He gave me a curious look. "Like Jake and Ruby? Jake makes Ruby Sorry Pasta when he knows he's been an asshole."

"I . . . guess I am," he admitted, but he sounded unsure. "So, is that a yes?"

"I'll put you on my dance card," I said, and his shoulders un-wound a little in relief.

"Oh, good. Why don't you take my umbrella and get your things from the Daffodil, and I'll close up and have a word with Butters about rooftops and birds."

I found his umbrella by the door, and left to go fetch my things and tell Junie the news. She seemed more than a little intrigued, wiggling her eyebrows at me as I left the inn, but I refused to think anything of it. The simple fact was: if I had to choose taking char-ity from Anders or another night in an inn with haunted plumbing, Anders was the sure bet. I'd at least get some sleep at the book-store. That was the only reason I even entertained the thought of the loft again. It wasn't because of Anders himself.

No, not at all.

When I returned, Anders must've given his cat a very stern talking-to, because Butters was curled up on his bedding by the window, back turned toward us, sulkily staring out at a starling taunting him from a streetlight. As Anders finished counting out the (admittedly unchanged) register, I gave the cat a gentle rub.

"Oh, don't fall for his sulking," Anders said, glaring at Butters. "He knows what he did."

I inclined my head defiantly. "I'm commiserating. We both know what it's like to get in trouble with you."

"Nonsense." He closed the register, and pinned me with those bright green eyes. "You've yet to lock me out of a window. But I'm sure there is still time. Shall we eat?" he asked, inclining his head for me to follow him through the bookstore to the back, and Butterscotch jumped down to follow. I hesitated for a moment, thinking that maybe I was in a bit of trouble, too.

Just an entirely different kind.

17

Cloudy with a Chance of Kisses

ON'T MIND THE MESS," he said as he welcomed me inside the small yellow two-story row house behind the bookstore.

The place was homey, decorated in a quaint sort of way, with plaid patterns and handcrafted furniture. The foyer led straight to a set of stairs, where I assumed the bedroom was. To my right was a doorframe leading into a small but comfortable living room, blankets neatly stacked on the backs of the couches, and to the left the green-tinted kitchen. The house was lovely, but in a detached Airbnb sort of way. There weren't any photos on the walls, and nothing personal on the side tables.

I sat at the table as he fed Butterscotch and muttered, petting his back, "We learned our lesson today, yes?"

In reply, the cat purred, neither agreeing nor promising to.

I propped my head up on my hand. "I really never pictured you as a cat person."

"Why, do I look like the dog type?" he asked, going to the

cabinet and taking out two jars of sauce—one Alfredo and one tomato—from the pantry. "Red or white?"

At first, I thought he was joking, but when he kept waiting for my answer, I replied with a very serious "Oh, dear."

"What?"

"Spaghetti sauces aren't like types of *wine*." I pushed myself to stand and took the jars of marinara and Alfredo sauces from his grip. "Do you even cook?"

He scoffed. "Obviously."

Liar.

"Right. Sit down, I've got this," I said, and motioned for him to take my seat instead. "And to answer your question—no. I didn't think you were a dog guy or a cat guy or a bird guy. I didn't think you'd have pets at all. Well"—and then I gave it a thought—"maybe a miniature pony. Named Ralph."

He narrowed his eyes. "Why Ralph? And why a miniature pony?"

"Have you had the displeasure of meeting one?"

"Can't say I have."

"Count yourself lucky. Once, Pru and I took a shortcut through a bit of farmland in our hometown. Forgot that the farmer had put out his ponies for the summer. The little shit chased us across the *entire field*. In the middle of the night." I took down a pot and started to fill it with water, my gaze a thousand miles away. "I still can't walk through a field at night without hearing the ghost of a neigh."

"And the pony's name was Ralph?" he deadpanned.

"Tiger Beat," I replied, which only baffled him.

His kitchen reminded me of my grandma's house, back when I was little and she used to take care of me while Mom went to work. The cabinets had creaky hinges, the stovetop was gas, the faucet took *forever* to get hot water, and everything was just a little rusted. He sat down in my chair and instructed me on how to turn on a gas stove, but I'd grown up with them. He, apparently, hadn't. Born and raised in the heart of Los Angeles. His father was an accountant for a big movie studio, and his mom was a Pilates instructor, which surprised me because Rachel *usually* orphaned her heroes. I guessed she wanted to do something different with him.

"And you . . . decided to own a bookstore? How did that come about?" I asked, taking a piece of spaghetti out of the boiling water and tossing it at the wall. It slid down, so the pasta wasn't ready yet.

"I'm going to pretend you didn't just sling pasta on my tile."

"It's how you tell if it's done," I explained. "If it sticks, it's done. You know the saying—throwing everything at a wall and seeing what sticks? What did you think that came from—Velcro balls?"

He thought about it. "I hadn't really thought about it."

"Clearly you weren't an English major," I replied.

"Journalism."

"Then how did you wind up here?"

His face pinched, and he sat back in his chair, as if trying to figure out what to say. I leaned against the counter, studying him as he did. There had to be some connection to the other characters. Usually, Rachel introduced the hero or the heroine before their book arrived, and so far there was no obvious heroine around. Lily had called him *uncle*, so maybe he was related to Thomas? But he didn't look like they were related, and as far as I remembered Thomas had the whole orphan backstory. But if not Thomas, then who? Anders felt familiar, like there was something so obvious, and I just couldn't put my finger on it. After a moment, he glanced up at me and nudged his chin toward the pot. "I think it's about to boil over."

"Oh, shit!" I grabbed the potholders and drained the spaghetti, and then put it back into the pot with the marinara sauce. (Pru would have been *beside* herself knowing that I didn't make it from scratch—she swore by this one celebrity chef's recipe, but all I liked from his cookbook was the lemon pie.) As I finished up, Anders took out a bottle of red wine from another cabinet, along with two wineglasses, and poured us both a drink.

"I might have overestimated my cooking skills," I admitted, putting the pot of spaghetti between us on a trivet.

"I'm serviceable at best," he replied, probably to make me feel better. "In fact, one time, Chel . . ." he started, but then he quieted, as if the name he was about to say had stolen all the wind out of his lungs, and shook his head. "I just burn everything."

"Pru says that it just takes practice, but I don't believe her."

"You don't seem like the patient type," he agreed, grabbing some tongs from the drawer and two bowls from the cabinet.

I mocked hurt. "I am the very model of a modern major general, why thank you."

He shook his head, amused.

We served ourselves from the pot. We didn't have meatballs, but I'd eaten just noodles and marinara sauce for so many years in undergrad that I didn't miss them. I motioned with my fork to his plate.

"So? Thoughts?"

He took his knife and fork like polished people did, and swirled up a bite of spaghetti with the kind of polite precision that was about to make me look like a Neanderthal. After a moment, he said, "It's decent."

I raised my eyebrows. "I hope that's high praise."

He chased it with a gulp of wine, which wasn't a great sign, so

I had to have a bite, too—and *immediately* realized what had gone wrong.

"Sugar," I groaned, realizing I must've used it instead of salt. "Why didn't you *say* so?"

"It's honestly not the worst I've had—perhaps some hot sauce will help?"

"*Hah*," I sighed as he retrieved the salt, and while the pasta still wasn't *good*, at least it was edible. After a few more bites, and a glass of wine, I admitted, "I wish I could say I've never done this before—but I have. For the book club. We all laughed so hard." I smiled a little at the memory. "I think that was the year we all read that vampire series and couldn't stop calling each other *suckling*, like the main vampire guy does."

He groaned. "I *hated* that series."

"The sex was decent."

"Ah yes," he said, adopting an offensively terrible Transylvanian accent, "'Come for me, suckling, moan for me, suckling, taste my nectar and beg for more, suckling'—it's *horrid*. I'm shocked you don't have better taste."

I giggled. "You're the one who memorized those lines, so who *really* has bad taste?" I tried another bite of the spaghetti, and made a face, pushing my plate away. "Okay. It was a valiant effort, but I'm not a cook."

He shook his head, and motioned with his fork to a few magnets on the refrigerator. "We can order in pizza, or there's a taco joint the next street over, but just don't bother looking at the menus. They're all gibberish, so it's impossible to order if you aren't already a part of the town, with it in your head."

"Everything feels half-finished," I muttered.

Quietly, he ate another bite, and then also gave up.

I leaned over my plate. "If there are so many other options, then why do you always go to Gail's? Is it just convenience, or are you waiting for something? Do you get lonely, without your fian—" I quickly shut my mouth, kicking myself. "I mean, faaaather, yeah. Father. Fiaaather. I've an accent sometimes . . ."

"I know Lily told you," he said, setting down his fork, and leaning back in his chair. "She is very good at meddling, just like her mother."

I cleared my throat. "Gemma *did* get Bea and Garnet together . . ."

He nodded, silent. "To be honest, it doesn't feel awkward eating alone at Gail's. Never has. I sort of stumbled into town by accident. The bookstore was vacant, so I asked Gail about the place. That was . . ." His voice turned tender as he tried to remember. "It was a long time ago."

I studied his face. He had to have come into town after the fourth book, when Bea and Garnet left, but by taking a look around, and talking with everyone—I couldn't get a sense for how long ago that was. A few years? A few months? Time felt strange here, like the longer I stayed, the less it moved, but that seemed characteristic of every small town in America.

I wonder what plans Rachel had for you, I thought. I hoped it was a better plan than what life had in store for me after Liam left. No one deserved that kind of heartbreak, not even Anders.

"Can I ask you a question," I asked, "and you'll tell me the truth?"

He took another sip of wine. "It depends on the question."

"Then will you at least tell me if you lie?"

His lips quirked into a half smile. "Sure."

"Everyone in Eloraton is where the author left them, aren't they?"

He looked away, running his thumb over the rim of his wineglass, thinking. "Yes," he finally said, and a knot wound tight in my chest because of just how sad that was—a story, half-done, like a theme park that never closed its doors.

Or a book that you never finished, lying open on the coffee table, half-forgotten and right where you left it years ago.

"And everything is good where it is."

In a town where the burgers at Gail's were always burnt, and the inn was in a perpetual state of disrepair, and Frank went fishing every weekend, and the rain always came at dinner and left by midnight.

Not perfect, but good.

Good enough to not want to dance around the idea of *better*.

"Now, if that's the only question, I need to find some *actual* food before my stomach eats itself," he said, pushing himself to his feet, grabbing both of our plates and putting them in the sink.

"You're the one who let me cook," I replied.

"You offered."

"Because you asked me red or white!"

He gave a lazy shrug. "Weaponized incompetence."

I threw my napkin at him, and he dodged it with a chuckle. The edges of his mouth quirked up in a smile he couldn't quite hide. It slipped across his face, slow and sweet, like molasses. I scowled, realizing that he was *enjoying* baiting me, and also that I was enjoying being baited by this infuriating, and handsome, fictional man.

Fictional, I had to remind myself. *He's not real.*

So I forced myself to my feet and toward the sink to discard any evidence that I had, in fact, been allowed in the kitchen.

"You can leave the dishes," he said, rolling up his shirtsleeves, and taking the sponge and plate from my hand. "You cooked, after all."

"You mean almost poisoned you with sugared spaghetti," I remarked, taking the dish back. "This is my penance."

He wrinkled his nose. "You won't take no for an answer, will you?"

I inclined my head. "No."

"Very well. You wash, I'll dry them? And then . . . how do you feel about pizza? I think Luigi's is still open for another half hour."

I finished scrubbing the dish and rinsed it off in the sink. "Pizza is agreeable," I replied—and turned off the water. Something was off. I listened, but at first I couldn't place it.

He took out his cell phone and punched in a number he got from a flyer on the fridge. "Pepperoni or—"

"Shh," I muttered, and pressed my fingers against his lips.

Out the window, dusk had slowly fallen into night, a bluish color that I hadn't seen since arriving here. Mostly because it'd been raining—

"Do you hear that?" I asked in awe, and looked up at him for confirmation—and realized just how close we were again. My fingers were still against his lips, and he hadn't made a move to remove them. I did quickly, and pressed my hand against my chest. My fingers tingled where they had touched his mouth. "Sorry, sorry— I just—I wanted to hear if . . ."

His gaze strayed to the window, too. His eyebrows furrowed, like he couldn't quite believe what he heard—or didn't hear, actually. He stepped close to the window and pushed it open. A strong, humid summer breeze swelled into the kitchen, carrying with it the scent of wet grass.

But it was no longer raining.

"Is this normal?" I asked, thinking that maybe the rain only came on certain nights, but the look on his face told me otherwise.

"No," he replied, and returned a puzzled look to me, as if I was a new detail in a story that didn't quite make sense anymore. "This is new."

"Do you want to . . ."

The moment he nodded, we abandoned the kitchen for the front door. Anders flung it open, and there were crickets and a night sky and the sweet smell of summer.

No rain.

No thunder.

I followed him through the bookstore, and came out the front, and down the stairs. The town was still wet, but the sky was already clearing up, stars peeking out. Anders stepped onto the sidewalk, staring up with confused wide-eyed wonder.

It wasn't raining.

It *wasn't raining.*

We made our way to the street, where Gail and her patrons had come out, too. Maya stepped out of the sweets shop, Junie from the garden shop, arms full of ferns for the inn, Lyssa behind her. We all stared up at the sky. And then someone laughed, and someone else cheered, and people were running down the street, arms out, because it *wasn't raining.*

For the first time in ages, there were stars.

And then I felt Anders's gaze on me, and I tensed. Was this my fault? Had I done this, somehow? Chased the rain away?

"Well," said Gail, putting her hands on her hips, "I think this means I can open the patio. Frank, you get off your ass and come help me get the chairs down—I don't *care* if you just came back from fishing. Up, up!" She turned back inside the bar, and the small patio beside the building flickered to life with hanging lights. I looked up at the thousands of stars, and the almost-full moon, relieved to find out that the sky I knew was still the same sky here.

Maybe the stars were a little brighter, the moonlight more silver, but still the same.

Anders's gaze hadn't left me, and finally, I gathered up my courage and returned it. He didn't look mad, at least.

"Well? Gail's, then? We can sit out on the patio," he said.

"I could go for some onion rings," I replied, and he went back inside and gathered his wallet and a light jacket, which he handed to me in case I caught a chill. I pulled the burgundy jacket over my shoulders, and we sat down on the patio and shared onion rings, and Gail kept serving us a steady stream of house wine and beer. Soon Will and Junie showed up with a dark-haired, gangly man in tow. Thomas, I guessed, since Gemma was at home with Lily watching *Jeopardy!*, and Maya came a little later, walking Houndstooth, her black Great Dane. We sat around the tables on the patio, the gas firepit crackling in the corner, and chatted—Anders and Thomas talked about a book they'd read, some memoir, and I couldn't help but imagine what Anders would look like, sitting at Pru's reclaimed wood dining room table, chatting with Jasper, stealing glances across the table at me.

He'd sneak a grin, maybe a wink, as Jasper waxed on about copyright law and evil corporations that are holding stories hostage, and I'd half listen as Pru ranted about her latest romantasy read, and the worst part was?

I could see it. Clear as day.

Which was a problem, seeing as how he was almost certainly the main character of the last book Rachel Flowers never finished, which meant he wasn't real. Long distance? I could travel. Language barriers? I could learn. But *fictional*?

It couldn't work out.

But . . .

I was gone tomorrow, anyway, taking the only road in and the only one out. Once I crossed Charm Bridge, would this town even be here anymore? I wasn't sure, and with mounting certainty, every fiber of my being wanted to just get *lost* in this book. For a moment. For a few hours.

For a night.

I grabbed another onion ring, and curled Anders's jacket tighter around me. It smelled like woodsy cedar and chamomile tea and the old, loved pages of a childhood novel. It was the kind of scent I could drown in. What if I did? I'd come back to the surface by morning, I was sure.

From across the table, Junie kept flicking her eyes between Anders and me.

She mouthed, "You two good?" and wiggled her eyebrows again. I rolled my eyes. I'm sure she would've pressed further, and maybe I would've caved, but the door to the patio flung open, and Ruby arrived like a hurricane.

"What sorry friends y'all are!" she declared. "Did my invite get lost?"

Will said, "I stopped by and told Jake."

"Well, Jake didn't tell me," she replied, and gave us a once-over. "Where *is* Jake?"

"Not here," Maya replied. "I saw him still at the cafe when I was closing up for the night." She, with Houndstooth sitting between her legs, leaned to the side a little to look around her gigantic dog, at Ruby. "I can go get him, if you want me to? Lyssa's not here, either."

But Ruby wasn't listening. She checked her watch and gave a sigh. "I should go help him."

"He's probably almost done," Will replied. "He'll come by after."

So Ruby stayed, and, like in the books, after a few drinks Ruby liked to sing, so she took requests as she waited for Jake. She waited for Jake as Maya finished her beer and called it a night, and Houndstooth made his slow round for all the pets he deserved. She waited for Jake as Thomas bade us goodbye, because it was almost Lily's bedtime and Thomas wanted to be there to read her a bedtime story. She waited for Jake until well past midnight, when Gail finally kicked us off the patio.

"Ruby, Ruby," said a very drunk Junie, as she leaned against Will, "you are so good at singing. You're, like, *radio* good. You've got a radio heart. You should look into that." She didn't notice the way Ruby frowned, and stopped twisting her hair, shifting on her feet, like the words had stabbed her in the side.

"C'mon, Junebug," said Will, and he coaxed her onto his back. "Let's go home."

"I like to sing, too," she went on as they shuffled away. "Want me to sing something for you?"

"What would you sing?"

"You and me, baby, are nothing but animals," she began, butchering the lyrics, and Will's laughter faded down the sidewalk.

Anders and I stood with Ruby for a little while longer, but she finally decided to give up.

"He probably went home," she said. "Goodnight, y'all." As she left, she pulled out her phone to check it.

And then there was just Anders and me. My head was buzzing from the wine—I couldn't remember how many glasses I'd had, and I was sure I'd feel it in the morning, but that was a problem for future Eileen. Current Eileen was feeling very good, wrapped in Anders's jacket, as he escorted me back to the bookshop. Current Eileen was thinking about drowning in his jacket and how nice it would be. The jacket was warm, and he smelled nice.

I couldn't remember the last time I liked someone's *smell*.

"Did you have fun tonight?" he asked, unlocking the front door.

I hummed in agreement. "I like you when you aren't so prickly."

He opened the door for me, amused, and he followed me into the store. It was cool and quiet, slivers of silver moonlight rushing in through the open windows, illuminating spines with half-hidden words. And this was my last night here. Tomorrow Frank would fix my car, and I'd be gone.

I shoved those thoughts far down beneath the warm buzz of house red wine. I wasn't going to think about that.

"I was prickly before?" he asked.

"Like a cactus," I confirmed, and then glanced over my shoulder to study him. "No, more like a briar patch—oh! Or a *rose*. A song once warned me they have thorns."

He chuckled quietly to himself, pocketing his keys. "You're drunk."

"Am not," I argued. "If I was drunk, I'd be ranting about Mary Shelley keeping the petrified heart of her dead lover in her desk drawer." I paused on the first step up to the second floor and turned on my heel to face him. With the step as leverage, we were almost at eye level. I studied his face in the moonlight, and oh, it struck me just how handsome he was. I felt so much like I had that New Year's Eve, running to kiss a man who would break my heart three years later. I wobbled a little on the stair, and Anders put a hand gently on my hip to steady me. "Though I might be a little tipsy," I admitted.

A laugh rumbled in his chest, and it made me want to hear what his actual laugh sounded like. Probably full and deep and lovely, the kind that made you want to laugh along with him.

Fuck, I *was* drunk.

What would he wax poetic about if he was drunk? Lord Byron swimming the English Channel? Keats writing love letters? Would he sit me down and tell me the long and complicated history of literature's most adamant archenemies? Or would he talk about his favorite book? It was probably some tome of dry literature. If I wanted to be salty, I'd guess *War and Peace*.

"What?" he asked, waiting for me to climb the rest of the stairs. There was a lovely soft blond curl that sat so delicately on his forehead. His hair looked soft. I was sure it was, if I ran my fingers through it. "What are you staring at, Eileen?"

I narrowed my eyes, deciding not to think about his hair. "I'm trying to imagine your favorite book."

"Why?"

"Because it's foreshadowing." Then I leaned in closer, and whispered, "You can tell me. A secret between archenemies."

"Rivals."

"Opponents."

He tsked, and then said in a low rumble, "I think I can guess yours."

He was so close now, I could study the lines of his face, the slope of his jaw. There was a soft rush of freckles across his cheeks, and they seemed to grow darker when he blushed, and an old scar on the left side of his lips from a fistfight or a fall. This close, so close I could count the individual blond lashes around his eyes. He struck me as the kind of quiet and stoic character who crept into your heart the longer you spent with him, steadfast like a dictionary.

His large hand never left my hip. It didn't move lower, but it didn't leave, either. It was constant and steady and warm. He could've inched closer, he could've come onto the step with me, but he didn't. He stayed eye level, equal, as if he preferred the view.

My heart hammered in my chest like a jackrabbit on the run.

Imagine me and you, I thought—and quickly reeled at the very *idea*. It was the house red getting to me. He was made for someone in the town, someone Rachel Flowers had planted at the beginning of this story, someone who fit perfectly into all of his crevices—

"I'm not into the whole tweed and argyle thing," I said aloud, not realizing I did until he leaned closer, his voice rumbly in his chest.

"Good, because I don't own any tweed *or* argyle."

"Lies." I swallowed. How was he so close? How was I? I tried not to stare at his mouth, but it was hard, and he had a wickedly charming quirk to his lips. "You're very much a tweed and argyle sort. From your polished shoes to your knife-pleated trousers to your *hair*, why is your hair so perfect—"

"Eileen?"

My voice came out in a squeak. "Yes?"

"I'm going to kiss you."

"You—yes," I managed, a moment before his hands caught me by the sides of my face, and drew me in for a kiss. And all notion that this was wrong, that he was off-limits, that tomorrow I would leave—left my mind in an instant. I didn't *care*. Every reader I'd ever known had wanted nothing more than to fall into the arms of a book boyfriend, some fictional Darcy, a shade of a Byronic hero, all their own.

So I did.

His mouth found mine, starved in the way a man drowning at sea starved for air. At first his kiss was timid, like he was holding himself back. I wanted to learn not only the contours of his face, but the taste of his tongue, the impression of his teeth as he nibbled my lip; I wanted to learn what would make him groan my name, what would make him come undone from that tense knot he kept himself in.

He tasted like onion rings and strong drink and sugared

spaghetti (and I'm sure I did, too), and smelled like oak and old books and the slightest hint of black tea.

His kiss turned wild and desperate, as he stopped holding back, and I found myself melting into him, grabbing hold of his starched shirt, his hands pulling around my waist, pressing me closer. He kissed like he wanted to devour me, eat me whole and commit me to memory, and I found myself matching his desire, as if some deep part of me had been shaken awake and risen to the surface. I couldn't remember the last time someone had kissed me that passionately—savored me, like I was the last sentence in his favorite book.

His hands lowered to my hips, and then retreated toward my lower back as he leaned into the kiss, cradling the back of my head with his other hand, as if he wanted to press me into himself, bring our hard-hammering hearts together.

His mouth was addicting. I'd never been kissed like this before, practiced and hungry, like he had been thinking about how to kiss me better.

As he leaned me against him, his chest sturdy, his arms strong, I pushed my hands into his hair—and *yes*, it was just as soft as I imagined. His curls wrapped around my fingers, loosening from their tame style. He nibbled on my lip, as if teasing, and I bit back, like a debate without words. Though what we were debating was very much one-sided.

And when I snagged his lip again, he groaned and held on to me tighter, breaking apart just long enough to growl, "Gentle, sweetheart," before he kissed me again.

And fuck, I didn't know if it was his main character magic, or the fact that I'd never been called *sweetheart* with such hunger, but it burned deep in my middle, below where the butterflies had burrowed and lain dead for years. His heroine could have him tomorrow. I wanted to have him now, this second, in my m—

Suddenly, there was a clap of thunder.

We startled away from each other. Our chests were heaving, our lips red and swollen from the kisses, his pupils blown wide as he drank me in, wanting nothing more than to taste me again, and I'm sure mine were the same.

But the bookstore had become dark again, the moonlight gone in what felt like the span of a breath. The bright, staccato beat of my heart was quickly drowned out by the rain as it pounded, heavy and fast, on the windows. Wind shook the panes, like ghosts trying to get in.

In that moment, he must've come to his senses. I did, too. A little bit.

"I'm sorry," I said, breathless. The bookstore was spinning, and so I finally admitted, "I—I think I'm drunk."

He cleared his throat, rubbing his mouth with his fingers, scrambling to collect himself. "Let me show you to your door." His voice was still gruff, barely constrained.

I gave a nervous laugh. "No, no. It's fine, it's right up there. I'm—I'm—" I stumbled as I turned around, and the next thing I knew he had picked me up in his arms and carried me up the winding staircase to the second floor, and across to the blue door of my loft.

Then he set me down. "There," he said.

I stared up into his lovely face, though admittedly I could only see what the lights in the loft allowed through the cracks in the door—which wasn't much. Still, I think I didn't mind it. "You . . . can come in, if you want?" I asked.

His mouth dipped into a frown, and his face pinched, like he was torn by the question, but finally he decided, "No. I don't think I should."

My eyes widened. "Oh."

Had I read the room wrong? Gotten the wrong vibe? Certainly he was very much into me, I could tell by his trousers alone, so what was stopping him? The rain pounded harder on the windows. The storm had come back with a vengeance, it seemed.

"I'm gone tomorrow," I said. "So it doesn't really matter if we . . ."

His mouth twisted further. "It does to me," he replied simply, and then kissed me on the forehead. "Have a good night, Elsy." Then he turned on his heel, and left me standing there in front of the loft, regretting my stupid heart, with the taste of him still on my lips.

Even a book boyfriend didn't want me.

18

Unintended Consequences

THE STARLINGS WERE NOISY in the morning. I groaned and rolled over in bed, feeling my stomach turn. The birds were singing that strange song again, and maybe I would've been able to place it if a jackhammer wasn't going off inside my head, and the birds just made it worse. At that moment, I wasn't sure what I preferred: a haunted toilet, or the starlings. I tried to bury my head under the pillows, but the second I moved, my stomach flipped again.

And this time it was coming up.

I barely made it to the bathroom in time before I got sick, and still I got sick on my shirt, too. I pried it off and tossed it onto the floor behind me, and pulled up my hair. Pru used to do that when we were in undergrad together. She'd use a mermaid clip, and rub circles on my back, and thank every god she could remember that they'd blessed her without a gag reflex.

After a while, there was a knock on the door. "Elsy?" the familiar voice of Anders called. Oh, good. Exactly the person I wanted to hear me retching the demon out of my body. Why did he have to come up here to check on me? For a second, I yearned for the Anders who hated me, but then I remembered the kiss, and I felt like I wanted to be sick all over again in a different way.

I'd actually *kissed* him, and it was one of those unforgettable sorts of kisses that even house wine couldn't erase. And then I'd gone and ruined it with my—well, with me being *me*. And then I asked him to sleep with me and he *rejected* me. Oh, god. Oh, fuck.

I could never show my face in this town again.

"I, um, have some tea here. And a doughnut . . . but I believe you will not want the doughnut," he added, a little quieter. "I wanted to check in on you. You had . . . a lot to drink last night."

I gently sat back against the wall, staring up at the smooth ceiling. My body felt like death. "Yes, yes, I did," I croaked. "Aren't you sick?"

"I learned from the house red a while ago," he replied.

"And you didn't think to warn me?"

"I tried. Quite a few times last night."

I thought back on it, but last night was all but a blur. I'd been too enthralled with either Houndstooth or Junie's hack of ranch on onion rings. Too bad I remembered the *rest* of my mistakes last night. Because the house red had made me make the most terrible, awful, no-good decision of the year. At least I was gone today, and I could put this whole mess behind me.

"Clearly," he went on, "I didn't try hard enough."

I laughed despite myself, and my middle hurt with the effort. "Prudence can't even stop me. Just leave the tea outside? I'll get it . . ." I glanced at my shirt on the floor. "Later."

"All right. If you need anything else . . ."

"I won't," I said, and swallowed, sick just thinking about the way he let me down last night. Was it because I was too drunk?

I currently hated past Eileen with a passion.

The floorboards creaked as he began to turn away. It felt like we were dancing around each other, tiptoeing, because of those awful, wonderful kisses.

"Look," I started, because I'd rather address this now with the closed door protecting me, when I couldn't see his face, "about last night . . ."

"We don't have to talk about it," he replied gently, returning. "Or if you want to, we can talk about it later. When you're not . . ."

"Puking my guts out?"

I heard the grimace in his voice. "Yes, that. I'll put the dough-nut beside the tea."

"Just to tempt me," I accused.

"To incentivize you."

I thought about the doughnut and immediately wanted to be sick again. "I will never eat again. This is all your fault."

"Yes, yes, obviously."

"You should've stopped me."

"I *tried*, I keep telling you."

"Likely excuse," I muttered, easing myself down onto the cool floor. I pressed my cheek against the cold tile, and it helped a little. My mouth tasted like . . . things I didn't want to think about, and my head pounded, and I was leaving today.

"You're cute," he went on, "when you're pretending to be angry with me."

I didn't feel very cute, tits out, lying on the bathroom floor with sweaty hair stuck to my cheek. But I felt myself blush anyway. "You can't even see me."

"I have a good imagination."

I felt my traitorous heart flutter in my chest as he walked away. When he was gone, I opened the bathroom door, grabbed the tea (pushing the doughnut as far away from me as I could), re-treated back into the bathroom, and made the decision to pretend like last night never happened—until *he* brought it up again. And maybe, with my luck, he wouldn't before I hunted down Frank and made him shock my Sweetpea back to life like some mechanical Frankenstein's monster. After a hot shower and some Tylenol I dug out of my duffel bag, I was feeling a little better, so I finally grabbed the doughnut, and made my way down into the bookstore. The doughnut was soft, dusted with powdered sugar and cinnamon, and the tea was strong and honeyed, which was a nice change from the motor oil I was used to drinking.

"Ah, you're alive," Anders noted as I shuffled to the front counter. He checked me over to make sure I was, in fact, alive. "How do you feel?"

"How do you *think*?" I croaked.

He snorted, and checked something off on his notepad. "I called Frank for you. He'll be around in a few to tow your car to the auto shop and get it checked out."

"Thank you." I noticed that he looked positively right as rain. There weren't even dark circles under his eyes. If there was an an-tithesis to a sexy goth vampire, he was it. A sullen, bookish anti-vampire. Though, he wasn't quite glowering at me anymore. In fact, his minty eyes looked softer than usual as he drank me in, all shitty five foot four of me. I said, "You must be one of those *morning* people."

"Only because I hate procrastinating, and there is too much to do," he replied, pulling up a stool to sit down behind the counter. Then he took out a pair of round glasses from his pocket and put them on to read a document of numbers on the computer. I had a professor once in college who wore round glasses. Almost every girl in class—including Prudence—fawned over him. They said he looked distinguished and made tweed coats fuckable. I didn't see it.

Until now.

Stop it, I scolded. I was hungover and halfway dead, and still my heart had the audacity to be horny. My brain was truly a traitor, and this town was getting to me, all the thoughts of romance and kissing and happily ever afters.

And I . . . I *liked* it. Imagining myself in a romance. I hadn't even tried in years, burrowing in some main character's love story instead.

He glanced up over his glasses at me. "Are you feeling ill again?"

"Huh?" I asked like an idiot.

"You're just standing there, looking pale and a bit sick."

I quickly turned away from him. "Sorry, sorry, I'm good. Lost in my head."

"Ah. What talent."

Yeah, that was it. *Talent.* A talent for daydreams. But it was a good one. I began to tell him that I was going to go pack up my things from the loft, when someone I could only guess was Frank appeared at the front door. He waved and thumbed behind him to the tow truck. Anders didn't even look up from the computer screen as I fled.

I'm sure I wasn't even a passing thought in his head.

I knew better than this. Besides, by tomorrow I'd just be a blurry memory of someone who came through town and stayed a few days in a story that never ended.

19

Unrequited Affliction

I T ONLY TOOK A glance under the hood for Frank of Frank's Auto Shop (and the infamous Frank's Hotties) to know exactly what was wrong with Sweetpea. "How on *earth* has this thing been running?"

"Duct tape and prayers," I replied, biting my thumbnail nervously. "So is she fixable?"

He closed the hood and lifted his green FRANK'S HOTTIES baseball hat to scratch at his forehead in thought. He was an older man in a bright Hawaiian shirt with khaki cargo pants, though you couldn't miss him even without the vacation print. He was a really big dude, with broad shoulders and a two-toned gray beard, the lighter strip running down the middle. In the third book, we find out that he had a stint in the WWE before he slipped a disk in his back. I mean, he didn't *really* have a stint in the WWE, but in the fictional world of Quixotic Falls he did, and he had all the charisma of Dave Bautista, and the swagger of Dwayne Johnson, and honestly, I'd buy a thousand hot sauce bottles from him if he asked.

He mopped up the sweat on his forehead and gave a shrug. "I mean, yeah, yeah, she'll take some finagling, for sure. But I can work with her."

I let out a relieved breath. "So . . . I'll come by later today to pick her up back up?" *And leave.*

"Sure, you can, but I'll probably be heading over to Coop's to try to salvage what I need, so you might wanna get the stuff out of your car that you want."

I didn't understand. "Salvage . . . ?"

He waved his hand at the front of my car, and paced back to his work desk at the head of the auto shop, swiping off bits of crumbs from the semi-clean piece of receipt paper underneath. "Your carburetor's blown," he said, testing three pens before he found one that worked, "and your girl's so old I don't got any spare parts lying around."

My shoulders sagged. "Wait, I thought you said she was fixable? Is she not?"

"No, no," he clarified, "she'll be a quick fix once I get the parts I need to rebuild the carburetor, but the earliest I can promise is . . ." He scratched something down on his receipt paper, sucking on his teeth. "Wednesday?"

Wednesday?

That was two days from now. Which meant . . . I was here. For two more days. *Two.* I chewed on my thumbnail. "And you're sure you can get it done by then?"

"Probably. In a perfect world," he replied, a little apologetically. "I'm a one-man band, ma'am, and this is gonna take a bit of time, but I'll have her fixed up as soon as I can."

I was being ridiculous, and it wasn't like anyone was expecting me at the cabin. The only person who knew I had still gone was Pru, and she was off doing Iceland with her boyfriend. Wednesday would be fine. But that meant . . . a couple more days with Anders, and my stomach twisted at the thought. Last night, I had kissed him knowing I'd be gone today, but now . . .

I wasn't sure what I thought.

Two more days with Anders. Two more days dancing around the thought of my own love story. Two days.

Two.

"Wednesday is perfect," I said with a fake smile. "Thank you. How much is it going to be?"

Frank tore off the receipt once he'd finished tallying up the expenses, and handed it to me. There wasn't a total on the receipt, only the work and, at the bottom—

TWO BOTTLES OF FRANK'S HOTTIES, $5.99 EACH.

"It has to cost more than that," I said, and he waved his hand. "I've not worked on a Pinto in years. You're givin' me a treat."

I felt bad anyway, because he was doing more work than he'd probably agreed to, and I was next to useless. "Thank you, really," I said, and went around to the back of the hatchback just to make sure I had already taken everything out that I needed. The box of books sat beside the crate of wine, and honestly I wouldn't have looked twice at them if the cover hadn't caught my eye. Curiously I pulled one out.

The cover was blurry—like someone had spilled water on it, but without the damage.

"It's not a problem, not a problem," Frank was saying, and I only half listened as he advised that I should get moving before the thunderstorm. "I hear it's comin' in from the north, so it'll be a doozy."

"Yeah, thanks," I said absently, opening the book.

There was nothing. No words. No chapter titles. Only, on the second page, where the title page should be, was my name— *To Elsy*. And at the bottom was Rachel's signature. The other three books were the same.

They were all blank.

Was that how Anders saw them the first night? Blank books with only a name and signature?

"Somethin' up, kid?" Frank asked, startling me.

I quickly put one of the books into my purse, and closed up the box. "No, no, everything's fine," I told him, and closed the hatchback. "Take care of her, Frank." I waved goodbye as I left the auto shop with a book that no longer had a story inside tucked into my purse.

~

NOT TWO MINUTES LATER, AS I WAS WONDERING HOW ANDERS would react to knowing I'd be here for two more days—happy that I would be, or nervous that I had more time to "cause ripples" in Eloraton, whatever that meant—I decided to take a shortcut through one of the side alleys behind the café to get back to the bookstore. I worried that the missing words were permanent. I hoped they weren't. These were all first editions.

The sky was clotting with rain clouds again. I guessed it was about time for that early afternoon storm that Frank talked about. A droplet hit my cheek, then another on my face, the storm coming on quickly.

I sped up my pace.

I didn't expect to stumble on Ruby and Jake behind the café, in the back alley by the dumpster. I recognized Jake instantly, because he was still in his work apron, his oversized white tank top grease stained, and dark messy hair pushed back over his forehead, his eyes bright.

I started to shout hello to them, when Jake's voice cut me off—

"Is everything all right?" he asked, lacing their fingers together. "You've been quiet lately. Are you getting sick? Hurt? Are you okay, sugar?"

In the books, the way he called her *sugar* undid her a little more every time. It made her feel like a part of a recipe, an ingredient in a life that tasted sweet.

The rain started to come down harder. Maybe if I headed back toward Frank's, I could duck under some of the awnings and make it back to the bookstore by the time the storm hit—

Ruby said to Jake, while holding his hands, "I love you, but I think I need to find out who I am again. The lines have blurred." Then she took a deep breath and said, "I want to take a break."

My heart slammed into my rib cage.

Shit.

I'd misheard. She must've meant something else. Yeah, she couldn't have meant, I mean, it couldn't have been—

Jake, thinking along the same lines, gave a nervous laugh and asked, "From . . . the café? Sure, sugar. We can make that work—"

"No," Ruby said, untangling her fingers from his. "Well, the café, too, but—" And she took a deep breath, looked him in the eyes, and said, "Us."

20

Four Shadow o'Clock

I DUCKED INTO THE BOOKSTORE, drenched from the storm, shivering in the entrance. I hadn't made it to the bookstore before the bottom fell out of the clouds, it'd come on so fast. Anders looked up from the book he was reading at the counter, his eyebrows raised in question, but I didn't know what to say, if anything. Maybe I'd misheard Ruby and Jake, or made it up, or maybe they were practicing for *Romeo and Juliet* at the community theater—

A rumble of thunder shook the bookstore. Anders raised his hand to still Butterscotch, who'd jumped up on all fours, his tail puffed out. We watched the ceiling, the dozens of colorful glass chimes trembling with the vibrations.

Anders checked his watch. "A storm this early?" he muttered, and made a soothing sound as he scratched his cat behind the ears.

A thunderstorm instead of a rain shower. A change in Eloraton.

His minty gaze settled on me, and I quickly swallowed down the nauseated feeling rising up from my stomach. And it wasn't from the hangover this time.

"It must be a change in the season," I said to Anders, my voice wobbling despite myself, and we both knew well it was the middle of June. My hands shook, but I curled my fingers into fists to keep them steady. Anders mistook my trembling for the cold, and produced a towel from under the counter.

"Here," he said, offering it to me.

"Th-thanks," I muttered, taking it to dry my hair. My brain was buzzing, fast and frantic.

Ruby and Jake broke up, it repeated, the phrase turning over and over onto itself. It morphed into *Ruby broke up with Jake*.

And then.

I broke up Ruby and Jake—

My words. She used my words—

"You really need to stop getting caught in the rain without an umbrella," he said. His voice was admonishing, but in a playful way. It made me feel worse, because the one thing he warned me about, the one thing he'd asked me to do—

Shit.

The rainstorms were coming and going at weird times. I'd kissed the hero of the unfinished last novel. And now I'd broken up one of the main pairings in Quixotic Falls. Anders had warned me about *ripples* but I hadn't thought—I didn't think that I could—

I wasn't important enough to change a story, and yet . . .

I needed to fix this. Repair Ruby and Jake and get out of the way of Anders's actual romantic love interest—whoever it might be—and back away slowly. Which also meant I probably shouldn't make out with him again. *Ever*. So when I found his heroine, he would fall for *her*.

Not that he *would* fall for me but—

I couldn't chance it. I didn't want to mess up my favorite romance story, even though I might have already. "Excuse me." I quickly disappeared down an aisle. I had to collect myself before I faced him, and it wasn't like I could just *not* tell him, right? He'd find out sooner rather than later that Eloraton's heartbreak couple had, well, ended in *heartbreak*.

I went down one aisle, and then turned and went down another, going deeper into the bookstore than I'd ever been, but I'd read about this place so many times, the labyrinthine maze of shelves was tattooed on the back of my eyelids. There was a little alcove by the fireplace that was quiet, with a small fainting couch that was soft and smelled of dusty books and smokey cigars. I sank down onto it, grabbed one of the red velvet pillows with golden tassels, and buried my face in it.

Breathe in.

Breathe out.

"Eileen?" Anders stepped into the alcove timidly, rapping his knuckles on the side of a bookcase like he would a door. I gave a start, whirling around to him. Rainwater still dripped down my face, and I quickly tried to wipe it away. "Are you sure you're all right?"

Tell him, I thought, but I couldn't. I didn't want him to hate me again.

He'd just begun to like me, too.

He tilted his head, waiting for my answer. I didn't want to tell him. But he was infuriatingly patient, and he crossed his arms over his chest, and leaned against the edge of one of the bookcases.

A sign that read MYSTERY hung above him. "Eileen, as long as no one's dead, it can't be all that bad. I'm sure Frank can fix your car."

My *car*? He thought I was upset about my car? I swallowed the truth with the rest of my mounting panic, and tried to think.

I could work with this.

I could fix Ruby and Jake.

I had a master's in English, was halfway to my PhD—whenever I could afford night classes—and I'd taken courses from some of the preeminent scholars of romantic literature. I'd devoured enough paperback romances to stock a small library. Happily ever afters couldn't be that hard to make, right?

They couldn't be.

I just had to get them there.

"Frank said it'll take a few days," I said, training my eyes on the damp towel in my lap, because Pru always said she could tell when I lied by the look on my face. Like I was in pain.

"A few days," he repeated, his voice purposefully level. I couldn't glean whether or not he was excited or disappointed. I hated that—he was so hard to read. If this was a book, I'd know him intimately, but now I was just feeling around in the dark.

"Apparently the town doesn't want me to go," I joked, and flashed him a hesitant smile. *He doesn't have to know.*

I expected him to sigh dramatically, and complain about me staying in his perfect town a little longer, but he didn't. He looked conflicted, however, and that seemed to surprise him. He cleared his throat and pushed himself off the side of the bookcase. "Well, I can't say that I'm not . . . looking forward to having someone else in the bookstore for a little while longer," he said, looking back at his cat. "You can have the loft for as long as you need."

The fact that I could still stay here filled me with both happiness and a particular kind of dread.

"I promise I won't be trouble," I told him, and he didn't seem all that convinced.

"You're already tracking water all through my bookstore, Elsy," he said, motioning to the trailing puddles of water. "I think we're well past trouble."

Surprised, I looked down at my damp self. "You don't like wet T-shirt contests?" I asked, feigning hurt. "I'm just practicing."

He gave me a look, the first one that wasn't level, wasn't controlled, and there was heat behind it. The kind I remembered from last night. "Get up," he said, and his tone brooked no argument, "you're soaking through the couch."

I popped to my feet. "I'll go change," I said, and started to move around him when I realized that all of my clothes were dirty. I stopped, and turned back to him. "Actually, you wouldn't happen to have a washer and dryer, would you? I didn't expect to stay somewhere without one, so I only packed a handful of clothes . . ."

He tilted his head. "I hope your underwear situation is different."

"Seven pairs, for each day of the week," I swore.

He chuckled, amused, and my heart did a little flip in my chest. I liked the way he laughed, soft and rumbly and warm, like—

Like *butterscotch.*

"Come on, I think I have something that'll fit you," he replied, nudging his head toward the back of the bookstore, toward his house, and I gratefully followed him. He let me borrow some sweatpants and a T-shirt while I shoved my damp jeans and soggy shirt in his washer. His sweatpants were too big, so I had to roll the waistband down a few times, and the T-shirt was laughably thread-bare, sporting the words CHESS CLUB CHAMPIONSHIP from fifteen years ago.

"Yours?" I asked, fingering the embroidered initials on the shirt pocket. A. S.

He shrugged. "I was decent."

Then left for the bookstore again.

I pulled my damp hair into a high bun and situated my bangs as best I could, but they were already curling in unruly directions on my forehead. Despite myself, I lifted the collar of his T-shirt to my nose and breathed it in. His shirt smelled like he did, like his jacket had the night before—of cedarwood and old books. *A. S.*—I'd seen those initials before, I know I had. Just in which book?

My mind was blanking on me, and it wasn't like I could consult the books.

They were *all* blank.

If I had cell service, the book club would know. Benji would have it highlighted, guaranteed. He was an editor at some major publishing house, after all. And Olivia would probably know how to get Ruby and Jake back together. Janelle could pluck random facts out of thin air like a walking wikipedia page. Aditi was a whiz at research. I could really use their advice right about now.

My phone sat on the side of the washer in his laundry room, at full charge since I couldn't do anything with it. I'm sure Pru had posted to the chat about Iceland and her trip, and everyone else about their life commitments, all wondering why I hadn't com-mented. Maybe Pru had told them we had an argument. Maybe she told them I'd gone up to the cabin alone, and everyone knew that cell service at the cabin was spotty at best—

They wouldn't be worried. Not yet.

I was alone.

Pushing my bangs out of my eyes, I told myself not to panic. Romance writers made happily ever afters all the time.

How hard could it be?

21

Sweet Tooth

FIRST THINGS FIRST: FIND RUBY.

I couldn't wait for my clothes to finish drying, so I set off in Anders's clothes to scope out the café. I was running low on cash, so I staked out behind an old brownish Buick across the street—the kind that should've been left in an eighties movie, though with the chrome detail and charms hanging from the rearview mirror, it looked well-kept. To be honest, it'd been sitting there since I pulled into town, and it never once moved, and now that I thought about it, that seemed a bit odd.

I stood there, leaning against the car, for at least half an hour until I saw movement through the café window. Jake took an elderly couple's orders, looking worse for wear. Ruby, on the other hand, was still nowhere to be seen. Was she already gone? I guessed I could ask Jake, but then I'd need a reason to look for Ruby, and I couldn't exactly tell him that it was my fault they broke up.

"How long have you been hiding there, Eileen?"

I gave a shriek, and spun around, met with the looming

presence of Anders, his arms crossed over his chest, his shoulders square, enhancing the outline of his biceps under the three-quarter-length sleeve of his Henley. He arched a single blond eyebrow, and I sank back against the shit-brown car in defeat.

"Oh," I sighed. "It's you."

He tilted his head. "Don't get too excited."

"I—I haven't been here long," I lied, because it'd most certainly been longer than I wanted to admit. "I was just . . . looking at this car? Yeah. This car. I saw it through the window and had an epiphany. It's been here ever since I got here, you know?" I patted the trunk of it. "I could steal the carburetor. I doubt the owner would notice. You know, I *do* miss the real world," I added, trying to make it sound like the truth. "All that . . . heartbreak and loneliness. My job." I gave a wistful sigh. "Who wouldn't miss it?"

"Your mouth is better at kissing than lying, Elsy," he replied, and as I gave a squawk of protest, he reached into his pocket for—keys. Car keys. Then he went to the trunk, unlocked it, and popped it open. "I would just appreciate it if my car wasn't caught in the middle of whatever you're scheming."

I winced. "It's a very . . . nice . . . car?"

He grabbed a tool bag and closed the trunk. Then, with one last quirk of his eyebrow—as if *daring* me to shenanigans—he went into his bookstore again, and I sank against the back fender.

Then the car honked as the locks slammed shut, startling me off.

"Fine, *fine*," I muttered, and glanced back into the café, but Jake had gone from the window.

Okay. Plan B, I guessed.

⌒

NEXT STOP WAS RUBY AND JAKE'S APARTMENT ABOVE THE movie theater. It was the art of elimination at this point.

I'd just march up to the door, knock on it, and tell her never to listen to anything I say ever again.

But Anders, oblivious, had other plans.

"Since you are here for a bit, would you mind watching the shop while I run to the hardware store? You *did* break my window," he added as I came back into the store to fetch my purse. He held up the broken window latch in his hand. "I won't be long."

I hesitated. "Well . . ."

"If you have plans, never mind."

That wasn't the issue. If he left the bookstore, he might hear about Jake and Ruby. This *was* a small town, and if my slap got around that fast? I'm sure Gail was consulting the phone tree as we spoke. "I can go for you?" I suggested. "I mean, I did break it."

"That's kind, but do you know what you're looking for?"

I inclined my head. "Are you saying that because I'm a woman?"

He narrowed his eyes. "You're so kind to offer since you did, in fact, break my window. Along with the latch, I believe a pane of my window is also cracked. I'm sure it won't be too expensive to re-place." He offered the latch to me.

Tricky, tricky. I returned his glare. "Fine," I said. "I'll hold down the fort."

He smirked and pocketed it. "Thank you. I'll only be gone about thirty minutes, and then you can . . ." He trailed off as a thought occurred to him. "I could take you around Eloraton, since you'll be here for a few more days. Give you a proper tour, in ex-change for your time. Grab some tacos, tour the clock tower."

"Will you glare at me grumpily the entire time?"

"I am not grumpy."

I stared at him.

"No," he caved. "I'll be good."

He sounded earnest, and I'd be lying if I said that the idea of him showing me around to all his favorite places didn't sound fun. It did. But if I said yes, it would make my problem with Ruby and Jake a hundred times harder. Then again, if I said yes, maybe I could figure out why he felt so familiar. He had to have been in one of the books somewhere. I just had to figure out his connection to Eloraton.

"Sure," I said, and retreated behind the counter. "I'll be here."

"Thank you," he replied in relief. "Don't burn the place down."

I mock gasped. "I would *never!*"

As I watched him go, I drummed my fingers on the shop counter impatiently. The hardware store was on the opposite side of town, so I had a feeling that thirty minutes was a bit of a lie. Which meant if I left now I had at *least* forty-five minutes to find Ruby, figure out why the hell she broke up with Jake, and fix it.

I counted to ten, and then jumped over the counter and pressed my face against the door just to make sure he was well and truly gone.

Coast was clear.

With my purse slung over my shoulder, I flipped the sign to CLOSED and slipped out of the bookstore. No one ever came to buy anything, anyway, so I was sure I wouldn't be missed for a *little* while. Everything would have been so much easier if she was at home, but when I rang the buzzer for the apartment above the movie theater, no one came to the door, so I decided to check the jewelry shop that her aunt owned, but the store was closed since Mercury was not in retrograde.

I chewed on my thumbnail as I started back toward the bookstore. The early afternoon thunderstorm had left the day muggy and gray, though the sun kept trying to break apart the clouds to no avail. I felt my sweat curling my hair against the nape of my neck.

As I passed Sweeties, the scent of melted honey dragged me from my thoughts. Wait—*Maya* might know where Ruby was! They were best friends, after all.

Perfect.

I hurried across the street and into Sweeties. "Maya, I have a—"

The woman at the register glanced up from counting out change. She looked a bit like Maya. They both had dark hair and warm brown skin, but her hair was long and wavy, and she always wore sword-shaped earrings that dangled just above her shoulders. Maya was a little taller than her, too, and had a more square face, but I hadn't noticed until I stepped inside that it was the older sister at the counter.

Gemma Shah, finally.

"Not Maya, sadly." Gemma looked up from the till, and her eyes lit up. "Oh! You must be the new girl. She's told me a lot about you. Heard about your car," she added, scrunching her nose. "That really sucks. I'm Gemma, Maya's older sister."

"Elsy," I replied, reaching over the counter to shake her hand. "I'm looking for Ruby, actually."

"Oh, she went with Maya today. Girls' day, because—" Gemma quickly snapped her mouth closed. Frowned. "You know, just a girls' day. They won't be home until tomorrow, probably. Ruby's got a cabin up at Stellar Lake, so they're probably staying there for the night."

Because she broke up with Jake.

Damn. I bit the inside of my cheek, trying to think up what to do.

Gemma said, as if reading my expression, "But Jake's off tomorrow—every Tuesday he is—so he'll be working on the inn with Will and Junie. Doing staining, or something. And trying

to figure out the plumbing situation—I mean, the *haunted toilet*."
She put it in air quotes, and rolled her eyes. "Leave it to Junie to
think up the wildest thing. It's probably a busted line, or a bad
pipe."

I didn't want to upset whatever spirit resided in the inn's plumbing, and I certainly didn't want it to come after me.

"Anyway, sorry, I didn't mean to yammer your ear off—
everyone says that's why Thomas and I get along. I talk too much,
he doesn't talk *ever*. We balance each other out. Thomas is my husband," she added quickly, and the more she talked the faster she
went. "We married a few years ago. Took over Sweeties from Uma,
but everyone calls her Granny Uma because, you know, she's like a
grandmother to everyone and oh my *god* I am talking too much."
She threw up her hands. "I apologize."

I giggled. Full on giggled. Because it felt like Gemma had just
walked off the page, all 153 excited pounds of her.

Pru and I had stood outside in freezing weather the morning
Honey and the Heartbreak came out. We were so excited, we beat
the owner to the bookshop, and warmed our hands on the Starbucks coffee we'd gotten across the street. Pru was neck-deep in a
job she hated, so as we waited outside in the cold, she vented to me
about the most horrid guests at the hotel where she worked.

"You wouldn't *believe* how many Jacuzzi rooms we had to take
out of commission after Valentine's on Friday," she had complained,
right up until we got our books in hand. "You're so lucky you do
what you love."

I nodded. I *did* feel lucky, back then. "I think I might apply for
the tenure track. Get a PhD."

"*Oh?*"

"Yeah, what do you think? Could you see me as a stuffy

old professor in thirty years?" I inclined my head to look more regal.

Pru snorted. "No offense, but *no*."

"Offense taken! I think I would be a pretty cute old professor lady. Crotchety. But I'd secretly sneak *Twilight* into all my required reading."

My best friend was absolutely offended. "You *wouldn't*."

"I would. It'd be payback for all the *their/they're/there*s they'll mix up in their essays that I'll suffer through."

She gave it a thought. "Fair."

After the sleepy bookstore employee finally drove up and opened the store, we got our preorders—and another few books, because neither of us could step into a bookstore without buying more—and left to go spend the day lost in Eloraton. But on the way home, I asked Pru, while driving, "Do you really mean it? I wouldn't make a good professor?"

She said, "I was just joking."

I gave her a look, because I knew better.

She caved. "I mean . . . I think you *like* teaching. I think you're *good* at it. I don't think it's something like you'll wake up in ten years and realize you made the biggest mistake of your life getting tenure, but I guess . . . I dunno. I feel like if your classics professor in undergrad hadn't pushed you to go to grad school, you'd be doing something way different."

"She said I'd do good in grad school," I pointed out, "and I did."

"Yeah but . . ." Then she shrugged. "What do I know? I've had five different jobs in two years."

Which was true, and I did love teaching, so I pushed it to the back of my mind. Besides, Liam was between projects again, and my paycheck was steady. That night, we ordered in Chinese and got lost in Eloraton with Gemma and a nerdy astrophysicist who came to town to study the comet that was passing through, and the book was quiet, with low stakes, and lovely. There were so many readers who hated this third book, because it was such a bold departure from the first two in the series. It was softer, like a waltz through Eloraton. In the first book, Junie had come to town in a whirlwind, and in the second book, Ruby rattled everyone with her songs.

Gemma was different. She had nothing to escape from, and no one to prove herself to. She just *existed*, with her daughter, Lily, and floated through the pages like time well spent on a lazy river.

When I first read *Honey and the Heartbreak*, I also didn't really like it. It was too slow, too quiet, too soft. I couldn't relate to Gemma at all, hung up over a heartbreak but not the man himself.

But then three years later, during the worst year of my life, I reread the series. I was fresh off my own heartbreak, drowning myself in happily ever afters so I wouldn't have to think about the failure of my own. I rarely left my apartment, except for teaching or getting takeout when Uber Eats didn't sound appealing. By this time, Rachel Flowers had died, too, and because everyone secretly loved a tragedy, her books shot onto bestseller lists and stayed there.

Rachel was divisive with her romances. She kept her readers on their toes, always a little more unconventional than most. Readers still didn't like *Honey and the Heartbreak*, but I finally understood it, and like the honey Gemma Shah's bees made, the story coated my soul and kept me warm. Not all love happens at first glance— sometimes, it takes a reread at the exact right (or wrong) time in your life. And sometimes, it takes a little help from your friends.

"What are you doing the second week of June?" Pru asked one evening in April, when I was right there with Gemma, falling head over heels for sweet and timid Thomas.

"I'll probably offer to teach summer classes."

"Well, don't."

I looked up from my book. "Why?"

We were curled on the couch, *The Bachelorette* murmuring in the background, a woman giving roses to charming men who hoped they could be her one. "Because we're taking a road trip up to the Hudson Valley."

"Why?"

"Because we're going to meet our book club."

"We can just Skype in," I replied dismissively. "It's a long drive."

"Elsy . . ."

I leveled a look at her. "Prudence . . ."

"Come on," she begged.

I whined, "I don't want to *go* anywhere."

"Not even to see our friends?"

No, I wanted to say, because I didn't want to leave the apartment at all. I hadn't, really, not since . . . well, not since Liam ended things. I hadn't even wanted to go grocery shopping, because what if I ran into him? Or his work friends? I didn't think I had the energy to act like everything was all right. Not yet, anyway.

Prudence began to hum that god-awful song.

"Please," I pled. "Stop."

But she just hummed it louder, and began to shimmy her shoulders to the song. "Come on, Eileen . . ." she said, taunting. And she knew it would work every time, because I always caved if it was something she wanted to do. I could put my wants and needs on the back burner and I'd grin and bear it and go off on adventures with her. It felt better, anyway, than thinking about my own life. If I could just live in her glow, bask in it forever, I thought that would be enough.

And for such a long time, it was.

But like Gemma realizing that her life went on regardless of whether she was in it, I began to realize my life wasn't stopping, either. It would go on regardless of whether I burrowed my head in the sand and stayed stock-still. I think that was why I decided to take the trip this year—it wasn't because I wanted routine or a week to read romances and drink shitty wine, but because . . .

My life *was* still moving, and deciding to still go was the first real decision I'd made for myself in . . .

In *years.*

So it was lovely, truly, to see Gemma Shah look so happy and at home in the place she cherished the most.

"Honestly," I replied, unable to stop smiling, "it's nice to finally meet you."

"Oh no, that can't be good. Has Lily been talking about me?" She arched an eyebrow, snapping the till closed with a flick of her wrist.

The sweets shop was empty, which was rare. She had on a red-and-white-striped shirt and high-waisted light-wash jeans, and a small golden coin around her neck, stamped with the outline of a honeybee. If Junie had been like a Monet painting, Gemma looked like the effortless happiness in Fragonard's *The Swing.* It was like she couldn't stand still, constantly in motion as she talked to me while she put on plastic gloves and grabbed a scraper, moving down the counter to where she and Maya made taffy on a long slab of marble.

"Don't believe everything you hear," she went on, pouring a pot of boiling taffy onto the counter. "She overexaggerates *everything.* And I mean everything. When she was three, she went fishing with Frank for the first time, and she caught a fish—you know how big it was?" She spread her hands apart as wide as they'd go. "This big, if you'd believe her."

I laughed. "What, it *wasn't* that big?"

"Sadly not, and I'm not as boring as Lily probably told you," she added. The ocher-colored taffy was cooling into a viscous puddle, and she scraped it together.

"She didn't say you were boring at all," I replied, "if that's any consolation. She did tell me about the mutiny of bees, though."

Gemma shook her head with a sigh. "If it's not one thing . . . Thank you for fixing her book, by the way. I've been trying to find another copy forever. You're a lifesaver."

"Nah, I had fun. Lily is adorable," I said as she turned back to the counter and returned to her cooling sugary puddle. Watching her work was fascinating. She went through the motions like she was on autopilot, having done it a thousand times before, scraping it together, turning it over, sprinkling a bit of flavor here, a dash there—like she was brewing a potion, and not a batch of taffy.

"Well, stay right there and let me finish, because I at *least* want to gift you some taffy for your troubles before you go," she went on, hooking the gooey taffy on the taffy hook hung on the wall, and starting to pull. "It seems like ever since you came to town, you've been shaking things up."

I looked away quickly. "I hope not too much."

She pulled on the taffy again, adding a strip of pink dye to the ocher. "I think this town needs a little shaking up," she finally decided, and flashed me a secretive smile.

I gave a noncommittal shrug. "Anders doesn't exactly think so."

She rolled her eyes. "That curmudgeon doesn't like anything."

"Really? But, he has such a great attitude . . ." I replied wryly.

She laughed. It was bright, like a bell. "*Doesn't* he? I think that's how he scared everyone off at first."

That intrigued me. "So, there *were* people crushing on him?"

"Oh god, yeah. Holly, Suze, Beanie—he chased them all away within the first week. But you . . ." And she wiggled her eyebrows. "You might have a chance. He doesn't scare you."

"Oh—oh no, we're barely friends now. I think that's the extent of relationship."

"Why?"

Because I almost ran him over with my car. Because I slapped him in the middle of town. Because he kissed me in a way that went all the way to my toes, and I can't seem to shake the butter-flies in my stomach that kiss bred.

"Oh, look at the time," I said, looking at my imaginary watch. "I think I hear Mephistopheles calling my name from the depths of hell, be seeing you!" I cried and escaped the candy shop as quick as I could. She serenaded me out, pealing into laughter as soon as the door swung closed behind me.

I didn't slow down my pace until I was a block away from the candy shop, and by then my cheeks were flushed from the exertion, and not the embarrassment. So, Anders *had* had people interested in him at first, but they all ran for the hills when he wasn't charm-ing or forthcoming or even a little bit *fun*. (Until he *was*, and then he was nicer, and thoughtful, and flirty.) He probably would've chased me away, too, if the inn wasn't haunted and he didn't have the only spare room in the entire town. Holly, Suze, and Beanie—those were the characters Gemma mentioned. Tertiary characters in the books, people with one scene or two, and barely mentioned again.

I tried to imagine any of them kissing Anders, riding off into the sunset with him, and the attempt made my hangover return with a vengeance—my stomach twisted, my chest hurt. Anders was probably on his way back from the hardware store by now, so

I sped up my pace. Butterscotch was lounging in a sun spot in the window. He gave me a lazy look, as if he knew exactly where I'd been and what I'd done.

And, to my eternal regret, so did his owner.

I froze in my footsteps the second I stepped inside.

Anders was reading at the counter. He languidly turned the page, his head propped up on his hand. The afternoon sun through the high windows turned his white-blond hair almost golden when it hit the light just right.

"Nice of you to finally return," he said nonchalantly. "Did you have a nice walk?"

I winced. "Sorry. I . . . forgot I left something in my car. So I went to Frank's to get it. I was just gone a few minutes."

He pursed his lips, like he knew I was lying, but he didn't call me out on it. He just asked, "Did you find what you were looking for?"

"No." At least *that* wasn't a lie, but still I couldn't look him in the eyes. Shame ate at the edges of my cheeks, red and awful. I hadn't thought about what would happen if I *didn't* come back in time, and now I felt like I'd let him down because—well, I *had*. "I'm sorry. How long have you been back . . . ?"

"A few minutes," he replied, standing, and gave a stretch—like a cat unfurling. His Henley rode up a little, coming untucked from his jeans, flashing a sliver of skin above his waistband. I immediately recalled our kiss, the way his chest felt with my hands pressed up against his skin, the solidness of him, the way he *smelled*—

I tore my gaze away. "Did they have the latch?"

"No."

"Ah." I shifted uncomfortably, remembering what Gemma said

about Anders chasing all the girls away. It wasn't hard for him. "You know the sign is still flipped to closed?"

"I know. I told you I'd take you around Eloraton when I got back, if you'd still like me to."

Oh, that just made me feel *worse*. I winced. "You really don't have to . . ."

He tilted his head to the side. "If you'd rather not, I understand."

"You're . . . not mad at me? For leaving the shop when you asked me to stay?"

"No," he replied, shaking his head. "You said you forgot something at Frank's, and it must've been important, so it can't be helped. Though, I'm sorry you didn't find it."

Shit. Now I felt even worse for lying. My shoulders sagged. "Yeah . . ."

He closed his book. It was an Ann Nichols novel—one of her newer ones. The cover wasn't blurry, and the pages weren't blank, so maybe it was just my Quixotic Falls novels? "So, where would you want to go first?"

I hesitated.

My gaze settled on the broken latch on the counter. I *needed* to fix whatever I'd broken between Ruby and Jake, but I *wanted* to go get tacos and see the clock tower. Besides, I couldn't really do anything else until Ruby came back, anyway.

Tomorrow, then. Tomorrow I'd talk to Jake, and Ruby, and help them sort it all out. Somehow.

I just . . . had to be on my best behavior tonight. Strictly Good Eileen.

"If it's that hard for you to decide . . ." Anders murmured, studying the crease between my brows, "I would suggest food first. Let me close up." Then he pushed himself off the counter and came around to lock the front door, but as he passed, he bent toward me, his shoulder brushing mine, and murmured, "You're still a bad liar, Eileen."

Well, I was certainly in trouble tonight.

And the worst part was, I feared I was going to like it.

22

Romantic Gestures

THE TACO JOINT WAS a small hole-in-the-wall place over on Four Shadow Street.

I got our sodas and found Anders at a table, with a greasy bag of tacos. The restaurant was filled with little knickknacks and paper streamers with the Mexican flag on them, and bobbleheads of mariacheros at the order counter.

If I was the nosy type, I'd figure out who Rachel dreamed up for him. I bet it was someone who was a foil, an opposite who drew out all the best and worst parts of him. So, basically an optimist who loved books and shook him out of his grumpy shell and had some sort of character flaw that was both a little endearing and very much annoying to him.

But I wasn't nosy—nosy was reserved for busybodies who poked around for their own self-fulfillment—no, I was *curious*, genuinely curious, and that was all the worse.

I slid into the chair opposite him. "There weren't any straws."

"There aren't any in Eloraton unless you ask for them," he

replied. "They're abysmal for the environment. You know, saving the whales."

"I have heard about that."

"My sister could give you a three-hour presentation on it, if you let her." He reached into the bag and divvied up our tacos. He got four to my two, and we split an order of nachos. Somehow, the revelation that he had *siblings* was more shocking than anything else about him.

"You have a *sister?*"

"Don't sound so surprised," he remarked dryly.

"Sorry, sorry." And then I schooled my face and said in my best impression of him, stoic and level, "You have a sister?"

He narrowed his eyes at me. "Hmm."

"Admit it," I said as he took his first bite of tripe taco with hot sauce, "I'm a better you than you are."

"Are you now," he replied, amused.

So I adopted his stoic voice and said, "Are you now." Then I grabbed a menu from the middle of the napkin holder and pretended it was a book. "Hello, I'm Anders the bookstore owner, and I like to glower and judge your favorite books."

He about choked on his food. "I do *not* judge someone by their favorite books, thank you."

"Unless . . ."

He inclined his head. "I don't."

"*Unless . . .*" I nudged again, because I knew there was an exception. There was always *one* exception.

And so he finally caved, "Unless it's one of those self-help-business-guru pull-your-self-up-by-your-bootstraps kind of books."

"Ooh, the kind where the author is always white, probably bald, middle-aged?"

"Standing in the corner of the book cover, arms crossed," he noted.

I could see it so clearly. "And he probably paid a ghostwriter not nearly enough money to repeat the same thing every other self-help business guru said in *their* book but with a different adjective?"

"And they all eventually start suing each other for copyright infringement and no one can trace back to who said what first?"

"How oddly specific," I noted, unable to hide a smile.

And he almost—*almost*—echoed it. I'm sure his smile was lovely, and I really wanted to see it. "My secret. I'll deny it if you tell anyone."

I crossed my pinkie over my chest. *"Never."*

"How do I not believe you," he noted, his eyes sparkling, and licked a bit of hot sauce off his thumb. His tongue was quick. I remembered the way it wanted to explore my mouth last night.

"So, where is your sister now?"

"Manitoba. Studying belugas."

"That sounds so cool. I've never seen a beluga before. Do you ever visit her?" I asked, picking at my taco. Maybe it was a hold-over from my hangover this morning, but I didn't really have an appetite. Or maybe it was nerves. Was this a date? No, no. It couldn't be.

If it was, it was the best date I'd been on in years. My only one, too, but never mind *semantics*.

"No," he replied. "She moved up there after I came to Eloraton."

"And you haven't left since?"

"No."

"Why?"

He shrugged, polishing off his second taco. "You should try the hot sauce. It's really great."

I eyed it. The cartoony logo of Frank's Hotties taunted me. "Nah, I'm good."

"Just try a little." He picked up the bottle and went to pour some on my taco.

"No! I don't want to leak!" I batted the bottle away. "How dare you."

He laughed, and we ate the rest of our meal, and chatted about our families. He told me about his parents, the accountant and the Pilates instructor, and how they'd retired to a cabin in the middle of the woods, where they raised chickens and a handful of very unruly goats, and they sounded like people my mom would have adored. I told him that she was divorced, never remarried, "And with her retirement, she decided to see the world. Meanwhile, I've never even been to New York City."

That surprised him. *"Never?"*

"Never," I confirmed. "It just seems so . . . *big*. Overwhelming. I'd probably have a panic attack right in the middle of Times Square."

"It *is* pretty chaotic," he agreed. "It's nothing like Eloraton. In the city, everything moves so fast no one even notices you—not even when you're gone. Here, it's impossible not to be noticed. If you're gone, everyone will know. It's . . . refreshing," he decided, though I had the feeling it wasn't the word he wanted to use.

I tilted my head. "Is that why you stayed?"

"One of them," he confirmed, and checked his watch. He wore it on the underside of his wrist, so the back of the watch face pressed against the soft inside. "If you're finished, we better hurry."

"I thought we were seeing the clock tower?"

He tossed our trash in the trash can. "Would I lie to you?"

he asked, and walked backward out the front door, and I hurried after him, a smile tugging at the edges of my lips.

THE CLOCK TOWER WAS SO TALL WHEN YOU STOOD AT THE base of it, like it stretched all the way into the evening sky. In the first book, Junie and Will snuck up to the top to see the town from the sky. *Sometimes all you need is to see life from a different angle, Will, to make it look new again.*

Anders nudged his head toward the maintenance door near the back of the building. "This way. We should hurry or we'll miss it."

"Miss what?"

He tapped his finger to his lips for quiet as he produced his keys from his pocket and unlocked the door. It was rusted, the hinges whining loudly as he forced it open. I turned on my cell phone flashlight, and followed him in. In reality, the clock tower was only five stories high, so the climb up to the top wasn't hard, but in the dark it took longer than usual. There were lights in the stairwell, but Anders said that we needed to leave them off.

"Unless you would like the town to know someone is in here?" he asked, which just told me that we weren't supposed to be here.

I gasped. "Anders, are we *trespassing*? Did you make me commit a *crime*?"

I could *feel* his eye roll as he said, "Oh yes, I made you. Watch your step," he added as we reached the top, where the turret clock sat. There were four faces, each of them with a spindle to a gear in the middle. It turned tiredly. He inclined his head toward the metal ladder on the far side of the room, and I climbed up to where the bell rested. Out of the arches, I could see the entire town, unfurling across the valley like a storybook. It took my breath away.

He climbed up after me, and wrapped his arm gently around

my waist to keep me steady. The wind was harsher up here, and it was so very, *very* far down, but he was solid and sure, so I wasn't afraid.

"This is . . ." I couldn't come up with the words.

"My favorite place in town," he replied, and carefully we walked over to the edge of the bell tower. The sun was slowly sinking down between the rolling hills of the Catskills, purples and blues and pinks. "I've never been up here with anyone else."

My heart fluttered. "No one?"

He shook his head. "But I thought you'd appreciate it."

I glanced up at him as the setting sun made the harsh lines of his face softer, the blond of his hair more gold. This was a special place—meant for a grand romantic gesture. It was a place wasted on me.

I was stealing all his heroine's moments, wasn't I?

It was a sobering thought.

"This is such a lovely view," I said, my heart twisting, "but you should've saved this for someone worth it."

To which he replied, cradling my face in his hand, searching my eyes as he did, "Aren't you? What are you so afraid of, Elsy?"

Right now? I was afraid of reaching out to him, I was afraid of taking his hands in mine. I was afraid of something—just *something good*—with someone. "Nothing," I said.

He ran his thumb along my bottom lip. "Liar . . ."

Was I imagining it, or was he leaning in for another kiss? He was, and I was, too, drawn like magnets, and all I wanted was to press my mouth to his and taste my name on his lips, and feel my blood coursing through my veins again—*finally*—like I was finally waking up from years of slumber.

"We can go back down," I said, moving past him toward the ladder, but then he caught me by the wrist to keep me.

"Wait, please." His grip was gentle, and I turned back to him.

The sun had set, and the oranges and reds were turning swiftly to purple and midnight blue as the moon grew brighter and brighter in the sky. "Anders," I began, but he led me toward the edge of the bell tower, and produced two pairs of earplugs from his pocket. I had a feeling that he hadn't gone to the hardware store just for the clasps, because this was too well planned, and that seemed just like him, through and through. Stoic, and thoughtful, and attentive, and even when he was grumpy, he made up for it.

"Put these in, it's almost time," he said, putting his own in, and I did, too. The world quieted, until I could only hear the blood rushing through my staccato heart. I opened my mouth to ask, loudly, what we were doing, when he held his hand up to his lips, and then—

All of the minute hands struck twelve at the same time.

And behind us, the bell pulled back and swung. Even with the earplugs in, the sound was so loud, it rattled my bones. At first, it startled me. I gave a yelp and grabbed Anders by the arm, curling close into his chest, and I think he started to laugh, but I couldn't hear it over the sound of the bell. It swung back and forth, in long and loud *gongs*, all the way to nine, when the bell came back to rest, but its reverberations persisted long after, like a sigh of a thousand bees. I took my earplugs out and the air itself seemed to *hum*, even down into my lungs, and every inch of me felt vibrant and—*alive*.

"What do you think?" he asked quietly into my hair, and I realized I was still clutching his shirt, leaning against him.

My body still tingling from the sound, I looked out over the town, and all the tiny little buildings and the tiny little cars and the people walking down the street, and the woods that crept right up to the roads, and the trees that filed up the sides of the hills, making them look like evergreen waves. I'd imagined Eloraton a thousand times, but it didn't even compare.

"It's . . . magical," I whispered.

"It is," he replied, though his gaze never left me.

～

THE NIGHT HAD COOLED WHEN WE FINALLY LEFT THE CLOCK tower, and found a seat on a park bench in the square. For the second night in a row, there wasn't a storm for miles. We sat silently, eating from the bag of taffy I'd bought a few days ago that I'd shoved in my purse. Well, *I* was eating from it. He stuck to his word that he didn't like sweet things.

"Did you used to live in New York City?" I asked, twisting the plastic wrapper around my finger. We were sitting so close I could just lean a little and bump my shoulder against his. He sat with one leg crossed over the other, bopping his foot up and down like he was nervous. *Was* he nervous? Why would he be? "You seemed to know it really well when we talked about it earlier."

"I did. Right on Eighty-Second Street on the Upper East Side."

"I have no idea what that means."

"It means I was close to the Met. I'd go there a lot to read."

I studied him. "You would."

"What does *that* mean?"

I pulled my legs up under me, angling myself toward him on the park bench. "Just that you enjoy quiet, nerdy places."

"Hardly quiet. The Egyptian wing is the best. The room is bright, and there are a lot of benches. There's so many people there, but it all just sounds like white noise after a while. I always went there to just . . . be beige for a while. A part of the scenery." I imagined that scene in *When Harry Met Sally*, when they were in that room, and tried to put myself there, too, but I didn't think I fit. He went on thoughtfully, "I miss the city sometimes. I miss the food—and the bookstores. Especially the bookstores. You'd love them," he added, glancing over at me, his eyes glimmering with excitement.

"They can't be half as good as Ineffable."

"Perish the thought—but they're good. They have character. Though, I've yet to meet a bookstore that doesn't."

I propped my arm up on the bench back and turned to face him. "Tell me everything about the city. Sell it to me like you would a book."

"That's a tough ask."

I smiled—I couldn't stop myself. "You like a challenge."

And for the first time, I think I saw what Anders looked like when he was happy. There was a new color to his face, painted in with excitement, like the thought of somewhere else had knocked the dust off his character and shaken him awake. "Well, first off, you need to go in the correct month. Everyone waxes about summer in the city, but they're wrong."

"Oh? Carrie Bradshaw *lied* to me?"

"Terribly so," he replied. "It's autumn that's perfect. Imagine your favorite watercolor painting, and then imagine it in hues of pumpkins and sunsets. All of the trees in Central Park turn orange and brown and yellow, and the leaves crunch under your feet, and the air smells cool and crisp. It feels like a Nora Ephron movie. I always used to get a dirty chai at this hole-in-the-wall coffee shop and walk from Union Square all the way down to Washington Square Park, and if I was lucky, there would be a really good food truck there selling fajitas." His eyebrows furrowed in vexation. "I miss it a lot, actually."

"I've never had a dirty chai before."

"I always get one on the first cloudy day of the season. They taste better when it's overcast."

"Maybe you can take me someday," I said before I realized how impossible that was, but once I'd said it I knew.

And he did, too, and we fell into an awkward silence.

He said, "Maybe someday you can take a vacation. I can give you a list of all the places you have to see."

"Are they tourist traps?"

"I'd never lead you astray."

"Hmm." I imagined going to New York and getting lost like the tourist that I inevitably would be. I'd take the subway too far, and I'd get on the express train instead of the local, and I'd have my nose buried in my maps app the entire time, forgetting that the most perfect part of the city was when you looked up—

And saw sky.

"Maybe someday," I replied. "You know, I almost took a teaching job in New York." It was after Liam broke up with me, when Pru had finally pried me out of my apartment, and introduced me to the world again. I had just wanted to leave, to go somewhere else. I guessed running was just instinct, at that point.

He asked, "Why didn't you?"

I shrugged, fishing another taffy out of the bag. Pru had asked the same thing, and I didn't really have a good answer. "What if I didn't like it? Besides, where I'm at now is just fine. Pru's close, and most of my colleagues like me. I teach English at a university," I added, realizing that I'd never told him. "The students are great. Not every day do you get to have a heated discussion about whether Dionysus and Apollo were in love in Ovid's *Metamorphoses*."

He nodded. "That does seem very invigorating. Is that your dream job?"

I snorted a laugh. "No. I wish it was, but it's just where I ended up, I think. I didn't want to be a librarian, and I didn't want to go to law school, so . . ." I shrugged. "I decided to teach."

He turned himself toward me in interest. His knee knocked against mine, and he didn't pull away. "What would you do, if you could do anything?"

"Anything?"

"Anything at all."

"I don't know." I shrugged again. He waited for me to answer, taking a taffy out of my bag. I was sure he'd win in a game of waiting. The truth was, I didn't *know* what I'd do. I hadn't really thought much about it. Because my mom had been a librarian, I'd gone into English thinking I'd get to a master's in library science, but as soon as I got into the grad program, I knew I didn't want to do that. My classics professor said I'd be good at teaching. So, I simply did that."

"Okay," he said slowly, popping the taffy into his mouth. "Where are you happiest?"

I thought about the nights Pru and I read quietly in our chairs in the dorm room our freshman year, and the years we'd start a new book at midnight and read until dawn. I thought about the book events we went to together, the uncomfortable seats and the stilted small talk with other nerdy bookish people who also didn't know the fine art of weather-related topics. How happy I was just to sit between aisles of books, breathing in the smell of newly printed pages and dusty old ones, binder's glue and cardboard and dust.

And I thought about Ineffable Books, and the way the sunlight streamed through the windows, making the motes of dust between the stacks sparkle. The way the spines of books felt as I ran my fingers across them, like a xylophone of words.

"A bookstore, I guess."

He said, "You couldn't leave it unattended, you know."

I winced. "Yeah, I would probably be very bad at it."

"I didn't say that," he replied, studying me with those bright mint eyes. At night, they almost looked like they glowed. "I think you can do whatever you put your mind to, Eileen. You're terrifying that way."

"That's nice of you to say, but it's not true. I'm not very good at anything."

He hummed. "You fixed Lily's book."

"Because my mom taught me how," I pointed out. "She's much better at it."

"You stayed an entire night at the Daffodil."

"I'd feel bad if I just left."

"And," he went on, "you've already gotten almost every main character to like you."

"And you?" I asked, searching his face. "Have I gotten you to like me?"

"Eileen," he said softly, his minty eyes having melted to pools of emeralds, "I'm not sure how many times I have to say it, but I'll say it as many times as you need: I never hated you."

"Not even when I almost ran you over?"

"I was in the middle of the road. In the rain. To be fair, I didn't expect anyone to come into town just then."

"And when I slapped you?"

"It hurt, but I understand that I upset you. I deserved it." Then he repeated again, slower, "I never hated you, Eileen."

I looked away, trying not to blush, because I'm sure he very much could. I wondered how he saw me. As someone who wasn't perpetually afraid of people she hadn't met yet? As someone who went into new places with hope instead of heartache? I wanted to meet that version of me, whoever she was. She could run a bookstore—I could almost see it. "It'd be small, you know?" I said, returning to the subject, and the tension between us eased a little. He sat back on the bench, listening. "Maybe one just for romance novels."

"What kind of romances?" he asked.

"All sorts. Sky's the limit. Romantasy to bodice rippers, for sure. Oh, and there would be a weekly book club."

He nodded. "Obviously, all good bookstores have one, but I'm a bit partial."

"So am I."

"And what would you name it?"

I scrunched my nose. "Shit, I don't know . . . *My First Bookstore?*"

He rolled his eyes. "You can do better than that."

"I don't know. I'm bad at names. Um . . ." I thought about it, glancing around the park, and then back at him. Every good romance had meet-cutes and love scenes and kisses. It had to have something to do with that. Maybe—"I'd call it the Grand Romantic."

A flicker of a smile crossed his mouth. "And you said you were bad at names."

I ignored him. "We'd host events for romance readers, and people would come from all over the country just to shop there. It would be the kind of place that made you believe in romance again."

He didn't say anything for a long moment.

So long that I forced out a laugh. "It's just a dream, though. I doubt any bank would loan me that kind of money."

"It's a good dream," he replied finally. "I'd be first in line."

I smiled at him, because that was kind. "In that tweed jacket I know you have?"

He sighed. "I'm telling you, I don't have one."

"Mm-hmm. Keep fooling yourself."

He laughed, a smile tugging at the corners of his mouth. A real one. For the first time. And it changed his entire face. The lines around his mouth, perpetually scrunched in a frown, vanished. The hard set of his eyebrows turned soft. He had a nice smile, too. *Charming.*

"So," I said, and I pulled my feet up and laid them across his legs so I sat sideways on the bench and could see him better, "what about you?"

He took another taffy from my bag. And here he said he didn't like sweets. "What about me?"

"What would you do, if you could do anything?"

In the book world, the sky was the limit, after all, and I wondered what piece of herself Rachel Flowers put into Anders. Her love for reading? (Obviously.) Her drive to write?

He sat back on the bench, rolling the taffy around in his mouth. "I already do it," he said. "Well, I *did* it. I had my dream job. I reviewed novels for the *New York Times*. Mostly thrillers and suspense, but sometimes I'd get lucky enough to review a romance. And there was nothing better." He frowned then, and for the first time in a few hours, a quiet coldness settled over his face again, though I knew him better now. It wasn't coldness. It was sadness. "But I haven't really enjoyed any books since . . . well, it just doesn't feel the same." He shook his head. "Time changes you. Stories change you. The people you meet change you. I'm simply not the same man that I was before."

Before—before he and his ex split? Who was she, and how was she so lovely, to make a ruin of him? Why did she leave? I couldn't imagine not being able to fall into the stories that kept me company in those long days after Liam left. I burrowed into them. I protected myself. To not have that . . .

"So all the books I've seen you with . . . you're not enjoying them?"

"I'm trying," he replied. "And, to be honest, I thought that maybe being around you would help because you just *exude* happiness. You don't notice it, but you're always smiling when you're in this town. When you're talking to Junie or Ruby or Maya, or walking down the street, or eating honey taffy—you're just . . . *happy*. I want to feel that again, too. So, so badly."

I reached over and threaded my fingers through his, and squeezed his hands tightly. "If I could give it to you, I would."

"It would taste sweet, I'm sure," he said, dropping his eyes to my mouth. "Like you."

My stomach burned. I wanted him to kiss me again, sitting on this park bench, on such a lovely summer night. The fireflies danced around us, the wind winding through the trees, and when he set his eyes on me, I felt like the only story he wanted to read.

And that was dangerous, because he was fictional and Rachel had written someone for him. Someone good.

And it wasn't me.

So I leaned forward and kissed him gently on the cheek instead. A compromise. "I had a lovely time tonight, Anders. Thank you."

"You are very welcome, Elsy," he replied, and seemed almost disappointed when I unfurled my legs from over his and pushed myself to stand. I outstretched my hand for him to take it so we could head back together, but he said, "I think I'm going to take a walk, instead. The bookstore is unlocked. I'll see you in the morning?"

"This time without a hangover," I promised, and started back toward the bookstore. I shouldn't have looked over my shoulder to see where he went, but I couldn't help myself.

I glanced back.

He had already left the bench, heading down the sidewalk toward the Daffodil Inn, and the graveyard of deleted things.

And unlike in a romance novel, he didn't look back at me.

A walk in that strange graveyard was odd at this time of night. Was he meeting someone? I had half a mind to just go back to the bookstore and go to sleep, because the starlings would wake me up at the most god-awful hour in the morning, but my curiosity got the better of me, and I snuck after him to the inn, where he hopped the fence into the garden, and disappeared through the pergola.

The kitchen lights were still on at the inn, and quiet music oozed through the open windows. I glanced inside as I passed through the garden. Junie and Will were slow dancing, her head on his shoulder, his arms around her waist, rocking back and forth to the slow, soft melody. And immediately, I felt like I'd just witnessed a private moment that wasn't mine to see.

I hurried after Anders, being sure to keep to the shadows, to not step on any sticks, to not get caught in the prickly rosebushes on either side of the pergola. When I got to the iron gate, I hid behind it. He sat down on the edge of the fountain and pulled out his cell phone, and called someone.

"Sorry it's so late," he said, and whoever it was caused a smile to curl across his mouth, for his eyes to crinkle. "Yeah, yeah. I'll keep that in mind . . ."

Who was he talking to that made him smile like that? Who would he call near midnight?

He chatted on the phone, but his voice was so low I could barely hear anything at all. I leaned against the iron gate, straining my ear—

My phone suddenly vibrated with a text message and gave a loud *blip*.

He snapped his head toward the noise, but I was already scrambling down the alley again, and through the pergola. I didn't stop running until I got to Main Street, where I bent over to catch my breath.

"The hell?" I muttered, taking my phone out of my back pocket.

There was a new text message, even though I had no service. It was from Pru, saying in all caps—

HE PROPOSED!!

I quickly grappled to reply—CONGRATS!!!

But as soon as I sent it, it came back. Message Unsent. Damn it, how had I gotten signal at all? Unless it was the courtyard where Anders took his call? But I didn't understand why that would matter. Anders could get his fictional cell service anywhere.

I chalked it up to a fluke and returned to the loft, but I didn't fall asleep until Anders came back half an hour later.

23

The Course of True Love

TODAY, I WAS GOING to fix everything. At least, that's what my partially sleep-deprived brain decided, because the starlings made it almost impossible to sleep in, even if I wanted to. Did they *have* to start their weird little song at 7:30 in the morning? Never mind Butterscotch, who had somehow clawed open the door and sat meowing on the window seat, looking up at the nest of birds, until I grabbed him and tossed him back into the bookstore.

After I got dressed and pulled my hair back into a high ponytail, it was still so early Anders hadn't come to open the bookstore yet, so I went to the Grumpy Possum to get us caffeine and bagels. Jake had the day off, and there was a squirrelly-looking teenager at the counter with a half-grown mustache, so he wasn't going to be much help. I studied the menu, but it was still no use. I couldn't read it even if I tried.

I dug my wallet out of my purse as the teen waited on my order. "Uh, a caramel latte, a black tea, a cream cheese bagel with lox and . . ." What kind of bagel had Anders eaten earlier? Right—"A bagel with chive and onion cream cheese." I put two dollars in the tip jar, and thanked him when he handed me a drink carrier with the drinks, and a warm bag with the bagels.

Anders had taken care of me yesterday morning, and I really did enjoy our date last night (*was* it a date? I shouldn't call it a date), so he shouldn't have been as surprised as he was to see me at the counter with a bagel and a tea for him when he rolled into the bookstore around eight.

He took a sip of tea suspiciously, and when he realized that it *was* tea and *wasn't* poisoned or cold or whatever, he opened the bag to see the bagel. Then he gave me a deliberating look. "What's your angle?" he asked.

"You're letting me stay in the loft for free. How's that for angles?"

"I'll believe it," he said after a thought, "but you're still suspect." He took his bagel. "Thank you, I'll treasure it always." Then he walked away with his prizes, and I bit in a smile.

"I think he likes me," I told Butterscotch, who was lying in his cat bed in the window. He gave me a bored look and put his nose under his tail.

Anders came back to the front after a while, and nudged his head toward the sign. "I've got to go run an errand, so why don't you embrace your bookseller fantasies for a bit? Try it on. See if you like it."

"An errand? Now?" I asked, checking my watch, because I had planned on going over to the Daffodil Inn soon.

"Now," he replied, taking his car keys out from under the counter.

"And you trust me not to wander off again?"

Twirling his keys around his finger, he turned back to me and gave it a thought. He cocked his head to the side, a lock of white-blond hair falling across his forehead. "I think you'll stay. For now."

And then he was gone, out the front door and into his old Buick. It started up with a whimper, and he backed out of his spot and drove off toward the main part of town. Curious. I wondered where he was going that needed a car to get to.

I was half-tempted to go to the inn now, but I still felt bad about leaving the shop unattended yesterday, and I didn't want to do it again. So I flipped the CLOSED sign to OPEN, and I spent the morning tallying inventory, and helping the few customers who came in to browse, and went about making new displays and finding books in strange places, and petting the best cat. It was . . . nice. Nice in the way I hadn't felt since I was a kid, sitting behind my mom's work desk at the library, scanning in books from the morning drop-off. With the sun streaming in through the windows, catching on the hanging crystals and chimes, it felt like time didn't matter. Like it was standing still.

Because this?

This was perfect.

It was so perfect that Anders caught me sitting on the counter, my head tilted back, enjoying the shaft of sunlight streaming in from the second-floor window, in the quiet. I hadn't even heard him come back, and only realized he was there when someone pulled themselves up to sit on the counter beside me.

I said, "Butterscotch had the right idea."

He agreed. "In my next life, I'd like to be a bookstore cat. Sunlight and books and naps."

"I dunno, I think you could do that in this life."

Closing his eyes, he tilted his head back, and the sunlight caught in his fair hair. "I could if I liked naps."

I opened my eyes and gave him a look of disbelief. "You don't like *naps*? What's wrong with you? Who hurt you as a child?"

He snorted a laugh. "That will take a few hours to unpack." Then, he opened his minty eyes, and caught my gaze, and held it. "But I have the time, if you do."

Yes, I found myself wanting to say, because there were so many questions I still wanted to ask him, so many things I still wanted to know. I wanted to puzzle him out, not to try to find who his heroine was, but just *because*. The more I knew about him, the less he felt like a fictional character, an archetype turned flesh. There were so many little flaws about him, so many inconsistencies that didn't tie up in a nice bow.

And, for a second, as we sat on the counter together, I could trick myself into thinking that Rachel hadn't had anyone else in mind when she made him—that maybe, just maybe, he was made for me.

No, Elsy, I thought, pulling myself out of that dream. But it was getting harder and harder to do that, and I was thinking about his would-be heroine less and less.

I was being silly.

And I'd had enough heartbreak for a lifetime.

"With all the things I still need to see?" I asked, breaking the moment, and he pursed his lips, as if he was a little disappointed. "Perish the thought. You know, all this talk of naps has me wanting to take one," I said, sliding off the counter. "After I come back— back *down here*," I quickly clarified, "we can think about dinner? It's my last night, you know. It should be special."

He gave it a thought. "I think we can do that."

"Perfect." I felt terrible lying to him, but *no* I wasn't going to overthink the flicker of disappointment in his eyes as I climbed the spiral staircase two at a time, and disappeared into my loft. Once the door was closed, I locked it and waited long enough for him to think that I probably had gone to bed.

Then I did exactly what my teenage self would have been proud of—I crept over to the window, missing all the creaky floorboards, and climbed out of it and down the trellis.

GEMMA HAD SAID THAT JAKE WOULD BE AT THE DAFFODIL working on renovations with Junie and Will. So with Ruby still MIA, that's where I started. I'd have preferred not to start with Jake's side, but beggars couldn't be choosers. Besides, maybe Junie had made some progress with the haunted toilet.

"Hello? Junie? Will?" I called, stepping into the inn. "Jake?"

"Is that you, Elsy?" Junie called from somewhere downstairs. A moment later, she poked her head out of the dining room, paint splatter on her shirt, a smudge on her face. "Oh thank *god*, you're just in time."

That wasn't a good sign. "For . . . what?"

"Jake is trapped."

I stared at her. Blinked. "Trapped . . . ?"

"In the dining room. With a can of wood stain."

"Oh, good, I thought you were going to say with a candlestick," I joked. She rolled her eyes and grabbed me by the hand, and dragged me through the parlor to the doorway to the dining room, which had been painted a lovely sage color, a new crystalline chandelier installed that refracted rainbow colors across the room, and most of the floor was a warm dark wood stain. Except for one small patch in the middle of the room, where Jake stood.

Unable to escape.

Will stood at the edge of the dining room, shaking his head, his hands on his hips. "Bro, you said you were an island unto your-self but this is a bit far."

Jake threw up a middle finger. "Just help me out."

"Gimme a sec, we gotta find some leverage—oh, Elsy! Perfect timing," he added as Junie dragged me up to the doorway.

Jake groaned. "Oh no, please don't tell anyone."

I crossed my heart with my pinkie. "Not a word but . . . yikes, dude."

He hung his head.

We ended up using a long ladder to stretch over the entire din-ing room, from the parlor doorway to the kitchen, and propped either side up on a chair. Junie and I sat on one side, and Will held the other still as Jake climbed onto it and made his slow crawl over the wet stained floor toward escape. He climbed off on Will's side, and collapsed onto the floor.

Junie sighed, and held the ladder up as her boyfriend started to reel it back in slowly but surely, taking care to not scuff up the newly stained floorboards. "And here I thought wood stain spon-taneously combusting was the most of my worries, not a heartbro-ken Jake trapping himself in my dining room."

"Heartbroken?" I asked, suddenly inspecting my nails.

"Don't tell anyone, but Ruby—"

"*Shush!*" Jake cried from the parlor. "No one needs to know!"

"—asked for a break," she finished in a whisper, and gave me a knowing look. "You're probably the last to know, since Jake spent most of last night at Gail's asking everyone he could find what he did wrong."

"Sad that I missed that . . ."

"Yeah, where were you? I couldn't help but notice Anders was also missing . . ." She wiggled her eyebrows.

"Nothing happened," I told her.

"Mm-hmm, I don't kiss and tell, either, but if I did, I would nod once if he's a good kisser or twice if he's not."

I gave her a deadpan look, and I had half a mind to ignore her completely, but come to think of it, this might actually be a way into what I was here to ask her to begin with . . .

So I nodded. Once.

She threw up her hands in victory. "I knew it!" she cried, reaching the foyer on the first floor again, and spun back to face me. "Was there tongue? Did you get to second base? Does he really taste like old books and dust?"

I cleared my throat. That I *wasn't* going to answer. "I don't—"

"Old books and dust? You gotta be talking about Anders," said Will as he came in from the porch, where he'd deposited the ladder. His cap was on backward, paint smeared over him like a Rorschach painting.

From the parlor, Jake yelled, "Did you get a paper cut?"

"Did you hear something? I could've sworn I heard a dude *who painted himself into a corner.*"

Jake rolled over onto his stomach and pushed himself to his feet. "I technically painted myself into the middle of the room. Get it right." He left the parlor, and went through the foyer and hallway to get to us in the kitchen. "Thanks for helping . . . I just realized I don't know your name," he added to me.

I held out a hand. "Elsy."

"Elsy." He took my hand and shook it. His grip was strong, his fingers scarred from all the years working at the café. "Sorry you had to help rescue me. The stuff with Ruby's got me in a twist."

"Nah, I told you not to worry, man," Will replied, slapping his friend on the back.

"How can I not? Just out of the blue she . . ."

"Called it quits?" Junie offered, to Will's utter dismay.

"I don't get it!" Jake cried, throwing his hands in the air, and she patted his shoulder comfortingly. Junie suggested that everyone take a break and drink some fresh-made lemonade, and Will agreed that it was a good idea, and I wasn't about to pass up Junie's lemonade. No one did. With a glass of lemonade in him, he seemed to be a little less frustrated, and a little more morose.

"She just broke up with me," he said, shaking his head. "I dunno what I did."

"You had to have done something, bro," Will said, pouring himself another glass.

Junie rolled her eyes. "Hush, you don't know that."

"You wouldn't break up with me for no reason, Junebug, and neither would Ruby."

Jake said, "That's the thing! I can't think of anything." But then he fell quiet, and scratched his chin in thought. "Well . . . I guess that's not super true. We haven't really been able to see each other that much. She works the mornings, I work the nights. I've been trying to get new people trained on those shifts, but it's been slow going. But she's perfectly cool with that."

Junie and Will exchanged a look, as if they knew there was something wrong with the math problem and they weren't all that positive of the answer. I guessed I just found the limits of authorial intent. I took a long sip of my lemonade. It was so sweet, I felt the grains of sugar crunch between my teeth. Well, Junie and Will certainly weren't going to be of any help.

"Have you asked her about it?" I asked, dipping my proverbial toes in the water, hoping it wouldn't scald me.

"We haven't really had much time to talk," he admitted.

Junie said, "That might be the first step."

Or just asking her what's wrong, I thought, a little frustrated, and sipped on my lemonade again. "Maybe she feels like your life would be the same with or without her, so what is the point?"

He gave me a baffled look. "Why'd she think that? She's my everything."

"When was the last time you told her that?" I asked.

Jake frowned. He thought about it and then, very quietly, muttered, "Shit. *Shit*." He threw back the rest of his lemonade and pushed himself to his feet, kissing Junie on the cheek. "Thanks for the drink, I gotta go fix this. Wish me luck!"

Then he was out of the kitchen and running down the hall and out the door.

Junie and Will exchanged another look. "How did you know?" she finally asked, looking at me strangely.

The simple answer? The starlings this morning had given me a lot of time to think and realize that Ruby wasn't the one I needed to talk to.

The harder answer was one I didn't like to think about—because recently, I realized, in my effort to be fine, to be good, to be absolutely copacetic, I wished I had told my best friend how I really felt about the cabin week being canceled. How I felt about feeling left behind, and the world spinning on without me. It was silly, because in hindsight I knew she'd understand. When it came down to it, though I adored Liam, in an effort to be right for him, I hadn't let him in. Just like I hadn't let Pru in, either. I hadn't told her so many things, like how much I loved her, and how much I appreciated that she kept me grounded. And the longer I stayed in Eloraton, the more I missed her. I wished I could text her, reply to her big news. This was the longest we'd ever gone without talking in . . . as long as I could remember.

But I didn't know Junie and Will enough to say all of that—I mean, I knew them intrinsically. I knew what made them tick. But I didn't know them like I knew a mirror, like I knew Pru.

I gave a self-conscious laugh, rubbing the back of my neck. "I read way too many romance books, I think."

Junie shook her head, in awe. "You and Anders both—"

Will put a hand on her arm. "Babe, do you hear that?" he asked, and her eyes widened at the sound of a soft hiss coming from . . . the basement. He cursed under his breath, grabbing a hand towel and a plunger from the hallway bathroom, and darted for the basement door.

Junie gave a weary sigh. "Not again," she muttered, going to fetch the mop. "If you specialize in fixing inns as well as relationships, let us know? We might have a job for you."

"I know nothing about plumbing," I said tragically. "Or exorcisms. Maybe someone took a really big poop, so big it grew a consciousness and now haunts the plumbing? The terrible turducken in hot poo-suit of the great shittening."

Junie threw her head back in a laugh, and followed Will to go fight the haunted toilet of the Daffodil Inn. And I had to get back to the bookstore before Anders found me missing—again.

The sky was still clear as the afternoon grew later, and I began to worry that rain wouldn't be coming today at all. Well, at least I wouldn't be caught in it without an umbrella this time, which was the smallest of blessings. I wasn't sure I'd be able to scale the trellis in the rain, anyway. Sneaking around was demeaning, to be honest, especially since I hadn't climbed in or out of a window since I was a teenager, when Pru and I snuck into a midnight showing of *Twilight*.

Looking up the trellis, I took a deep breath, and started up the side. The vines were thick, disguising the latticework, so I guessed where to put my feet. I hoped there weren't snakes in the vines. Were there snakes up in New York?

I didn't remember.

Then, halfway up the trellis, I lost my footing.

With a scream, I slipped. I squeezed my eyes shut. This was going to hurt. This was going to hurt so—

Someone caught me.

Strong arms held me up and brought me close to an equally solid chest. The first thing I noticed was that he smelled nice—like oak and motor oil. I cracked open an eye.

A man with soot-black hair and eyes just as dark looked down at me. He had an eyebrow piercing, and a thick, short-trimmed black beard that stood out against his pale skin. He was tall, his leather jacket clinging to his broad shoulders, and it struck me just how enthralling he looked, because there was always something new to see. The piece of gray in his hair, the light brush of freckles across his cheeks, the helix in his left ear.

It was Garnet Rivers.

His smile was slow like molasses. "Good thing I caught ya."

I nodded, breathless, though whether it was from the fall or because he was just so freaking gorgeous, I wasn't sure.

Garnet Rivers—this was *the* Garnet Rivers. The man who rode off into the sunset with Bea. His jaw was sharp, his nose crooked from where it'd been broken in one too many bar fights. You could see the resemblance between him and Ruby; they were fraternal twins, after all. But if he was here, did that mean Bea was back in town too?

"You okay?" he asked, finally setting me on my feet.

I nodded again.

He laughed. It was a deep rumble in his chest. A shiver curled down my spine.

"Hello?" came the voice of Anders, having heard my scream, as he rounded the outside of his bookshop. "Is someone—oh." He froze in his footsteps, and studied the scene in front of him. There was something foreign in his face. Panic? Anger? It was strange. But as soon as it was there, it was gone again, and he schooled his face into that indifferent mask he always wore. "Garnet," he greeted. "I heard you might be home."

"My reputation precedes me." He held me tight as he gave Anders a once-over. "And who're you?"

"I own the bookstore," Anders replied.

"Ah." Garnet slid his lazy gaze to me, then back to him. "So I guess she's yours?"

He visibly went rigid. "She's staying in the loft. As a guest."

"Huh. What kind of guest uses the window?" he asked, and my cheeks flushed a deep shade of red. I wanted to tell Anders I could explain, but he wasn't even looking at me anymore.

"The kind who likes to climb trellises. But she can use the front door," he added, and then promptly turned on his heel and left.

No, wait, I can explain, I wanted to say, but what good would it do?

Garnet set me down finally. "He seems like a real piece of work," he replied, and he was right, but he really had no business talking. Because last I knew, Garnet Rivers had gone off on a road trip with Beatrice Everly, and now he was back—seemingly alone. Everyone knew at the end of *Return to Sender* that Bea and Garnet would be a happy for now because Bea was too smart to fall for Garnet forever, and Garnet loved his freedom too much to stay with Bea. But seeing Garnet back without her . . .

It was a complicated feeling. I'd hoped that they'd stay together, that Garnet would realize that Bea was the best he'd ever get, but everything about *Return to Sender* was about journeys, and paths not taken, and how you can walk with someone down a road for a little while and then pick a different path. It didn't make the time less worthy, but it did make it sad.

"You good?" Garnet asked.

I blinked, wrenching myself out of my thoughts. "Thanks for the catch," I said.

"I mean"—and he looked at me under those long, dark lashes, his eyes like pools of oil—"I could treat you to dinner as a thank-you . . ."

"Don't you mean I could treat you?"

"You're already a treat, sweetie."

I laughed—literally laughed aloud in his face. He looked very put off by it, but that was fine. I wasn't looking to start a love triangle with both the grumpiest man in town and everyone's worst mistake. That would've been entertaining, but it wasn't me. I patted him on the shoulder. "That's a good line. Save it for someone else, though."

His eyebrows furrowed in confusion, and I left him to it. I had some explaining to do to Anders, and I'd better do it sooner rather than later.

24

Sub Plots

ANDERS," I CALLED AS I flung open the front door to the bookstore. The bell above me chimed brightly. "Anders, I can expl—"

Suddenly, there was a rumble outside. At first it sounded like thunder, but it didn't fade. In fact, it sounded like it was coming *closer.* Out the bookshop window, a beat-up baby-blue Ford truck roared into a parking spot in front of the Roost, and the second Ruby slid out of the passenger seat, wet hair pulled up in a messy bun, still in her bathing suit top and damp high-rise jean shorts, Jake tore out of the café like a man on a mission. He'd probably staked himself out at a window booth and waited for her since he left the inn. The fact that he wasn't wearing a baseball cap meant that he was serious. That, and the bouquet of wildflowers he held.

I perked up, like a dog offered a bone.

This was it. The *moment.*

Don't mess this up, Jake, I prayed.

"C'mon, you can do it, buddy," I muttered under my breath as he presented her the bouquet of wildflowers. I couldn't hear what he said, but Ruby seemed surprised by the gift. He motioned with his head, and probably asked her to walk with him.

At first, she looked like she didn't want to, but then she caved and handed Maya the flowers. She followed Jake down the sidewalk, and turned the corner into an ivy-filled side street. I debated whether to leave the bookstore to follow them. No, I just had to hope that Jake did this thing properly.

And I had to find Anders.

He was busying himself toward the back of the bookstore with an end cap, where he tore down a display offering BRIGHT SUMMERY READS and built a new one promising THRILLING ADVENTURE. It was mostly dinosaur books. I watched him, chewing on my thumbnail. He was upset, I could tell because he wouldn't so much as look at me.

"I didn't *mean* to fall into Garnet's arms, if you're wondering." I said to him, but he didn't even turn around as he arranged Michael Crichton on the top shelf.

"It's not my business. I'm not your keeper."

"You would be a pretty hot chaperone, though."

His molten glare turned his minty eyes dark, and he rolled the new display books over to the endcap. At least he *looked* at me. That was a start. "The bookstore *does* have a front door, but if you prefer the window, who am I to argue?"

"I . . ." I stared at him. It clicked. "Oh my god, you're *jealous*."

He scoffed, turning away. "I'm not *jealous*."

"You are!"

"I don't care if you go off and do whatever you want with Garnet. It doesn't matter. He'll be gone by morning, anyway," he added with a sneer.

"Well, maybe I will!"

"Then go right ahead."

"Fine."

"Fine!"

"Fine—"

"No, it's not fine," he caved, whirling around to me. "Because just the thought of another person doing things with you. For you." And his voice dipped into a growl, his eyes darkening with the promise. "To you. It drives me crazy."

His confession made me suck in a breath. "But you could have already."

"Yes, but I want you to remember when I do." He took a deep breath, steeling himself. "I just don't want a one-night stand with you."

My eyes widened.

Oh.

"Then," I said, my voice quiet and shaky, afraid to ask, "what do you want?"

He came up to me, and bent a little so that he could look me in the eye—the same way he looked at me that night on the stairs—and he kissed me lightly on the lips. Softly. Gently. Like I was made of spun glass. So featherlight, and yet I felt it all the way to my toes.

"This," he whispered, a secret between us. "Repeatedly. Until we are so sick of each other—"

The front door flung open, and Maya came in like a storm. Anders and I jumped away from each other like we'd been burned. He quickly shoved his hands into his pockets, and I busied myself with the end cap.

Maya didn't suspect a thing.

"Girls' night!" she cried, inviting me to drinks over at the Roost. Her cheeks were sunburnt, her short black hair curling around her ears. She and Ruby must've had a great time at Stellar Lake. "You're in, right?"

"I . . ." I hesitated, glancing at Anders.

"Oh, come on! This might be your last night here! Celebrate it with us?" she asked, taking me by the arm.

Behind her, Anders mouthed, "Go," with a relinquishing nod, and returned to his endcap Michael Crichton display. He began to glue up tiny cutouts of *T. rexes* eating men on toilets across the top of the shelf.

"Sure," I told her.

"Excellent! Only girls, sorry," she added to Anders.

He put *Jurassic Park* face-out. "I'm hurt, Maya, I thought I was an honorary member?"

"Times they are a-changin'," Maya replied cryptically, and pulled me out of the bookstore and across the street to the bar. I glanced back one last time at the bookstore, and Anders was framed in the window, watching me go.

❮—❯

I WISH I COULD SAY THAT I WAS LOOKING FORWARD TO GIRLS' night, but my mind was still in the bookstore, staring into its owner's lovely green eyes. He *liked* me—he actually liked *me*. I didn't quite know how to feel. Elated? Nervous? Scared that he liked *me*? Happy that he did? I'd read such declarations a hundred times over, but none of them prepared me for it. He wasn't real, yet the butterflies in my stomach most definitely were.

Gemma and Junie were already set up at a table, drinking a beer and a mojito, and I wondered when I could return to the bookstore. They waved me and Maya over, and Maya was impressed that her sister had actually closed the shop early to join them for drinks.

"Once in a blue moon is fine," Gemma chided. "You make me sound like a workaholic."

"Just the busiest of bees," Maya replied, grinning, and her sister shoved her playfully in the arm.

Okay, I couldn't go back to the bookstore—I didn't want to miss *this*, either.

There had been a few girls' nights in the books: All of the heroines were best friends. Junie, and Gemma, and Ruby, and Bea, and Maya. I guessed I was taking Bea's spot, since she'd left town. But before she had, they had always gathered around the front round table in the bar, ordered an extra-large plate of onion rings slathered in cheese and chili, and sought assistance or camaraderie, or therapy, from their friends. It was a lot like my book club, I realized, and as the women all laughed and gibed each other with inside jokes, I found myself missing them. I wondered how they were faring without the Super Smutty Book Club readathon this year and my box of Riesling to get Matt through Janelle's Cock Count tally. (She made a mark every time the word "cock" was used. Last year, we got up to sixty-nine times. It was nice.)

"Bea said she wants to come home to visit soon," Junie said.

Gemma asked, "With or without Garnet?"

Maya knew that answer. "Without. Ruby said that her brother rolled back into town today, grabbed some clothes, and left for the city. Living that punk rock dream," she added dolefully, giving rocker horns. I took a large gulp of wine, because apparently I had the honor of seeing him for the two seconds he was back in town. Lucky me.

Junie rolled her eyes. "Bea's the best he'll ever get."

"But she can do better," Gemma replied.

I said, without thinking, "I think they were perfect for each other at the time. Happy, for a moment." When the women gave me a curious look, as to wonder how I knew about Bea, I lied. "Anders told me about her."

"Really? She left before he came to town," Junie said, frowning, "but he is really good at picking up on things. I feel like he always knows more than he's letting on."

"Ruby is convinced she knows him from somewhere—elementary school, maybe? Because he's so familiar." Maya sipped on her drink, and flagged Gail down to order some onion rings with chili and cheese.

Gemma agreed. "You know, I thought I was the only one who thought that. Where *is* Ruby, by the—oh." At the front of the bar, the door swung open and Ruby came in like a hurricane. "Never mind."

Ruby climbed up onto the barstool with a dramatic groan. "Oh my *god*, Jake just split me like a *tree*."

Gemma almost spewed her mojito, and Maya handed her a napkin. *"Ruby!"*

"It's true!" She drank a sip of Maya's rum and Coke, and crunched the ice between her teeth. "I haven't had sex that good in *years*."

I tried not to choke on the complimentary peanuts that were, very quickly, becoming hazardous to my health. "You don't say."

"I just don't get it," she went on, flagging Gail over to order herself a beer. "I love Jake, but he's never been very attentive, and suddenly he just *knew* what I was upset about. Like he was paying attention."

"Oh, Ruby, you know he was paying attention the entire time," Gemma said, finally recovering herself. "Weren't you just saying last week how he always set the timer for the coffeepot for your morning shifts? And he premade all the scones?"

She replied, "But that was for the café. I didn't think . . ." She shifted on her barstool. "I guess I didn't realize that it was mutual. That he missed our time alone together as much as I did."

"And everything is okay now?" I asked tentatively.

She turned her kohl-rimmed eyes to me and narrowed them. "No," she replied, and leaned toward me, "it's *better*. We're actually going to go on dates again, and he's planning a vacation—just the two of us! And oh my *god*, I have to tell you, the way he used his mouth—"

"Okay," Gemma interrupted loudly. "We're good. We don't need a play-by-play."

Ruby sucked in a breath through her teeth. "Ooh, your sex life that vanilla, Gemma?"

"It's perfectly acceptable," she replied quickly. "We don't really get to do . . . *it* . . . a lot, you know, with Lily."

Maya said, "Sis, you *can* say 'sex.' It's not a bad word."

Junie, who had been abnormally quiet as she texted someone on her phone (probably Will), agreed. "There's also plenty of other words you can use." Then, to Gemma's utter horror, she began to list them off on her fingers, "The horizontal tango, slamming the clam, schnoodlypooping, boning the graveyard, feeding the kitty, the ol' in and out—"

Gemma buried her face in her hands. "I hate all of you."

"—filling the creme doughnut, stuffing the taco, the forbidden polka—"

"We *get it on* perfectly fine, thank you."

"—skeet shooting, parallel parking, hot yoga, making whoopee—"

Ruby said, "Lust and thrust."

"Ooh, that's a good one."

"Spelunking," I added, and everyone murmured with a nod.

"Parking the Plymouth in the garage of love," Maya said with a wiggle of her eyebrows.

Gemma replied, looking like she was regretting ever leaving Sweeties today, "No one says that."

"Foxtrot Uniform Charlie Kilo," Ruby added. "Extreme flirting."

Gemma said, "I don't understand half of these."

Ruby tsked, shaking her head. "You're so boring, Gems. I bet you and Thomas cuddle for hours and talk about bees. Not a single safe word in sight."

"We're not kink-shaming at this table," Junie said in a matronly fashion.

Ruby put a hand on her chest. "I would *never*!" Then she grinned at Gemma and leaned over the table, a spark in her eyes. "I just want to give pointers."

I sat back with my drink, and listened to them, best friends chatting like it was any old day in the neighborhood—and for them, it was. The way they gave each other sideways looks, rolled their eyes, laughed, it reminded me of gossiping with the book club, and most importantly, Pru. I missed her.

I missed her so terribly, and I wished I could send her a text or a voicemail, and tell her how happy I was that she was finally engaged. Truly happy. Ridiculously happy. Because her story wasn't going to end like mine. Hers was going to be good and lasting.

The more distance I got from Liam, in the years that went by, I began to realize that I'd never really looked too far ahead when I was with him. I was always too obsessed with following wherever he led, making sure that he was happy, that he was loved, and I never thought to want anything in return. Coffee and bagels in the morning, or earplugs for a clock tower, or simple faith that I could do whatever I set my mind to.

It was refreshing, and nice, and sweet—to be given something so I didn't have to want it in the first place.

"Well." Gemma tilted her head in thought, boring her gaze into her half-drunk mojito. She shifted in her seat, a little uncomfortable with any talk of intimacy. It wasn't that she was against it, just that she was private about it all. "Thomas and I really never switch things up . . . I think he's just safe doing what he knows. You know him, he doesn't like variables."

"You never know until you try," Ruby pointed out. "Right, Maya?" she glanced over at her best friend, who was looking down the bar at something. Or, more aptly, some*one*. "Maya?"

In the back of the bar, near the TVs, Lyssa Greene sat with her dad, Frank, sharing chili-cheese fries and watching a wrestling match.

Maya jerked her gaze away quickly, like she'd been caught stealing something that wasn't hers. "Yes, absolutely. One hundred percent agree."

Ruby glanced down at Lyssa, then back at her best friend. "You know, you can go over and just talk to her."

"What? No, no no no," Maya refused. "I can't. Not after . . . I can't. I'm mortified that I told her that I liked her at all. She's my best friend—I mean, besides you, Ruby, but Ruby is *Ruby* and Lyssa is . . . like a moon you just want to be in the orbit of, and what if she thinks I was only friends in hopes of dating her someday? I feel sick to my stomach just thinking about it."

"Then *tell* her that," Ruby said, and Maya shook her head.

"But what if I do, and she still doesn't want to be friends?"

"So you'd rather leave all this in limbo?"

"It's not so bad," Maya said quietly.

No, I thought, sipping my wine. *It is awful.* A romance without an ending—without even a good beginning! Rachel Flowers would never just leave bread crumbs and forget about them.

"And anyway! We're not here to talk about the sorry state of my love—"

"It is, though," Junie interrupted, and began to pick at the label on her beer bottle. She'd peeled half the label away, so I suspected I knew the culprit of all the hot sauce labels. "It is bad to not know the ending. I mean, what if she's not around tomorrow?"

Ruby scowled. "Lyssa isn't going to *die*, Junie. You've been playing around with that haunted toilet too long," and in reply Junie groaned, reminded about her plumbing, and put her face in her hands.

At the head of the bar, Anders stepped in, and noticed me at the table. He gave the slightest nod before he took his usual seat at the very end, and ordered his burger.

"Okay, well, thanks, everyone, for your support but I choose to not talk to Lyssa." And to change the subject, Maya dug her wallet out of her back pocket and took out a few quarters. "I'm gonna go pick some tunes. It's too quiet in here."

Ruby finished the rest of Maya's drink and slid off her barstool. "I'm coming with. You pick the worst songs."

"I do *not*!"

"Sure, sure." She laughed, and together they disappeared toward the nearly defunct jukebox at the other end of the bar. I remembered that it always took Maya and Ruby *ages* to pick songs, because their taste in music was like oil and water.

Junie got us a flight of shots, and Gemma ordered another basket of onion rings, and when Ruby and Maya returned with their songs picked, they all asked me about my life, and whether I had kids or pets or a boyfriend, and we all fell into a cadence of conversation well into the night, and yet my mind kept going back to what Junie said about not knowing the ending, and how ironic that was in a story that didn't have an end.

25

Something Wicked This Way Comes

I STUMBLED INTO THE BOOKSTORE around ten, my head swimming with lemon drops and one too many stolen sips of mojitos and rum and Cokes. The girls made sure I was inside before they turned down the street and made their way home, singing Fleetwood Mac like I always imagined they would.

The bookstore was dark and cool, and the silence was so welcome after the heady noise of the bar. I stood there for a long moment, letting the ringing in my ears fade to the creaking quiet of the store. That was when I noticed that there was a light on in the back alcove with the couch. Anders was still awake?

I should've gone up the stairs and straight to bed, but my curiosity got the better of me.

He was stretched out on the threadbare couch, reading a book, a glass of whiskey in his hand that he swirled slowly, the ice clinking in the glass. In the soft light from the lamp behind him, he looked content as he turned the page, his once-sharp edges softer in the dark.

I wondered what kind of person he'd been before he came to Eloraton, why his ex left, and who Rachel Flowers had imagined for his future—was she stoic to match his silence, or were there laughter lines around her eyes like there were his? Did she carry herself with as much rigidness, or was she a little looser—did she dance? Or stand on the sidelines and watch? How did she like to be kissed? Did a shiver crawl up her spine when he purred her name into her ear?

Could it ever be me?

"Eileen," Anders said without looking up from his book, "if you keep undressing me with your eyes, I'm going to catch a cold."

Then, slowly, he turned his minty gaze up to look at me. He thought *I* was undressing *him*? That single look stripped me bare. A flash of heat crawled across my cheeks.

I replied, "Then you shouldn't be reading."

His eyebrows raised a fraction, amused. "Is that your thing?"

I wasn't sure if the alcohol that warmed my stomach and made my head buzzy was the cause of my bold sass, or if it was just his haughty attitude, but I marched over to the couch and fell onto the other side. "It helps if he's wearing a tweed coat."

He rolled his eyes. "Again with the tweed. No matter how many times you ask, the answer's the same."

"Pity. I guess you're not the kind of guy I'm looking for."

"Pity indeed," he replied, and returned to his book. "How was girls' night?"

"Oh, you know, we plotted world domination and discussed the best poisons to kill our husbands."

"You don't have a husband," he tsked.

"I almost did," I replied, half joking, but mostly not. His eyes flicked to my face, studying me. I took his glass and downed the rest of his whiskey. It burned all the way down. He gave me a disapproving look, and then poured himself another from the decanter on the coffee table.

"He was a fool, then," he said, "whoever he was."

"To marry me?"

"To not."

I smiled, despite myself. "He'd say differently."

"He doesn't matter. He let you go." Anders said it so simply, it felt like the truth.

My stomach burned, wanting nothing more than to lean over and kiss him again, and taste him, too, and breathe in the woodsy scent of his aftershave, and the smell of old books that clung to his clothes. And maybe he would've leaned in, too, and kissed me, if I hadn't said—

"I'm leaving soon, so even if you wanted more, if I wanted more, we . . ." I pursed my lips, and looked away. "What do we do?"

He inclined his head, and his silence spoke volumes. Finally he said, "Someone once told me that we can only take on as much as we can carry with us."

I curled my legs up under me, watching him in the low light. "Would you carry me with you?" And then, because I couldn't bear the weight of this conversation, I added, "Like in a satchel or . . . ?"

He laughed softly, probably made easier by the whiskey in his hand. "If you'll let me, I'll carry you here."

And then he picked up my hand, and kissed my palm, and placed it over his heart. And I felt his heartbeat under my fingers, bright and strong, and his skin was warm, and I couldn't imagine for a moment that this man could ever be fictional when he was so very *here*. He had blood, and bones, and a beating heart, and calluses on the tips of his fingers, and a curl that never quite left his forehead, and eyes that weren't quite green and weren't quite gray, but a bright mint that was quickly becoming my favorite color.

After a moment of feeling his pulse, I whispered, "I would like that."

Because he was right: sometimes people came into your life for brief moments, and changed you forever. I think he was my person.

And he didn't even exist. He came from the mind of an author I'd admired so much—who had changed my life with her books, so of course I would fall for a man she created. His backstory, his witty banter, his minty eyes, even the way he *smelled*.

I laid my head on his shoulder, and it was so comfortable. As rain began to patter on the windows, we talked about being a book critic, and how it was similar to being an English professor. We argued over the definition of literary classics, and the best condiment, and whether books were more aesthetically pleasing arranged by *color* or by title. Butterscotch found us halfway through and joined us, and by then Anders's body had settled into the weight of mine, as if welcoming it. He was warm, and we breathed in tandem, and it all felt so natural, so much so that I didn't realize I'd dozed off until I blinked awake again what felt like only a few minutes later.

We were still on the couch, but I was curled against his side, my head on his chest, while he was propped up against the arm of the couch, one arm behind me, the other holding open a book as he read. The lamplight was low, the fire out, and from the heaviness around my eyes, I knew I'd dozed off for longer than a few minutes.

Mortified, I started to sit up, but he gently tugged me back down.

"Go back to sleep," he said, and turned the page.

"I'm sorry—I didn't mean to doze off," I quickly said. "I'll go to bed—"

"You're fine," he interrupted gently, quieting my worry. Then he added, "You haven't started drooling yet."

"Oh, so I'm just free to sleep here until I start slobbering over your shirt?"

"Shh," he said, and guided my head back onto his chest. "Stop talking. I'm at a good part."

I glanced at the book, and by just a paragraph I knew what it was. "The dragon's about to find him."

He scowled down at me. "I let you sleep on me and *that* is how you repay me? With a spoiler for *The Hobbit*?"

"It's not a spoiler if you've read it before," I admonished.

"Semantics." He licked his thumb, and turned the page again. "Though, if I were Bilbo, I would've never gone on this awful trip."

"He didn't know how bad it'd be." I sank back against his chest. "Though, arguably, it turned out to be worth it in the end."

"Did it?"

I thought about my trip, driving out of Atlanta in agonizing slowness, hoping that Pru would call and tell me that she'd canceled her trip to Iceland, but by then she and Jasper were already halfway to the airport, bound for Reykjavík. I thought about all the miles up to the Hudson Valley when I wished the car would spring a leak, or lose a tire, excusing me from having to do this alone. All alone.

I wanted adventure, like my mom, but I always found excuses not to take them because I was afraid of getting hurt. Like Bilbo in *The Hobbit*, safe in the burrow of my home where no one but bookish villains and paper cuts could hurt me.

But I'd made it, and I'd gone on an adventure, and now I was here on the couch with a stranger, and my heart was fizzing in a way it hadn't in a long time. And while I didn't need to . . . I think I *wanted* to fall in love. Madly, truly, deeply. And that scared me the most because, like Bilbo discovered, the heartache was worth the adventure.

"I think so," I whispered into his shirt.

26

Pineapple

THE GOOD NEWS WAS my thirty-two-year-old body could absolutely still function after two nights (not in a row) of heavy drinking. The *bad* news was that my thirty-two-year-old body could not function *well*. Where I'd had a hangover the first time, this time I just *hurt*. Everywhere. As soon as the starlings started to sing their maiden call at the most god-awful hour on Wednesday morning, I wanted to find their nest and punt it across town. This morning they did, in fact, sound like chain saws, grating against my migraine like a serrated knife. At this point, I hated whatever tune they sang. It was incessant. Eternal. *Awful.* When I couldn't take it anymore around 10:00 a.m., I rolled out of bed and dragged myself into the tub for a quick shower. I thought it'd help.

It did not.

I didn't even remember how I got to bed. The last thing I remembered was . . . a lemon drop? No, the bookstore. Chatting with Anders. Falling asleep on his shoulder—oh my *god*. I wanted to die.

After I pulled my unruly hair into a bun and changed into a T-shirt and frayed shorts, I wandered down into the bookshop. There, Anders was dusting the shelves with eagle-eyed precision. He worked so hard to keep this place looking lovely, but there wasn't a lot of foot traffic, and most of the series didn't revolve around this store at all. It was just a footnote in most of the novels, a fun date place, a scene with some key dialogue and nothing more, but he kept it clean and tidy like it was his own even though it wasn't. There was something endearing about that, the way he was just so meticulous and caring. Every detail seen, every corner known.

It was so foreign to me, because I could barely recall the color of my desk in my office, or the color of pen I used to mark up essays. My head was full of useless things—the books I read, characters' favorite colors, lines that felt lyrical and significant and slid off my tongue like honey. I could recall my favorite page in *The Song of Achilles* by Madeline Miller, I could remember my favorite rhyme in Percy Shelley's catalog, my favorite thoughtful mediation in any bell hooks text. They were things that were selfish and insular. I cared for words with a reverence I rarely shared with anyone—how could you share them, anyway, when words were imagined things?

Perhaps that was why I never really thought to share any of it with Liam. Maybe if I had, we'd still be kissing each other good night, and sleeping with our backs turned, and waking up tangled in the sheets, but I was being too generous, and clinging to the parts of him I still loved. Which were getting smaller by the day. And the more I thought about it, the more I became convinced that eventually, as I tried to keep being the girl who had kissed him at midnight, I lost myself in the process. And lost what I really wanted—a partner, not someone I had to take care of. Liam was kind, but he rarely asked how I was. He gave great gifts, but never personal ones. We hiked together, and when I fell behind, he kept marching on. I used to think it was because he knew I'd catch up eventually, so he wasn't worried, but maybe it was because he didn't want to be bothered to slow down and take in the scenery together.

It was the first sign, or maybe the fifth, but I hadn't seen any of them.

The bell above the front door jingled, and the tall and scrawny outline of Thomas came in. He changed out his sunglasses for his regular ones, and waved to Anders.

"Thomas, this is a bit of a surprise," Anders greeted, retracting his duster and stashing it behind the counter. "What can I help with?"

"Bees," Thomas replied, going straight to the nature section on the far left wall. "I need something about *bees*. There's about to be a mutiny, Anders, and I can't have that on my watch." He plucked a book off the shelf and flipped through it, and then put it back. Then did the same to another one. "Hmm."

Anders glanced up, and found me standing on the second-floor balcony, at the rail. His eyes held mine, bright pools of minty herb, like fresh grass on a hot summer day. He wasn't surprised to see me. He must've heard me come out of the loft and walk across the second floor—the boards were a bit creaky, and I was too lost in my own head to notice. Not surprised, then, but . . . relieved? Like he had been waiting all morning. I remembered how he smelled last night, like cedarwood and black tea, and how warm I felt against him.

"Sleep well?" he mouthed.

I mouthed back, "Tylenol?"

He nudged his head toward the counter and nodded. "And

coffee." Be still my heart. I couldn't come down the stairs fast enough. As I passed him by the nature section, he said, "Good morning, Elsy."

"Morning, Anders," I greeted. "Thomas."

"Morning," Thomas said absently, and plucked another book from the shelf. "No, nothing here, either . . ."

While Anders helped Thomas try to find a book on beehive mutinies, I dug around behind the counter for the Tylenol. It was in one of the cluttered drawers, under a bunch of half-legible bookmarks. I shook out two, and shot them back with a gulp of lukewarm coffee from the Grumpy Possum Café. Anders had probably gotten it for me much earlier, but it'd sat out by the till for at least an hour, so it tasted a bit stale. Still, it hit the spot, and it was the thought that counted.

Maybe after the Tylenol and caffeine, my head would stop throbbing.

"Is that all?" Anders asked, noticing how Thomas kept glancing over at the self-help section. More importantly, the shelf about relationships. "I'm sure I could help you find whatever you're looking for."

"No, no, this is good . . ." he replied, and then flicked his gaze to me. "I'll just get this," he added. "I don't want to bother you too much."

"Fine. Elsy, since you're at the counter." He motioned to Thomas's book.

"You trust me to do money?"

"I suppose it's a hard ask for someone haunting the checkout counter's only barstool."

Nursing my coffee, I glanced around and—no, he was right. I was sitting on the only stool behind the counter, and I was a little afraid if I moved too much or stood too long, my stomach would have a very hard time staying, uh, *settled*. "Consider me a wizard with money. A magician of pennies. A—a—"

"Witch of one-dollar bills?" Thomas suggested, and I gave him a finger gun.

"You get it."

Anders rolled his eyes, and took up his duster again to pursue another thin layer of dust on a shelf in the religion section.

Thomas made sure he was far enough out of earshot before he leaned toward me and said, "Actually, I'm sort of here about a . . . *problem*."

Oh *no*. I froze as soon as I grabbed his book to scan it. "A what?"

He shifted nervously. "Jake said you helped him yesterday with, erm, with Ruby. That you're really good at giving pointers. So I just thought . . ."

My stomach twisted—and it wasn't from the hangover. "Is something wrong?"

"Wrong? Oh no, no no no," he quickly replied, shaking his head. "Gemma and I are good! I was just . . ." He glanced nervously in the direction Anders had gone, and said in an even quieter voice, "I figured, since you're just passing through, you can help me. I know Anders. Asking him about this might be a bit, erm, awkward."

And asking me *wasn't*? I wasn't sure I liked where this conversation was going. "Uh . . ."

He swallowed thickly, darting his eyes about again. There was a thin line of nervous sweat on his upper lip. Oh, poor guy. He never was good under pressure.

"Whatever it is, Thomas," I said sincerely, "I can help—"

"Sex," he blurted.

I didn't think I heard properly. "I'm sorry . . . ?"

"Okay, so"—and he pulled his fingers through his hair, and the sweat on his hands accidentally made it stand up like a mad scientist—"last night Gemma came home, and Lily was already in bed, and so Gemma wanted us to . . . try something new. I'm not good at new. I'm good at routine. I'm good at history. I'm good at things that are constant—stars, for instance. Bees, when they're not trying to mutiny their queen. Schedules and orders and . . . I guess what I'm saying is, I wasn't prepared. I froze up. I know this sounds very strange, and this is not a conversation strangers have, I realize, but—I'd rather have it with you than Anders."

Because I was going to leave, and he'd have to carry on his friendship with Anders—which I'm sure most people could do. But Thomas? He was awkward enough as it was. He didn't really mess with things that didn't have an equation to them. And I was an outlier.

So, in a somewhat sweet way, him choosing me for this plight made sense.

It didn't make me any less mortified, because *he* didn't know that I knew way, *way* more about his and Gemma's romantic life than anyone else in town, which was just really ironic.

And tragic.

For me.

"So," he asked, pleadingly like a lost puppy, "can you help?"

How could I say no, respectfully? If anyone knew how to help him, it was me. I held up a finger, and slipped away for a moment into the self-help and relationships section. It took a few scans, but I plucked one out from one of the bottom shelves.

"Not that one," said Anders, materializing at my side.

I shrieked, and then punched him in the arm. "Stop doing that!"

"Ow, what did I do?" he asked, rubbing his arm.

"Snuck up on me! *Again!*" I hissed.

He rolled his eyes, and reached over my shoulder for another book. He was so close, I could smell his aftershave, and the woodsy paper smell that lingered on his clothes. "This one is better."

I took it. On the cover was just a zipper running all the way down. Admittedly, it did have the better cover than the one I'd picked out, which was of a man in a hideous spray tan, grinning at the camera. I looked at both of them. "Is this a personal suggestion?"

He gave a shrug. "Pineapple."

Which was a very well-known safe word. I chewed on the inside of my cheek, trying to hide a grin. "I'll take it on good faith, then." Then I returned to Thomas, and handed him Anders's suggestion. He bought both the bee book, and the sex one, acting a little more confident than he had before.

"Jake was right," Thomas said with a grin. "You're good. Thanks, Elsy—see you, Anders!" He raised his hand in goodbye just in time for me to notice that the bookshop owner had been close enough for the tail end of our conversation.

I winced as the door closed.

Anders came up to lean against the counter, closing his dusting wand again. "So," he said.

"So . . ."

"'Jake was right'?" he quoted.

I feigned innocence. "I have no idea what he was talking about."

"Eileen."

Uh-oh. He used my full name. I twisted the lock of hair around my finger nervously, chewing on my bottom lip. "Okay, look . . . I might have caused some . . . *ripples*."

He didn't look all that surprised. "Go on."

"So I went about trying to fix them." I glanced out the door after Thomas, and then back at Anders. "I'm sorry I didn't tell you."

He didn't say anything for a long moment, tapping the dust wand in his open palm. But then he set it down and said, "I knew about Ruby and Jake."

My eyes widened.

"And that you tried to fix it."

"I did!" I clarified. "I *did* fix it."

His lips twitched into a ghost of a smile. "All right, you did."

"And you aren't mad?"

In reply, he leaned against the counter beside me. "At first? I was a little annoyed. You left my bookstore *unattended*, after all, and you're a horrible liar."

I winced.

"But you keep surprising me."

"Like a plot twist," I said, tongue-in-cheek.

He took my hand in his, conflict furrowing his brows. "Yes, well, speaking of plot twists—"

27

Good Bones

THE BELL ABOVE THE door jingled again. "I've got good news!" Frank crowed as he flung the door open and stepped inside. His combat boots made hard *thunk*s on the hardwood floor, leaving a trail of mud behind him.

Anders's words caught in his throat. He closed his mouth in frustration, and turned toward our new guest. "Frank, hello."

"Anders, Anders, I'm a genius," he said, slapping him on the back so hard he almost knocked Anders's glasses off.

Anders pushed them back up his nose. "Was that ever in question?"

Frank grinned, showing the gap in his front two teeth. "Maybe tell my daughter that." Then he spun to me and threw up his arms. "She'll be ready *tomorrow* morning!"

"Your daughter?" I asked, perplexed.

"No, your car! I thought it'd be ready *today*, but heh, who's not a day off once in a while? After searching everywhere, I finally found a carburetor I can work with," he said, and gave Anders a wink. "She'll be ready to send you on your way in the morning."

My eyes widened. "O-oh."

Sweetpea was almost fixed? I didn't know what to think. To be honest, I'd sort of forgotten that I was stranded here at all, and not staying of my own accord. And tomorrow, I'd finally get to go to the cabin. Start my vacation—

Leave.

The word felt heavy on my chest.

If my true feelings about the news reflected on my face, Frank didn't notice. He told me he'd bring the car around tomorrow morning, with some extra Hotties in the back seat (wink, wink), and I'd be on my way. Then, just as quickly as he'd come, he left— like a tornado. Upending everything in one fell swoop.

When he was gone, Anders and I stood awkwardly for a long moment.

"Well," he began, breaking the silence, as he put his hands into his knife-pleated trousers. Honestly, I missed the jeans a little bit, and how good he looked in them. The better he dressed, the more it felt like armor. "Seems like—"

"Excuse me," I muttered, quickly leaving from behind the counter, and fled out the front door before he could say anything else.

My chest felt tight and squirming, like worms had burrowed their way inside my rib cage. The sun was hot and almost directly overhead as I made my way down the sidewalk. I curled my fingers into fists.

I was acting foolishly. I couldn't stay here forever—I didn't want to—but I didn't want to go yet, either. I'd fixed the mess I'd made with Ruby and Jake, but there were too many questions that I wanted *answered*—too many plot threads left open. What would happen to Maya and Lyssa? Would the inn ever open again? What was the ending that Rachel Flowers had in her head for this town, these people? Who did she write for Anders? I still couldn't find her (though I hadn't really been looking all that hard, if I was being honest). So much of the real world was built on half-finished stories and bitter endings, I didn't want to leave this one without knowing.

My feet carried me down the sidewalk, my head spinning, and I didn't stop until familiar voices shouting dragged me out of my thoughts. I'd walked all the way to the Daffodil Inn, halfway across to the clock tower in the center of town, when Junie burst out the front door.

She yelled behind her, "Sometimes good bones aren't enough!" As she descended the stairs, she kicked a decorative white rock on the path, and it skittered into the yard.

Then she noticed me, and—without knowing what else to do— raised her hand in greeting. "Erm, hello."

I echoed the wave. "Hi." I crossed the street and leaned against the white picket fence. The tower in the square tolled noon.

After the buzzing had receded, and the town quieted with the echoes of the bells, Junie said, "There's water everywhere. Puddles of it coming from the toilet. We don't understand it—we've checked it *all*." She made a noise of frustration, and then took a deep breath, and collected herself. "Sorry, I know you don't want to hear this."

"It's all right. For what it's worth, I didn't mean to eavesdrop."

"Can hardly call it eavesdropping when I'm yelling."

I shrugged, and looked down at my sneakers. "Frank came by the bookshop. Apparently, he'll have my car fixed by tomorrow."

Junie perked. "Oh, that's fantastic!"

"Yeah . . ."

She studied me for a brief moment, before guessing, "You aren't excited?"

"I am—of course I am. But I . . . it sounds silly," I admitted, and she bumped her shoulder against mine.

"Nonsense. What's up?"

"I . . . don't think I want to go?" I said, half question, half statement. The sentence felt like a precious secret, one that I hadn't really dared to even think about yet. "But I know I have to," I added quickly. "I have friends who are probably already missing me, and I have a job to get back to, and a life but . . . it's so tempting to just get lost here, and stay forever."

She tilted her head. "Then why don't you?"

"I mean, my friends and my career and—and *everything.*"

She shrugged. "Well, I did. I stopped through here, and I just never left."

"Yeah, but you're—" *Not real.* I bit my lip. Looked away. "Braver than me."

"Oh, no. I'm not brave. Chaotic, sure. But brave? I don't think that's what you should call people who jump before they look. I think I was running," she decided, "and maybe I just made excuses to stay. Maybe I thought I could have a happily ever after in an old, decrepit inn with my best friend." She turned her gaze to the beautiful Victorian house, with its pastel paint and crisp white latticework. "And maybe it's all just catching up to me now. Maybe it's time to find a new dream." She took a deep breath, and then pushed herself up off the fence. "One that isn't leaky."

No, wait, I wanted to say. I wanted to take her by the wrist and pull her back to face me and look her in her eyes. *You're Junie Bray. You have a happy ending sewn into this story. If yours doesn't come true, if you can't be happy, what chance is there for the rest of us?*

"Anyway," she went on, putting her hands in the back pockets of her paint-splattered shorts, "I won't fault you if you stay, is what

I'm saying. Follow your heart. Even if it leads you wrong, will you really regret it?"

I wasn't sure.

"Do you?" I asked.

She smiled knowingly. "Not one second. Either way," she added, "see you at the café tomorrow morning? As a going-away breakfast?"

"I'd like that."

"Good. See you at nine sharp!" As she waved goodbye and retreated down the garden path, back to the house that was supposed to be her happily ever after, I wasn't sure of the answer to the question she posed—*would* I regret it?

My heart had already led me astray once with Liam, but no one had ever posed the question of whether I *regretted* him.

I pushed myself off the fence, and wandered back toward the bookshop. I regretted things, sure. Words said, words not. Words I could have—should have—said differently. But did I regret those years as a whole? The years we held hands, and he led while I lost myself in book after book, dreaming of the stories we'd make together, and never did?

I . . . didn't know.

I looked up at the clear blue sky, remembering the first full day I was here, when Eloraton was still stuck, still stagnant. The clouds had gathered like a murmuration of starlings, quick and loud, bringing with them scheduled rain. Though, it hadn't rained in the early afternoon for a few days now as the town began to change, and slowly start to move again. The clouds passed, and the sun was hot, and the sound of bugs and rustling leaves and open air filled my ears.

It *was* my fault everything was moving. That there was no rain at noon. That Ruby and Jake had broken up—and gotten back together. That Gemma wanted to explore her and Thomas's relationship.

That Junie began to think her home—her happy ending—wasn't the Daffodil Inn.

For everything I stitched together, something else just seemed to fall apart. Had I missed something? Done something wrong?

And then there was Anders . . .

If this was a book, I'd know the information I'd need to sew this story together. I'd know the hints Rachel Flowers dropped. I'd see the foreshadowing. I'd predict the ending, and see it through.

I was good at reading between the lines, at interpreting the yellow wallpaper.

But this . . . this felt like being in the middle of a story, between one sentence and the next, not sure where to go.

Here, I was little more than a woman who'd come in from out of town—someone not quite a friend, but not a stranger, either. A visitor, here for a moment, just passing through.

A secondary character.

And as I passed shop after shop, street after street, watching the town breathe, and shift, I began to think . . . I could just stay here. I might have been an errant puzzle piece belonging to a different puzzle altogether, but even lost puzzle pieces were put back in the box when you were done with them. I could just be another secondary character, a blurred figure in the background of someone else's story.

That didn't sound too bad.

When I was on the block with the bookshop, I noticed that Anders's Buick was gone. I stared at the parking spot where it used to be, the only thing left was a huge oil stain from where it'd leaked there for months. Behind me, the door to the bookshop opened, the bell jingling, and Anders stepped out.

I asked, "What happened to your car?"

"It was bound for the junk heap anyway. It barely ran."

"But it did run," I said, and I frowned, remembering Frank's strange wink to him when he came into the bookshop earlier. "You didn't—you didn't give your car to Frank to fix mine, did you?"

"You have people waiting out there for you," he replied, and that was all the answer I needed.

"I didn't *ask* you to—"

"But I did. And I got quite a few cases of hot sauce in return." He put his hands into his jeans pockets. He'd changed out of his business casual into a Henley and sneakers, his fair hair disheveled in that infuriatingly artful way.

"But—but . . . what about your car?" I asked, my voice breaking.

"It's fine. I never used it anyway, and it was ugly."

It was, but . . . my bottom lip wobbled. I blinked tears out of my eyes.

Anders gave a start. "You're—why are you crying?"

"I . . . it's . . . why are you so thoughtful? You shouldn't be so *thoughtful*," I croaked, because I hadn't expected this at all. I'd gone through so much of my life filling wants and needs for other people, I hadn't . . . I didn't . . .

It was thoughtful, and I was thankful.

And confused.

I sank down onto the curb, pushing the tears out of my eyes, and he came to sit down beside me.

"Hey," he said gently, "you're allowed to be cared for, too. You don't have to do everything alone."

I set my jaw, and picked at my fingernails. "I was engaged once," I began, as if that explained my outburst.

"I know," he replied.

"We were perfect together, I thought. He was lovely, and talented, and good-looking. Whenever we would go out on our anniversaries—all of them, three-month, sixth-month, a year, four years—people would tell me how lucky I was. Except I'd always be the one to make the reservations. I'd always be the one to get both of our cards. I'd buy the Christmas presents. I'd book the vacations . . ."

He could have asked me why I thought he'd care about this history, but I felt it was important—a part of me that was the kind of broken that couldn't be fixed with a cup of coffee or a few pretty words. But he was silent, and attentive, and he listened.

"He broke up with me a week before the wedding. Moved out that night. Because I'd done everything else for the wedding, I had to call everyone, *both* of our families, and help them get some money back on their plane tickets and hotels. And the thing is—I thought it was me. I thought it was my fault, that I was defective or something, and I couldn't deal with it so I just—I just stopped. My wedding dress is still hanging up in my closet, my wedding shoes in their box. I just froze everything. I put it on ice. Me included," I added. "Maybe that's why I read romance novels so often, because they're pretty stories clearly shelved in fiction, and that's where I wanted to be. And then I came here, to a fictional town, and I think . . . in the back of my mind I just . . . I knew I wanted to stay. I wanted to stay in a world where the plots are predictable and the endings are happy. Somewhere just as frozen as I am."

Quietly, he reached down and took my hand, and flipped it over, palm facing up. "My mother once told me that you can tell a lot about someone by their hands." Gently, he traced the long crease that ran from the middle of my palm to just beneath my first finger. "She never meant mystically—lifelines or luck lines or love lines. But by the scars, and the calluses, and the efficacy."

"Then mine must look pretty lazy," I commented, but my heart had started to race. He held my hand so tenderly, brushing his thumb across my palm so lightly I repressed a shiver.

He shook his head. "Your hands are gentle and cold. You use them a lot, but no one ever holds them to keep them warm."

Then he raised my fingertips to his lips, and kissed them.

"Fictional men can't hold them," he added, and my heart lodged in my throat. "There's someone for you. Someone real."

"Did my love line tell you that?"

The edge of his mouth twitched. "Call it wishful thinking." He sat back on the curb, and we watched a couple walk down the street on the other side, and disappear into Lyssa's vibrant garden shop. "But what I can't guess, is of all the book series in the world, why this one? Why do you love these stories so much?"

I studied the town square, wishing I could soak in everything—every color, ever sound, and heartbeat. "It's silly."

"I doubt it," he replied.

So, I took a deep breath—and I told him. "I think . . . it's because of the way anything feels possible. The soft tenacity of the narrator, the cozy familiarity. Like when the author told the story, she was telling it to *me*. Only me. It's like she wanted me to come to Eloraton, and she took me by the hand, and we went through story after story, and I didn't have to worry about if there would be a happy ending. I knew there would be."

Year after year after year, books that ferried me through heartbreak and hope and those terrible nights after Liam left. They were words that tucked me into bed at night when I was alone, they were words that played the soundtrack of my heartbreak, the what-ifs, the second-guesses, the nights I sat alone and wondered, *Why not me?* Those books were like arms I fell into, armor that protected me from the world when life got too hard.

"It was a love that I knew wouldn't fail me. It was safe. It was a comfort when I was heartbroken and yearning to feel something *good*, because I couldn't imagine it on my own." I leaned forward a little, blinking back tears. "I think that's why I love these books so much. Because even when I felt broken, Rachel Flowers was always there to show me that there were still happy endings to be found . . . even if they weren't mine."

He said quietly, "She was magic that way."

"Yes, she was."

We sat there for a long moment, watching the couple on the green kiss, and split a sandwich. I dried my eyes and felt a little better.

After a while he asked, "Do you want to go on a walk with me?"

"Is it one to remember?" I replied, unable to hide a clever grin.

He groaned at the pun, and then pushed himself to his feet. "You have to ruin everything, don't you?"

"*I* thought it was a good joke." I stood with him, brushing the dirt off my jean shorts.

"Of course you do. Come on," he said, and nodded toward the far side of the town square. I wasn't sure where he was leading me, until I saw the trailhead at the edge of town—

QUIXOTIC FALLS—1.2 MILES

I stopped once I read it. He didn't notice until he was already a few feet into the trail, and then he paused, and turned back to me. I remembered how adamant he was about not going to the waterfall, how it wouldn't fix my life—but of course it wouldn't. And even if that was why I wanted to go in the beginning . . .

I just wanted to see it now.

"Well?" He outstretched his hand to me, and it reminded me so much of the way Liam used to as well, our fingers intertwined, leading me up around mountains, down rolling hills—and my heart twisted. But, I must not have learned, because I took his hand, expecting him to pull me up the trail, but he just held it and said, "I'll follow. I think you know the way."

Those words settled against my anxious heart like a salve, so powerful that even though I only knew the way to the waterfall through pages in a book, I set off up the trail with him at my side.

The day grew warmer as the sun made its slow progress across the sky, and the leaves somehow seemed to turn greener. The trail was shorter than I imagined—or maybe time just flew by as we walked in silence, listening to the hum of the woods—but finally we came to the top, where a wooden sign read QUIXOTIC FALLS, with an arrow pointing left, over a rickety wooden bridge.

He let me go first, and I didn't think anything of it until he hesitated on the other side.

"Everything all right?" I asked. He shifted nervously on his feet, eyeing the wooden bridge. "Haven't you done this before?"

"No," he replied truthfully. "Never really had a . . . *reason* . . . to come up here."

I inclined my head. "Why now?"

He took a hesitant step, and then another, white-knuckling the rope handrails as he made his way over. His eyes were glued to the ground. "Because I didn't want to come alone."

"You could've asked Maya, or Junie, or—"

He scowled. "They've all *been* here before."

"So?"

"So"—another nervous step, then another—"it was a waste of their time."

"*Or*," I supposed, leaning against the side of the bridge on the other side, making it sway a little, much to his distress, "you didn't want to go with someone who'd already seen it before. But that can't be right."

"Why would you think that?"

"Because you seem like a guy who doesn't care much for firsts."

He reached the other side and bent down to me. He said, low and serious, "I care very much about firsts, sweetheart. Also"—and he slapped my hand off the bridge rope—"you're the worst." Then he stalked ahead of me, and I bit the inside of my cheek to keep from grinning.

I liked his grumpiness, I finally admitted to myself, almost as much as I liked the view of him from behind.

It was a short walk from the bridge to the waterfall, and I heard it long before I actually saw it, a loud, roaring sound that reverberated like rolling thunder. We passed under an outcropping of rock, and then there it was on the other side.

Quixotic Falls.

It took my breath away.

The waterfall was so tall, I had to crane my neck to see the top of it. Shimmers of a rainbow reflected in the mist and sunlight, and the air was cool and damp. It felt good in the humidity of the afternoon. I closed my eyes, and enjoyed the mist that clung to my skin, coagulating into droplets. We walked along the underside of it, and the sunlight hit the falling water like it was glimmers of glass. The tunnel between the rock face and the waterfall was smooth and rounded from thousands of years of erosion. Vines crawled across the rocks—morning glories and four o'clocks and honeysuckles. The waterfall poured down into a small watering hole that then slowly wormed its way into a larger river down the mountain. I knew this place would feel whimsical. Surrounding the swimming hole, the bright pink heather and stark white yarrow mixed with coneflowers and black-eyed Susans.

"I wish Pru could see this place." I reached out and ran a hand under the waterfall. It was sharply cool, like sticking my hand into a bucket of ice. Remembering all of the books, all of the days I hid inside pages, trying to find some sort of happily ever after when reality refused.

"The water's colder than I thought," I said.

He stepped up beside me and reached his hand into the waterfall, too, at first to test the pressure and the coldness, and then laced his fingers through mine. "It feels nice," he remarked, though I suspected he didn't just mean the water.

My throat stung. My gaze shifted to his profile, as he looked up at the towering waterfall. "Yes," I agreed in a small, unsure voice, the warmth of his hand in stark contrast with the water, "it does."

He turned his face toward me. He leaned closer—or was that me leaning closer? He concentrated on my lips, so close now I breathed in the scent of his aftershave. We retracted our hands from the waterfall, our fingers still laced together.

"I thought you didn't want me to kiss at the waterfall?" I asked. The roar of the water was so loud, it drowned everything else out in a rush of white noise. Everything but me, and him.

"No, no, I didn't," he replied, his words hot against my lips.

I eased back then, because nothing good could come from this. Nothing at all. He had a heroine out there somewhere, a happy ending who would come waltzing into town and steal his heart, and I did not have the strength to suffer that again. Not a second time. "Well," I said, letting go of his hand as I turned away, "perhaps we shouldn't—"

He grabbed my wrist and spun me back, and pulled me tight against him. His peridot eyes were dark, almost the color of pebbles at the bottom of a river. "Perhaps I just didn't want anyone else to kiss you."

I didn't give him the chance, because I grabbed him by the front of the shirt and pulled myself up onto my tiptoes, and crushed my mouth against his first.

28

Don't Go Chasing Waterfalls

H E TASTED LIKE MINTS and black tea.

It felt like he was waiting for my mouth to find his. For a second he was surprised, but then he held me tighter against him and melted into the moment. And he kissed—oh, *fuck*, he kissed like he made it his mission to read kissing books every day of his life. It was gentle at first, questioning, until my fingers curled up into his hair and he took that as a yes. Because it was. My mouth parted, and he tilted my head back and deepened the kiss. My ears rang with the sound of the waterfall. It was thundering, but so was my heart, and I wasn't sure which was louder.

When we finally came up for air, I gasped.

"I never get tired of kissing you," I murmured, tugging at the collar of his Henley.

"I could say the same," he whispered, his pupils wide, blotting out the minty green completely. His chest rose and fell quickly, his breath hot against my mouth. "Though I could do so much more."

"Then do it," I whispered, and pushed him backward.

He fell through the waterfall into the pool on the other side, and I followed. I gasped as I hit the icy water, gooseflesh prickling up my skin. He came back to the surface with a gasp, and pushed his hair out of his face.

"How dare y—"

I wrapped my arms around his shoulders and drew myself up to kiss him again. The contrast of his warm hands on my body in the cold water made me shiver.

We made ripples in the water.

His hands slipped down to my waist, his mouth on the side of my neck as he kissed me there, then lower at my collarbone, the base of my throat. His teeth skimmed my skin as he carried me over to the bank of the plunge pool, and pushed me onto a patch of aster and grass, his hands feeling up my thighs. I curled my fingers into his hair, and brought his head back up to mine, and kissed his mouth again.

I didn't like the taste of black tea, but I fucking loved the taste of him, and when I bit his lip, I loved the sound of his moan, too.

"Fuck, Elsy," he growled, looking down at me, framed in the asters, "go a little slower."

I smiled against his mouth. "Am I too fast for you?"

"Yes," he replied, lifting himself up off me, his hands planted on either side of my head, and nibbled on my earlobe before he whispered into my ear. "I want to savor this."

The barely restrained want in his voice made my heart slam against my chest. He wanted to savor this, but clearly he sounded like he wanted me as soon as possible. There was something so infuriatingly sexy about that patience, so much so that it just made me want him more. His hands traveled down my torso as he nibbled my neck again, breathing into my hair.

"I want to savor you," he murmured, burying his face in my

hair, "sweetheart." The way he growled it sent my heart skipping like a stone.

"I thought you didn't like sweet things," I said, trying to keep control of myself, though all I wanted to do was drown myself in his touch.

His lips pressed against my ear. "I like you." His hands worked to unbutton my shorts and slide them off. Water droplets slid to the ends of his hair, glistening in the afternoon sunlight that shone through the trees.

My chest felt like it was full of butterflies. I pushed him off me, and rolled, so that I straddled his hips. My hair fell down over my shoulders, framing my face in curtains of curly copper. "You can't mean that."

"I do." He looked up at me with eyes like molten emeralds. "How do you want me to prove it?"

I traced the line of his jaw. "Do you have any ideas?"

"I could serenade you with words," he supplied, taking my hand and kissing the palm of it, never letting his gaze leave mine. "If I was a poet, I could liken love to your eyes. If I was a gardener, I could plant a kiss on all the places you despise on yourself." Slowly, he pulled me down on top of him, pressed against him. "If I was a writer, I could write epics to your lovely lips." He kissed me again, and his words were hot against my mouth. "If I was a painter, I could explore every bend and curve so when my eyes failed me, I would paint you by memory." His hands slid along the length of my sides, dusting softly against my thighs.

Then he wrapped his arm around me and rolled me onto my back, his mouth on mine, and gently took off my shirt, and I unclasped my bra, and he planted a kiss on my left breast, and then my right.

"Lovely," he murmured, and flicked his tongue against my nipple. My fingers buried into the heather beneath me.

I sucked in a breath. He felt my chest rise, and it only made him plant his hands on my waist and do it again, so I couldn't squirm away.

And like a painter, he explored every part of my body. Like a writer, he muttered manifestos to my elbows, my knees, my ankles. Like a gardener, he planted kisses on my stomach and under my chin, in all the places that the world told me I shouldn't love. And if there was love in my eyes, he was a poet, too.

I'd distanced myself from love for so long, told myself that I didn't need it, didn't *want* it, that I wasn't so sure I knew what love looked like anymore outside of a book. I'd grown to care about this man, somehow, over the last few days. I'd gotten used to his wry charm, and his sarcasm, and I found myself looking for his shadow at the bar, and the bookstore. And I knew that whenever I thought of that road that wound up to Charm Bridge, a heavy stone sank in my stomach.

No, I wouldn't think about that now, because he was here, and he was with me. No one else but me.

As his hands traveled down, I caught them. "Wait," I whispered, and swallowed the trepidation growing in my chest. "Wait, we should probably . . ."

"Right," he added. He reached over to his damp jeans and pulled out his wallet, taking a condom from where the bills were supposed to be. It was an act that was supposed to be for his heroine, for the woman Rachel Flowers wrote for him.

Not me. This scene, these kisses, they weren't meant for me. They were for—

"I'm sorry if it isn't your preference," he said, beginning to tear the wrapper open, but I stayed his hands. He huffed, "It's hard to find different kinds in El—"

"No, no, that's not what . . ." I hesitated. Bit my lip hard. I looked up to the waterfall and said, "Are you sure you want to do this with me?"

His gaze softened. "What kind of question is that, sweetheart?"

Shit. I squeezed my eyes closed. "I just mean . . . I'm not supposed to be here. And you have someone else—someone you're supposed to—"

"Eileen," he interrupted, his voice barely restrained, and my gaze focused on him again, and his handsome face. He pushed a lock of hair off my forehead, and then kissed it. "I want to do this with you. Do you want to with me?"

Oh, what kind of question was that? I studied him, his soft hair and his angular face and his lovely mint eyes.

I nodded, feeling the butterflies in my chest grow wilder. "More than anything."

His expression turned serious. "Good," he rumbled. With his free hand, he slid his finger from my neck, down between my breasts. He tilted his head to the side, as if debating something in his head. "But how badly . . . ?" His fingers slipped down beneath my underwear, and he stroked me gently with one finger, then two.

I stifled a gasp. *Oh.*

"I didn't hear you. I guess not badly enough . . ."

He began to pull away, when I grabbed his hand and forced it to stay still. "Don't you dare stop."

His eyebrows jerked up. "Is that a request?"

"A demand."

"Bossy little thing," he murmured, and obliged. He stroked me with his long fingers, working me agonizingly slowly.

"Faster," I said.

So obviously he didn't.

"It isn't a race, sweetheart," he admonished with a tsk, and then that awful mouth of his twisted into a smirk, and he lowered it onto my skin, and kissed the place between my breasts. "Because I want to know how long you'll last."

The realization dawned on me with a rush as he moved against my clit still so slowly. "You are the *worst*—"

"Am I?" He went even slower.

"Anders—"

"I can do worse," he said, and as he stroked me, it felt like my entire body was inching closer and closer to bursting into flames. "I can make you come undone piece by piece. I can fuck you until you can only see stars and me. Now be quiet," he said, and sank himself lower against me, his lips trailing down my stomach, "and let me make use of this mouth of mine."

I curled my hands around the flowers, and felt the earth shiver as he spoke in the language of pleasure with his tongue. I died a little in those wildflowers, surrounded by the rush of water and damp moss and sunlight, and felt for the first time in my life—

That I didn't want to skip to the end, I didn't want to reach for the past. Now was enough.

And when we were done, and spent, and he lay on the heather beside me and traced the freckles from my shoulders to my collarbones, I said, "I thought it'd be bigger."

He raised an inquiring eyebrow.

"The waterfall," I clarified, motioning back to the titular Quixotic Falls. "I thought it'd be bigger."

He laughed, and pulled me close, the smell of wildflowers heady and sweet, and kissed me again.

29

Plumb Luck

EVENTUALLY, WE DRIED OFF and put on our clothes, and made our way down from the waterfall.

And eventually, we returned to the bookstore. We ate dinner in his apartment, and shared a bottle of wine, and when he walked me back to the loft that evening, we somehow found our way into bed together, too. The sex was even better a second time—though maybe that was because we were in a *bed* rather than on some weeds in nature, or maybe it was because we were finding a rhythm with each other, exploring each other's bodies, noting what made the other gasp, what made us groan.

And, after, like a romance novel, I fell asleep in his arms, and I couldn't remember the last time I'd ever felt so alive.

Sadly, the starlings were loud the next morning, singing that almost-familiar song. I think I would've recognized it then, if I'd given it any more thought, but the sunlight was too bright, and it was warm, and the hour was much, *much* too early. Anders had fallen asleep with his arms around me, and now he groaned with his face burrowed into my hair, my back against his chest.

"I forgot about the *birds*," he bemoaned, and pushed his face into my shoulder.

I yawned. "We can eat them later."

He snorted, and with a sigh uncurled his arms from my middle. I turned over to look at him. His hair was a mess, his eyes sleepy. I could stare at him for hours. I might have, honestly, if he hadn't been staring at me, too.

"You're beautiful," he murmured.

I blushed, and turned my face into my pillow so he couldn't see. "Stop it, it's too early."

"Fine, you're hideous, then."

I barked a laugh. "Much better." The bed was so warm, and comfortable, I could stay there forever. Except—

My car would be ready today. The realization was like a stone in my stomach.

He began to turn to get up, when I grabbed him by the arm.

"Can we stay like this a little while longer?" I asked quietly, and then—so he wouldn't see the real reason—I lied, "You're so warm. And I'm comfortable."

He shifted a little in the bed beside me, and for a moment I thought he was going to leave, but he just readjusted his arm, and nuzzled his face into my hair. "For a little while," he agreed.

I closed my eyes, trying to lie to myself that this was fine. That the relief I felt was normal for anyone who didn't want to get up in the mornings. That my wanting to stay here, beside him, forever, was just . . . a symptom of Eloraton, and not my own traitorous heart. I would miss so much of him, but most of all the way he smelled, like black tea and cedarwood and old, forgotten books, things that only book characters could really smell like. And because of that, he also smelled like memories. The good, sunlight-faded kind, the only sound the soft turn of the page.

"She wrote you so perfectly," I whispered against his collarbone, his fingers combing through my hair.

He froze. "What?"

"It's okay, I know. This was supposed to be your book," I said, looking up into his face, and his minty eyes widened in surprise. Like he really thought I wouldn't find out. I was an *English professor*. I knew foreshadowing. Occam's razor. Chekhov's gun. I've played the game Clue. Read "The Yellow Wallpaper." "Your unfinished happily ever after."

"It's not my story, Eileen."

Of course it is, I thought. *You just don't see it.* I doubted main characters ever realized they were in their own story until it began, and his had yet to. He'd meet the heroine Rachel Flowers picked out for him, and he'd fall in love with her—could it be me?

Every romance needed a happy ending, after all. It was a rule.

"I could stay," I decided. "I don't have to go." Then, quieter, "I don't want to."

"Eileen . . ." Something unreadable flickered through his eyes. No, it wasn't unreadable. I knew that expression. It was the same kind of look I'd seen before, when I'd told Liam that I loved him, and then again the look on his face in the barn, under that ridiculous antler chandelier, that he wanted something different.

"I could work at the bookshop," I went on. "Find an apartment. I could—"

Suddenly, he swung his legs over the side of the bed and pushed himself to his feet. "I'm sorry," he said as he put on his jeans, slipped on his shirt.

My heart dropped into my toes. I crawled up onto my knees, wrapping the duvet around me. "It'd be that bad?"

"No, that's not—I . . . I'm sorry," he repeated, but it wasn't an answer. I needed an *answer*.

"Anders. Anders, *talk* to me."

"I—I have to go." He put on his shoes as he hopped to the door, in such a fluster to leave he almost forgot to close it behind him. His footsteps faded away, the floorboards creaking as he descended the stairs to the first floor. I waited for the back door to open—which it did—and shut again, and the telltale sound of the lock clicking, before I curled my knees up to my chest and buried my face in them.

"I just want to stay," I muttered to the empty loft, but the only answer was silence.

A FEW HOURS LATER, I FINALLY CRAWLED MY WAY OUT OF BED, and took a hot shower, and packed everything into my weekender. I kept waiting for Frank to pull up with Sweetpea, running as good as new, and hand off the keys.

I got myself the corner booth at the Grumpy Possum and ordered the strongest coffee they served and a Honey Surprise, but Jake said they were all out of honey—something about the mutiny, he sighed—so I ordered a muffin instead. I couldn't read anything else on the menu, anyway.

Jake took extra-good care of me—I *assumed* because he thought I worked magic on his relationship. I just sort of wished I could've helped Gemma and Junie, too. Especially Junie. Leaving the inn in disrepair felt . . . consequential.

And Maya, oh, *Maya*. I wished I could just shove her and Lyssa into a room, and tell them to kiss it out. Lyssa loved her, too, I was sure of it. Didn't she?

Lost in thought, I didn't notice Maya until she slid into the booth across from me. "Penny for your thoughts?"

I glanced up. "Anders said I needed to start charging more."

She laughed. "Inflation gets you every time. So, today's the day."

"Today's the day," I echoed. Thanks to Anders's Buick, may it rest in pieces.

"Do you think you have room in the trunk for me?" she joked.

"Wanna go in my stead?"

Maya frowned. "Then stay, if you wanna stay."

"I can't."

"Why?"

Because Anders didn't want me to. Because, if I thought about it for two seconds, I *couldn't*. Not responsibly, anyway. But what would I really leave, if I did? A job I half hated? Friends who, for the most part, lived five hundred miles away? Pru, who was moving on with her life, going to the next phase, leaving me behind? I'd checked my phone countless times to see if the text ever went through, and it never did. I couldn't even consult her, so I picked at my muffin.

"Wow, what's with the long face? Are you *that* sad Gemma figured out how to stop the bee mutiny?" Ruby asked, sliding into the booth beside Maya, flipping up her sunglasses. She was dressed in paint-splotched shorts and a shirt that read, in big red letters, HONKERS. She gave me a once-over. "You'll get wrinkles if you keep frowning like that."

I asked, surprised, "The bees aren't mutinying anymore?"

"Nope," Ruby confirmed.

Maya added, "Apparently they just really didn't like all the rain." And it hadn't been raining as much since I arrived. I guess I had inadvertently changed that, too, but . . . that wasn't such a bad thing. Then she told Ruby, "She's leaving today."

Ruby whistled. "So it's a bon voyage breakfast? That sucks. If I knew, I would've made you a going-away present."

"Rubes, you suck at arts and crafts."

"It would've been store-bought," she amended, and Maya rolled her eyes. "I've got so much time now that Jake and I are figuring things out. He even asked for morning shift, and we're taking the *entire weekend* off." She waved to her boyfriend across the café, one finger down at a time, smiling. Then she said under her breath, "I'm going to ride him raw."

I almost spewed my coffee, and Maya pushed a few napkins toward me.

Ruby waved at someone who came in, and both Gemma and Junie slid into the booth with us.

Gemma put her purse on the hook on the corner of the table. "Sorry we're a little late," she supplied. She had on her Sweeties uniform, her wavy hair pinned back with bobby pins. It wasn't hard to tell that she was positively glowing. "I got a late start this morning, and Lily found her new obsession."

"A late start," Maya said to Ruby, wiggling her eyebrows.

I grinned. "Did those books help Thomas study up?"

Gemma plucked the menu from behind the napkin holder and dutifully ignored us. "Lily thinks she wants to be a wildlife vet now."

Junie asked, after flagging Jake over to order a round of coffees, "I thought she was into tardigrades?"

"That was last year. This year it's something that you'll really love, Jake," she added as he came over with four mugs, and filled them with coffee. He stood, rapt, waiting for the answer. Gemma finally revealed: "Possums."

Jake groaned, and walked away.

Gemma went on, "Did you know they have opposable thumbs?"

"Yes," Ruby deadpanned. The look in her eyes was almost like she was reliving wartimes.

"*And* that they can swim up to *fifteen feet* underwater without coming up for breath? Lily was telling me about a story where a baby possum came up through a *toilet*."

"That's frightening," I said grimly.

"Oh, I've got a better one. One time . . ." And Ruby began to recount her and Jake's first run-in with the grumpy possum of the titular café. I'd read this story a thousand times, so my mind began to wander.

Out the window, Anders left his shop to take his morning stroll, and met up with Lily and Thomas coming out of Sweeties, and I wished I didn't know how solid his chest was, or how warm and gentle his hands, or how he tasted—but I did. And I only had myself to blame.

Whoever coveted a book boyfriend was a fool.

"Well, hopefully by the next time you come, the bed-and-breakfast will be open," Maya said, "so you don't have to stay in a place that smells like dusty old books."

"*If* she ever leaves," Ruby pointed out cryptically.

"I did tell her she could stay," Junie added.

"Don't curse her like that." Maya scowled. "People rarely leave. It's one of those things—like the Hotel California. And not in a good way."

Ruby nodded. "Bea's even coming back."

That would be nice, to meet Bea, too. In interviews, Rachel always said she felt most like Beatrice Everly. She wrote herself the most in her.

I couldn't imagine why Bea would leave Eloraton to begin with, because I'd been searching for a way to stay. Every morning was bright and sunny, the honey taffy always sweet, the burgers at

Gail's always burnt, the smell of freshly cut grass and honeysuckle in the wind like a familiar perfume. I couldn't imagine anywhere more perfect. Even sitting in a café named after a certain famed rodent—

I slammed down my mostly empty coffee mug.

Oh my *god*.

That was it.

"The possum," I blurted.

The girls looked at me like I'd grown another head.

"What?" Maya asked.

"This place is named after one, yeah," Ruby said.

"No, no, possums can swim up to fifteen feet without needing air."

Gemma nodded, trying to understand. "Yes, I just said that. Lily is obsessed—"

"I know! That's it. That's *it*," I repeated, more to myself than to them. "Rachel Flowers *did* leave threads. We just had to find them!"

It made sense. It made total sense, but none of them understood what the heck I was going on about. It didn't matter. I was on a roll.

I could fix one last thing before I left, tie up one last loose end.

"Junie, come on," I said, climbing to my feet in the booth and then hopping out of it. I grabbed her by the arm, and pulled her to stand, "we need to go see a ghost about a toilet."

～

THE DAFFODIL INN WAS VIBRATING WITH PEOPLE. EVERYONE was all-hands-on-deck the moment I told Junie my revelation. And when I did, it was like something clicked in her mind, and she immediately called Will, who came over with every handyman he knew, and a tiny woman who was the town's pest control.

We *scoured* the plumbing.

The toilets upstairs. The kitchen sinks. Wherever there was a hiccup, a strange change in water pressure, we'd follow the line down, and if my guess was correct then the nest would be—

"There," Will said, pointing behind the haunted toilet.

The pest wrangler held up a hacksaw, and with a solemn nod she stepped toward the wall and sawed it open.

At first, there was no sign of an infestation—and then there was a hiss.

The pest control woman gave a triumphant, "A-*ha*!" and reached into the dark, haunted abyss with a gloved hand, like she was reaching into an oven full of molten lava. It took a moment, but when she pulled her hand back out, she had hold of something. A chunky possum with a missing eye and singed whiskers.

No one said anything for a long moment, and then Junie turned to Ruby, and put her hand on her shoulder and said in a grave, slightly broken voice, "We've found your possum, Ruby."

"And it's a girl!" the pest control woman cried, because there were at least three baby possums clinging to the big one for dear life. She turned to Ruby and added, "Mazel tov!"

Indeed.

With the possum brood found and put (safely) into a cage to be transported to their new home, Maya and a few of Will's contractor friends patched up the back of the haunted toilet with minimal argument from Junie. Though that might've been because she was still shocked that the ordeal was over. The plumbing was fixed. She went around to each toilet and faucet twice, and tested each one, until she was satisfied, and by the time she'd finished her second round and returned to the foyer, the hole in the haunted toilet had been patched, and Will was waiting for her at the front door, grinning ear to ear.

"It's done," she muttered with that far-off battle-scarred look in her eyes. "It's done?"

Will took her face gently, and pressed their foreheads together. "Yeah, babe, it's done."

"It's done," she repeated, a little flicker of life in her voice. Of hope.

"It's done," he repeated with a smile.

A laugh bubbled up from her throat. "It's done!" she cried, and kissed him fiercely on the mouth. Maya and I looked away to give them a little privacy, but Ruby watched and nodded, like she was appraising a diamond.

"Nice," she murmured, thumbs up.

Junie and Will broke away from their kiss, and he sank down on one knee. She smiled so wide she couldn't help it. "You've done this already, babe. I already have the ring."

He brought her hand to his lips and kissed the engagement ring there. "Let me ask again?"

"You already know my answer," she said in a laugh filled with love.

"That was a lifetime ago, and I want to be sure."

She took his face in her hands. "That my answer didn't change?"

He smiled, a little hesitantly. "Did it?"

"Of course not, silly goose," she replied, and kissed him again. "I'll say yes again and again and again. And I don't want to wait anymore. Let's have a wedding—tomorrow."

"Tomorrow?" Will laughed. "That's so soon."

"So? Everyone we love is already here. Why are we even waiting?"

In reply, he picked her up and spun her around, and kissed her fiercely on the mouth. "I can't hardly wait, Junebug."

I felt my stomach twist, my heart burn. Was this what it looked like, true enduring love? Because it was something that I couldn't describe, something that I had never felt—not once—in my life. And I wanted to. So, so badly.

We decided to give Will and Junie some privacy after a harrowing few hours, and the possums needed to be relocated back toward the café. We weren't quite sure *exactly* where to put them yet, but Ruby said that she had some ideas.

After all, the café was named after the possum.

Then she bade me goodbye, and hurried back toward the café to tell Jake the good news. I stood on the sidewalk, vibrating with excitement, because I'd done it. Junie and Will were going to be okay—they could keep their dream, live their happily ever after.

What was a love story without a perfect ending, anyway?

And now there would be a wedding. I couldn't help but smile. The actual *wedding*. The one that had been alluded to for four books. The one I never thought I'd ever read.

That wedding. The wedding Eloraton was waiting for.

The wedding at the end of it all.

And just when I thought things couldn't get any better, Lyssa Greene met me on the sidewalk and held up the keys to my Pinto. There was a strange look in her eyes, one I couldn't figure out. At least, not until she said—

"Can I ask you a question? About leaving? Because I think I'm in love."

30

Lyssa Greene Is Not Okay

I STARED AT HER. "IN love with . . ."

She nervously tugged on her long vibrant red braid, and muttered a name under her breath.

I leaned closer. "Who?"

"Maya."

Of course she loved Maya, that wasn't a question, but . . . "What does that have to do with me leaving?" I asked.

She shifted nervously on her feet. "Because you love Anders, and you're leaving, and I just want to know *how*? How can you do it?"

I went through all the excuses in my head, everything I could think of to say—but nothing seemed good enough. And knowing Lyssa, she wouldn't believe any of them, anyway. She had a knack for sussing out lies, and it was one of the (many) things Maya loved about her.

I chewed on the inside of my cheek. "I wouldn't say *love* exactly, but . . . how do you know?"

She gave me a level look. "The entire *town* knows at this point. You're like peas and carrots."

A small smile flickered across my mouth. "I guess so. Let's walk?" I suggested. "Around the clock tower? One last lap before I go," I added, and she caved and followed me into the shade of the tower. The afternoon had grown pink and gold as the sun bobbed above the trees. "So . . . the simple answer is—I don't want to. But if I stay here, then I'll never see my friends again. I'll never see Pru again," I said, realizing it myself as I did. "I'll never hear her voice or watch terrible Hallmark movies on the couch with a box of wine. I won't be at her wedding or . . . anything."

We wouldn't read books together anymore, or talk about Quixotic Falls, or roll our eyes at how popular the series got after the author died, because people loved to love something that was no longer there.

And that was it. I knew what I had to do, why Anders walked away—there was only one ending here. And it wasn't mine. We ended our walk at the bench I'd sat on the first day I was here, when Anders found me and held an umbrella over my head as the rain dried up. Now, the sky was clear and the air smelled like dry summer, and it was strange how fast things changed.

"I can't stay," I said, finally. "No matter how much I want to."

Lyssa sat quietly on the bench beside me for a long time. This was the first real conversation we'd had since I arrived in Eloraton, and I hated that it was. She took a deep breath, absently picking at her cuticles.

After a while, she asked, "But aren't you scared that he might be the one? And if you leave him you'll leave every good thing behind, too?"

"Yeah."

"And still, you . . ."

"Yeah," I admitted.

"*How?*"

That was a good question, and one I didn't know the answer to, because I couldn't predict the future or how I would miss him when I took the only road in and the only road out of Eloraton, so I told her exactly that. "I don't know. What's stopping you from telling the person you love that you love them? Taking a chance?"

"Only *everything*. What if Maya and I don't work out? What if her sister and my dad get into a condiment feud? What if we have to pick sides? What if—" She stopped herself, and took a deep breath. "Anyway, thank you." Lyssa took my keys out of her pocket, where she'd stashed them, and held them out to me. I took them, and they felt heavier than I remembered.

"I'm sorry I couldn't be more help," I said.

"Pru must mean a lot to you," she inferred.

"She does, and we left on kind of bad terms," I admitted. "She hasn't heard from me in a few days, so I'm sure she's worried—I'm sure the whole book club is." I hoped Pru chalked up her unanswered text to me having spotty reception. I hoped she wasn't waiting for my response—she was off in Iceland, after all, climbing glaciers and floating in hot springs. I'd text her as soon as I got reception, I promised myself. It was all I *could* do, as I pushed myself to my feet, and wondered if I should say goodbye to Anders—and *how* I could say goodbye to Anders.

A part of me wondered if I should just get in my car and go. I would just be a chapter in his life, anyway, perhaps not even that. But it was a good chapter. A lovely paragraph. A blissful mention.

She stood and dusted off her skirt to leave.

"You know," I said thoughtfully, as I remembered the way Anders kissed my shoulder in the morning light, the way his fingers fit in mine, the sun lingering in his white-blond curls, "it's okay to not know how something is going to work out. If I've learned one thing about being here, it's that it's worth taking the chance even if it's the wrong one. *You're* worth that chance. And so am I."

She smiled. "Thank you. Dad parked your car in front of the bookstore. It runs as right as rain. Safe travels," she added, and left for her garden store again.

I twirled the keys around in my hand, watching Eloraton, committing every bit of it to memory. The buildings. The the way the streetlights popped on one after the other like dominos. The soft whisper of summer wind through the trees. And when I was satisfied, I pocketed my keys.

There was one last place I needed to visit before I left.

31

Statues and Limitations

I STEPPED THROUGH THE PERGOLA, and down the shadowy alley to the courtyard. The soft trickle of the fountain rebounded off the brick buildings, and a starling trilled in one of the trees. In my pocket, my phone vibrated. I took it out.

There was another text from Prudence—How's the trip?

And then a third—Hello???

So there *was* reception here. But why? The deeper I went into the alleyway, sure enough the half a bar turned into a full bar, then two.

My phone vibrated twice more as a text and an email came in. The email was from my dean, asking me when I was coming back to campus because she needed someone to fill in for an adjunct professor in Summer II sessions, and the text—

Well, there were actually a lot of them.

First one from Olivia, then Ben, then three from Aditi, and a few Ron Swanson GIFs from Matt. I decided to let them all come in before I tried to decipher what was from whom. At least I knew my friends were worried about me—though, of course they were, they were my friends. And, from a cursory glance, I knew that Pru had told them I'd taken the trip alone.

Why didn't Anders tell me I'd get a signal here?

I texted Pru first—

Hi, I'm alive! Sorry for worrying you. <3 And CONGRATULATIONS!!! I am so, so happy for you both. Can't wait to hear the details.

The message went, and I waited for her to respond as I made my way toward the fountain. The forgotten courtyard looked peaceful in the late afternoon. The shadows from the trees were long, painting everything a lovely shade of gold, speckled with flares of awakening fireflies as they drifted across the tall grass.

And if Anders had only come to town after Bea left, after the last book in the series, and this courtyard with it . . . they had to be connected somehow, right? The statues half-buried in the four o'clock felt more than a little important now. Were all the statues of Anders? As I pulled the vines off them, some of the faces were still strangers to me. Again and again, repeated with slightly different variations and then discarded, like the sculptor couldn't quite get any of them right. Some of them had scratched-out names on their palms, or behind their ears, but I could only make out one—

A. S.

Those initials. The same from Anders' chess club T-shirt. A was his first name. Anderson. S was . . . Smith? No, Rachel Flowers would never.

I traced the stoic brow of one of the half-buried statues of Anders, when my phone pinged loudly. It startled me out of my thoughts, and I quickly checked the screen. It was the book club chat.

You owe me a drink, Janelle texted. I lost ten years of my life worrying!!

Matt texted, WE THOUGHT U WERE DEAD.

Aditi added, I read a true crime story where they found BODIES in OIL BARRELS. It was in New Hampshire but that's close right??

I found myself smiling as Olivia chastised Aditi over geography, and Janelle asked if I'd heard the news.

I did!! I texted. I'm so happy for her.

ABOUT. DAMN. TIME, Janelle agreed. And you're okay? Pru told us . . . are you AT the cabin?

No, I replied truthfully, but figured the rest of it might've been a little more unbelievable, so I told them the simple bit: my car broke down in a small town, and I'd been waiting for it to get fixed ever since.

Cute town?? Olivia asked.

Then Benji, sweet and attentive Benji, texted, What's the name of the town? Do you need a ride?

Right, because he lived in New York City. I winced. No, I texted back. And I can't remember the name of it—I'm fine! The bookstore owner here rented me the loft above his shop. I'll text y'all when I get to the cabin. It won't be the same without everyone. <3

Next year, Janelle swore, and I liked the sound of that.

I sat against the fountain, and tilted my head all the way back to look at the stars. The sky was beginning to clot again with rain clouds, though it was becoming a normal sight for me. It must've been the slowly changing rainstorms blowing in for the evening. I knew I should leave before the rain started. So I grabbed my purse and opened it up to put my phone into the front pocket, when I noticed that the book inside had a title on the spine again.

DAFFODIL DAYDREAMS

My heart leapt into my throat. I scrambled to take it out. The cover was there again, too, no longer a blur, and when I opened it up—

The words, all of them, they were there. The dog-eared pages, the coffee stains, all of it. I buzzed through the pages, the sound filling my soul with happiness, until it rested on the dedication page.

To A. S.

Thunder rumbled overhead, and a raindrop fell onto my cheek, another onto my nose. Before I came to Eloraton, Anders said that every day was the same. A storm blew in at twelve, and then one in the late afternoon. Gail always burnt her burgers, and the taffy was always sweet, and the inn was always in a constant state of restoration—

As though the author had left midsentence.

Because she had, and who else would want to guard it?

The looks he gave the townsfolk when he thought they didn't notice, the way he knew everything about them, his patience with Lily. How he'd come in only after the last book, having no connections with anyone, no roots, and yet he felt so at home. How he'd come to the town and hadn't left—not once—even though he had a sister who wanted him to visit. His soft asides about the author, the way he looked at her signature when he opened my novels, like one ghost finding another.

It was right there. It was all right there and I couldn't *see* it.

I ran out of the courtyard, my heart pounding. It couldn't be him—it *couldn't*. He would have told me, right?

My sneaker caught on the curb, and I stumbled out of the alley. The rain was coming down harder now, drenching the town. It hadn't rained in the afternoon in a few days. Not since things began to move again. Not since I had accidentally jolted Eloraton out of its perfect little time capsule.

I knew now why he wanted to keep everything the way it was. Why he didn't want ripples.

Everything was just the way she had left it. It was perfect, still, in its own little garden.

Then I'd come, and I ruined it while thinking that I was helping, and the worst part was—I *understood*. Because my wedding dress was still hanging in its bag in my closet, my wedding shoes in their box. I still had my registry saved on my phone, I kept a save-the-date postcard in my underwear drawer, so everything would stay exactly the way it was, exactly the way Liam left it—when I was still happy.

Anders stood at the counter, like he had every afternoon since I first came to town, his head propped up on his hand, reading another romance. He looked so at home here in the bookstore that it had tricked me for days. I thought he looked at home here because that was how Rachel wrote him—because he belonged.

But I was wrong.

His fiancée hadn't been his *ex*, his fiancée was . . . she was . . .

The bell above the door jingled, and he glanced up in surprise. "I . . . I thought you were gone."

"I just realized," I gasped, trying to catch my breath. The coldness of the bookstore, coupled with my wet clothes, gave me a chill. "I never asked for your last name."

Understanding flickered through his green eyes. He closed his book, and pushed himself up straight. "Ah," he murmured, frowning. "Sinclair," he said, as if he knew the consequences would break the spell. He curled his hands into fists as if steeling himself for the revelation. "Anderson Sinclair."

I already knew, but hearing his name from his lips made it real. I never could figure out who he was in this town because he wasn't anyone—no, he was in Rachel's real story. He had been part of her life, her happy ending—cut short.

"You're . . . the person she dedicated all of her books to. She was your fiancée."

"She was," he said, "once upon a time."

32

The Last Manuscript

"WHY DIDN'T YOU TELL me?" I asked.

He rubbed the back of his neck. "Because . . ." And he went quiet, as if trying to find the right words as he stared down at the books in his hand. "I liked that you didn't see me just as someone whose fiancée died. You saw *me*."

But that wasn't true. Not in the least. I studied him, wondering what else he had omitted, what he hadn't said. Rain ran down the sides of my face, and dripped off my clothes. I must have looked like I had that first night—a drowned cat coming in from the storm. It would have been poetic, a perfect circle, if I didn't feel so utterly tricked. "I only see the parts you let me," I said, shaking my head. "I should go—"

He blurted. "My favorite color is blue."

"*What?*"

"My favorite animal is a platypus. The only time I've ever ridden a horse, it bucked me off and I got a scar right here to prove it." He pointed to the scar on his upper lip. "I went to NYU for undergrad, and then Columbia for grad school. I wanted to be as far away from my parents as possible."

"Those are just facts," I said. "I could probably *google* you for those."

So he asked, imploringly, "Then what do you want to know?"

Everything, and that was dangerous because I was leaving, and the more I learned about him the harder it would be to let him go. But . . . I looked down at the book in my hands, and then back at him.

"Can you tell me about her?" I asked, curiosity getting the better of my judgment. The less I knew about her, the better, but I couldn't shake her ghost from my thoughts. "I mean . . . I know her but . . . but I don't."

He nodded, closed his romance novel. "We were neighbors as kids. We went to the same middle school, the same high school. I started dating her two weeks before prom. I never imagined she'd say yes to a pimply, scrawny kid like me," he began, and when he spoke about her, he put reverence in every word, like to savor her memory he also savored her words. "She made me feel like a better person by just being around her. Whenever she got angry, she got this little wrinkle between her brows, and her feet were ticklish, and she laughed at every dad joke." The remnants of a smile crossed his mouth, and I didn't think he noticed, too lost in his memories.

I studied that half-forgotten smile. It was bittersweet. Heartsick. "You miss her."

And he would never stop missing her, because that was what loss was in the end—breaking of a piece off yourself that you'd never get back. There were people who tried to fill that hole with work, and there were people like me who tried to fill it with stories; people filled it with whatever could fit.

"Of course I do. Sometimes, here, I can almost trick myself into thinking she's here, too." He shook his head, at a loss for words. "But, none of it is any excuse, and I'm sorry."

I swallowed the knot in my throat. "I think I understand. You just wanted to live in her story."

"Next best thing to making one with her, right?" he asked, and it was heartbreaking how his voice cracked at the end. I began to reach for him, but he stood from the counter. "I want to show you something. I should have shown it to you before," he added, and motioned for me to follow him to the back of the bookstore. I wasn't sure where he led, until he opened the door to the back office, and came back with a manila folder and a towel. I sat down on the couch, where I wrapped the towel around my shoulders, and he handed me the folder. "Here."

Inside, there were printed computer pages. The pages were all curled and worn, marked up with tabs.

I frowned. "What's this?"

He sat down beside me, and motioned for me to open it. "It's Rachel's last book. Or, at least, half of it."

Curiously, I opened the folder. I didn't know what I expected to find—but it wasn't this. **Maya Shah Gets the Girl by Rachel Flowers**, the title page read. I turned to the first chapter.

Maya Shah never cried.

"This . . . this is the last story?" I asked, my voice sounding like it was a thousand miles away.

"Most of it," he clarified, and I flipped to the last page, and quickly found out why. It was a book almost done—the story left on a sentence that wasn't even completed.

A romance left without a happily ever after.

Looking at the pages, I remembered what Maya had said to me, about feeling stuck, like nothing ever moved, nothing ever changed. And then what Lyssa said, about feeling lost. They were the only ones, aside from Anders, who were cognizant of it, and I now realized why. Because this was *their* story. Left off right at the worst part.

I'd been wrong this entire time. Anders had not been the love interest of this story—Maya was.

"Rachel never finished the book," Anders said, watching me flip through the pages. "The town was, for a very long time, frozen exactly where she left it. Where . . ." He looked away, and the frown that tugged on his lips took on a bittersweet taste. "Where she left *me*. Then you came along, and things began to move again."

The bookstore was silent, as if the stacks were leaning in to listen.

"I ruined it for you," I muttered.

"No," he replied, and took my hands in his. I couldn't look at him, still lost in the pages on my lap. He squeezed my hands tightly, finally dragging my attention to him. His eyes were kind, imploring me to listen. "If you read those pages, you'll see that Ruby and Jake were already inching toward a breakup, and Gemma and Thomas were growing bored, and the Daffodil Inn was almost—*almost*—open again, and Maya and Lyssa were in the throes of . . . I think Rachel always called it the dark night of the soul? I remember that she was frustrated because she didn't know how to pull them out of it. She tried everything, and she said nothing felt good." He pursed his lips, because it was clearly uncomfortable for him to talk about this—about Rachel Flowers. His fiancée. His best friend. His . . . *everything*. "After, I didn't know how to live in a world without her. I didn't think I wanted to. And then I realized I no longer remembered her laugh. Her smile. I was losing her, one day at a time. So I drove back to where—to where the accident happened," he said a little quieter, and swallowed thickly. "I don't know why I did. I didn't know where else to go. But, instead,

I found Eloraton, and everything was *exactly* where she left it. Everything—every little piece. Even the deleted drafts, the ideas that never happened—"

"The courtyard," I realized.

He nodded. "Yes. It was all there, and I thought . . . I could just stay. For a little while. And a little while turned into months, then a year . . . then two. Every day was the same, where the burgers were always slightly burnt and the taffy was sweet and it rained in the afternoon. I knew it all, like clockwork."

He ran his thumbs over my knuckles. "The evening you came in to town, I knew better than to get caught in the rain. But I did, anyway. Just for something different, I think. To remind myself of something new. Then you arrived, and everything began to change."

"I didn't mean for any of it to happen." My voice shook. *That* was why he didn't want me to mess anything up, because this town was everything he ever loved about the love of his life. I closed the manila folder, feeling sick to my stomach. "I should've just left when you told me to. I should've—"

He leaned closer, imploring me to look at him, and only him. "You're not listening, Eileen."

"Of course I am!" I pulled my hands out of his. "I think I'm finally *listening* to you! You told me to not mess with anything and then I go and—"

"You brought the town back to life," he said, desperate. "You got it moving again."

"You told me not to!"

"And I was wrong," he admitted.

That made me tongue-tied. He . . . he *what*?

"I was wrong," he repeated, and moved the folder to the coffee table. He threaded his fingers through mine and squeezed them tightly. "I was afraid that if this story was finished, that would be it—there would be no more stories, and no more Rachel—but I was wrong about that, too. Because her stories live on in you, and your friends, and everyone else who reads her work. She's gone, and she's not. She's dead, and she'll never die, and that is the part about stories that I'd forgotten. And you helped me remember. Perhaps this ending isn't what Rachel had in mind, but I don't regret it."

My throat felt tight. "Why?"

"Because in this love story," he replied, taking my chin in his hands, angling my face up to his, "I met you." If I let myself, I could get lost in those peridot eyes.

My heart skipped. Did he really mean that?

His thumb ran along my bottom lip, and the featherlight touch reminded me of the hours we spent at the waterfall, and later in the loft. What his hands could do. "For so long, I just . . . *existed*. I just stayed where I was, and everything stayed, too. Exactly where she left us. My life became a memorial. It wasn't mine anymore."

I knew that feeling—being frozen because you hurt too much to move. Life just felt easier when nothing changed, but that was only because you'd grown numb to the world around you.

"But you reminded me that things didn't always have to be good, over and over and over, but they could be great, some days. Perfect even. I spent so long trying to blend into the background, I forgot what this feels like."

My throat tightened. "This?"

He motioned between us. "*This*. When I'm around you," he added, his tight shoulders unwinding, and turned those minty eyes back to my face to study it—my eyes, my nose, my mouth. Very much my mouth. "I feel like someone again."

My heart thrummed, bright and loud, in my throat. "Like a main character in your own life?"

"Or . . . just someone important in yours," he muttered, and as a surprise to us both, he bent close, but so did I, like two stars falling into each other's gravity—

From the foyer, Lily shouted, "Uncle Andie! Uncle Andie! Do you have any books on *bees*?"

He groaned in exasperation. *"Lily . . ."*

A part of me was glad he didn't kiss me, the other part of me bitter Lily had interrupted. He pushed himself off the couch, the moment gone, and I breathed out a sigh of—relief? *Was* it relief?

I told myself it was.

"You should get dried off," he said, "and stop tracking water through my store."

I put on a smile. "Ah, there's the Anders I know. I'll get changed and be on my way."

He looked confused. "Oh? Will I have to find another date for tomorrow?"

I sat up a little straighter. "I . . ."

"Unless you already have plans for the wedding."

I had a cabin to get to and books to read and a best friend to call and apologize to and . . . "No plans," I said.

"Good girl," he replied, and left for the front of the store. "Coming, Lily," he called, and when he was gone, I fell back against the couch and sucked in a deep breath.

Then let it out again.

My heart hammered. My head felt like it was in the clouds. Why couldn't my mind stop spinning? Why did it remind me how green his eyes were, how soft his lips when he kissed me last night? His laugh? His *everything*? And why did it hurt thinking about saying goodbye?

And the realization hit me like a train on a track—

I was falling in love with a real person, utterly and irrevocably against my will.

33

All Roads

JUNIE AND WILL WED the next night, on a perfect summer eve-ning. We'd spent the entire day decorating the Daffodil in deep purples and sunny yellows and aquamarine blues and sage greens. Sometimes, Anders would steal a glance from across the room, or we would brush shoulders in a hallway, touch hands, and each little bit of him sent shivers down my spine. Every time I thought about kissing him, touching him, being *with* him, my chest wound so tight I could barely breathe.

I didn't want to be in love again, because what if it all went bad? What if Anders saw some flaw that I hadn't seen and, like Liam, knew he could do better? But what if he left with me? What if things turned out *good*? I wasn't sure I could handle that, either. It was my anxiety talking, I knew it was, but there was no one else in my head to tell me otherwise.

I was scared. I didn't *need* love.

But oh, oh, how I *wanted* it.

I borrowed a floral dress from Gemma, and a pair of Ruby's heels that were a bit too big, and thought about the wedding dress still hanging in my closet and the shoes still in the box, and how that life would have been so much different than the one I lived now. I wouldn't be the same person. I wasn't sure I'd even recognize myself. But I knew, deep down, that this was me. This version, mangled with heartbreak and hope all twisted together, and I liked this me.

I liked this me very much.

The ceremony was loud, and joyous, and I would never forget the look on Will's face when he saw Junie for the first time, gracing the stairs on the way down to the first floor, framed so perfectly with her best friends on either side. Lace dress hemmed to the knees, long lacy sleeves, a flower crown of bright yellow daffodils, and those threadbare pink Converses.

They said their vows tearfully and kissed, and for a while after, as we clapped and cheered, they pressed their foreheads together, and he whispered something soft, something that made her smile, and my heart ached because I wished I knew what he said. I wished I knew what she replied. I wished the scene could have been painted in Rachel Flowers's words, and I wished I could've been reading them from my perch on my floral sofa, Pru on the other side.

I wished I could hear her commentary, and I wished I could've handed her tissues one last time, and I wished we could've talked all night about the meet-cute, the delicate turns of phrases, the happy ending.

Pru would've sighed, content and wistful. She would've said, "Oh, how corny," and loved every word.

Behind me I heard Jake whisper something to Ruby, and I glanced over my shoulder as they disappeared out of the back and stepped into the garden. I didn't know what they said, but I knew Ruby was smiling as he kissed her fingertips delicately. I wasn't very good at reading lips, but I could read his—

"It's you," he said to her. "Wherever, whatever, with you."

She cupped his face in her hands. "Then let's get the fuck out of here, babe," she replied, and crushed her mouth to his.

I took a glass of champagne from the catering table, and all around me, stories were meeting their ends, circles were connecting, periods and last pages and the soft *thump* of a book well loved and closed in adoration.

As it turned out, the story didn't need me at all. It just needed someone—anyone—to turn the page.

In a corner of the parlor, Frank was chatting with Gail, rosy cheeked and laughing, and Gemma was dancing, with Lily on her feet, and the air was bright and everyone was loved.

I wouldn't fault Anders for wanting to stay for so long.

In another life, I'm sure I could've written myself into Eloraton and become that quirky English professor who lived in the loft of an independent bookstore, searching for her great American novel. I didn't have to be anyone else. Defined by few adjectives and a name, padding other people's stories so they didn't feel so empty. It would have been a good life. But I wanted a little more.

Anders slipped up beside me, and offered me his hand. "Care to dance, Miss Merriweather?"

My chest grew tight, and I told myself to enjoy this. "Why, Mr. Sinclair," I replied, placing my hand in his, "I thought you'd never ask."

He led me into the parlor, and we slow danced cheek to cheek. I closed my eyes and decided to commit this to memory. The way his clean-shaven face felt against mine, the smell of his aftershave, the soft curl of his fair hair. Eventually, we danced our way out onto the veranda. He began to hum to the music inside—and I recognized it, finally.

It was the starlings' melody.

"Come on, Eileen."

I held on to him tighter. "I think," I whispered, "I'm falling in love with you."

To which he replied, not missing a single dance step, as if he already knew, "I'm not a book boyfriend, you know. I'm real."

"I know," I agreed, and with my cheek against his, enjoying the smell of his aftershave and the warmth of his skin, and the way, when we danced, we seemed to breathe together, too, "and I think you're worth the heartbreak."

However hard the heartbreak would be.

When the dance ended, we broke away. "C'mon, Eileen," he said, mirroring the starling song, "they won't miss us. There's somewhere I want to show you."

Then he took me by the hand, and pulled me out into the garden. The night was cool, and dark, and the fireflies flitted from rosebush to hydrangea to the oaks that lined the back of the garden. We slipped through the overgrown archway into a shadowy courtyard.

I knew where we were. The forgotten place, framed with those lost statues and half-deleted thoughts. Now that I could compare Anders to the statues with his face, I could see what they all had been missing. The parts that were already in Eloraton—the parts she gave other characters. The gravestones were drafts she buried into folders on her desktop or deleted or lost, though **THISDRAFT SUCKS_V4_FINAL.docx** had to have turned into something.

"Well, it's not much of a surprise," he went on, turning on his heel to walk backward and face me. He arched an eyebrow. "I believe you already know this place."

"You aren't very subtle at sneaking," I pointed out.

"Neither are you."

I smiled. "We're a pair, then. What, oh what will you do once I leave?" I meant it as a joke, but his face grew somber.

"I think . . ." he began, sitting down at the fountain. In the distance, through the alleyway, the inn's windows glowed brightly with life and laughter. "I think I'm going to leave, too. Do you have room in your car since I sacrificed mine for yours?"

My heart jumped into my throat. "You mean it?"

"Yes," he said. "I think I've spent enough time lost in a book."

"But . . . if you leave, what if you can't come back?"

"I know. And when I first came here, I would have been very scared of that. But everything moves on. And I want to move on, too. I'm tired of living the same page every day. I want something new. I think Rachel would want that for me, too. I just stayed for so long because . . ." He chewed on his words, choosing them carefully. "I thought that if I stayed here long enough, I'd find where she wrote me into her books. I'd find a character like me, and I'd feel how much she loved me one last time. There are so many of our friends here, or at least large pieces of them. But . . ." He frowned, as if he was trying to hold back a strong emotion, and he wasn't quite sure what it was. "But I'm only in this graveyard of ideas— I'm not even in the town. She put everything she ever loved in these books, all the way down to the French toast and the starlings, and I'm not here."

That baffled me. Not that she hadn't put him in the town, but that he couldn't see it.

I reached out, and took him by the hand. "But you are."

His eyebrows furrowed in confusion.

I cupped his cheek with my hand. "You're everywhere in this town," I said. "You're in Jake's stubbornness, his smile, and you're in Thomas's genius and his gait, long and limber like he's always late for somewhere. You're in Will's dedication, and in the love in his eyes, and the scar on his lip," I said, and traced that fine hairline scar, "and I'm sure you looked at Rachel the same way he looks at

Junie, and Anders—*Anders*—it's the kind of look that moves mountains. It's the kind of look of someone who gave up their whole life to live in an unfinished story. She wrote you in all of it. You can't see it because you're too close, but believe me, she loved you. She loved you so much."

His green, green eyes grew wet with tears. "I never realized . . ." He laid his hand atop mine on his cheek, and held it tightly, and kissed the palm of my hand. "Thank you."

"You're welcome," I whispered.

And I knew Rachel was here, too. When she first died, I started to wonder what happened to the story she left behind. Would it just disappear when she did? Be forgotten? But I'd been here for long enough to know that when I finally took the only road in and out of Eloraton, and crossed Charm Bridge, I'd never come back. I was sure—but that didn't mean the story stopped. It wouldn't, because we kept it alive—by reading her novels, by imagining what came next—and so because her work lived on, so did she. In little ways.

In little ways, she stayed.

Even as the story moved on.

Anders leaned over and kissed me. His mouth tasted a little salty with tears, mixed with the bubbly champagne from the wedding. It was a bittersweet combination. It tasted hopeful. I pulled away. He felt it, too. The start of something, of a story, if we let it.

"Do you think they're missing us yet?" I asked.

"Maybe. I *do* have impeccable music t— Do you hear that?" He cocked his head.

"Hear wh—"

"*Shh,*" he muttered, pressing a finger to my mouth. "Someone's coming."

"Maya?"

In reply, he took me by the hand and pulled me back behind an overgrown hedge. Inside of it was a couple in an embrace, their faces covered by vines. We quietly parted the leaves as Maya and Lyssa came through the arch, into the courtyard. They were whispering, and giggling, and there was a new openness to Lyssa that I hadn't seen before.

"I'm sorry that you waited so long," Lyssa said, taking Maya by the hands and threading their fingers together.

"What changed?" Maya asked.

"Someone told me that love is worth taking a chance, even if it's the wrong one."

Hurt flickered across Maya's moonlit face. "You think you'll regret me?"

"No," the gardener replied, and came closer to the girl she had loved for years, though she'd never given her heart the chance to admit it. "I think I'll regret never doing this."

Then she kissed Maya Shah in the forgotten courtyard. And the summer hummed on, humid and clear, without a cloud in the sky, and the fireflies lit on the edges of too-tall blades of grass, and so, so quietly, the wind that sighed through the trees sounded like the turn of a page.

It was a thread that Rachel had put in motion in the first book, one that came together even without my help.

Because sometimes things just fell together. Sometimes things were meant to be.

Anders smiled at me, and I returned it, and we knocked our fists together.

A truly happy ending.

"Let's sneak out?" he mouthed.

I nodded.

We were almost caught when Anders tripped over a bust of his own head, but Lyssa said it was probably the possum, and kissed her girlfriend again. We hurried out of the garden, and back up the veranda to the inn, where the soft golden glow of light illuminated the porch. Anders's fingers were woven through mine, and it felt natural.

It felt fated.

"Has anyone else called shotgun?" he asked jokingly.

I gave it a thought. "You might have to fight with the box of wine . . ." I trailed off as I noticed a figure at the front gates of the inn. Tall, thin, curly dark hair. I saw her a moment before Anders did, and when he did, he looked like he had seen a ghost.

Because Beatrice Everly stood at the garden gates, returned home.

34

Rachel Flowers

I NEVER ARRIVED FOR ANYTHING on time.

School? Casually late. College clubs? You had to tell me to arrive, at *least* thirty minutes early. Christmas Eve? New Year's? Doctor visits? I laughed in the face of calendar appointments, just like my mother had before me. I was either too early or too late. There was never an in-between.

The only time I'd ever been on time for anything was the night Pru and I met Rachel Flowers. It was an event in a small, unassuming bookstore in Decatur, where there were as many indoor plants as books, and enough chairs set out for a small horde of fans.

None of them showed up—with the exception of Pru and me.

We began to get an inkling that this event was going south when we took our seats in the front row (Pru *always* insisted on getting the best seats no matter what, so being blissfully comfortable in the back of the room was never going to be my lot in life) and the closer we got to the event start time, the more apparent the empty chairs around us became. Some customers came in to buy books, and a few asked what the event was for, but when they heard it was a "romance author," quite a few of them looked amused by the idea but never lingered.

But while I grew worried about the turnout, Pru was just blissfully excited. She didn't care if there was one person in the audience, or ten. She held the new book—*Return to Sender*—to her chest and waited in nervous anticipation. We'd never met an author before, at least not one that we loved. (I had, sadly, met quite a few that I didn't like at all, and that was rather unfortunate in my line of work.)

"I've got so many questions to ask her," Pru told me, squirming in her seat like a child. "A hundred questions! Do you think I should make a list of my top ten?"

I glanced around at the empty seats. "I think she might have time for one or two."

Pru laughed.

"I feel bad for her," I said. "No one's here."

"Yeah but *we're* here."

"We're just two people."

"Two people more than zero," she replied simply, and then gasped. "Oh, there she is! How does my hair look?" she added, facing me, and when I told her she looked fine, she turned back to the front and excitedly waited as a tall, thin young woman with dark hair and glasses came and sat down in a plush chair set up in front of us. She shifted a little nervously, looking at the two of us, and no one else. We were all the same age. We could've gone to the same school, been in the same college classes. We could've all had sleepovers and painted our nails together, if we'd been in the same town.

It was a little startling, seeing her in person, because she looked so . . . normal. Like the rest of us. I knew that sounded silly, because authors and artists and movie stars were like the rest of us, but it was a revelation nonetheless. Here we were, sitting across from each other, all human and flawed and *real*.

What was also very real was that no one else was here—and I mean *no one*. It was like the second the clock struck seven, everyone vacated the business so that there would be the least amount of eyewitnesses possible.

Rachel Flowers's searching gaze settled on someone in the very back, and whoever it was seemed to give her heart, because she smiled and then greeted us.

"Well, I guess it'll just be us tonight. Can I . . ." And then she went over to a concessions table where the lone, sorrowful bookseller had opened a bottle of chardonnay, expecting a lot more people. Rachel took a cup, tucked the bottle under her arm, and came over to sit beside us in the hard metal chairs.

"That's better," she said, and outstretched her free hand. "I'm Rachel. Do you drink?" And she filled my and Pru's cups up again, and for the next hour and a half, we chatted about books, and stories, and favorite authors. Pru had forgotten every single one of her questions, and she didn't remember them until the next morning, when she complained that the cheap chardonnay had given her a migraine.

When I thought back on the event, I remembered that the time flew by so quickly, it surprised me when a man came up behind Rachel and put a gentle hand on her shoulder. "The bookstore's closing soon, Chel."

The man had probably been Anders, but my memory of him was blurry at best. The only thing I could recall for certain was Pru's excitement even after we'd been shown the door and were on our way to our parking spot in a nearby garage. She overflowed with joy—she practically vibrated with it, and it was infectious. I don't know if it was the three glasses of chardonnay or the fact that the night ended up being cool and crisp and basically perfect, but that was one of the best nights of my life.

Not because we got to meet and have a one-on-one chat with our favorite author (okay, maybe that was a *little* bit of it), but because the evening had just been . . . nice. Really, and truly *nice*.

In the end, I'd apologized to Rachel Flowers about the horrible turnout, but Rachel had just smiled and shaken her head.

"It was perfect. I don't write to be everyone's favorite novelist. I write because I love this." And she motioned to my best friend and me. "It sounds like a silly Hallmark card, I realize, but it means I get to meet you two." She added, a little quieter, "I actually prefer smaller events. Less of a chance of me making a fool of myself."

"You're so cool," Pru had gushed. "How could you ever? You're perfect."

"My fiancé would say otherwise. Apparently I snore."

I said, "Where is he? I see him, it's fight on sight."

She laughed. "I'll warn him."

Then she'd thanked us, and said she hoped to see us at another event.

Just because we spent a couple of hours with the author didn't mean that we knew her, obviously. I'm sure Rachel Flowers separated the person she was in her career, and the person she was in private—sort of like the rest of us. I rarely showed my full hand to anyone who wasn't my best friend; I rarely bared my insecurities. There was a mask everyone had to put on to live in the world and guard their hearts; the only difference was some people were just more public than others. Pru and I were lucky—we'd always worn our hearts on our sleeves when we were together. The rest of the world might not understand, but it wasn't *for* them.

"Did I ask anything stupid? Was I annoying?" Pru asked me,

and the answer was no. Of course not. "I hope she has a very nice rest of her tour events," she went on, and then cursed.

I asked, "What?"

"I forgot to ask her about my theories on the end of the series! I need to know if they ever find that damn possum."

"I guess you'll just have to wait and find out," I'd replied smartly. "Don't worry, I'll read the last page first and let you know."

She gasped. "You wouldn't *dare*, Eileen Marie Merriweather!"

"Oh, I absolutely would."

Because Pru and I were opposites, and we were best friends, and sometimes in life, that was all you ever needed to get through the really tough bits.

A few months after the event, Rachel Flowers passed away in a car accident. A drunk driver T-boned her and her fiancé as they were coming home from dinner. The fandom mourned. They sent flowers to the publisher. They held vigils at their favorite bookstores.

And through the overtures of sadness, the series went viral. Everyone wanted to read about the kind of series that could evoke that sort of dedication. My best friend supposed it was half FOMO—the people who didn't know to mourn wanted to get in on the mourning—and half coincidence.

The first book hit the *New York Times* bestseller list. Then the second. Third. Then the entire series. The books, and the author, had never found success while she was alive, but dead?

She was remembered.

And there was something startlingly bitter in the sweetness of that. We would never get more books from Rachel Flowers, we would just get the echoes of them.

Because even after the people were gone, there were still stories. There were always stories. Other people took the heart of her books, and kept them close, and nurtured them and grew into something new, because nothing could ever stay in stasis. Nothing ever stopped. Nothing was permanent. Art lived and breathed, like love, like friendship.

Life—like works of art—was transformative.

It persisted.

And through them, so did we.

35

The Only Road Out

T HE WOMAN AT THE front gate noticed us and waved. "Hello there. I think I'm a little late to the party." She had a kind smile and a gap in her front two teeth. She carried a suitcase with her and a bag slung over her shoulder, and almost dumped both of them down as soon as she let herself in through the gate.

Anders quickly moved closer to her to take a bag. "Let me help . . ."

She held up a hand. "Oh no, I'm fine. Thank you, though." She re-situated her bag, and then looked him up and down, and stretched out her hand. "I'm Bea."

"Anders," he replied, taking her hand.

I watched them from the shadow of the garden, feeling my heart swell and sink at the same time. Rachel Flowers once said in an interview that she rarely wrote herself into novels. She likened different characters to putting on different wigs and stepping into different kinds of shoes.

"None of them are *me*," she had told an interviewer once, when asked which character was most like her. But then she had paused for a second, and thought about it. "But if I had to choose, I'd say Bea is the closest—though don't ask me to sew anything!" she added with a laugh, and the expression on her face settled into a content grin. "She's the life I'd have loved to lead if I didn't happen into this one. I like this one too much, though."

Even in stories they found each other.

Anders and Bea looked at each other for a little too long in the soft and warm light of the inn, as though they'd seen each other in a dream.

Bea asked, smiling, "I'm sorry, but do I know you?"

"I . . . don't think so," he replied, his voice tight.

"You just look so familiar is all," she added, and then turned her gaze to me. "Hi."

"Hi," I replied, waving. My chest felt tight. I could barely breathe. "Everyone's inside. They haven't cut the cake yet."

"Oh, excellent! I love that part," she added, dipping around Anders with one last lingering look, before she hurried up the steps and pushed open the front door. A moment later, there were cheers and shouts of "Bea!" and "You made it!" as everyone came in to hug her and welcome her home, like a lost family member homeward bound.

The reception would last well into the night. I could stay, and see what happened. If Maya and Lyssa would dance together, if Gail and Frank would finally settle their war of condiments, where Ruby and Jake disappeared to, if Beatrice . . .

A knot formed in my throat.

No, I didn't think I wanted to know, even though it felt like closing the book just before the last page.

"I think I have to go," I said, deciding in that moment.

Anders gave me a confused look. "You don't want to see how it ends?"

"No. You coming?" I asked.

He hesitated, glancing back through the open door to the wedding, to Beatrice, and that was all the answer I needed. It was the only answer he could give.

I gave him a smile that meant it was okay—because it *was* okay, because this was different than the last time I'd had my heart broken. This man was kind, and he was sad, and if he could find a happy ending in his past, then who was I to stop him? "Go get her, tiger."

To that, he kissed my forehead in that bittersweet way goodbyes always were. "Find me in the romance section," he whispered.

And I braced myself for my heart to break—

But it didn't.

Maybe I was stronger than I gave myself credit for. Or, maybe, whatever I was leaving was worth it, because ahead of me was Pru, and the book club, and my story.

Whether or not tonight had a happy ending, I wouldn't be around to find out. Maybe that was for the best. Maybe, in some stories, the ending didn't matter as much as the journey. It was a romance, after all.

They all had happy endings eventually.

Don't look back, I reminded myself as I put Ruby's shoes by the front gate, and started running down the sidewalk toward the bookstore. I changed out of Gemma's dress, and said goodbye to Butterscotch.

It was time to go.

Sweetpea was exactly where Frank had parked her yesterday. He'd even buffed out the scratches I'd gotten in Atlanta traffic. True to his word, there were two bottles of Frank's Hotties in the glove compartment, along with a note—

Lovely workin' on this old lady! Safe travels!

I slipped the note back into the glove compartment, and put my weekend bag in the passenger seat, and situated myself behind the wheel. Adjusted the rearview mirror. And inserted the key.

I turned the ignition.

The car gave a rumble, and came to life.

I pulled out of the parking spot, and I took the only road in and out of Eloraton.

I tried not to look back.

As the red covered bridge approached, I reached up to the rearview mirror to see if I could angle it back and see the town—but then I stopped myself.

The bridge came, and I passed over it.

And I turned the page.

36

True Love

I PARKED IN THE GRAVEL lot that, in any other year, would be full with a white Prius and an SUV rental, but this year it was vacant. The A-frame cabin sat dark in the shadow of the moon. It was a gorgeous house. Olivia had found it a few years ago, and we'd stayed here ever since. There was a Jacuzzi on the back deck that looked out across the green hills of the Catskills.

I cut off the engine.

Took a deep breath.

Everything looked just a little different outside Eloraton. Just a little louder, a little more vibrant. The town had already begun to feel like a dream, where I remembered snatches of things, but with every mile I put behind me, another small thing was lost. The smell of rain on the damp grass. The sound of the starlings in the morning. And whenever I tried to hang on to those memories, those moments, the feeling of warm sunlight on my skin—it began to sound like the rustle of paper, and the scent of old books, and the feeling of pages between my fingers.

The one thing that remained—the only thing—was Anders. His taste, his touch, the rumble of his laugh. I had been right all along, hadn't I? He was going to make a dreamy hero, once he found his happily ever after.

And I was going to finally find mine, too.

Unbuckling myself, I stepped out of my car, and I got my things from the trunk. The books were sharp again, the words back on their pages. I flipped through *Daffodil Daydreams* and paused on a page with the first mention of Junie's name, as she wondered if she'd ever fit in there in that small town of Eloraton. I smiled, remembering her and Will framed in the soft glow of their wedding, surrounded by an entire town of people who loved her, and I thought—

It was a good ending. Or maybe a beginning.

Either way, it was good.

There was a sound of a door opening, which was wrong—I knew it was wrong—because no one was here, and we had rented the cabin for one more day. *Bear?* I thought, but bears couldn't open doors . . . right?

"And here I thought you'd never show," said a familiar voice, and my heart leapt into my throat. I closed the hatchback quickly, and there, framed in the doorway to the cabin, was my best friend, still in her faded college sweatshirt and pants she'd worn threadbare. Her dirty blond hair was pulled up into a ponytail, greasy from travel, her eyes tired like she'd just gotten off a red-eye.

And she had.

I couldn't believe it. I blinked a few times, just to make sure. "Pru . . . but—but what happened to Iceland?"

"It's still there," she replied. She held up her hand, and the engagement ring on her finger. "I'd kick myself forever if I missed this week with you."

I started toward her, and she swept down the steps. She was here, she was here, my best friend—

We collided and held each other tightly, and she started to cry, and I started to cry with her, because things weren't perfect, and endings weren't always happy, but it wasn't always the destination that mattered.

It was this.

Pru and book clubs and burnt hamburgers disguised in hot sauce and poorly attended author events and cheap chardonnay and loud music and summers driving down country roads with the windows rolled down and engagement parties and nights with wine and hot tubs and good books.

It wasn't the end that mattered, but every word leading up to it.

37

The Montage at the End

WE DROVE HOME THE next morning with the worst hangover of Pru's life. I'd, thankfully, already had that at the *beginning* of my week, and I think my body had decided that I needed a break from feeling dead. Pru likened it to the night Liam broke off our engagement, but it felt more like a few days ago after girls' night. When we got home, she posted on social that she and Jasper were engaged, and showed everyone the ring, and told them all how he proposed—

On an iceberg, just as I predicted.

(As it turned out, while Pru flew to New York, he flew home to Atlanta, and paced nervously back and forth in their tiny cottage in Marietta until we rolled back into town.)

A week after we came home from the cabin, Pru asked if I was really okay. "Because, you know"—she hadn't known what to say, or how to say it—"we were always . . . we always did everything together."

"We still do," I replied. "I'll always be right here with you for every anniversary, birthday, new house, wedding—whatever. We're still in this together."

She cocked her head to the side. We were sitting in the back of Sweetpea, the hatchback open, watching *Mamma Mia!* at the local drive-in's "HELLO SUMMER!" movie marathon. "What changed?"

I wished I could tell her—I wanted to—but I knew how my story would sound. Then again, I couldn't lie to her, either. I couldn't tell her that romance novels with Fabio on the cover and music playlists featuring Stevie Nicks singing about men who didn't deserve second chances cured me of whatever hole I had sunk into since Liam. I was still in that hole, to be honest, but I was learning how to grow and nurture some vines to climb out.

"Something happened the week you weren't at the book club cabin," Pru went on. "I know you. You're not telling me something."

"I doubt you'll believe me."

She seemed perplexed. On the screen, all the guys were high-kicking themselves across a pier. "Whenever have I not?"

She had me there.

"What happened?" she asked again.

Everything. Nothing.

I was tired of being stagnant, I thought. *I wanted to be a main character in my own life again.*

And, deep down, I still missed Eloraton terribly. I would go back to the series, and flip through it sometimes, and smile as Junie stumbled into town, and Ruby fell in love with Jake, and Gemma kissed Thomas under the stars, and Bea rode off into the sunset with a happy for now, only to come home when her adventure ended. I'd pause at the dedication sometimes.

To A. S.

I hoped Anders was all right.

I hoped he found his happy ending.

"Okay," I said to Pru, "but I warned you. Remember the cases of hot sauce you found in my car?"

"Yeah. It was supposed to be wine. What's that got to do with anything?" She angled herself toward me and waited patiently. We'd seen this movie a thousand times before, and no one else was within earshot anyway. So, I took out another two wine coolers from the Yeti stashed in the back seat, and took a deep breath—

And I told her about a town that didn't exist.

PRUDENCE DIDN'T BELIEVE ME AT FIRST. SHE THOUGHT EITHER I'd hallucinated a lot of it, or what had *actually* happened was so heartbreaking that my brain came up with a new story. At least, not until I went on my first date since Liam a month and a half later, during the first days of the fall semester. The man was handsome, and he taught English in the same department as me—and the second he showed up at my apartment and saw my bookshelf, he laughed.

"You turn them around when guests come over, right?" he asked, motioning to the sanguine embraces and lusty women across the covers. He plucked one off the shelf—a vintage-looking bodice ripper with Jason Baca on the cover, inches away from dragging his tongue across the woman's neck. "This Fabio's not exactly a Chuck Palahniuk."

"That's not Fabio."

"My mistake, they all look the same."

I sighed. "Well, that's a pity."

"Why?"

"Because you have to leave. The door's there, if you've forgotten."

He chuckled nervously. "I didn't . . . You're kidding."

"No. I didn't judge you when you said you collected *swords*. You don't put them away when company comes over, do you? Besides, romance outsells every other genre—by a *lot*, and it's still growing even when sales in every other genre are declining. In the US alone, romance sells about nineteen billion units a year." I plucked the paperback from his hand. "You can take that to your next fight club. Now there's the door."

The next time I saw him in the hallway, he didn't even look me in the eyes. That might've been for the best, anyway.

That could've been chalked up to a one-off, but then I told my department head that I wasn't taking that 8:00 a.m. English 101 class that she always sloughed off onto me. I told her to let one of the newer adjuncts teach it and she seemed positively gobsmacked.

And so did Pru when I told her.

So she knew something was up. She told me that, finally, when we'd met for dinner the next week—book club week—and shared a large Nacho Supreme together before our Zoom meeting. She was still hunting for a job—*again*. It felt like an eternal, cursed task for her.

"Eloraton changed you," she commented, scooping up a lot of cheese on a chip, and shoving it in her mouth. "Academia better watch out."

"I'm just tired of sacrificing myself all the time," I replied. "I sort of felt like the Giving Tree, chopping myself smaller and smaller, and I guess I finally realized, if I kept this up, I'd be nothing but a stump by the end."

She wrinkled her nose. "I think you'd at least fashion yourself into a comfortable *chair*."

I gave her a look.

"Straight mahogany. Vintage. You'd be a classic."

"Aw, thanks," I said, batting my eyelashes.

"Only the best for my best friend," she said, and leaned her head on my shoulder. "It's nice to see you're back. I've missed you."

"I've been right here."

She shook her head. "No, you haven't. Not since Liam."

It still hurt, sometimes, to think about him, but not in a way that made me freeze anymore. I had buried my head in stories so long that I'd forgotten to live the real thing. I fell in love with the Liam in my head, the story of who we could be together, the possibility of it. I had ignored the rest.

Until I no longer could.

I shrugged. "I think I just finally figured out what love actually looks like."

Love looked like a man who had coffee ready for me in the mornings even though he preferred tea, and remembered exactly how I took it. Love ate my sugary spaghetti, and held an umbrella over my head when it rained, and apologized when he knew he was wrong. Love was inquisitive, and mindful, and—somewhere beneath the grumpy exterior—sweet. Love was tricking yourself into doing something you didn't want to do, because you loved the person who did.

Love was a bunch of small things that added up to bigger things.

Love was feeling valued. And accepted.

Just the way you were.

It was never feeling too much, or not enough, even though often you were both, because Love loved you anyway. Not in spite of it, but *because* of it.

Prudence studied me for a long moment, and finally said, "I'm so mad you let him go. I mean, he could open up a bookstore in Decatur. There's already a thousand of them—but he could open up one more."

I rolled my eyes.

"Maybe he could've hired me," she added with a sigh. "I'd be a cute bookseller. Are you done?" she added, getting up off the couch and motioning to her to-go container. I handed it to her and went to go put the rest in the fridge for breakfast, while I grabbed my computer. We had a Zoom meeting in five minutes, and I was determined *not* to be the late one for once.

An idea began to form in the back of my head. It was crazy, but the more I thought about it, the more I began to wonder . . . what would it hurt?

When she sat back down and pulled a blanket over her wrinkled interview skirt, I gave her a thoughtful look.

"Why don't we?" I asked her.

"We what?"

I bumped her shoulder against mine. "Why don't we open up a bookstore?"

"You're kidding." She laughed. "Us?"

"Why *not* us?"

Her laughter died in her throat, and she gave it a thought. "I . . . huh. Why not us?" she echoed.

"It could be an adventure," I said.

"It could be a disaster," she replied.

I grinned. "Sounds fun." We logged on to the Zoom, and were the first ones in the room. "Did you finish the book for book club, by the way?"

"Yeah, waiting for the interview today. I hated the ending."

"Why?"

She scowled. "Ghosts should stay *dead*. It was a total cop-out.

And they fell in love *way* too fast. It was too insta-love-y for me. And? No one says *doggo* anymore."

"I say doggo," I replied.

She scrunched her nose. "Ironically?"

"Totes—"

Olivia came into the Zoom and said, "There's a difference between insta-*love* and insta-*lust*. A lot of people mistake the two."

Prudence frowned and looked back at the screen. "Are you saying—oh my god, Liv!" she gasped, holding her hand up to the screen to block her view. "Are you in the *bath*?"

"You can't see anything," Olivia replied, piling more bubbles atop her chest. "It's lavender-scented."

Two more people entered the Zoom: Aditi and Matt. They were absolutely unfazed by Olivia's view.

"Good morning—or afternoon, wherever you are," Aditi greeted, and Matt waved with a grunt. "Is Benji here yet?"

"Not yet," I replied.

"This is exciting," Matt said, putting on his glasses to finally see everyone. "Look at everyone's faces! And, uh, other parts. It's been too long. Next year, we'll all be back at the cabin. No buts!"

"Already in my calendar," Aditi said.

"And requested it off," Janelle added, logging on from what looked like her car. She was slurping up instant ramen, still in her nursing scrubs. It must've been her night on call.

Then another video joined the fray. Benji, his glasses low on his face, and beside him was his fiancée. Apparently she'd been a ghostwriter for the famous Ann Nichols, and we all swore that we wouldn't read Ann in the book club. No, instead we read the ghostwriter's most recent novel—

"And there's the author herself!" Olivia crowed. "First off, I just wanted to say what a *lovely* style and voice you have, Florence."

The blond woman blushed. "O-oh, thank you very much."

Benji leaned toward the screen, squinting. Then he cleared his throat. "Liv, are you . . ."

The woman grabbed something off-screen—it was a huge margarita pitcher with an umbrella at the top and a swirly straw. She took a long sip and said, "Drinking? Absolutely. I've got three foster kittens and two of them had explosive diarrhea today."

"No, I mean—" Benji started, but his fiancée elbowed him in the side. "Good choice, Liv."

In reply, the woman saluted him and sank down a little lower in her bath. Matt clapped his hands together, and looked down at his notes. "So, who wants to start . . ."

Aditi rolled their eyes. "Who put Matt in charge this time?"

"Well, do *you* want to lead the discussion?"

"Fuck no."

Prudence leaned forward. "Okay, okay, before we start, can I ask you guys something?"

Everyone looked at her expectantly. Benji even lowered his glasses to look more attentive.

Pru scooted to the edge of the couch and asked, "What do you guys think if we opened up a bookstore?"

Benji blinked. "How did this come about?"

"We were just talking," I began, but Prudence interrupted me.

"The guy Elsy fell for in the Hudson Valley was a bookstore owner and it got us thinking—"

Matt held up his hand. "Hold on. The guy Elsy . . ."

"Fell for?" Olivia finished, sitting up a little taller in the bath, making sure to bring the bubbles with her. "Like, *fell* fell?"

"Oh yeah," Prudence, the traitor, confirmed.

The gasp that tore through the speakers was so loud, it crackled the mics. I slid a glare to my best friend, and she gave me the *if you won't care, we will* look, and unscrewed the wine she brought, and took a swig right out of the bottle. And so the questions began, and no one discussed the book that evening, instead asking the important questions like—

"Can he cook?"

(No, but he did eat my horrible spaghetti.)

"Was he cute?"

(What kind of question was that?)

"Did he have a *scar* anywhere . . . ?"

(He did. And I'd traced it with my tongue a few times.)

"How was the sex?"

(Perfect, under the waterfall.)

"Wait, you had sex under a *waterfall*?"

(It's a long story.)

"And you let him go?"

Of course I did. What other choice did I have, hold on to him until my hands turned white, until I choked the love out of him? No, love wasn't a trap, something you had to crawl out of later. If you loved something—someone—sometimes you had to let them go. And if they loved you, too, they'd come back.

Love—true love—always came back.

38

The Grand Romantic

THE DAYS GOT COOLER, and the leaves turned orange, and for two whole weeks we got a lovely and brisk fall. I broke out my warm cardigans, and bundled up in scarves and knit caps, and taught English 101 at 10:00 a.m. sharp, and, in the evenings, Pru and I began to renovate the small storefront we leased. It took a minute to scrape together the funds, but Benji was the one who suggested a crowdsourcing campaign, and who knew so many people wanted to help out? Between that and the small business loan we got with Jasper's help, we managed. So we spackled the walls, and we hung the light fixtures, and when Jasper could take off work, he helped us install the hardware and laminate floors. We painted murals in the few places we couldn't fit bookshelves, and set about ordering every romance novel we could think of. The entire thing was tiring, and some nights when a shelf fell down, or we found an infestation of cockroaches in the break room, we wanted to quit. But we didn't. We put on a steamy audiobook, and critiqued the sex scenes late into the night as we painted, and sanded, and plotted. We discussed Nora, and Ann, and Beverly, and Rachel, and we compared covers and marketing tactics, and how the genre had transformed itself over the years to its current iteration.

That fall, I told my dean that I wasn't signing a new contract for the next year, and she did everything to try to get me to stay, but nothing would.

"You'll regret it," she said. "You're so close to tenure!"

I doubted it.

And then we were a week from opening, and I'd just painted the bookstore name above the storefront window, and it didn't look half-bad.

Jasper frowned at the name. "Like, a meet-cute?"

"At the end," I supplied. "It's when Darcy tells Elizabeth he loves her most ardently, when Mark brings Bridget a new diary, when Harry tells Sally he loves her, when Will buys Junie the inn." I smiled up at the name, putting my hands on my hips. "The grand romantic gesture."

So, obviously, we named the bookshop the Grand Romantic.

We opened the bookstore at the end of a rainy October. Benji and his fiancée flew down from New York, though that might have been because she was the guest on our opening night. The others in the book club also came, and Pru and I were afraid that they'd be the only ones.

"Even if they are," Pru said, adjusting my silver-sequined jacket, and gently pulling my braid free of the sequins, "then it's going to be the best night of our lives." She was dressed in a pastel mauve dress with tulle at the bottom, flowers in her recently cropped hair. "Now, I'm going to go out and mingle, and you should, too."

"I will," I replied, though I felt a little sick to my stomach at the thought of walking out, and seeing no one in the store.

What if our bookstore failed? What if—

Stop, I forced myself to think. I was getting ahead of myself.

Life wasn't about the ending. It was about everything else. And tonight, it was about opening a bookstore with my very best friend.

Pru turned and began to leave the back area that was closed off with a curtain. There was a threadbare fainting couch there, and a water dispenser, and a calendar where we'd already written down about a dozen events—and prayed to *god* people attended.

"Hey, Prudence?" I asked.

She glanced back at me, halfway to pulling back the curtain to go greet our guests. "Yeah?"

"Thank you. For going on this adventure with me."

She smiled, and reached out her hand, wiggling her sparkle-tipped fingers, imploring me to take it. "Come on, Eileen."

I folded my fingers with hers, and we stepped out into the bookstore.

It was crowded with people.

My heart was so full, it felt like it might explode. Pru squeezed my hand tightly.

"See?" she mouthed, and wandered into the crowd, leaving me to my own devices.

Most everyone was familiar—my colleagues at the university, and some of my students, and most of Jasper's law firm. Everyone congratulated me, shaking my hand, telling me how beautiful the bookstore was, how unique the selection. Everything was hand-selected, from traditionally published romances to self-published to vanity presses. Pru and I had done our homework, and we'd scoured the internet for a well-rounded collection so that there was a little bit for everyone. Most people kept a wide berth from the MONSTER COLLECTION kiosk that Pru had lovingly created, but those who came up to explore the selection ended up chatting with each other, comparing their tastes.

I sipped on my champagne, and made sure that people found what they were looking for. A few customers came up to me, asking about Quixotic Falls. They'd read about it in a piece in the *New York Times*. Obviously I was thrilled, but as I was about to ask what the article was, I saw a familiar man near the front of the store. I thought my heart would jolt, my breath would hitch, but . . . seeing Liam Black for the first time in a year and a half did nothing for me. Absolutely nothing.

It wasn't him who came over, though. It was his wife, Bethany. "You must be Eileen," she said. She was petite and fit, with long black hair and wide eyes. "This place is gorgeous. Congrats."

"Thanks," I replied, wondering why she was here. To gloat that she'd gotten Liam? To show me her ring?

She held up an Ann Nichols book. "I've been dying for a romance bookstore. I saw on the sign there might be a book club? Liam doesn't really read, but I'm *voracious*."

I glanced back at Liam, and he seemed keen on simply ignoring me. It was very clear that he'd come because of her, and whether he wouldn't look me in the eye because what he did to me was shitty, or because he simply didn't care—

Well, it wasn't my business anymore.

"The book club's starting next week, actually. You're welcome to come. We've got about twelve people signed up," I added.

She glowed with excitement. "Oh, I'm *so* excited. Do you have any Mafia romances?" she asked, a little quieter. *"Fated mates?"*

I pointed her in the direction of where she'd find them, and she disappeared into the stacks with her husband in tow, and they drifted off into my bookstore. When they were gone, I realized my heart was racing, and I tasted panic in my mouth.

Deep breath, Eileen, I thought. It was fine.

My mom found me a few minutes later and topped off my

champagne glass. "Did you see him? The bastard," she muttered, like the busybody she was. "I should carve him up and—"

"He's here with his wife." I drained my flute, and held it out for another refill. "She's nice."

She obliged. "Oh?"

"And I'm over it. I'll do better," I said, and she smiled and patted me on the cheek.

"I've always said that, darling. I'm so proud of you," she said, and wrapped her arms around me. She squeezed me tightly. In the back of the store, we were planning on setting her up with a small booth where she could repair well-loved novels. We'd already gotten a lot of interest in it, but Mom was very particular about her tools and her work hours. We'd figure it out. "Now, I'm going to go make sure everyone's having a blast, and you just enjoy yourself."

"Thanks, Mom," I replied, and she kissed my cheek and left to go play host in my stead. She was the people person, anyway. Get her going on her travels, and she could talk for *hours*. I pitied the people who'd get trapped listening to her recount her trip to Alaska.

Toward the end of the night, Liam's wife came to say goodbye and how much she was going to thoroughly enjoy the bookstore. She'd bought five Greek god romances, thanks to Pru, and was excited to get to "the one with the tentacles and the happily ever after."

Liam looked bored, and so I eyed him and asked, "Not your speed?"

"I like whatever she does," he replied, prickling a little, and then shook it out. He said earnestly, "I'm glad you finally found something you wanted. You look . . . happy."

"I am," I assured. "It was nice to see you, Liam. Bethany," I added to her, "book club's next week. Six p.m. sharp—you'll be there?"

"I wouldn't miss it," she replied, and grabbed Liam by the arm, and they left the bookstore together, heads bent toward each other, with an ease that Liam and I had never had.

After Florence Day's event, the store began to clear out, and I would be lying if I said I wasn't looking for a familiar silhouette between the aisles, but of course I never saw him. I smiled to myself, remembering the night Anders asked me what I'd name a bookstore, and I guessed it was more than a little wishful thinking that the Grand Romantic would live up to its name. I shook so many people's hands, and learned so many people's faces, that they all became a blur by the time the last customer left.

After they were gone, I went to help Prudence and Jasper find all the plastic champagne glasses people stuck between stacks of books, and hunted down all the errant napkins, and tossed it all in the trash. After we set the display tables back into the center of the store, and fixed up the endcaps again, I told Pru that she and Jasper could go.

"It's almost nine, and restaurants will be closing soon. You should go get something to eat and celebrate," I said.

"But the cash register still needs to be counted out and—"

"I got it," I said, motioning for them to leave. "*Go.*"

Prudence said, taking her purse from the register, "You don't have to tell me twice. I'm *starving.*"

Jasper looked up from fishing a used napkin out from between Nora Roberts's ample bibliography. "Oh, thank *god*. I was about to start chewing on a book."

"They're not very nutritious."

"I survived off Monster energy drinks in law school. My body would make do," he said gallantly, and she laughed, and he went to get their coats.

"Hey, Elsy?" Pru asked as she came up to me, and wrapped her arms around me tightly, squeezing so hard I felt my ribs creak. "I love you."

I returned the hug. "I love you, too, Pru."

"Even if this business fails, we'll blame Jeff Bezos and stay friends forever, right?"

"Absolutely," I promised into her hair. We finally unwound from each other. "But . . . let's not jinx it? I'd rather stay in business."

She held up her hand, and her fingers were crossed. "All the precautions," she replied. Jasper came back with their coats, but as they turned to put on their coats to leave, I called her name. "Hmm?" she asked, turning back.

"The starlings didn't mean anything," I told her. "In the books. They were just birds."

"Maybe to you," she replied, and gave a wink as she curled her arm around Jasper's and they left the Grand Romantic.

The door swung shut, and silence filled the bookstore.

I closed my eyes, and if I listened really hard, I could hear the sound of crystal chimes in the rafters, and starlings in the eaves, and remember how the sunlight slipped through the windows, and shimmered in the bookstore owner's pale blond hair.

And I was home.

39

Book Ends

I RAN MY FINGERS ACROSS the spines of the books as I took one last curving route down every aisle, picking up any remaining champagne flutes and discarded napkins, turning covers face out, and righting stacks. In the contemporary section, my fingers paused on a small paperback tucked into the shelf, the first in a series of five that was never finished. Even as I took it off the shelf, and flipped through the pages, I already knew the first line—

There was only one road in and one road out of Eloraton, New York, and most people never took it.

But I had.

The bell above the front door jingled. I gave a sigh and closed the book. Returned it to its place on the shelf. "Forget something, Pru?"

"I'm afraid I did," said a soft, stoic voice. Not Pru. Not at all.

I looked over—and froze.

A man stood in aisle, between the Noras and the Beverlys, just so comfortably, like he belonged in a bookstore—*my* bookstore. His hair was cut shorter, still that pale blond that tended to curl around his ears, and his reading glasses sat tucked into his tweed coat pocket. Dark jeans that fit nicely and a heather-gray Henley and black boots laced with sage-green shoestrings. He looked nothing like the man I remembered, and exactly like him at the same time, a mirage standing there, his hands in his pockets.

My heart beat loud in my ears.

"I'm looking for a book," he began, his minty eyes bright and glimmering. "Do you have a recommendation?"

"What are you looking for?" My voice was barely more than a whisper. Was he really here? Was it him? I wanted to believe my eyes, but my heart didn't want to admit it.

"Something I've never read before," he replied.

"Well . . . I might know a story you'll like. It's a little odd, though."

He studied me for a thoughtful moment. "I like odd."

"And maybe a little boring."

"Oh, now you're really selling me. What's it about?"

I took a deep breath, and stepped closer to him. "A woman who stumbles into a strange town, and almost runs over a strange man standing in the rain."

"What makes him so strange?"

"He doesn't own tweed," I said, "and he looks like he definitely should."

"Ah, well," he replied, and stepped closer to me, so close I could smell the cedarwood on his skin. He was here. He was real. His fingers lightly brushed a lock of hair out of my face. "I'm sure he rectifies that."

"He does." I gently curled my fingers into the lapels of his tweed coat, and pulled him closer. "You're here," I whispered, reaching up to his face and cradling it in my hands, as if he'd disappear the second I blinked.

He pressed his hand on mine, holding it against his face, and kissed the base of my palm.

"I'm here," he replied. He held on to me tightly, and pressed his forehead against mine. Out of Eloraton, he looked different. His hair wasn't as bright, and his eyes weren't as green, and a few fine wrinkles had appeared on his forehead and around his eyes, and I loved every one of them. He wasn't a romance hero, but he was mine. "However, opening an entire romance bookstore is a bit overkill. I just said the romance *section*."

I laughed. I couldn't help it. "I never do things by halves. You know that," I replied, still unable to take my eyes off him. I swallowed the knot in my throat. "But . . . why? I thought—what about . . ."

"Some stories end," he said, "and I'm not Bea's happily ever after. I was Rachel's, for a little while, and I never want to be that again."

Oh. I dropped my hand from his face. "So . . ."

"I want to be a beginning, and a middle," he went on. "I want a first chapter, and a second and a third—those long chapters, you know, the ones you have to take a break from halfway through. I want all of it, not just the end." He looked down at my hands, and took them in his, and squeezed them tightly. "And I want it with you."

With me?

"I love you," he said, and it felt like a phrase he'd uttered a thousand times even though I'd never heard it before. He said it like it was part of a grocery list, like it was a greeting, and a good night, and a promise all in one. Three words that were everything, and anything. "I love you," he repeated. "I love the way your mouth always slides into a smile, even when no one's looking. I love the way you go out of your way for people you've barely met. I love how your hair always curls right here, at the nape of your neck"—and he ran his fingers along the side of my neck. "And I love how you make me want to see the world in color, and I love how I feel when I'm with you. And maybe we won't work out, but maybe we will—and I'll run across cities, and I'll show up with boom boxes outside your window, and I'll meet you at the tops of buildings, and I'll kiss you in the rain just to remind you that you're worth every moment." He bent and kissed my cheeks, and I realized that he had kissed the tears off them. I was crying, and I couldn't stop.

"How long have you been rehearsing that?" I asked, sniffing, trying to stop crying.

He laughed, and pressed his forehead against mine. "You're worth every second I did."

"I know," I replied, and pulled him down to kiss him again. The kiss was slow and languid, like he suddenly had all the time in the world to kiss me.

And I really hoped he did.

I traced the curve of his jaw, drinking him in in the soft fluorescence of the bookstore. There was a buoyancy to him that there hadn't been before, a boyishness, as if he'd reined himself in while staying in Eloraton, and put himself into a box that now no longer fit. I imagined this was the man whom Rachel had once fallen in love with, or closer to him than the stoic and sour owner of Ineffable Books.

I took him by the hands and squeezed them tightly, unable to keep from smiling. "Can I show you around?" And I barely gave him a chance to nod before I spirited him along all the aisles, and showed him the murals, and the DATE A BOOK BOYFRIEND display with books wrapped in paper, the love interests mocked up like a dating profile. I showed him the colorful crystal chimes I'd found at a garage sale, and the book spinners for the mass-market paperbacks, and the old cashier's till Jasper found in his granddad's decrepit shed.

"It's a beautiful store, Elsy," he said, running his fingers along the spines of novels. "It feels like you."

"It still needs a little work," I replied, rounding the tiny checkout counter, and popping out the register to count the money, "but all good things do."

He agreed.

"Do you miss yours?" I asked.

"Yes, but I left it a while ago," he said, and when I gave him a strange look, he explained. "I left town with Butters as soon as Frank could find a new carburetor for my Buick. It took about a week digging through the junkyard, but it was worth it. Besides, I had to find someone to take over the bookshop."

"Who did you find?"

"Thomas," he replied.

I smiled. "I bet Lily loved that."

"You have no idea," he agreed, and came over to lean against the counter while I tallied up the bills. "They were all very sad you left, by the way. I told them you'd be back around."

"In a way," I replied sadly. "Do you think the town is still there?"

He shook his head. "I went back a few weeks later, after I'd thoroughly cleaned my apartment in the city and got everything in order, and the town was gone. The only thing left was the waterfall, which was the only real part of the town to begin with."

I let out a breath, and I hoped it didn't sound too sad. "So it really is over."

"It was a good ending."

"It was," I agreed, and finished cashing out the drawer. I put the money in the lockbox under the counter, and went to go return a few of the novels to the display table in the middle of the store. The pink neon sign behind me flickered tiredly. "What took you so long to come find me, then?" I asked, my back turned to him.

He followed me to the table, rubbing the back of his neck in thought. The soft light of the bookstore made his fair blond hair almost silver. "I wanted to set my life in order again first. When I left, I left everything."

"Except Butterscotch."

"Except Butterscotch," he agreed, "who misses your pets, by the way."

"I do give the best scritches."

"I wanted to come find you the second I left Eloraton," he went on, "but I . . . I also wanted to come find you as the man you deserve. Someone who has a life. A story. Who has his feet firmly planted on the ground. So I did that. I started my life again. I read books, I learned how to write critiques again, I caught up with my parents, I visited my sister in Manitoba. I learned to be Anderson Sinclair again." He took a deep breath. "So . . . what do you think? Was it worth the wait?"

I studied him as I leaned back against the display table, in that tweed coat that really looked awful on him. "Well," I began, as I took hold of his jacket, "almost."

I took his tweed jacket off, and pushed his hair out of his face.

"There," I whispered, and he bent down and kissed me. Slowly, savoringly. And he tasted like black tea and new beginnings. He cradled my face, fingers curling into my hair, releasing it from its bun. My copper hair fell down across my shoulders, wild, as he grabbed me by the waist and lifted me up onto the table, toppling a few books off the edges. He pressed himself against me, wanting to be nothing but closer, and gladly—wholeheartedly—I melted into his kisses like ice on hot pavement.

"I love you," I felt more than heard Anders say against my lips.

"Every day I spent knowing you were out there, that you *existed*, and that I wasn't with you, drove me mad. I never want to spend another day like that again."

I pressed our foreheads together, breathless, breathing in the scent of him. My cheeks were flushed, and his minty eyes had turned forest green, drunk on me. "Promise?"

"Promise," he echoed, and snagged my mouth with his again, this time hungrily, passionately, and I let myself lose all sight of the plot.

He remembered my body like Eloraton had been yesterday. He knew where to put his teeth so that I gasped, he knew where to place his hands, how slow to unzip my dress. He remembered it all, my curves, my edges, and all I could do to not lose my mind was to try to work my fingers down the buttons of his shirt, undoing them one by one. He pressed his lips against my neck as his fingers slipped between my thighs and stroked me, and my heart went spinning. I gasped, pressing the side of my face to his, wrapping my arms around his neck. He was so delicious, and so thorough, he had to do it again just so I could pay attention the second time. He muttered affirmations into my hair as he kissed me, and taught me things about myself that I had yet to know, and I taught him things, too, and that was love.

Love was patient and meticulous and it never ceased to surprise me. It wasn't something that I needed, something that I *deserved*, that I was *worthy* of—love was what I wanted. Anders was who I wanted. For now. For a day. For a week—for *years*. A story written in the language of kisses, and read to me in sweet, soft sighs.

And though I didn't know the ending, I didn't need to. Because this?

This was enough.

A Beginning

THERE ONCE WAS A TOWN.

And it did not exist. Not on maps, not on roads, not on the internet. It lived, quietly, in the pages of a novel, and there it stayed. The grass always smelled fresh and the hamburgers at the bar were always burnt and the taffy always stuck to your molars and sometimes—in my daydreams—I visited it. I walked along the sidewalks and I listened to the clock tower chime on the hour, and I fell again, and again, and again, into the pages of my favorite books.

There was once a town that didn't exist, and it used to feel like home.

But now there was a bookstore with hundreds of happily ever afters sitting on the shelves, and a woman with dirty blond hair and a tricky smile sitting at the counter, daring you to take a chance on a book you've never heard of, and a part-time book critic who kept the shelves in alphabetical order and made the best tea, and sometimes when it rained he would pull me out into it and steal kisses that tasted like summer days in a town that didn't exist. And an old orange cat would sit at the front door and demand pets from everyone he met. And there were book clubs and midnight release parties and fae court galas and on the days that were so slow that no one came in, I would turn on an old pop song and sing at the top of my lungs. And everything was good. Not perfect all the time, but real life was never meant to be perfect—where the burgers were always slightly burnt and the taffy was sticky and the weather predictable—but it was close.

Because this story was good, and it was sweet.

And it was home.

Acknowledgments

Every book is a little different until you read the acknowledgements. And then in that regard, every book is the same: an author nervous-sweating in the pages, hoping they remembered to thank everyone who had some hand in their book.

You'd think I would have a list by now, so many books in, or I would learn to collect names and dig them out when the acknowledgments are due. But I am nothing if not a creature of habit, so after every book I find myself staring at a list of names, armpits sweaty, knowing that I have *absolutely* forgotten someone but I have no idea who.

It's the tragedy of the acknowledgments section.

So, I'm going to list the village that raised my book in painstaking detail, and I'm going to try my hardest to remember everyone, and I'm going to inevitably fail. The names are in no particular order, but whether you're the first or last I name—I want to thank you from the bottom of my heart for helping bring this book to life.

I might have written down a few silly little words, but you made it a *book*.

Thank you.

Amanda Bergeron. Holly Root. Sareer Khader. Tina Joell. Jess Mangicaro. Danielle Keir. Craig Burke. Jeanne-Marie Hudson. Alaina Christensen. Angelina Krahn. Abby Graves. Megha Jain. Vi-An Nguyen. Christine Legon. Daniel Brount. Nicole Brinkley. Katherine Locke. Kaitlyn Sage Patterson. Ashley Schumacher. Mike Lasagna. Eric Smith. Rachel Strolle. Shae McDaniel. Jarad Greene. Ada Starino. Savannah Apperson. Cera Peters.

And finally, my parents, Cheryl and Randy Poston. Thanks for instilling a love for reading in me from a young age.

No—wait! One more!

My favorite author. I'm glad I found your books. They kept me afloat through the worst years of my life.

Thank you for your stories.

ASHLEY POSTON

READERS GUIDE

Books and their Readers

I REMEMBER THE FIRST TIME I met my favorite book.

I can't tell you where I was or what clothes I had on or how old I was—though I think I was about twelve—but I can tell you exactly how I felt. I can tell you the feeling that raced through my body, from the top of my head to the tips of my toes. It was the kind of feeling that felt like walking into a house you've never been in before, but immediately feeling like it was home. It's the feeling of eating your favorite ice cream on a humid summer afternoon. It's bundling up in your favorite blanket, warm and comforting. It's a kiss goodnight, the first rays of sunlight you see in the morning, streaming through the window; the first taste of snow; the feeling of warm spring rain after a terrible winter—

It's exhilarating, and comforting, and magical all in one.

There is just something enchanting about meeting your favorite book, like locking eyes with a stranger across the room and knowing—immediately—that they are the other half of your soul. Books are magical that way, how they can hold small bits of you, written by people who never knew you existed. A turn of phrase can encapsulate a part of your heart you never knew how to put words to, a line of dialogue can echo a part of your soul whispering in a language you never knew.

I like the idea that once your book is published, it is no longer yours. It's yours in the technical sense—the copyright is in your name, you get paid royalties (hopefully)—but the book itself belongs to a version of you in the past. A version of you that, day by day, gets further and further away from the you that you are now.

I also like the idea that once your book is published, it belongs to the people who read it. It occupies a spot on their shelf, just like it once occupied a piece of your life. It finds a home elsewhere, in other hearts, in the hands of readers who will interpret and imagine your words in their own unique way.

Since becoming an author, I realized that I'm the only one who will ever experience my story the way I wrote it. Only I will take the journey with Elsy and Anders, and climb the trail to the waterfall in the way that I imagine it. But that also means that every reader after me experiences the exact same—something wholly rare and unique to them. Something sacred.

I think that's what makes your favorite book even more powerful, because not only did you read it and experience it in the only way *you* can, but it lit the exact right parts of your soul to make you fall in love. You, in all the world, found home in that moment. You found comfort in a set of words written a year, two years, ten—a hundred years ago—and there they are now, echoing in the chambers of your heart, whether it's a literary classic or a forgotten novella buried in the stacks of a used bookstore.

Every reader deserves that.

An author might have their name on a novel, but it's the readers who bring those slices of dead trees to life. It's the readers who forge an author's legacy and keep them alive long after they've gone.

That's the magic of stories.

They entertain you. They challenge you. They comfort you. They transport you to somewhere only you can find, and somewhere you can stay for as long as you like.

The author of my favorite book is gone, but her words echo on in my rib cage, and stand the test of time on my shelf, and keep me company, even though I've never met her, and she never knew I existed.

Like a tattoo on the heart, the story stays.

Discussion Questions

1. Elsy loves the Quixotic Falls series because it has been with her through much of her adult life. Do you have a special series or standalone novel that you reminisce fondly about?

2. Ruby Rivers' original ending in her Quixotic Falls book is a happily-ever-after, but who does that HEA benefit the most? Do you think her new ending is more satisfying to the readers, or her original one?

3. Why do you think bookstores and cats go together like peas and carrots?

4. Elsy fondly remembers reading her first romance. What was the first romance novel you ever read?

5. Think about your favorite tropes—the boy next door, enemies to lovers, grumpy/sunshine, secret royalty, hot priests, bodyguards,

hurt/comfort, among hundreds of others. What draws you to those tropes? And what books would you recommend to someone looking for them? No judgments!

6. If you could spend a day in your favorite fictional place, where would that be, and what would you do?

7. Elsy realizes her dream is to open a bookstore focused on romance. If you opened a bookstore what would it look like, and how would you curate it?

8. Rachel Flowers lives on in her series, but her readers are perpetually left without a proper ending. Would you rather read a book series that will never have an ending, or a book series with a disappointing end?

9. What will you read next? And where did you hear about it?

A Recommended Reading List for Books about Books

- *Howl's Moving Castle* by Diana Wynne Jones
- *Emily Wilde's Encyclopaedia of Faeries* by Heather Fawcett
- *Ex Libris: Confessions of a Common Reader* by Anne Fadiman
- *The Ten Thousand Doors of January* by Alix E. Harrow
- *The Very Secret Society of Irregular Witches* by Sangu Mandanna
- *The Neighbor Favor* by Kristina Forest
- *Inkheart* by Cornelia Funke
- *The Banned Bookshop of Maggie Banks* by Shauna Robinson
- *Yellowface* by R. F. Kuang
- *Between the Lines* by Jodi Picoult and Samantha van Leer
- *Sorcery of Thorns* by Margaret Rogerson

ASHLEY POSTON is the *New York Times* bestselling author of *The Dead Romantics* and *The Seven Year Slip*. A native of South Carolina, she lives in a small gray house with her sassy cat and too many books. You can find her on the internet somewhere, watching cat videos and reading fan fiction.

VISIT ASHLEY POSTON ONLINE

AshPoston.com
🅕 🅞 HeyAshPoston
🐦 AshPoston

Learn more about this book
and other titles from
New York Times bestselling author

ASHLEY POSTON

SCAN ME
or visit
prh.com/ashleyposton